T0304410

Praise for *The Infernal Riddle of Thomas Peach*:

'Treadwell's book is a magnificent pastiche of 18th-century fiction'

Sunday Times

'An extraordinary novel . . . a tour de force'

Andrew Taylor

'*Tristram Shandy* meets *Jonathan Strange and Mr Norrell* in a novel that addresses dark disturbing themes with tremendous wit, charm and elegance'

Daily Mirror

'This novel is a virtuoso performance . . . he must be heartily congratulated both for performing an extraordinary feat of literary ventriloquism and also for reminding us what historical fiction does best: create an entirely convincing vanished world while also using that world as a lens through which to view the present day'

Guardian

'A clever, playful mystery'

Daily Express, Books of the Year

'Part historical pastiche, part gothic horror, this is an ambitious and stylistically bold 18th-Century adventure with shades of *Jonathan Strange and Mr Norrell*'

SFX

'Entertaining, often amusing and definitely intriguing. I particularly liked the way I became totally immersed in this 18th Century world – the author's attention to tone and detail is impressive'

Concatenation

A Fire Beneath the World

Also by Jas Treadwell

The Infernal Riddle of Thomas Peach

A Fire
Beneath the World

Jas Treadwell

**HODDER &
STOUGHTON**

First published in Great Britain in 2024 by Hodder & Stoughton
An Hachette UK company

1

Copyright © James Treadwell 2024

A CIP catalogue record for this title is available from the British Library

Hardback ISBN 978 1 529 34737 1
Trade Paperback ISBN 978 1 529 34738 8
ebook ISBN 978 1 529 34739 5

Typeset in Sabon MT by Hewer Text UK Ltd, Edinburgh
Printed and bound in Great Britain by Clays Ltd, Elcograf S.p.A.

Hodder & Stoughton policy is to use papers that are natural, renewable
and recyclable products and made from wood grown in sustainable
forests. The logging and manufacturing processes are expected to
conform to the environmental regulations of the country of origin.

Hodder & Stoughton Ltd
Carmelite House
50 Victoria Embankment
London EC4Y 0DZ

www.hodder.co.uk

A FIRE BENEATH

THE
WORLD

Gentleman, of C___ton B___, Somerset-shire;

With an *authentic account* of certain

NOTORIOUS
EVENTS

occurring in that county

anno *Domini* 1785

Containing also some *metaphysical* discoveries,
of a very remarkable nature

Midnight and summer rain. All the palace windows are dark. The river stinks.

A broad quay separates the river from the palace, its August dust turning to mud. The boatmen and stevedores have long since gone to bed. Now this downpour has emptied it of everyone else: revellers, promenaders, orators, conspirators. For several days sheets of paper have been whirling up and down the quay, blown into short-lived clusters as though forming cabals or starting brawls. They stick to the earth and commence dissolving.

'One should gather up the more substantial of those pamphlets,' observes the senior member of the Committee of Public Security of the Museum Section (Nocturnal Division). 'They might feed our fire.'

His proposal is advanced without amendment, and voted on, and agreed. One of the junior members is dispatched into the mud to reap its crop of print, while the rest of the Committee maintains watch on the palace gate.

Their fire is for illumination not comfort. In Paris, in August, even the rain is warm; but the boulevards are murky and there are plotters all around, lurking wherever the light of patriotism does not reach. The Committee's purpose is to keep vigil over this single modest and overlooked exit from the palace, during those hours when the quay is deserted. The king and queen have already made one shameful attempt to flee the embrace of their own people. Who knows when they might try again?

The exit is a tunnel of sooty stone protected at the outer end by an iron gate, with a narrow door at its inner terminus. Even by daylight it is largely invisible. Some say it enters into kitchens, others into cellars; to a dungeon, declares a third party. This is the extremity of the riverside wing of the Tuileries Palace, overlooking the noisy quay and the reeking Seine. No guards ever stand here, and neither the iron gate nor the narrow door have once been seen to open. No matter. They provide access from palace to street; therefore they must be policed.

The junior member returns with an armful of spattered papers, adjusting her cockade, which is much too big for her. She is seven years old, or eight, or nine. She tosses her gleanings into the sputtering fire, immediately extinguishing a large portion of it, earning the execrations of her four fellows of the Committee. The senior member bravely puts his hand among the flames to extract some of the papers. He hangs them around their small shelter to season them a little before allowing them to burn. He picks up one particular sheet, whose heading is printed in great characters. WHAT IS TO BE DONE WITH THE REFRACTORY PRIESTS? — By, A Citizen.

The member examines the smudged lines of ink for several seconds with a superior frown.

'Bah,' he says. 'Treasonous libels against the people. This author should hang.'

The others nod eagerly. No vote is required. None of them contest their leader's opinion, for they cannot read.

'I shall add his name to the list of the proscribed,' the senior member announces. With a sharpened stick he scratches a few charcoal marks on the lid of a crate, recently obtained by the Committee for this purpose, though they will shortly need to find another, having nearly covered the original with smears and squiggles. The marks are generally shapeless and indistinct, but it is of no significance: the senior member can no more write or read than his associates. He is Antoine, a shoemaker's boy, twelve years of age according to his mother, though he declares himself eighteen and a full-grown citizen of the new nation, with all the natural and inalienable rights they speak of in the meetings of the

Museum Section, to which he listens through his neighbour's window.

A rattle and a creak.

'Hush!' Antoine commands. 'What is that?'

Another creak, followed by a rusty groan of hinges.

'Devil!' cries Blandine, who is Antoine's younger sister and a very great patriot. 'It is the door. The king and queen attempt another flight!'

Since nightfall and the coming of the rain she has been working on sharpening a stick. She takes good hold of it and peers across the boulevard into the dirty tunnel, where a crouched and shadowed figure has emerged from within the palace. This figure approaches the iron gate. They hear his gasp of revulsion as he notices its adornment.

Some weeks past, by dint of exceptional efforts, the Committee of Public Security of the Museum Section (Nocturnal Division) succeeded in obtaining the head of a traitor, during the disorder subsequent on that traitor being torn limb from limb by the mob. The members of the Committee were able to use their small stature to their advantage, darting between the legs of clumsier and more drunken souvenir-hunters and so making away with the prize, which the junior member hid in her skirts in the very instant that the actions of the crowd caused it to roll against her foot. This trophy they have impaled on the spikes atop the palace gate, facing inwards. They intended it to warn the king and queen of their certain fate, should those personages foolishly attempt to escape the Tuileries by the exit where the Committee keeps vigil.

It appears that Louis has tired of his monstrous German harridan. A single person only is making this particular attempt: a man. He fumbles at the lock of the gate.

'Not so fast, sir,' says Blandine. At the sound of her bold but piping threat the king peers out from under his capacious hood and curses.

'My faith,' he mutters. His voice is tremulous, his accent pronounced. 'Can one no longer take a step in this whole city of

Paris without being inconvenienced by the effrontery of urchins?'
He pushes the gate open, propelling little Blandine backwards
into the mud. At this offence to one of their number the rest of the
Committee surge forward as one, surrounding the monarch.

'By order of the citizens of Paris,' Antoine says, brandishing his
charcoal-tipped stick, 'you are not permitted to depart the
Tuileries. Your majesty shall also apologise to my sister for
knocking her into the unclean street.'

The cowled man laughs. 'By our Lady, you are brave children,
to accost the king of France in such language!'

'The so-called king of France,' Antoine replies, with great
contempt, 'is a citizen of the nation, no greater in dignity than
any of his fellow-men.'

'That may be so,' the man concedes. 'But, my young patriots,
let us agree that though he is no better than others, and, the good
God knows, is certainly no worse, he is nevertheless a distinct
personage, not identical to those fellow-men you speak of; and, as
you may see' — he pushes back the hood, revealing a pinched,
balding face, lined with age, and a wooden crucifix hanging at his
neck — 'I am not he.'

The members of the Committee, now including Blandine, who
has risen from her indignity, crowd close around the man and
examine him by the light of their struggling fire.

'Then what are you about, sneaking away from the palace in
the dead of night?'

'I do not think myself obliged to give explanations to a gang
of children, who ought to be in their beds, if their mothers and
fathers knew how to exercise the authority they so noisily
claim a right to. But you may guess my business from my habit,
which ought to command your reverence, not your
impertinence.'

Beneath his travelling-cape the man wears a black robe, belted
with rope.

'A priest!' exclaims the junior member, and retreats, crossing
herself.

He looks at her approvingly. 'God in Heaven observes your awe, child, and will remember it when you come before Him.'

'Perhaps,' says Antoine with a sneer, 'or perhaps not. What is certain is that we attend this gate and will not permit it to be used to offend the will of the nation. Declare your purposes, priest.'

The man's unpleasantly bulbous eyes look rapidly from one to another of the upturned little faces. The rats of revolution, he thinks. Beady, hungry and savage. Paris is overrun with them. When they swarm together they fear nothing.

'Well then, young citizen, be content to know that I have this night heard the confession of a person too noble to be named in such a place. I was called to the palace for that purpose, and, my sacred duty complete, I now return to my home in the north.'

The mere reference to a *noble person* arouses an instant emotion in the members of the Committee, equally compounded of curiosity and rage.

'The Count of Artois?' says one of the children.

'The Duke of Enghien?' suggests another.

'The *queen*?' says Antoine, jabbing the unfortunate priest with his stick. At that hated word the whole company hisses and growls.

'Pestilent infants! Remove yourself from my path at once!'

'Is he a refectory priest?' cries the youngest member. She has scented the possibility of battle, perhaps even of an impromptu hanging.

'*Refractory*,' Antoine corrects her. 'I trust, father, that you have sworn your oath of obedience to the constitution of France as required by the decrees of the National Assembly, which is the sole legitimate authority of the land?'

'The refractory priests,' says Blandine, also pressing the point of her sharpened stick against the priest's robes, with an eagerness he begins to find alarming, 'are vipers and cockroaches.'

'What is your name, priest?' Antoine demands.

'Unhand me! Grace of God, is this what France has descended to, that an old man is to be abused in the street by ignorant children under the very windows of the abode of monarchy?'

'The queen might have sent him with papers,' says Blandine, who during the two months since the royal family attempted to escape the country has listened with the utmost eagerness to every rumour of their further villainous plots. 'He must be searched.'

The man's hollowed features appear suddenly anxious, as though he has realised that the Committee is not to be trifled with.

'Your name?' their leader again demands.

'I, young brigand, am Pierre Quemener, brother of the order of St Benedict.'

Antoine repeats the Breton surname with a certain difficulty. He turns to one of his colleagues, a thick-necked warty lad. 'Consult the list of those priests known to have refused the oath of loyalty to the constitution. See if this Pierre is among them.'

'At once, my captain,' says the boy. He dashes to the fire and plucks up one of the smeared pamphlets drying by its edge. For several moments he makes a show of reading it. Then he adopts a face of triumph and points his slab of a finger towards the middle of the sheet. 'There!'

'I knew it,' cries Blandine. 'Let us tie his feet and throw him in the Seine.'

The priest's offended dignity has given way to palpable alarm, which, fortunately for him, clears his wits. 'Dear children!' he says. 'There is surely some error. Please, bring me your list.'

The warty boy looks uncertain. Antoine, mollified by the change in his captive's tone, hesitates also. The priest seizes his moment. 'Alas,' he says, 'it is my great misfortune that I almost share a name with a disloyal priest. A rogue, God forgive him, called Pierre Kéméner. Here — good citizen—' He takes the curdled pamphlet from the hands of the boy and shuffles closer to the fire. He pretends to examine the paper. He sighs and points.

'It is as I thought. Citizens — observe, here. The name printed on your list is Kéméner — not Quemener. Regard this character — the K—'

Antoine snatches the paper and studies the incomprehensible bumps and loops of ink. Sensing that he has been bested somehow, he angrily throws it into the mud.

'Very well,' he says. 'But you shall be searched nevertheless from crown to shoe.'

Blandine exclaims with disappointment at the escape of her intended victim. In compensation she begins thrusting her hands among his robes. Her fellows are quick to follow her example, appreciating, with the unerringly rapid instinct of children in such matters, that this will be the limit of the violence permitted on this occasion, and determined to make the most of it. They prod and pinch the old man unmercifully, encouraged all the while by Antoine in the name of their duty to the nation and the people. Their enthusiasm goes so far as to threaten the priest with entire disrobing, until the narrow palace door slams open and a new and furious voice bellows from within.

'Imps! Lice! Hands off the holy father, or by Saint Louis I'll beat you all back to your sewers. Back, small pigs, back!'

The newcomer is a sturdy woman in a smock, armed with a rolling-pin which she brandishes tremendously. At once the members of the Committee turn to front her, snarling at this fresh challenge. Here, though, is a different sort of enemy. Kings, queens, priests and nobles they do not fear at all. Everyone knows that since the revolution of two summers past the common people are raised above such contemptible aristocratic relics. An angry kitchen-servant threatening a beating is quite another matter. The children are reminded of their own fathers and mothers, who administer heavy punishment with tools very similar to that wielded by the stout woman. She throws the gate open so fiercely that the traitor's head is almost dislodged from its spikes, and advances. 'Devils! Savages!' The Committee gives ground, its courage wavering. Blandine is last to retreat, which unfortunately leaves her within range of the rolling-pin. It crashes hard against her ear. Shrieking, she flees to the shelter, where the fire sizzles unhappily, and crouches, holding a hand to her bleeding skull while her colleagues surround her.

The victorious kitchen-woman scowls at them before addressing the priest. She helps him rearrange his garb. When she is sure he is unhurt and ready to endure the rainy night, she withdraws a parcel from her smock.

'A pastry for your journey, good father,' she says, pressing it into his hands. The members of the Committee watch, their mouths suddenly wet with hunger. The pastry shell is as big as their heads. Its warm buttery aroma competes for a beautiful moment with the odours rising from the Seine. The priest thanks and blesses her, gathers up the edges of his cloak and hurries west towards where the watchfires on the Royal Bridge send columns of sparks up into the rain.

His rescuer turns to the cowering and starving children and scolds them loudly for several minutes, ending with the advice that they should go home to their mothers, for if she catches them lurking outside her kitchens again she will give each one of them a blow on both ears, this time with an iron pan instead of a pin of wood. On her way back inside she plucks the shrivelled head from the spike where the Committee so carefully placed it and hurls it into the knot of children. They scatter, screaming.

Brother Quemener scurries along the right bank of the river, hugging his fat pastry, cursing the rain and the revolution. Its men — impious fools. Its women — jackals, hyenas! But ah, its children are the worst of all. They are incarnate devils. His breath is unsteady. He avoids notice. Even at this hour and in this weather there are throngs in the Tuileries garden, bawling insults at the royal guards and giving obscene gestures towards the windows above. Along the quay are barrels and boxes, masses of shadow. He directs his way among them. Those which were not moved during the daylight hours are already plastered with paper: filthy cartoons, libels, calls to arms.

Two or three times he is accosted, largely on account of the pastry, which he has to beg not to share. Good sirs, he pleads, good citizens, I am a humble Breton, far from home, who must walk all through the wet night, for my vows preclude me from paying for a bed at the inn. The heartless Parisians have no respect for his vows. But at the appellation of Breton they nod, and confer, and agree that he shall keep his pastry. It is common knowledge that the deputies sent from Brittany to the National Assembly are among the most unbending in the cause of the nation, the readiest to give the king and his lackeys a bloody nose. Brother Pierre praises the maxims of Sieyès. His interrogators slap him on the back, wish him joy of his road. 'Only, sir, you had better eat your pastry before you are far from Paris, or robbers will eat it for you!'

He tucks the pastry into his satchel.

From the windows of the Faubourg St Honoré come sounds of domestic riot. Songs, chants, curses. Here no one cares who passes the fetid alleys in the dark. He is undisturbed until he attains the western margin of the city, where the roads are watched.

These are men of the National Guard, not packs of drunken citizens or feral urchins. True, the distinction is more subtle than it ought to be, but Brother Quemener has anticipated a formal style of interrogation and is prepared. He submits as calmly as his pounding heart allows. He must show the letter with his commission at the palace. Because he has been there he must be questioned closely. His satchel is to be investigated. Has he sworn the oath of loyalty to the nation required of all priests? He cannot stain his conscience with a lie on so grave a matter: he has not. Then his person must be examined as well as his satchel. Ah, sirs, he sighs, may God forgive you the trouble you give a poor old man. He lifts a mournful glance heavenwards like the suffering saints in the pictures. While he stands patiently, they inspect cloak and robes. Why do you not swear the oath, they demand? Good sirs, because I cannot: I am enjoined by sacred vows and holy writ to elevate no law higher than the law of God. But, he says, for everything our National Assembly has done to ease the sufferings of the poor and temper the arrogance of the great, I bless them and offer prayers for their good endeavours.

This is an untruth, but cunningly worded, so that Brother Quemener is content to make his conscience bend around it. It serves the greater good, he tells himself. The effect on the guardsmen is remarkable. They approve his sentiment with cups of wine, and after only the smallest discussion among themselves send him on his way, though they tell him he is a fool to travel by night, even so small a distance as to the abbey at Noyent. He tells them he will trust in God and his little lantern.

His greater trust, not confided to the guardsmen, is in the boy paid to wait for him a mile beyond the limit of Paris. From towers at his back he hears bells toll the appointed hour. He quickens his pace along the dark road. Surely the lad will wait a while? He cannot guess the distance in so vile a night. He has begun to fear he is abandoned, and will certainly be robbed if he does not die of the wet, when a torch appears among the trees, and there the boy is, leading two horses.

They turn off the road. The boy knows every track among these pastures, as well in the dead of night as by day. They cannot go faster than a cautious plod but there is no longer any need for haste. No one stirs but farmhouse dogs, growling across the dark. The lad knows which ones are too old or lazy to do more than growl and which to steer away from.

An hour or more passes. They arrive at the sad hovel where the boy lives with his mother. The old woman has stayed awake, transported with anxiety. She throws herself to her knees at their coming and kisses the priest's hands. There is tepid soup and bad wine, each of which he receives gratefully. He hangs his sodden cloak by the fire and takes a chair. He will pray, he says, while the woman and her son sleep.

When he is alone and at least partly dry, and the house is quiet, he withdraws from his satchel the cold and crumbling pastry. He sighs once more and breaks it open.

Inside the crust is a wadding of mere dough, almost raw. At the centre of the spongy mass there is a hollow, occupied by a small packet wrapped in cloth. Floury lumps adhere to it. He picks them off, throwing the remnants in the fire, where the crust already smokes and oozes.

The packet is a bundle of papers tied with a white silk ribbon. A wafer of impressed wax seals the knot. It is not for Brother Quemener to break the seal. He is no more than the humblest messenger, the least of the tools employed by the hand that wrote the letters. Nevertheless, his eyes moisten as he contemplates his secret burden. He bends and kisses the seal, daring for a moment to imagine he kisses that very hand — ah! So white, so fair! So noble, and cruelly persecuted!

From hand to hand the secret letters go, westwards and northwards. They enter a venerable house of contemplation by the orchard gate, in the pocket of one dressed as a common labourer, and leave the next day packed in the straw at the bottom of a cask of apples. Where even the churches are not safe from the eyes of so-called patriots, they pass by barge down the Eure, between fields of thin wheat where every other stalk has begun to rot in persistent rains. The harvest of the year 'ninety-one will be poor: fateful circumstance, for the author of the letters and many thousands more! They are brought one night in utmost secrecy to a Normandy convent. In her private cell the abbess breaks the seal: the first of the messages is for her. She weeps as she reads, pitying the good Catholic queen of France, no better than a prisoner in her own palace. If she dared reply she would send back a letter watered with her tears, placing her own house at the disposal of anointed authority. But she need not. It is understood. When the time comes, when refuge and disguise are required, the abbess will do her duty. So the queen writes, and so the venerable mother swears, on her knees before the image of the Mother of all suffering women.

Now the remaining letters turn north, seeking the shore. Every caution must be doubled. The towns and cities cannot be thought of. They have fallen one and all to the new men of France, who issue daily proclamations regarding this and that, and hold their lords temporal and spiritual in open contempt. From Caen it is reported that the mob tore down a statue of the king himself. Fires have been set in churches, where the only crime of the curate is to refuse a sacrilegious oath. Furthermore, these leagues of France, from the grisly rock-strewn barrens of Brittany to the Picardy marshes, overlook the Sleeve: that shallow sea which is her only protection from the most barbarous, despicable monsters ever birthed from the belching sewers of Hell to crawl out and deface the Earth: the *English*.

There is not a man, woman or child in the duchy of Normandy who does not hiss at the name of their ancient foes: not even a dog or a cat. If the letters were by mischance discovered, and it became known that the queen of France appeals for aid and rescue, to a milord of *England* — !

Even those to whom the packet is now entrusted do not suspect it. They know only that its secrecy must be protected to the last extremity; with their lives, if required. It is a holy struggle. The chattering monkeys and braying asses who appoint themselves France's new nobility are acolytes of modern philosophers, readers of impious books, repeaters of atheistic slogans. To die in the course of resisting such fiends would be martyrdom.

In Brittany, and now, it is rumoured, in Normandy also, there is an agent of the National Assembly sent to scour the true faith from the land. His black heart is filled with particular malice and cunning. No one sees him at work. No one knows who he is. Some call him the priest-killer. Pious women will not speak the name except in their prayers, begging God to strike him down. When a secret mass conducted by one of the honest curates who refuse to swear the accursed oath is inexplicably discovered and betrayed; when a devout old couple, who keep a portrait of his sacred majesty Louis beside their little engraving of Saint Agatha, are broken in on and marched to prison on some confected charge; when signs appear at the graveyard gate proclaiming that 'DEATH IS NOTHING BUT AN ENDLESS SLEEP'! — then people tremble and say it must be the priest-killer's work. No secret is so jealously protected but he seems to know it. He inflicts his oppressions mysteriously, without warning, like a supernatural being. He burns with tireless hatred for all God's servants from the highest to the humblest. My faith! — is he not a very demon?

Abbot Basculin is a wise and learned man, not given to superstition. Yet even he grows anxious at the tales spreading among the lay brothers and the more impressionable nuns. For several days he has been hidden within the walls of a modest conventual foundation, obscurely sited among the sturdy hedges and rich fields of the Norman hinterlands, not far from the sea to the west. He has not troubled to attempt disguise. He is too old. Besides, everyone knows him. His piety is renowned from the Seine to the Vilaine. At that fatal moment two years and more ago when the king summoned the States General, abbot Basculin went to Versailles among the delegates of the First Estate and laboured with all his spirit to assist the reconstruction of France. But now the guidance of priests, like the honour of nobles, is not wanted. No: it is despised. The windows of his house were broken with stones while he sat at dinner. He has determined to go into exile, like so many of the former props and pillars of the kingdom.

Within his sanctuary he paces, prays and waits. He cannot simply pack up his retinue and secure passage from Caen or Cherbourg. The people have become angry and impertinent. They resent those who flee to England. It is a slight upon their nation, they say, and therefore also an insult to us, for as the National Assembly declares, the people are the nation and the nation no more than the people.

Absurdity! Old abbot Basculin shakes his grey head at their folly and includes them in his prayers. Nevertheless, he will not risk their indignation at the harbours. In every town of significance, he has heard, clubs are forming, to see the will of the people enforced, with sticks and stones; with pitchforks and ropes!

'It is mere brigandage, dear sisters,' he tells the nuns who bring his evening meal (a fine fat pheasant tonight, with acceptable wine, as well as bread and legumes). 'As though France had not laws already. And the law of Heaven above all.' The sisters have been instructed not to converse with their guest the abbot, but they murmur agreement as they set the dishes down.

He has resolved to depart France in secret, with his household goods to follow later by equally discreet means. Two months ago he sent word to trusted friends at court requesting advice and assistance. In reply he was summoned to Rouen, for a private audience with a man of great eminence and holiness. The eminence looked on him gravely and asked: will abbot Basculin consent to place himself in the service of one too noble to be named? One who asks no more of him, than to convey some letters across the Sleeve, in the most extreme secrecy? One whose best hope is the loyalty and faith of such friends, for this person is surrounded day and night by packs of wolves, and, though among the greatest names in Europe, counts themselves scarcely better than a prisoner?

Before the image of Our Lady he knelt and made his vow.

Go then, the eminence instructed him, make your preparations and await the letters. Since that day Basculin has felt himself young again. His soul is tossed up and down like a lover's. Every dawn glows with possibility. At dusk each night he is tortured by dread. No letters come. My God, suppose that fiend the priest-killer has uncovered the plot!

'Father?'

'Yes, dear sister?'

A downcast face whispers at the grille in the door. The abbot is surprised. It is late; he heard compline while he ate. The excellent pheasant is picked clean. Perhaps this sweet child has come to take away the carcass.

'There is a man at the gate. He is very insistent, and asks for you by name.'

My faith! Is he discovered? He will not answer. Let the sisters deny that he is there. Even the brutes of revolution will surely not drag him by force from among holy women?

Or could this be the messenger he expects?

'What sort of man? How does he look?'

The sister does not know. She hastens from the door. From the sound of her voice she is not much older than a child, a simple country girl.

Abbot Basculin goes to the gate. The night is wet again and very dark for the season. His belly roils with fear and undigested meat. He farts shamefully.

There is only one man, holding in one hand a lantern and in the other a leather satchel.

The letters have come at last. The messenger speaks no word, nor lets the light fall on his face. He has trudged many miles in the rain by remote paths and has as many again to trudge home. The curate told him his sins of the past three years would be forgiven in one stroke if he did as he was told. He is a simpleton, and, alas, uncommonly lustful. His sins are numerous. There are also several months remaining in the year, he knows, and he plans to sin prolifically, knowing that nothing will be held against him until after Christmas. So he follows his instructions perfectly. The curate told him he must never speak a single word of this deed to anyone. He does not answer the old man at the gate, not even when offered coin, but only presents the satchel and turns back towards his distant bed.

Into such hands are fallen the hopes of the queen of France.

Three nights later, corresponding to the day and hour specified in the letters, abbot Basculin approaches a beach.

By the mercy of God it is not raining, though the air is damp and a thin mist, settled on the sea, makes cautious explorations into the adjacent plain.

As promised, a ship waits some distance offshore. All the fishermen have long since gone to bed. Only this one vessel breaks the virgin dark of the sea. Lanterns at stern and prow make a pair of illuminated clouds out of the light fog.

The abbot has a small escort comprised of the more worldly and adventurous sisters. His old friend the superior is forbidden such nocturnal expeditions by the state of her joints, but she has instructed several of her charges to lead their guest to the appointed place and see him safely embarked. For his own part, Basculin thinks the commission would have better suited two or three of the lay brothers. Perfect secrecy, however, demanded otherwise. Avowed sisters will not tell tales. So it falls to them to traipse across pastures and between scrub and dune, despite the offence to modesty. They are all Norman girls under their veils (which for the sake of deference they maintain, even before so venerable a man as the abbot), and shrink not at all from a quantity of weeds and coarse sand. They chatter among themselves. From time to time there is laughter, at which Basculin frowns.

The beach is long and desolate. A rowing boat leans on its side against a tussock. The surf advances and falls back. It is difficult to make out the ship at anchor; the mist has thickened. He raises the sisters' lantern on a piece of wood and gives the signal, before the vapours can condense into a true sea fog. After an anxious minute, answer comes from the vessel. His old eyes are too weak to be sure, but his companions assure him a new light has appeared there, waving up and down three times.

'Now, dear children,' he says, 'you must all leave me. Our Lord and his Mother protect you all.'

Alas, alas, good father! They kneel one by one before him in the sand, weeping. May God protect you among the heathen English! They cannot bear to think of so pious a man compelled from France. He must pray for a swift return to his devoted people. They become severely emotional and manifest a reluctance to depart. Were they not enjoined to see their holy father safely embarked?

'But, my small daughters in Jesus, a boat will soon arrive, sent from that ship, rowed by ruffian sailors and Englishmen, before whose eyes it is most unfit that you should appear. Leave me, I entreat you, or I shall have to command it. I do not wish to mar this tender farewell with the stern exercise of paternal authority, even as my heart overflows with chaste love for you all.'

Ah, father! Ah, best of men! We shall cry unceasingly for several days! But though they wail and cling to his hands they are at last persuaded to leave. With a pang of distress he reflects that the cry of those sweet innocent children — 'Farewell, adieu!' — will be the last words he hears spoken in his own tongue on his native soil, for the good God only knows how long.

He waits.

The interval becomes cold despite the season. The ship's lights are now no more than obscure smudges. He can discern no other lantern, but perhaps the rowers have no need of one. Nor can he hear the sound of oars or gruff voices; but his ears are as old as his eyes. The sisters required their light to return to their house. He is in darkness. It seems unwise to call out, but as minute after minute goes by he can think of nothing else to do. 'Ahoy, ahoy!' *Sshhh*, reply the breeze and the slithering waves.

Now he is certain the rowers have lost their way in the mist. He decides to march up and down the shore. If he does not walk, my faith! — the night will consume his old bones. He touches the packet of letters sewn inside his cloak, remembering the cause for which he suffers.

He sets off towards the sound of the tide, but has gone no more than ten steps before someone behind calls, 'Father?'

It is one of the sisters, returned without the rest. Her only light is a single candle sheltered in her hand.

'Dear one! This is no place or hour for you to be alone.'

'I feared the boat might miss you in this fog,' she says, 'and so returned to assure myself of your safety.' Her accent is strange. He does not recall any of the sisters speaking in such rough ungainly tones; a little crow in a flock of thrushes.

'The sailors have difficulty finding the place, it is true, but they are doubtless close. I am much more concerned for your position than you ought to be for mine. Gladly I will give you my blessing again, but you must rejoin your sisters at once. There is nothing you can do here.'

'To the contrary, father,' she says. 'Before I wedded myself to Jesus I was the daughter of a fisherman, his only child, and would often row our boat. There is just such a boat here at hand upon the beach. I will row you a little way out towards the ship, from where you may hail them.'

'Faugh! Impossible!'

'In Christ nothing is impossible, according to the gospel.'

The abbot Basculin thinks there is something very strange about the manner of this veiled girl.

'You do not have the accent of the Normans,' he says. 'Was your father, God bless him and his labours, a man of Brittany?'

'Not of Brittany, but of Britain,' replies the curiously bold sister. By what art she prevents the damp night air from extinguishing her little candle, Basculin cannot guess. 'I passed my childhood on the far shore of this sea.'

'An English novice! I had not heard there was such a one among the Order.'

'It is an accident of birth only, father. Come. I shall push the boat.' She passes the candle for him to hold, which requires him to stand quite still, crouched over, with his back to the breeze. He attempts to remonstrate, but in vain, for the ugly-voiced novice already strides over the sand and within moments is heard dragging the boat towards the sea. By Saint Cyr, but she is strong, for so slight a creature!

'There is a skill to it,' she says, returning to him. 'Any fisherman's child will tell you so. It is the same with the management of the oars. Enter the boat, good father. I shall assist.'

They stand at the edge of the rising tide. Only the faintest suggestion of lantern-light shows out in the bay. Otherwise there is nothing, except the persistent questioning of small waves against the shore. Old Basculin protests that the sister's plan cannot be seemly. But he is aware of the damp penetrating his skeleton and the letters folded invisibly in his cloak. If none come from the ship to rescue him he will catch his death on the beach and his sacred vow will not be fulfilled.

'You will only row us a little distance from the shore, so I may call to the ship?'

'Precisely so, father.'

The sea appears tranquil, and the English girl most certainly knows how to handle a rowing-boat, for — picking up her robes, though she remains modestly veiled — she has stepped over the stern and set the oars in place.

Lord, along what strange paths you conduct us! With an additional prayer for his safety the abbot enters the boat. The sister offers her hand in assistance. He should not accept it. It is a grievous wrong to touch the flesh of a novice. Yet when the moment comes he does not resist.

How cold her hand is!

'You may sit there in the stern,' she says, and almost before he can gather his cloak under him she has settled to the oars, her back to the great dark sea, and they are gliding into its embrace.

'You row as well as a ferryman, beloved child.'

'My father used to say so. He would call me his little Charon.'

The abbot shivers. It is no time to be reminded of the boatman who conducts the souls of the dead. In this dark one could easily imagine the waters beneath to be dread Styx itself. Already he cannot distinguish the shore.

'What is your name, sister, that I may pray for you?'

'I am called Sister Maledicta.'

She leans forward and back, raises and dips her arms, patiently and smoothly. Her head remains very still.

'My hearing is dimmed with age. I thought I heard you say Sister Maledicta!'

The sister does not speak. If she smiles at his little joke, it is concealed by the veil.

A small gust blows across the boat. He has been inattentive. The candle is suddenly extinguished.

'Curse it!' he exclaims.

'Have no concern, father,' she says. 'I can row equally well in the dark.'

'This is far enough, I am certain.' The abbot peers over her shoulder, looking for the stain of light which indicates the position of the ship. He cannot see it. To the devil with this fog!

'A little further,' she says.

'Are you certain?'

'Quite certain.'

'I cannot make out the lanterns. You have erred in your direction, foolish child.'

'I have not,' she says, quite imperturbable. 'It is often the case that as one approaches a ship at anchor, the direct view of its light is obstructed by the body of the vessel.'

'Then we are close enough to hail?'

'Very nearly. Do you know who commands that ship, father?'

'A strange question! What concern is that of yours?'

'He is an Englishman,' the sister continues, without regard for the abbot's rebuke. She converses as she rows: steadily, relentlessly, following her own course. 'A nobleman, it is rumoured, though no one knows his true identity. They call him the Forget-Me-Not. He has adopted the flower as his symbol, I believe. It is a jest of sorts.'

'What nonsense is this you speak?'

'Is it nonsense? The rumour says that very many priests and nobles who flee the revolution have been aided in their escape by the gallant and mysterious Forget-Me-Not.'

'My dear child, these are not matters for you to speak of. I fear you are deficient in your attention to the love of Jesus, which ought to be the whole business of your mind and heart.'

'This English nobleman the Forget-Me-Not, they say, is most particularly devoted to the queen of France.'

'The queen of France?' A strange dark chill has seeped into the abbot. It touches his heart.

'Precisely, father. He adores her image as the knights of romance adored their ladies. Everyone whispers that the Forget-Me-Not has sworn several oaths to liberate the queen from Paris, and conduct her by stealth to England, where he will prostrate himself at her feet. This plan is even now supposed to be in secret preparation. Do you really know nothing of the tales? They are rumoured high and low.'

The abbot has difficulty answering in correct grammar. 'Profane matters—' he says, stumbling over his own tongue. 'The queen — child — You are not to think of — Stop rowing. Stop, I command you! I must call out in the instant.'

Most surprisingly, the sister obeys. The oars cease their motion. So little of the light of moon and stars penetrates the fog that he is better informed of it by his ears than his eyes. All is suddenly very still.

'I am astonished, father. I thought the good abbot Basculin was known as a friend of the queen, and one interested in her affairs. But we have reached the place. I suggest you stand and face over the stern. The ship of the Forget-Me-Not is but a small distance in that direction.'

'Stand? I can barely see!'

'I shall maintain the balance of the boat by means of the oars,' she says. The abbot reaches a hand to the thwart and very cautiously attempts to lift himself upright. His legs are trembling but the boat seems steady.

'Then you have no knowledge at all of the queen's plots, father? How wise and unworldly you are!'

The abbot thinks it was an evil omen that he misheard her name as *Maledicta*, which means *accursed*. He would rather have the company of English sailors, no matter how brutish, than this iron-voiced and brawny-armed novice! Why does she speak of the splendid and oppressed Marie-Antoinette, as though by diabolical insight she knows the very mission to which he is sworn?

'Ahoy, ahoy!' he calls out. 'I, your appointed passenger, am here!'

'You must turn yourself around, father, and lean over the stern. In this fog all sounds are dulled. Also your voice is by nature weak.'

He means to rebuke her severely for this disrespectful remark but finds he either cannot or dares not. With tiny shuffling motions, so as not to disturb the boat's tranquillity, he rearranges his stance.

'Well then,' comes the patient voice from behind the veil. 'If you are ignorant of the queen's doings, and that bold hero the Forget-Me-Not, you must surely have heard stories of the *priest-killer*?'

'Silence! In God's name, silence!' The abbot feels for the stern, leaning forward. He will shout loud enough to rouse the drowned from their slumbers! He will not endure another moment in this boat.

There is a small noise at his back, the creak of an oar swiftly raised from its resting-place. In the next instant its tip presses against the base of his spine. A third instant and the oar pushes with irresistible force, propelling the abbot Basculin and his secret parcel of letters over the stern and into the sea. For a brief while he struggles, his old limbs given unnatural energy by the prospect of extinction. But the tip of the oar descends from above, prodding and nudging him under. The sea is shallow here, but deep enough, exactly as deep as a grave.

CHAPTER ONE

Consider, reader, the WORLD, and all the people in it.

Now, observe —

Do you not see, that the whole race of mankind is divided into exactly *two* classes? and that every rational creature that walks the globe, belongs either to the one, or the other?

We have once or twice advanced this theory of ours, during our rare sallies into society, and been mocked for it. Our accusers do not say, we are *wrong*. — The proposition itself is not in dispute, among persons of any degree of education. No — they laugh at us, for daring to repeat a trivial observation, as though it were some profound discovery. Ha — they say to us — They take a pinch of snuff, or flutter a fan — Ha — Will you attempt to astonish the world with the assertion, that it consists of *men* and *women*?

There is no use trying to enlighten such people. The labour of *Sisyphus*, would be less discouraging. —

Our theory does NOT refer to the distinction of the sexes. Any body with the smallest experience of the world, has learned for themselves, that although some are created to bear children, and others to engender them, you may find every conceivable kind of person, in the ranks of either — Every shade of ignorance, folly, selfishness, cupidity, and meanness of spirit — along with, we suppose, their opposites — Regardless of the arrangement of the organs of generation. Moreover, every body knows there are such things as *manly* women — feminine men — Mere beasts, of both sexes. — No — We shall not seek a proper understanding of the great division of mankind, in so superficial a distinction.

Strip away all accident and ornament. Direct your search, to the *inward* heart of each individual nature —

The abysmal deeps of Personality*

— and you are compelled to admit, that all your fellow-creatures, without exception, belong to one or other of the two orders; —

EITHER, those who declare that the Revolution in France of the year 1789, was the most fortunate event in the whole of human history; that, by overthrowing a sclerotic and corrupted hereditary monarchy, and proclaiming instead the universal RIGHTS OF MAN, the people of that country made an example for every other nation to follow, which, if repeated, would usher the great brotherhood of mankind towards an age of universal justice, enlightenment, and peace;

OR, those who believe the same event to have been a miserable catastrophe, founded upon specious principles, enacted in orgies of barbarous violence, which by its reckless contempt for established authority threatened the very ground of good order and lawful rule, and threw into bloody confusion all the connexions that bind together the elements of society, thus changing a proud nation into a desert of savages, and the habitation of wolves.

We offer no additional defence of our theory. We have not the time. — It is simple and self-evident truth. *You*, reader, we trust, are wise enough to acknowledge as much without further debate.

We think we know you — do we not? Your face —

Alas, so many faces come and go before us. An endless phantasmagoria — Faces from the past — the present — From — dare we say it — *futurity*, in momentary glimpses —

---

* A noble phrase, borrowed from one of our modern poets. We do not name him — In case the name be destined for obscurity.

In London, towards the latter half of the year 1791, no one disputes our claim. Over the intervening decades, the truth of it has turned secret and subtle, though no less perfect; but at *that* time — the time of our tale — it is known as plainly as the soil beneath your shoe. The two orders of mankind have divided between them, every domain of human existence. Each inhabit their separate hemispheres, from which they look with utter disdain at the occupants of the other, and exchange frequent volleys of hostile language. They attend distinct gatherings, in different houses. At the theatre, and the pleasure gardens, and other public assemblies, they sit apart from one another. They promenade in opposite directions around the walks of the Pantheon, or at Ranelagh. They bestow their patronage upon, or offer their services to, members of their own class exclusively. Their kind of musical performance is applauded; the other, vehemently hissed. A foaming torrent of tracts, journals, pamphlets, and books, pours from the presses, destined for one camp or the other, bursting with execrations against the opposing side.

Our book — we assure you, reader — is one of those rare productions, which may be read with pleasure and profit, by EITHER sort. —

For the most part, in the year 'ninety-one, the adherents of each party do not meet one another. In our own times, and, we suppose, in the ages to come, the two races of mankind no longer exist in a state of open warfare. Indeed, the mysterious progress of history is such, that there are now very many of our fellow men and women who *do not themselves know* to which they belong! — a most remarkable circumstance, which tends, among other things, to the maintenance of peaceful relations between them. But at the time of our story, the great cataclysm of 'eighty-nine is fresh in the memory — uppermost in every mind — And those who consider the age they live in to be the *best* of times, will have nothing to do with those who think it the *worst.* — Or — we need hardly add — *vice versa.*

Woe betide the man, who enters a room, where Dr Price's Sermon Before the Constitutional Society is eagerly discussed and approved of, bearing under his arm, his private volume of the Hon. Mr Burke's Reflections on the Revolution in France!

Alas for her, who announces her approval of Miss Wollstonecraft's Vindication of the Rights of Woman, in the company of subscribers to Miss Hannah More's penny tracts!

It is no use affecting, that one *has no opinion*. Every body has their opinion. One might as well find oneself — greatly, perhaps, to one's surprize — standing in incorporeal form before the gate of Heaven, with St Peter gazing on in severe enquiry, his pen poised over the ledger of the blessed and the damned, and declare oneself *a sort of deist — of no particular religion* — though I've nothing against it, mind — one wishes all the religious fellows could be less determined with all their *bally-hoo*, what?

Well — we hear you ask — for it seems to us we *do* know you, reader! or one who was very like you — Well, but of which of the two orders of mankind is THOMAS PEACH?

The case of that remarkable man is, we confess, an unusual one. — Ours is not the only theory, which the history of Mr Tho.s Peach threatens to undermine.

But — He is not, at this moment, the principal actor in our play.

Are you impatient, reader, to renew your acquaintance with the gentleman? Do you chafe to learn, what sway he holds, over the events of the hour? — For — you wisely deduce — in this crisis of the world, a man of exceptional talents — a man, who considers more deeply, and sees farther, than others do — a man, whose penetrating eye has pierced the veil, of *death itself* — A man, in short, such as our Mr Peach — He, you may well suppose, has no small part to play, in the great drama now unfolding.

Alas — We must beg your patience nevertheless.

Remember, good reader, that Thomas Peach, for all his talents — Powers, which, if he chose to exercise them in public view, would raise him among the Titans of the age! — Is, by temperament, a modest and retiring soul. — One of those, that love nothing so much, as to sit by their fire-sides of an evening, with only a volume of some favourite author for company. The events of the hour he is content to let pass, outside his door — which is locked. — Beyond his windows — which are shuttered.

Remember also, that six years have come and gone, since we saw him last. Six years, of determined retirement — Deliberate seclusion —

His retreat, has not been altogether tranquil.

Let us be candid, reader — for you would do well to fortify yourself, against what lies ahead. Since we last bade farewell to Mr Peach, six years past, he is fallen deep into a certain *obscurity*.

Darkness attends him. —

Now, reader — You may object, that Mr Peach was always OBSCURE, and ATTENDED BY DARKNESS.

If so — we congratulate you, on your understanding of that portion of the history of this extraordinary man, which we had the honour of laying before you, in our former volume, some years hence.*

It is true, that Thomas Peach lived always in quiet retirement, in the country — the better to practise arts, not fit for the eyes of the vulgar.

It is likewise true, that he was *attended*, by a domestic servant, of an unusual nature — That famous, or infamous, *Miss Clarissa Riddle*, of whom it may be said with confidence, that if ever there was a creature *of darkness*, young Clary is that creature. — That much we pronounce with certainty, though little else! — for the exact nature of Miss Riddle remained as mysterious to us, at the conclusion of our former history, as it was when she made her ill-starred entrance.

---

* *vide* The Infernal Riddle of Tho.s Peach, Esq., of Somerset-Shire. — A lurid title, we confess, and perhaps not intirely according with our own preference. — But the whims of the book-sellers are not to be contradicted, by a mere *author*.

Nevertheless, we insist, that there has been a change. — And, not for the better.

You may judge for yourself, reader, when the time comes to disturb Mr Peach's retirement, by paying the gentleman a visit, in our next chapter.

Do not be alarmed — We shall do so, in the company of *a lady*.

Her acquaintance, we shall renew with pleasure unalloyed. — Indeed — you are not required, to defer that pleasure, until our next — For she is to make her appearance here, in our opening chapter.

With that happy promise, permit us now to conduct you, good reader, to *London* — where Mr Peach never goes, though he has often been invited — requested — Summoned, even, by the more peremptory sort of correspondent.

Among the latter we number one Monsieur de Charizard. A man of France — a petty nobleman, or *seigneur* — And, as our story begins, an *émigré*. — That is, one of the many Frenchmen, of the privileged and wealthy classes, who found the loss of their privileges not to their taste, and have removed themselves beyond the borders of their nation, to a place where they can enjoy their wealth in peace.

The Monsieur was assisted in his decision, by the partial reduction of the Château Charizard to ruin, at the hands of a mob of excitable peasants, in the summer of 'eighty-nine. He suffered no injury himself, for, like all Frenchmen of distinction, or any pretensions thereto, he dwelt exclusively in Paris and Versailles, and seldom visited the castle of his ancestors, which lies, at any rate, upon a crag of granite, in a remote and rough part of Brittany, surrounded by gloomy forests; the whole situation distressing to any refined sensibility.

His family likewise escaped any indignity, because — he has no family.

Monsieur de Charizard is known to be a *libertine*.

Not for him, the common satisfactions of domestic existence! The Monsieur will drink life to the dregs — Refill the goblet, and quaff again — And to the devil with those who disapprove!

He is said to have been an associate of the notorious *Marquis de Sade.**

Certain it is, that his intellectual pursuits have led him in regions unknown to orthodoxy, and proscribed by polite society. For, upon his first arrival at London, two winters past, he sent a letter to Mr Tho.s Peach, Esq., the *English magician*, requesting in the most elegant and charming terms the honour of a visit, at whatever day and hour might be convenient.

Black rumours have been attached to the name of de Charizard, for generations. In the town of Charizard-in-the-Wood, below the granite outcrop, deep within the gloomy forest, they speak of a compact made with the Devil — A curse, inherited by each successive *seigneur*, with his title.

The present holder is rumoured to interest himself, in occult practices, of the boldest sort.

Monsieur de Charizard's letter received no reply. — Not so much as an acknowledgment. The Monsieur was quite shocked.

He considered making a journey, to the rural parts of England. — Considered it briefly; for he has heard the rustic Britons are scarcely distinguishable from bears, in manners, appearance, and intellectual capacity.

In the following summer — the summer, of the year 'ninety — an opportunity arose, to pursue some further enquiries, without exposing himself to the British peasantry. Monsieur de Charizard was invited to join a party, at Bath. — A place, he had been informed, of fashionable entertainment — And a mere few miles distant, from that obscure nook of the country, where the so-called magician is said to reside.

The fashionable entertainments excited only his disdain. — These English, they have no more understanding of *la mode*, than buskined Germans!

---

* Our reader looks quizzical. We do not blame you in the least. The notoriety of this Marquis, is of so utterly *French* a nature, that it cannot be translated. — May, indeed, be perfectly invisible, to the British eye.

His enquiries, however, were not altogether fruitless. He learned, that Mr Thomas Peach was a notable eccentric of the country. — His company, never sought, or, if by some accident requested, always refused. — His house, universally shunned.

Monsieur de Charizard had at least the satisfaction of learning, that his was not the only letter, addressed to that man, to go without reply — Indeed, that Mr Peach was known to avoid correspondence of any sort, as rigorously and inflexibly, as though he had taken an oath against it, like some hermit of the pen.

The only reason Mr Peach is spoken of, in Bath, at all, is — That he is known to be in some sort under the protection of a rich Englishwoman—a female *poet*, no less!—A certain Mademoiselle Farthingay — a person of fashion and distinction, by the standards of the country, despite the acknowledged fact, that her father was — a *tobacco-merchant!*

M de Charizard would laugh at the pretensions of these barbarians, if he were not more inclined to weep at them.

He has been forced to exchange the court of Versailles, for this!
—

Accursed revolution!

How, he wonders, came the mysterious Mr Peach to be connected, with — he hides his smile, as best he can — so *distinguished* a person, as this poetess, the Miss Farthingay?

— Well, monsieur — Her parents, you know — both dead, some years past — Bad business — Both of 'em at once, in their beds — Nasty rumours — This Peach fellow, of some assistance to the lady, in the crisis — One don't like to enquire too close — Not genteel, what? — Beneath the lady, to conern herself with such a fellow, hey? — But a dem handsome woman — Dem handsome! —

Monsieur de Charizard could only conclude, that the rumours which had reached him, in the libertine salons of Paris, concerning this English adept of the occult arts, were quite phantastical. — That the so-called magician, was no more than some rustic madman, kept by an eccentric English lady, for her own amusement.

The lady, however, aroused his passing interest — For she is unmarried, and not yet thirty — and universally agreed, to be a beauty, according to British canons.

On returning to London, the Monsieur sent for a book of her verses. He understands English tolerably well — but could make nothing of them. The language seems to him quite unfit for poetry. — Nevertheless, it is plain enough from Mademoiselle the Poet's titles, that she is infected with revolutionary fervour. 'The Harp of Liberty' — 'France Unchained: A Sonnet' — 'Lines, Written upon Receiving the News of the Destruction of the Bastille' —

Pah! — M de Charizard tosses the volume upon the rug, and takes up his glass instead — and forgets the whole affair.

There is not the slightest question as to which of *the two orders of mankind* includes our Monsieur. — And as little doubt, regarding the poetess.

It's therefore impossible, in the ordinary course of things, that they should ever set eyes on one another. Like planets, they move in separate spheres. — The Monsieur, we fancy, would do for *Mercury*. — And, if the rule held true, we should have no tale to tell, for our beginning hangs upon the conjunction of these two bodies.

But — how often is it the case, in every matter connected with the affairs of Mr Tho.s Peach! — on a certain ill-fated evening of the London season, in the year 'ninety-one, some strange power has intervened, to make possible that which should not be possible, if only for a few hours, across one small fraction of the metropolis.

Behold the fraction in question. — A fashionable terrace, in *St James's*.

Carriages pull up before a fine mansion, disgorging their various cargoes. Some of the vehicles are magnificent, and produce persons of distinction. Others are mere *hackneys*. Further visitors to the house arrive, on foot! — the majority, persons of suitably *pedestrian* appearance and station; although, as it happens, the Monsieur de Charizard has also arrived without a carriage. His apartments in the city are not far distant, and he enjoys promenading among the commoners and middling people of London town — Which is fortunate, since he disdains the use of the public conveyances, and, being in exile, has no equipage of his own.

He is dressed with his customary brilliance. Even his valet — who accompanies his master, each time the Monsieur ventures out the door — wears a refinement of tailoring few Englishmen dare aspire to. They attract much notice in the streets, wheresoever they go. Monsieur does not care in the least, that the astonishment he and his valet provoke, is not infrequently attended with laughter — mockery, even — or shouted insult.

For Monsieur de Charizard, there is positive delight in provoking the *canaille*. To offend the opinion of the masses, is an article of faith with him — Perhaps, his *only* article of faith.

It is quite otherwise with his valet. But the poor fellow's opinion is not asked, and, if given unsolicited, would count for nothing.

Let us step inside the mansion, and investigate the lure, that has attracted so mingled an assembly.

The scene within is curious indeed. Those who present their cards of invitation, and proceed to the grand room above-stairs, share no visible ties of rank, distinction, or amity. The highest of the high are not represented, nor, of course, the lowest of the low — Nor even the highest of the low. But of all the gradations between, almost every one has sent its ambassadors. The *beau monde* is on display, as always — the intire purpose of the *beau monde* is, to be on display — But there are also two or three elderly fellows, who by their appearance might as likely be found driving an hackney-carriage, as stepping out of one.

The guests are not numerous. Most seem to be strangers to one another, or, if they nod acknowledgment, perform the gesture in a manner that proclaims them *not friends*.

M de Charizard knows two or three, by sight. These are persons every body knows — Every body who is any body. A minister at the pleasure of His Majesty — A bishop, or some such — The Monsieur cannot exactly recall which offices they occupy, but he recognizes them as servants of a crowned head, and understands therefore, that he is among allies.

And yet! — over there, across the splendid room, where that gay circle forms — Is that not Lady____, and others of her *Whiggish* set? — who dress in absurd Grecian styles, and are loud in praise of the revolutionaries? He has heard that the scribbling fire-brand M Danton, so hot in the cause of the commoners of Paris that even the National Assembly is outraged, and has forced him to leave France — that Danton is received by Lady___, at her dinner-table.

Diable! — and who is that handsome dark woman, with her own hair piled loosely above her head, tied with no more ornament than a single scarf?

Reader — With this single look of the libertine monsieur, towards the handsome Miss Arabella Farthingay, of Somerset-shire, our tale properly BEGINS. — And — we think we hear you murmur — *not before time.*

Fatal glance!

Heaven and earth trembled no less, when the young prince of Troy first laid eyes on Helen of Greece —

M de Charizard cannot remove his gaze from her. — *Magnifique!*

Remember, reader, that he knows her not. How much better, had it stayed so — had strange fortune never brought the twain together at all! Yet certain conjunctions, are fated — Of too great significance, to be left to the whims of accident.

The tale we tell is one such, reader. — Never think, we have taken up our pen again, merely to amuse you.

Monsieur de Charizard insinuates himself among the general company, and begins making enquiries.

But what can be the occasion for a gathering so heterogeneous? — A dance is not intended. — There are no musicians. No tables are set for dining, and besides, the hour is too early to dine, except for those unencumbered by the slightest acquaintance with the decrees of fashion.

Let us inspect the adjacent room.

Here is a place of gilded magnificence. The windows look over Pall-Mall, with a lordly regard — while painted cherubs and nymphs in their turn look over the room, from the ceiling.

The furniture is all pushed back against the walls, to make a clear space in the middle, protected by a circle of velvet rope.

Within that circle are four chequered tables, each set for the game of chess. — The white army and the black, facing silently across the squares between, and a chair behind each, where their generals shall sit.

By twos and threes, the guests migrate to this room — In mixed procession — The minister, and the bishop, and the hackney-carriage drivers, side by side. Conversation descends to a murmur, as they approach the tables. The unkempt elderly gentlemen have fallen silent, and stare over the boards with something akin to hunger, like pagan worshippers, in the presence of their idol.

A bell chimes.

An announcement is made — General applause. — Four players step out from the crowd, and take seats, at each of the four tables. Two will play the white pieces, two the black.

The murmur descends again, to an expectant hush. The four stare at the pieces, as though delivering silent exhortations to their soldiers. — Be brave — fight well — to the death!

But where are their *opponents*?

The gilt and ivory clock on the mantel ticks on, in silence. —

A door in the panelling opens. Into the room steps an old man, plainly though neatly dressed, supporting himself with a black cane. An eruption of applause greets him. — *So that's the fellow! — Lord! he's so ordinary-looking — Nothing like his picture —* &c. —

It appears the old gentleman is to play four games himself, two on the white side, two on the black, passing from table to table.

He is introduced to each of the other players in turn — Bows — shakes hands — Receives their compliments — It is an honour — The honour, the gentleman replies, speaking with a pronounced accent, belongs entirely to me.

Our venerable chess-player is another Frenchman. Monsieur de Charizard eyes his countryman with an intent look. — Intent, and not altogether friendly, we should say. He watches the chess-players, like a cat watching a mouse-hole.

The elderly player speaks quietly to an assistant, who fetches a chair, and places it — facing *away* from the tables. Here the Frenchman sits himself.

He sighs, and wiggles his head, and nods to the same servant, who now produces from a pocket a length of black silk. Of this the boy makes a blind-fold, which he proceeds to tie, respectfully but deftly, at the back of the old man's head.

At this remarkable sight, further murmurs circle the crowd. The blind-folded player raises an arm, for silence — Which falls again, at once.

He has the room under a kind of spell.

— *Alors, Messieurs*, he says, in a firm voice, I am ready. Mr Monckton, your opening move, if you please.

One of the white players — whose bearing and dress proclaim him a person of no particular distinction, except among *chess-players*, where his name is as universally known, as it is feared — calls out, as though he expects the Frenchman to be deaf — Sir, I advance my king's bishop's pawn two squares. — And, having proclaimed his move, adjusts the corresponding piece on the board.

— Very well — says the blind-folded man. — Then I beg you will do me the honour of advancing my queen's pawn, by two squares.

Mr Monckton moves the black piece as instructed, and bends over the board in fierce thought.

— *Et maintenant*, the Frenchman says — without stirring from his chair, or removing the blind-fold — I commence the contest with you, milord Trent, by the advance of my king's pawn, two squares.

— An excellent beginning, Monsieur Philidor, replies Lord Trent, and moves the white piece towards his own black army. — I shall approve it by imitation, which is the sincerest of compliments. — The peer smiles around at the company, who applaud his remark, and moves the black king's pawn to face its opponent directly. — King's pawn to the fourth rank, Lord Trent says, in case his meaning should not have been clear to the Frenchman.

— Trent'll have him, murmurs someone near Monsieur de Charizard. — He's the devil of a player. I hear he's done nothing but prepare for the match for a week. Fifty pounds for Lord Trent.

The Monsieur is momentarily tempted to address himself to this booby, and accept the wager. These English fools cannot possibly understand the genius of Philidor. He himself, Hippolite-Aimant-Louis de Charizard, who has studied the mystery of chess with inconceivable devotion, still does not understand it. — Though he has suspicions.

Yet — in the present situation — even M de Charizard's confidence wavers. *Four* games, played simultaneously, *without once looking at the pieces* — Holding the changing position of each game, within his imagination alone — It is impossible the old monster can win them all, against the finest players in England — Impossible! He will mistake the disposition of the pieces — Confuse one game, with another. — No human brain can be capable of doing, what Philidor has proposed to do to-day.

Now, if it was that handsome woman, with her black hair bound like a goddess of Greece, who proposed the wager — *Diable!* he would accept in an instant, and contrive to lose, so he might observe her fine eyes sparkle in triumph, and her complexion flush.

He must have her — name!

To Hades with des Sables — What has the boy been doing? — The Monsieur looks around the room in search of his lavishly costumed valet, whom he instructed to gather information concerning the fascinating beauty, but des Sables — so we name the valet — is nowhere to be seen. Poor fellow — He is experiencing some difficulty in fulfilling his master's commission, for, despite having accompanied M de Charizard to London two winters past, he remains largely ignorant of the English language. — And moreover, the native valets, and footmen, and door-keepers of London, treat him with utter contempt, on account of the elaborate silks and baubles in which his master clothes him, and also because of the girlish beauty of his features.

This des Sables is a remarkably comely youth — Is he not, reader? — Quite remarkable!

The four games continue, in the manner already described. M Philidor, the old Frenchman, never moves from his chair, or touches his blind-fold. He holds his cane between his knees, twisting its head from time to time, and calls out his moves on each table in turn, one after the next. Initially his opponents reply without hesitation. The second white player, a Mr Goodacres, is seen to smile. A note of triumph creeps into his tone as he announces his seventh move. His neighbour Captain Anson, who, like Lord Trent, commands the black pieces, glances at Mr Goodacres's board, frowns, and reverts to the study of his own position.

Some of the crowd lean as far across the velvet ropes as they can, and stroke their chins, or bite their lips. — What can the old fellow be doing? — His knight — there? — The majority cannot see the boards, nor care to. Their amazement is aroused by the mere performance. They cannot refrain from whispers, until a perpetual tide of muttering flows around the circle — *Lord! how does he remember the moves? — I declare, there must be a trick — That blind-fold is only thin stuff — Has he a mirror in the ceiling?*

He has not a mirror in the ceiling.

M de Charizard cannot help himself. As though by mesmeric power, he is drawn to the front of the crowd. He would rather not see the tables — By his life! he would much prefer only to observe the laughing woman in her Grecian dress — Yet a terrible compulsion grips him. The imbecile Goodacres, who thinks he is winning, stands on the verge of swift and humiliating defeat. He has thrust his pieces into attack, neglecting the security of his king. Monckton has won a *chevalier*, without noticing how much he has lost, by snapping up the temporary advantage. — Philidor's pawns are now arranged in immovable formation in the centre of the field, and the white pieces will shortly be unable to move to advantage at all. Milord Trent stares at the board as though imploring the pieces to speak. He has not made any move at all, for fifteen minutes. He clings on — he will fight — But, by Hades! he will lose. They all lose to Philidor, just as he himself, the *seigneur* de Charizard, has lost, each time they played, in the salons of Paris, before the fool king and his spineless Swiss functionary Neckar permitted Paris to fall into the hands of snakes and donkeys.

It is beyond the bounds of nature, what Philidor does. — So M de Charizard avows.

Our Monsieur is not alone in his opinion. As the games proceed, beyond the tenth moves, and the fifteenth — and the four seated players grimace, and pick their lips, and snort in frustration — As Mr Goodacres cries in rage, and pushes back his chair, and races from the room — and handsome Lord Trent, the hope of British honour, is seen to shake his head, with a rueful smile — the whisper in the crowd rises to something like a roar — *I can't scarcely believe it — No one I tell will believe it — Lord! I declare he must be a wizard!*

The death-blow to Lord Trent, when it comes, is exquisite — A simple shuffle of an humble pawn, unlocking the attack of the bishop behind it, while in the same move opening a path for the entry of a castle to black's position, and undermine it as thoroughly, as though it carried several bags of powder. Applause rings out. — De Charizard cannot restrain his favourite oath — *Diable!*

M Philidor cocks his head, and again requests silence.

— Do I discern the voice of my old acquaintance, the noble Monsieur de Charizard? — The old man rises and removes his blind-fold. Though Lord Trent, among many others, hastens to congratulate him, M Philidor scans the assembly, until he discovers his fellow-countryman, to whom he directs a species of bow — Perhaps somewhat sardonic in character. — It is difficult to be certain, with French manners.

— I fear you had better withdraw, Monsieur, says a female voice at de Charizard's shoulder. — He looks as if he might select you for his next opponent.

M de Charizard turns to see who has dared to address him so freely.

Diable! it is the handsome woman with the Grecian hair! —

With that rapidity granted only to Frenchmen in such situations, he conceals his surprize, his pleasure, and his access of urgent lust, and is immediately charming.

— I would present merely a trifling dessert to Monsieur Philidor, madame, after the feast he has made of your countrymen. But if he does me the honour of requesting to devour me, I shall not attempt to flee, like man of ginger-bread.

The handsome lady laughs. — How it gratifies him! Laughter is not deemed polite at Versailles, or in the highest London society. But this woman's stile of dress declares her one of those, who adhere to the maxims of *Rousseau*, and embrace what is natural in man. — There is a freedom about her manners and her motions, thinks Monsieur, which quite entrances one. — How delightful it would be, to tame such a spirit!

— You play the game, monsieur?

— Always, madame, he replies, and allows his look to become penetrating and significant.

— Gracious! I hope you do not think to make *me* a piece in your sport. Do not say, *You shall be my queen*, I beg you. Think of something wittier.

Diable! but these English women are bold as sailors!

— On the contrary, madame, it is I who would gladly enlist under your colours, as the humblest *pion*. But I must beg you to forgive the observation, that you hint at some offence I may have most inexcusably given? I shall exist in the utmost agitation until you condescend to enlighten me, for I cannot attempt to clear the stain upon my honour until I am conscious where it lies.

— Pray, Monsieur de Charizard, do not be agitated in the least. Your honour is certainly as spotless as it was when you entered the room. I understand nevertheless that your valet, who appears to be an angel in human dress, has gone up and down the house enquiring after me.

— An angel? The boy is a very devil of hell. I shall beat him without mercy, madame, for his gross impertinence. I shall strip him naked and thrash his tenderest flesh to ribbons. — Des Sables! — The Monsieur again scans the room for his unfortunate servant, thunder in his eye.

— Heavens, monsieur! you may spare the boy. I meant only to save him and yourself any further labour, by resolving the mystery myself.

M de Charizard bows very low, with the correct sweep of his arm and fluxion of his backward knee. — These English cannot make a proper bow, any more than they can write proper poetry. Their flesh is by nature as incapable of one, as their tongue of the other. — He declares himself mortified — infinitely obliged to the lady — her servant for eternity. She is amused by the performance, exactly as a woman of spirit should be. — The game of honour and *politesse* is to be played, with a smile, and a wink. There is no use at all in a beautiful woman, who is *too* polite, and guards her honour with frigid severity. — No use, except the enjoyment of breaking them at the last; but that particular enjoyment our Monsieur reserves, for low-born ladies, whose husbands may be bought off, or, if they insist on a duel, killed without scandal.

The lady gives her name as Miss *Farthingay*.

To the devil with these English consonants! It is like swallowing one's own tongue.

The name, Monsieur reflects, has a ring of familiarity. He has heard of the woman — But cannot recall where.

Is it possible she has *a certain reputation*? She is by no means of the youngest, and yet unmarried. —

Once, in the days when France was still France, Monsieur de Charizard knew what those simple observations signified. He might then have disdained the conquest of such a woman, as too easy an adventure. But that was before the chains of custom were broken, and the world turned upside-down. — Who now knows, what a woman is?

— I have been making enquiries of my own, monsieur, Miss Farthingay says, her eyes still alive with amusement, in a manner which threatens to arouse the soul of M de Charizard to a phrenzy. — You are not come to London as an ambassador of the National Assembly, I may suppose.

— And dare I trust that you will be so infinitely obliging as to pardon the observation, that you would receive such an embassy with favour?*

— One ought not argue so great a question as the merits of your National Assembly in this company, says Miss Farthingay. — We are here with no purpose but to enjoy a game, are we not? — She gestures to the men gathered by the tables, where M Philidor continues to receive the congratulations of the company.

— Ah! cries Monsieur de Charizard — You believe the chess nothing but a sport?

Miss Farthingay is surprized. — Shall I understand, monsieur, that you do not?

— A *game*, of kings and queens, and knights, and jesters, castles, commoners? Milady — Consider the nations of the world,

---

* Forgive us, reader. — Our duty as historian demands, that we record certain parts of these conversations, in full. It is difficult to credit, that only a few decades since, men and women of a certain station were required to employ these absurd circumlocutions, in order to speak to one another without giving offence. We shall paraphrase where we can — And hope, that our tale proceeds swiftly to less honourable forms of conversation — Which, as you will have deduced, is certainly the intention of Monsieur de Charizard.

in these present times. Can any one maintain the chess is nothing
but play, when it shews, that a mere *pion* may in time become a
queen, or imprison a king?

— The views of Monsieur de Charizard, says a new voice,
regarding the game of chess, are notably eccentric.

The newcomer is — Monsieur Philidor himself! — who has
politely made his way through the throng of admirers, towards
his fellow-countryman. Miss Farthingay greets him gracefully,
with compliments on his astonishing performance. M Philidor
declares himself *enchanté* — &c. — The crowd gathers around,
among them the defeated Lord Trent, who, in common with
several other young men of good family or fortune, is solicitous in
his attentions to Miss Farthingay. He wonders, whether she will
favour the world, with a commemoration of M Philidor's fourfold
triumph, in *verse*?

Diable! — The Farthingay! — She is the poet! — the patroness,
of Monsieur Peach!

But — hellfire and damnation! — she is now in conversation
with the lords and ladies — while he must defend himself, before
the accursed old goat Philidor!

M de Charizard explains, for the benefit of those assembled
nearby — raising his voice to as melodious a pitch as the English
words will suffer, and decorating his speech with whatever poor
flourishes the lumpen grammar of the language allows, in hopes
of recapturing the attention of the infernally charming
Farthingay — Explains, that chess is not merely a set of pieces,
governed in mechanical fashion by another set of rules, like one
of their British steam-engines — But, a *mystery*. — That its
origins are entwined with the Eastern religions, and that the
prophets and wise men of the orient created it as an oracle. —
That in the course of its transition to Europe, through the
centuries, its true meaning was obscured, and it became merely
a past-time — But its secrets, though veiled in age, may one day
be rediscovered — Most of all at the present moment, for who
cannot see in the recent history of France, certain patterns that

play across the chess-board? — the advance of *pawns* — the retreats and counter-attacks of royalty — the evasions of cavaliers — the plans of the jesters, which you English mistakenly call bishops —

— *Comme on dit*, Monsieur Philidor says, lifting his cane a little — Quite eccentric!

Several of those listening are moved to smile, or hide their mouths. By the fires of Phlegethon, thinks de Charizard — He would call them out, if this were private company, and dare them to mock him to his face! — call them out, and kill them! for the English are as inept in the duel, as in all other refinements of honour. — He remains perfectly courteous, and debates for a while with old Philidor — who insists, as for all his damnably long life he has insisted, that the game of chess is perfectly and exclusively *rational*; comprises no more, than the execution of its rules, which, though subtle, are neither numerous nor complex; and that his own mastery derives merely from understanding how the rules are best applied.

Monsieur de Charizard knows otherwise.

He is certain — he is most profoundly certain — that Philidor has struck a bargain with supernatural powers. There is no other explanation. The old fiend makes moves no other person can see — Wins games, with half the pieces his opponent employs — Wins while *blinded*, by Hades! — Can none of these buffoons see what is plain before them? Philidor has been granted the antient secrets of chess. De Charizard is as sure of it, as of Satan himself. — But he has not the *proof*! — and must therefore endure the laughter and slights, perpetually suffered by those, who see deeper than the *canaille*.

Diable! —

— May I hope, says Philidor, with a rogueish wink, quite disgusting in one so far advanced towards his grave — May I hope, monsieur, you have been fortunate in your search for those particular chess-pieces, in which you were once so excessively interested?

M de Charizard bows again. — Smiles, in the correct manner — that is, without exposing his teeth, as the English barbarians do — And steels himself to endure further mockery — Inwardly raging.

— Monsieur de Charizard, continues Philidor, for the benefit of the assembled rabble, Was once most diligent in the effort to obtain a certain set of pieces, which he credits with magical powers. — Philidor embellishes the concluding English words with a discreet raising of his eyebrows, and pretends an expression of solemnity.

— I would happily assist Monsieur de Charizard in his search, says the smiling Lord Trent. — He and I have equally concluded, that we shall never win a game against Monsieur Philidor, except by *supernatural* means.

Feeble as this sally is, all the company applauds it. — Ignorant dolts! sneering imbeciles!

Our Monsieur is in a most vengeful mood, when at last he takes himself home. He struts along the public roads with particular emphasis, to the burning embarrassment of his young valet.

The poor youth des Sables fears worse may follow within-doors. Alas! he knows his master's moods. — He foresees himself tied in silken ribbons, with an apple or an orange placed between his teeth — the orange is somewhat the less objectionable of the two — Lashed upon the buttocks, and then treated, as his master assures him, in the fashion the heroes of antient Greece treated their favoured servants —

We shall not stay to discover, whether his fears prove groundless. What passes among *Frenchmen*, is not our concern, thank God!

We are grateful for our licensed indifference, to French matters — Though we anticipate, that it may present some difficulties, in the execution of our tale — For, a considerable portion of what follows, is destined to take place upon French soil.

But, we shall find a way —

Or, *a way shall be found for us.* —

In this matter at least, we are of the opinion of Monsieur de Charizard, not Monsieur Philidor. — There are arts and mysteries, which elude or transgress the rules of perfect reason. Our own efforts witness it — And the forces, that direct our narrative, have a potency we cannot ourselves explain —

Ah! — THOMAS PEACH! — What dark principles have we imbibed from you!

Most reasonable of men! — Wise and moderate, in your conduct — benevolent, in habits — Enlightened, in principles! Yet how mysterious the revelations consequent on your history, and how obscure the shadows that attend your name!

You are the pattern of light and dark together — Like the chess-board —

Forgive us our simile, reader. The curious scene just passed, has as it were imprinted it, upon our mind's eye — Black against white, like printed pages.

Let us shake from our brain Mr Peach and his riddling shadows. Our duty, reader, as we advised you, lies not with him — But, for the present, with his friend and patroness, the poetical Miss Farthingay — handsome, witty, and gay! — In whose company we hope for livelier entertainment, than can be expected from a man of solitary habits, and strange pursuits. The *queen*, is the brilliant ornament of the chess-board, always busy, and ranging far and wide — while the *king* hides in his corner, fearful of notice, and crawls unwillingly, if he be compelled to move at all —

How rich in figures is this game of chess!

We declare, reader — We should not like to decide, between the interpretations of messieurs de Charizard and Philidor — The light of *reason*, and the dark of *mystery* —

A month goes by after the hasty flight of abbot Basculin. His friends thank God that he is safely across the Sleeve, for the revolutionaries grow hotter against established religon with every passing week.

All hope of his prompt return is surrendered. In the depths of September, when the air turns cool and unpicked pears and apples spread a sweet stench of rot over the fields of Normandy, news comes from Paris that the king has given his solemn oath to abide by the constitution. The revolution is complete. Centuries of monarchy are terminated. Already several town notaries and the like have put their names forward for the approval of men of even less significance, hoping to be elected to the new Assembly. Within two scant years the nation of France has been turned end over end like an infant's toy, and eminences like Basculin, once raised to its head by their wisdom and piety, are now to be kicked in the mud.

'This new Assembly will order that all prisoners be freed,' says Gaspard Lesinge to Cochonne. 'Depend upon it.'

Cochonne feels a flutter of hope in her heart. 'It is true?'

'Most certainly true,' says Lesinge. He raises a finger, a gesture of instruction. 'It has been the custom to free the prisoners on occasions of national celebration since the time of the Roman kings. The days of Jesus himself.'

Cochonne makes the sign of the cross over her breast. 'How many things you know,' she sighs.

Lesinge sidles across the floor of his cell, bringing himself closer to the barred aperture in the door through which he and Cochonne converse.

Gaspard Lesinge has been in prison for many days now. No one comes to see him but the jailer's daughter. Therefore it is upon the jailer's daughter, extraordinary specimen though she is, that he must practise his arts.

'In the language of the Romans,' he says, 'it was called the *jubilee*.'

Cochonne repeats the strange word.

'I would go so far as to wager that the decree has already been made. We may expect the order to arrive from Paris within two days. Three, if the roads are wet and the messengers lazy.'

'I shall hurry to my father,' says Cochonne, 'and ask him about it.'

'Bah!' Lesinge exclaims, wagging his finger. 'There is no need to wait for the permission of that old tyrant.'

'Nevertheless, sir, he is the jailer. The message from Paris will be given to him first.'

'What does it matter which person receives the message? It is the decree itself which signifies. Now that it is made — and, my dearest Cochonne, it most surely has been made — ought it not be put in force at once? The law is too great a thing to be delayed by roads or weather, or the whims of its petty ministers.'

'Sir,' says Cochonne, slowly, 'is it perhaps possible, that you invent this *jubilee*, to persuade me to set you at liberty, without the authority of my father?'

'Outrageous suggestion!'

'My form may be monstrous, but I have a heart of tenderness. Do not wound it, sir.'

Lesinge falls to his knees on the rough stone. 'On my honour!'

'I shall consult my parent,' says Cochonne.

Her parent is a notable farmer, who keeps his grain and the fodder for his cows in the disintegrating castle that has for centuries overlooked the town and the crooked arm of the harbour below. The castle was raised in the time of Charles the Wise, when it presented an impressive appearance, ringed around with towers, commanding the whole coast from Coutances to Saint-Jean. On the day the last stone was laid its long decline began, as all creatures commence their dying the day they are born. By the reign of the thirteenth Louis it had already fallen into senescence. The townsfolk adopted its failing structures for barns and byres. This was lucky for the castle, since it spared the people the necessity of overrunning and destroying it in the summer of 'eighty-nine, when their rage boiled against all symbols of the old regime, especially the property of those to whom the regime demanded they pay their tithes and taxes.

Cochonne's father fell by accident into the position of custodian of the weed-strewn castle grounds. For want of any better he is therefore also the jail-keeper, since the ruins preserve at the base of one of their towers a handful of cells where prisoners may still be kept.

Before the revolution the office was almost ceremonial. But in these two years of turmoil and suspicion the cells have rarely been empty. For this reason the farmer presses his daughter into service. She takes food and fresh straw to the imprisoned men, and attends to other menial tasks, so that he and his sons may continue the more important work of plough and churn.

Not every father, even among the peasantry, would send his daughter of nineteen years to wait upon criminals. But Cochonne is no ordinary girl.

She is a colossus. 'Piglet girl,' they called her almost as soon as she was born, for she came from the womb huge, fat and squealing; an infant of such dimensions she cost the mother her life. As she began, she continued, growing prodigiously. Her baptismal name is long forgotten. She stands well over six feet tall, with shoulders that beg to be yoked to a cart. Her father has surrendered all hope of finding her a husband. She would be far better than an ordinary wife, he used to say to the men of the town. She will do a man's work when needed, and for the rest, think of the sons she would give! But Normandy is as full of sweet apple-cheeked girls as of apples; no one wants to wed an Amazon. His daughter is an embarrassment and an encumbrance. His wife — his second wife, mother to his two dutiful human-sized sons — also despises Cochonne, and thinks her best off up in the castle ruins where no one sees her except the prisoners. She would persecute the girl thoroughly if she dared, but is afraid of her, as are her sons. When Cochonne was fifteen the boys tried to tease her by tying her up and lowering her on a rope into the castle well. She broke the wrist of one and the nose of the other.

Those sins she confessed. She was truly sorry for them at the time. She even wept a little as she said her rosary. She used to think God would permit her no longer to be a monster once she stopped growing, if her heart was good, as the curate assured her it was. But now she is nineteen and nothing has changed. Her legs are as thick as a man's. God has ignored all her prayers.

Therefore Cochonne no longer confesses every small thought which perhaps harbours a sin. This new prisoner, for example, who tells beautiful stories, and can shape his hands so their shadow becomes the head of a quacking duck, or a wolf curling its muzzle: she has told no one of the pity his plight arouses in her, nor how she blushes to hear his words of admiration. Her father says the man is a common brigand, arrested for robbery on the road. Her own heart tells her it cannot be true. If only she could free him, as he has once or twice begged her to, in passionate whispers!

But Cochonne, though a simple tender soul, is not absolutely stupid. She knows to her sorrow that the regard he professes for her is feigned. All her life she has been informed of her unspeakable ugliness.

Yet while a barred door stands between them, what harm is there in pretending that the stranger honestly means the fine words he says? — as long as she is never foolish enough to open the door and put them to the test.

Poor Cochonne!

She finds her father by the old castle gate, his sickle on his knees, plying a sharpening-stone. Is it true, she asks, that the new lords in Paris will declare a general amnesty of prisoners, to celebrate their victory over the king?

He laughs at her for pretending to understand men's business just because she is formed to a man's size. 'Better to drag all the rats from their cells and toss them on a fire, hey? There would be what I call a celebration!'

'The man here will not be freed, then?' For a moment her look lingers on the bunch of keys her father wears at his belt.

'Freed!' He coughs, spits into the weeds. 'He will be hung. What is a prisoner for if not to hang?'

Thus Cochonne has confirmation that she has been imposed upon.

She is more sorrowful than angry. When she goes to the castle tower that evening she does not answer Lesinge's greeting or even meet his eyes. 'My beauty!' he cries. 'My Penthesilea!' He often calls her by this name. She thinks it magnificent though she cannot pronounce it. It means, he says, a queen, a great warrior queen from the days of heroes. She supposes this is another lie. The word is probably some coarse insult and he secretly mocks her with it, as everyone mocks her.

She extinguishes the lantern at the foot of the stairs with relish, and leaves the prisoner to reflect on his sins in the dark.

That night the young men of the town have their own plans for their captive.

This town, like every other town in France, is in ferment. Each time news arrives from Paris it comes as though brought aboard a merchantman in the crooked harbour. The true news, stacked in the hold, is unloaded, opened, eagerly consumed. But alongside that cargo the ship brings all the usual detritus: contraband in the master's cabin, fleas on the mariners, weeds and barnacles clinging to the hull. So the intelligence of the king's solemn oath to uphold the constitution is attended with trains of pestilential rumour and scabbed with crusts of ignorance. The king's vow, it is said, was witnessed by Jesuits. Everyone knows that the creed of the Jesuits is casuistry and oath-breaking. The king's brothers, the Count of

Artois and the Duke of Bourbon, have publicly declared that the constitution will be overthrown and the people taxed again, at twice the rate they were before. The priests are hoarding all the corn. The queen has given birth to a baby wolf. The English devil called the Forget-Me-Not goes about Normandy disguised as a milkmaid, stealing all the muskets and cannon to prepare the way for an invasion. All this and more is reported as common knowledge. In brief, there are dangers and enemies everywhere. If the revolution is not defended with force of arms, my faith! — the rich men will rush back from exile, and there will be no more bread.

At the meeting of the town's Society of Patriots, solemnised by wine and candlelight, the young men come to their resolutions. The first matter is to deal with the prisoner up at the old castle. Most certainly he spies for the queen or is an agent of the Count of Artois. It is time, my brothers, to take up torches and reaping-hooks, and shed blood for justice!

The young men march first to the house of Cochonne's father. Here they inform him of the decision of the Society of Patriots, and demand the prison keys. If any of you brainless wastrels would consent to marry my daughter, the old farmer thinks, you might have them, and a horse to ride away on too. But they are merely boys, drunk on the promise of violence. He tells them to go to bed and slams his door.

The fury of the patriots only increases. The filthy old farmer and his sons, are they not hoarding grain, in secret chambers of the ruined castle? There is some argument over whether his house should be set aflame.

From a room above Cochonne hears the rough language of the young men and sees their torches spitting in the fine mist. She does not hesitate. The face of her prisoner comes before her like a vision. His intelligent eyes! That mouth, so mobile and expressive! Lesinge is not young, and the face, considered as a totality, is not beautiful. Still, when she watches him speak her heart trembles.

Ignoring the indignation of her stepmother, she rushes out of the back door, bare feet splashing in mud and filth, and up the winding lane to the castle.

When the mob arrives several minutes later, it finds her stationed at the entrance to the tower stairs, holding a long-handled rake.

The young men bump and nudge one another.

'Stand aside, woman, in the name of France!' says the most eloquent among them. His father is the schoolteacher.

'No,' says Cochonne.

'Disgusting boar!' shouts a less eloquent patriot. He scoops a handful of mud and flings it at the girl. 'Pig-woman!'

'The prisoner,' says the teacher's boy, 'is declared an enemy of the people. Justice must be served.'

'I shit on your justice,' says Cochonne.

'Aristocrat!' cries an enraged youth. This boy has long nursed a special hatred for the giantess because of her naked piety. His own father, a cobbler and from time to time a binder of books, taught him that priests leeched all the wealth of France and are to blame for every one of her ills. He breaks ranks with his companions and rushes forward to knock Cochonne out of the way. His bravery earns him no better reward than a crushing blow from the handle of the rake.

'Ow! Demon!' he wails, from his position in the mud.

Though the mob is not large, it decides that against a single opponent it must prevail by mere force of numbers. The Patriots make a disorganised charge, impelled with more energy by the rearguard than those in the van. One, two! — the farm implement fells the first pair of boys to venture within range. One howls and clutches his head, a sticky mess coming away on his palm. The other tumbles silently. When he pulls himself to his knees he has no recollection of where he is or how he came to be there. He sees his friends withdrawing in haste and crawls after them, mystified by the refusal of his legs to carry him upright.

'I took you for a queen of the Amazons,' says Gaspard Lesinge to Cochonne, the next day, 'but now I believe you are no less than the goddess of victory.' Though she has not boasted of her triumph, Lesinge naturally overheard the tumult outside the tower. 'I owe you my life, fair one. How richly I would reward you, if only I were freed from this whore of a prison!'

Cochonne snorts.

'You doubt me?'

'I think, sir, you will tell any lie at all to save yourself from hanging.'

Lesinge laughs. He is by no means a handsome man. By nature he is cautious, cunning and stealthy, like the rat, and his features are moulded accordingly: sharp-nosed, eager-eyed almost to a grotesque degree. Days of incarceration have cast a ghoulish pallor over his complexion and left his hair long and foul. His face, however, is unusual in animation and expressiveness. There are not many who can laugh in a cell. Cochonne has overseen a number of prisoners these last two years, and every one has in some degree been rendered dull and despairing by their situation. The vital spark fades. They slump into sacks of clothed flesh. Never before has she met a man like Lesinge.

'And do you blame me for it, goddess?'

'A man ought not to lie. Also, this word, *goddess*, I do not like it. It is impious.'

He bows in his cell. 'If it displeases you, there! — it is banished from the vocabulary.'

'You should learn humility, sir. With such words you make sport of Cochonne.'

'By Our Lady, I do not. Though I will admit I find difficulty in being humble. If you knew me truly you might learn the reason.'

'Pah. A common brigand, a prisoner? What does such a man boast of?'

Lesinge again comes close to the aperture in the door.

'Do you truly think Gaspard Lesinge a common brigand?'

'Father says you rob travellers in the road like a bandit.'

'And is it now a crime in France for a man of honour to reclaim by arms what mere thieves first stole from him?' Lesinge leaps up and paces the cell in agitation. 'If my accuser dared face me before the parliaments, ah, then the world would hear the truth. *One* would be compelled to acknowledge himself a robber, and it would not be Lesinge!'

Cochonne knows it for a sin, but cannot help herself: her heart thrills at the noble passion in his words.

Lesinge appears to recollect himself. 'But what use are these protestations? Your father, fair one, like the rabble of this town, is settled on my guilt. The friends who might have testified to my name and title are vanished. I shall perish here, in this excrescence of cow-farmers and cheesemakers, and the line of my ancestors will be extinguished in me.' He drops to his knees and covers his face with his hands.

Ancestors? thinks Cochonne. My title? For what species of imbecile do you take me, sir?

To forestall any further action on the part of the mob, her father thinks it prudent to have the prisoner examined again at once. He convenes the town officials. Gaspard Lesinge is permitted to wash, cut his nails and comb the lice from his hair. Under questioning he insists that he is an honourable burgher of Picardy, the victim of outrageous theft, who pursued the criminals across half the north of France in order to reclaim his stolen valuables. The so-called robbery for which he has been arrested was, he swears, nothing other than an effort to recover his own property. His present mean appearance he accounts for as a consequence of the length and difficulty of his pursuit and the buffetings of unkind fate. The sad tale is related with such energy that half his hearers are convinced it must be authentic, and the other half that it is all invention.

The notables of the town resolve to send enquiries to colleagues in Picardy. While they await answers to their letters the prisoner shall return to his cell, where no one needs to think about him at all except Cochonne.

'Alas!' he says to her. 'I shall pass the remaining years of my life in this dungeon. It will be for you to bring out my cold corpse, when death comes at last to relieve my despair.'

Cochonne is moved. 'The good God forbid it,' she murmurs.

Lesinge sighs. 'I accept my doom,' he says. 'Fate has never looked with kindness upon Gaspard Lesinge. There was one, he believed, who seemed not entirely to despise him. One who might have changed the course of his destiny. But she favours him no more.'

'Ah, sir, then you had once a lover? And she was faithless?'

'That also is true. But I was not speaking of her. You, Cochonne! — it was you in whom I placed my hopes. It is you who has destroyed them!'

Cochonne disdains to be persuaded by such language. Nevertheless, she loves to hear it, and returns, evening after evening, staying a little longer each time, without noticing what she does.

A day arrives when Lesinge's manner is unusually grave.

'My Penthesilea,' he says. 'I wish to entrust you with a secret and a legacy. You are my sole remaining comfort in this life, which I feel must soon draw to its conclusion.'

'Do not say so!'

'I do. I sense the cold shadows approaching. Every day I pass in this prison invites them nearer, and no one can release me.'

'Poor sir, I know well enough you want me to steal the key from my father. I am not the fool you think I am. But I cannot do it, though I pity you.'

'Never,' says Lesinge, with passion. 'I, impose on you, who are my only friend left in the world? Gaspard is not so vile a man.'

Cochonne knows quite well that he is lying. But she cannot be angry. Her heart is naturally formed for pity, not disdain.

'Bring the light,' he whispers, 'and come close to the door. I must show you something.'

She takes the lantern from its hook at the base of the stairs and holds it up to the aperture. By its light she sees a small thing in the man's hand. It gleams soft and linen-white like the early autumn moon. Where it has appeared from she cannot guess.

It is a statue the size of a finger, made from some kind of smooth pale wood. It represents the head and neck of a blinded horse, rising upright from a simple circular base. Lesinge turns it in the light. There are tiny notches and curls and hollows carved along its mane, which make the gleaming white wood look so smooth and flowing she longs to feel it. The muzzle of the horse is beautifully carved as well. Each nostril flares slightly, as though the head were about to lift from its bowed posture and whinny. Where the eyes should be are two little empty sockets. The blindness of the noble horse is so sad that Cochonne cannot speak.

'All these weeks,' Lesinge says, 'I have hidden it in my shoe. No one but you knows of it.'

'I have never seen anything so beautiful.'

'Imagine how fine it would be if the stones that made its eyes had not been prised out. They were two miniature jewels of polished jet, each worth forty pounds.'

'Ah, then he was not always blind?'

'No, truly. A blind cavalier would be little use in the battle.'

'A cavalier? I do not understand you.'

'My poor Cochonne, how little you know of the world. This is a piece from the game of chess. He is called the white cavalier. He once had thirty-one fellows, some ivory like himself, others black serpentine. The white and the black would war against one another across a chequered plain. A fine spectacle! But they were scattered apart by robbery and other misfortunes, and my white cavalier now has only me for his companion. When I die, fair one, I wish you to look after him, injured as he is. Take him from my corpse. Keep him always, and remember Gaspard Lesinge, whom God and His saints forgot!'

Captivated, the giantess gazes at the tragic white horse, so permitting Lesinge to study her expression. His brows contract. His rat's eyes narrow. A sharp and calculating look comes over him. Cochonne has never seen this look. He does not allow it to appear when she is watching. By the time she raises her eyes in a few seconds it will have vanished. For now the man analyses, calculates, with the rapidity of a crude but agile and practical intellect. She wavers, he is thinking. Two days more, or three, and the she-monster submits to your will, Gaspard, you ingenious fellow! He permits himself an unseen smile.

At precisely the same instant, one hundred and seventy British miles to the north and east, across the grey waste of the Sleeve and the timid shires of England's south, the piece that is twin to Lesinge's blind horse turns in the fingers of the Sir de Charizard, while the windows of his apartments shudder in an autumn gale. The other white cavalier is much cleaner, and retains its eyes, which glitter by the light of the fire.

Sir de Charizard spins the piece around and around and stares into the hearth. The wind forces its way down the chimney, causing the flames to shiver.

'More wood, boy! By the devil, if that fire blows out we shall not rouse it again, and this damnable weather of London will kill the both of us.'

De Charizard is out of humour with England and the English. Were he in the France of his forefathers he should not have so much trouble in the pursuit of one woman. A woman not even married; not even, as rumour and his own fine instincts inform him, a virgin! But these English, they are fishes, cold and bloodless. Their fogs and drizzles have infected them and doused their vital fires. To the simple conquest of a woman such as this damnably handsome poet, the Miss Arabella Farthingay, their customs as well as their laws give a dreary *Thou shalt not*. If he wants her, he is to woo her. By Charon's beard, he is expected to play the part of a prospective husband!

There is no creature on earth the Sir de Charizard holds in such entire contempt as a husband.

Merely to access the salons Miss Farthingay attends, and the dances where she is on display, he has had to pretend sympathy with the revolution. Thank Hades, there are French tailors in

London. Without them it would have been impossible to obtain his new dress, in the colours of red and blue as well as good Bourbon white. He would no sooner be clothed by English bunglers than go about in a smock.

He has challenged several Englishmen whom he observed paying Miss Farthingay particular attentions. All refuse to meet him. The ground of their pusillanimity is that no offence has been given. 'My dear fellow — 'Pon my word — You know, you needn't go about offering to kill every man in London — You Frenchies ought to stick to killing each other, what? Ha, ha, ha!'

The Farthingay herself is not impressed by his demonstrations of valour. Nor does she warm to his revolutionary sentiments. She says she suspects them insincere.

As if a man of wit and fashion should be expected to mean what he says!

In the extremity of his frustration, Sir de Charizard resumed his study of miss's poetry. He learned some of it by heart. At appropriate moments he repeated choice lines in company.

Never before has he so abased himself in pursuit of his desires. Yet all these efforts have advanced him not a step nearer the delightful goal. There has been not so much as an accidental brush of her glove against his hand; not a single private smile, let alone the whisper of that exquisite female *No* whose true meaning is *Perhaps; in time; continue the contest, sir, and you may be victorious at the last.*

Devil! What is the use of playing, when none of these English boobies understand the game?

For all that, he does not give up the chase. His code, the code of the libertine, demands one thing only. Victory! — no matter how lengthy the battle, nor what means are necessary to triumph. Or what would distinguish him from cowards and slaves, kneeling Christians or prostrating Mahometans?

So he sits by the fire, turning the white knight in his fingers, thinking.

Gallantry has failed him. Therefore he will use other means. Oh, the cowards and slaves mock him for these as well, led by their wheezing jester Philidor. *Magical chess-pieces, ha, ha ha!* Let them laugh, these asses who think themselves so wise and good. Let them sneer at what they call superstition even as they cringe before their so-called saviour on his cross.

Soon enough their laughter will change to tears.

De Charizard is sure of it. It has been foretold to him, by the great Infernal Master to whom he is secretly sworn. The gates of the world below are to open and the fallen angels be summoned, and all pious cowardly fools will be thrown down.

These are not idle prophecies. The Master already walks the earth in human form. De Charizard has witnessed it and knelt before it, though he kneels to no other, and been granted assurance of hell's impending triumph!

Because he knelt, it has been given to the Sir to invoke certain powers in aid of his desires, as long as those desires are anathema to the pious. Well! — and what is more hateful to the trembling slaves of religion than the ruin of a woman's virtue?

He will no longer shame himself and his libertine creed by courting the Farthingay in the manner of ordinary men. Better that irresistible powers compel her to fall.

His blood beats hot at the thought. The windows rattle. The chimney moans.

This is an evil night, thinks his handsome valet, loading wood onto the fire.

'Dismiss the other servants,' says his master. 'I shall not dine this evening. Bring brandy as well as wine.'

'As sir wishes.'

'And fetch the chess-table.'

Des Sables dusts off his hands. 'Does sir expect company?'

The master laughs. 'No, boy. And yes. There! A riddle. Do you enjoy riddles?'

'Not at all, sir.'

'Why not?'

'If one hears *no* and *yes* at the same time, one does not know where one stands. One's head is in a confusion.'

'You are a simpleton, des Sables.'

'As sir says.'

'A bumpkin. If your empty head was not so very pretty I would have sent you back to your family's pigsty years ago.'

'You still may, sir.'

'Ha! Are you so eager to leave my service?'

'It is not for me to say.'

'You wish to be kicked from the door like a dog and left to fend for yourself among the English brutes? They would not be so tender to you as I am. They would snatch you from the street before you had gone as far as the corner, dress you in women's clothes, and hire you to any who pays. Is that what you wish?'

Des Sables shudders.

'Never fear,' says the master, throwing back a mouthful of wine. 'I shall not part with you. Not until you are old and ugly.'

'Sir is very good.'

'Sir is not good in the least. Your hint of unwillingness arouses in me a contrary spirit. It is my pleasure to frustrate your desire and make you serve when you do not wish to.'

Des Sables recognises this mood of his master's. It is better not to answer at all.

The Sir swills his glass and empties it. 'As well as brandy and the chess-table, I also require the casket of my ancestors.'

'But no, sir!'

'What?' The master leaps from his chair, raising his cane, at which des Sables cowers. 'Did I hear you say the syllable *no*?'

'Think what you do. I implore you.'

'Ha! And what do you imagine I have been busy at for three hours but thinking? Dog! Go, send away the servants, before I beat you from the room.'

Des Sables hurries downstairs. If he had only a little more resolution he would not stop in the room where the cooks and footmen gather, but would run to the door, and out, never to return. Once, in Paris, he fled his master's house, but the women and boys of the streets hooted at him for his dress and threw mud and the excrement of horses, which frightened him so much he ran back in. And that was Paris, where the people, though rude and cruel beasts, at least spoke rational language. Here in London — No. Whatever devilry the Sir intends to conjure in the house tonight, it cannot be a worse prospect than going alone and penniless into English streets.

He knows he is a coward. He weeps a little for it.

The cooks and footmen snigger as always. 'Yes, yes, madam,' they say, in their execrable mockery of French words. They pretend to curtsey like women. Then they make remarks in English which turn the sniggers to roars.

However much they despise him, he despises himself more.

On the day he went into service with the Sir de Charizard his grandfather's blind eyes ran with tears. 'That cursed house!' the old man said. 'That name of evil! Alas, our sweet young cabbage is lost for ever.' In villages all across the northwest of France the reputation of the de Charizards is black as storm-clouds. Centuries ago, when Francis I was king, the lord of Castle Charizard had a barren wife and no cousins or nephews to prolong the family. In return for the gift of a son he promised his whole lineage to the devil. The prince of hell heard his oath, granted the bargain, and ever since then the de Charizards have been proverbial for wickedness.

Young des Sables laughed at these peasants' tales. He despised his grandparent's superstitions, as the young thoughtlessly despise the old. There were grapes and sweet oranges at his new master's table and he had a dazzling costume of silk to wear, in colours his grandfather had never set eyes on in all his life. His master occupied a splendid Paris house and would be visited by gentlemen and ladies of the highest fashion.

How much better if he had heeded the old man's warning!

The old tales were true after all. The fashionable ladies and gentlemen who attended Sir de Charizard turned out to be devotees of grotesque pleasure and depraved luxury, who openly scoffed at common morals. And the Sir himself embraces his cursed inheritance and makes adorations to the Devil.

Des Sables has been compelled to attend certain rites in his own person. He is always blindfolded and so cannot say what they consist of, which is one very small consolation. The language the depraved ladies and gentlemen speak during these ceremonies is all Latin, of which des Sables knows not a word. But he hears the name *Satana*, which needs no translation. Besides, he thinks it cannot be a well-intentioned ritual which requires him to be naked, apart from the blindfold, and which demands the death of a goat, an event from time to time perceived by his ears and nose though his sight is blocked. And the signs painted in blood, which the following day he must efface from the floor, with pail and sponge! — des Sables's only comfort is that his grandfather has now gone to rest in the earth and the remainder of the family know nothing of his shame.

Sir de Charizard's flight to England had the benefit of sparing his poor valet the repetition of these horrible practices. But although many things were left behind, the master would not leave France without the evil old box he calls the casket of his ancestors. For all des Sables knows there may well be some bones of the original wicked lord kept within, among the strange inscribed stones, the five-pointed iron pendants, the ancient crumbling pocket-books, the miscellany of chess-pieces, and all the other evil relics which are Sir de Charizard's most treasured possessions, and which he wasted a great part of his fortune on acquiring.

Even to touch the box repels des Sables. Nevertheless, he fetches it from the trunk in the private chambers and brings it to his master, though he holds it as far from his face as he can.

The chess-table has been brought already and is set before the Sir's chair, with two brandy-glasses laid out beside. The little white horse sits on its starting square, alone on the field.

Des Sables does not himself understand chess, but he is familiar with the usual arrangement of the board, thanks to his master's passion for the game.

'If I may observe, many pieces appear to be missing.'

'Then,' says de Charizard, drawing a black velvet blindfold from his pocket, 'we must call on them to take their places, is it not so?'

'Sir, I beg you, no.'

'Oh, you beg me, do you?'

'A million pardons, Sir, but I implore you, do not call on diabolic powers for mere sport. Your own reason surely advises against it.'

At this plea the Sir flies into a violent passion. He curses both reason and the name of Heaven, defying either power to tell him what is wicked and what is not. Most vehemently, he curses his valet, threatening the cringing boy with torments and murder. He pulls des Sables by his long golden hair and swats him about the shins with his cane until the boy shrieks for mercy, promising to endure every command in obedient silence.

As he removes his clothes and accepts the blindfold, des Sables thinks: The fire is warm at least, and I shall be standing near it.

Despite the heat of the flames he trembles. His flesh, exposed to the air, seems to pull away from his bones. He clasps his hands behind him as he has learned. Whatever will now happen in the room, the best he can hope for is not to be noticed. If he has no part in any of it he will count himself lucky. Though the blindfold obscures his sight completely he closes his eyes. He tries to imagine he does not exist at all.

He hears a sinister creak. The horrible old casket has been opened. The master commences incantations.

There is the word again, *Satana*! — Des Sables wishes he could put his hands over his ears, but that would earn him another beating, or worse. At least there will be no goat.

Indeed, the whole performance seems to him somewhat desultory. Unaccompanied by his fashionable accomplices of Paris, muffled by the heavy English cloths, diminished in comparison with the noise of the wind, his master's chanting sounds faintly ridiculous. Des Sables becomes aware of an itch on his buttock. Surreptitiously he disengages one hand from the other and scratches.

Necessity and experience have attuned him to his master's moods. Even without the use of his eyes he senses a mounting disappointment.

Possibly, des Sables thinks, the absence of the goat renders the performance ineffectual?

The incantations cease. Some minutes pass during which only the weather makes noise. At last des Sables hears a body descend with weary emphasis into a chair, and smells brandy.

'Pah! Remove the blindfold and take yourself away. I do not wish to look at you.'

Des Sables fills with joy though he is careful not to show it. He obeys with all haste, gathering up his discarded clothes before he leaves the room.

A few more minutes later, dressed again in everything but shoes — he wishes to move without any noise, the better to be ignored for the rest of the night — he repasses the door to the room. It remains slightly open. He cannot resist a stealthy look.

Sir de Charizard is still in his chair, staring into the flames, a crystal goblet raised absently. He has very much the look of one who might dash the glass into the fire in rage or despair. The chess-table sits before him. One piece only has been added to the board, the valet observes: the black queen, staring across the field at the white knight. Between them is an object he trembles to see.

There is nothing obviously sinister about it to explain the horror that grips him. It is an irregular lump of some milky or cloudy crystal, about the size of a large man's fist, not brilliantly cut like the brandy-glasses but coarse and dull. It could have been pulled yesterday from its seam deep in the earth, if it is a stone of earth. De Charizard swears it is not.

One morning, when he was unusually drunk after his breakfast, and des Sables was still new in his service, he boasted that the ugly rock bequeathed to him by distant ancestors was worth all the diamonds in the world put together. How can that be, Sir? Because, beautiful slave, it is a piece broken from a comet, and therefore comes from beyond the world itself. Innocent as he was in those early days of his ill-omened employment, des Sables reached out a finger. His master pushed his hand away. You would not think of touching it, he said, if you knew its power. What power is that? It appears quite inert, like any stone. But no, de Charizard said, with a drunken leer, it is not at all what it appears. It comes from the supernatural regions, and is gifted with the power to give access to them. Speak the proper words, and this stone becomes like a door to hell itself. To hell! And do you know the proper words, Sir? Why, des Sables, should you like to see hell, where you and I will one day go? Shall we ask to see the apartment prepared for you? There will be a warm fire burning in the grate, by Hades!

'Des Sables! What are you doing?'

The valet starts from his reverie and shrinks from the door.

'Damned spy! Do not think I cannot see you skulking there.'

'I only passed the room for a moment, sir, on my way to my poor cold room above. I thought to look in, in case master required anything.'

'Lying rogue. But since you are so diligent in your attentions you may fetch a second bottle of the brandy.'

He returns from the cellar with the bottle, having stopped on the way to put on his shoes. The master has returned his disappointed gaze to the fire. He holds out his glass without looking up and sighs while des Sables fills it.

'By the black waters of Lethe, how this Englishwoman torments me.'

'The sex,' des Sables says, 'is formed to be the pleasure and pain of man, or so I have heard it said.'

'What must I do to have her, little philosopher? I shall have her, by one way or another. I shall. I vow it on my soul.'

The instant he completes his oath the doorbell rings with frantic violence. Des Sables starts so abruptly he almost spills brandy on his master's sleeve, a crime for which he knows he would be caned.

'Devil!' De Charizard is just as surprised, but the emotion that suddenly possesses him is excitement, not fear. 'The door! Down, boy, and open it, quickly!'

An evil light glimmers over the cloudy skin of the summoning-stone. The bell clatters again, as though the person who pulls it outside was fleeing from a pack of wolves.

'But,' stammers des Sables, 'I have not had the opportunity to rearrange my dress.'

'Imbecile!' The master leaps from his chair. A strange unhealthy vigour has come over him. 'To Hades with your vanity. Go down and answer the door!'

Des Sables protests that the household domestics have all gone home, that the house is not prepared for company, that at this hour it can only be rogues or villains seeking entry. He would find further excuses, but they are interrupted by the swish of the cane on the back of his legs, which sends him yelping and limping down to the hall at the front of the house. Let the rogues and villains have us, then! — he thinks as he draws back the bolt. If they come to rob this devil of a lord I will not stand in their way.

He pulls the door open an inch or two.

With a great roar the wind seizes it and throws it wide, knocking him backwards to the chill marble floor. He has the confused impression of a single faceless figure all in black. The candles all blow out at once. Some entrance occurs in the sudden dark, a swift motion towards him. The door slams shut with tremendous violence, as though the same wind that thrust it open so violently had gained the power to pull as well as push.

De Charizard calls down from the apartments above. 'Devil! What an infernal commotion. Who is it, boy?'

The hall is completely dark. Des Sables stumbles to his feet.

'Tell your master,' says a grating voice, 'the black queen is arrived to treat with him.'

Des Sables has endured many grotesque and revolting surprises in the service of the Sir de Charizard, but never until the present moment has he felt his heart almost stop with fear.

'Des Sables! Answer, damn you!'

He hears the rustle of female clothing. The owner of the voice has stepped past him in the dark.

'I will announce myself,' the voice tells him. It is a vile ugly flat voice, like a death's-head speaking French, or an English person. The rustle proceeds up the stairs, unhindered by the extinction of the candles. Some gleams of firelight escaping into the hall above allow him to discern a silhouette ascending; a veiled woman, moving with unhesitating purpose. He wants to cry a warning to his master but cannot. He is having difficulty with his breath and appears to have fallen to his knees.

The black queen!

Then the enchanted chess-piece and the horrible old summoning-stone have effected their unholy work! — despite the absence of any goat.

From above he hears his master's cry of astonishment.

Leave this damned house, the shade of des Sables's grandfather commands. Save yourself, small cabbage, while there is still time! An apartment in hell is indeed set aside for you, unless you turn away from the cursed de Charizards!

Though des Sables reads only clumsily and with much effort, he has attended gatherings of Parisian servants who interest themselves in their betterment, and heard recitations of some of the pamphlets of Voltaire as well as extracts from the great Encyclopaedia. He does not subscribe to the simple religion of peasants and old men. Nevertheless, he is inclined to accept his grandfather's ghostly advice. I will, he thinks, crawling towards the door. I will go out at once, even in this weather, and dressed as I am. Better to be sodomised by the brutes of London than risk an eternity in the tar-pits of Satan!

He reaches for the handle. Unfortunately he has mislaid himself in the pitch-dark hall. His arm comes to rest instead upon the bottom stair. He looks up and sees the glimmer of light and warmth, and the way towards his own room under the eaves.

No! cries his grandfather's shade, diminishing to nothing.

Des Sables pulls off his shoes again with trembling fingers. It is another two or three minutes before he dares commence a silent crawl up the stairs. By the time he reaches the mid-point of the ascent he can hear his master and the black queen speaking, though he cannot yet distinguish the words.

On hands and knees he inches along the gallery. He tells himself to pass the half-open door without a look. He must be silent and invisible as the cat. But his exhortations are of no use. He cannot help lifting his eyes towards the firelight, and then he is drawn towards the door like a moth to flame.

The Sir de Charizard, whose usual posture is the perfection of disdainful ease, stands almost on his tiptoes in eager excitement. He has moved to the near side of the chess-table; his back is to the door.

Facing him across the board is a woman dressed head to toe in black. Layers of black lace cover bosom, shoulders and neck. Black satin gloves conceal her hands. She wears a dainty bonnet decorated with black feathers and flowers of black crêpe, to which is pinned a veil that hides her face completely. Not an inch of her natural form is visible — if, des Sables thinks, she has one.

The grim apparition extends a finger and points at the lump of rough crystal in the middle of the board.

'The demonoscope,' she says, in her horrible voice.

De Charizard flinches. 'But no,' he says. 'Ask anything else. I cannot bargain for the stone of my ancestors.'

'The demonoscope, or there is no bargain at all.'

'I have in my casket of treasures an emerald from the sceptre of Hermes Trismegistus. It is worth forty times the value of that stone. You shall have it, or any other marvel you select. Allow me to bring the casket.'

Des Sables's heart leaps as his master begins to turn towards the door. But the black queen takes hold of his wrist. De Charizard gasps at her touch as if it were cold as frost.

'The demonoscope or nothing,' she says. 'But you may keep it until the day I return to collect it.'

'And when shall that be?'

'When I choose.'

'A week? A month? Many years?'

'Perhaps a week. Perhaps many years.'

'Devil! I cannot surrender the summoning-stone. For centuries it has belonged in my family.'

'Then you shall never have the woman.'

'Flames of hell! You are cruelly inflexible, whoever you are.'

The black queen waits several seconds and then starts towards the door, sending des Sables scuttling out of sight. He hears her say in her mangled French, 'I go. You shall never see me again.'

'Stay!' cries de Charizard. 'I agree to the bargain. Promise me the woman and the stone is yours.'

Terrified of making the smallest noise, des Sables shrinks down in the shadows.

'Your hand,' he hears the black queen say. He supposes his master offers it, for the Sir gasps again.

'Like ice!' he exclaims.

'It is done,' the apparition says. 'The bargain is agreed: in return for the demonoscope, the woman you desire. You may now tell me her name.'

De Charizard speaks through clenched teeth. 'An Englishwoman. The famous Whiggish poetess, Miss Arabella Farthingay.'

The silence following these words extends so long that des Sables wonders whether the two of them have been spirited away from the room. He uncurls himself and crawls with infinite caution towards the door again.

'Arabella Farthingay,' the black queen repeats at last. The name which costs Sir de Charizard so much effort to pronounce comes easily to her mouth.

'She will fall to me? I will have her unreservedly, as a man desires to have a woman?'

'The bargain is made,' the black queen says.

Her steps approach the door. Des Sables looks left and right in panic and discovers that fear has rooted him in place.

'What must I do?' says his master. 'When will the conquest be?'

'You must wait,' says the black queen, very near the door. She is leaving without any ceremony. Des Sables presses himself to the floor and prays for shadow to swallow him whole.

Too late! — she has come rapidly out into the dark hall and will surely notice him, and reduce him to dust with a gesture and a diabolic word! But the black skirts rustle past towards the stairs.

As she hurries by, perfectly sure of her way despite the extinction of every candle, he has the distinct impression that she mutters words beneath her veil.

His terror makes it difficult to attend to any noise except the pounding of his blood in his ears. Nevertheless, when he reaches his bed at last and reflects on everything that occurred, he cannot rid himself of the thought that the black queen's mutterings consisted of a single English word, continuously repeated.

Des Sables does not know many English words. There is, however, one which he hears all the time in the mouths of the footmen and porters of London, a coarse and vulgar monosyllable. He thinks his ears must have deceived him, for it seems improbable that the sinister apparition should say that particular word over and over again under her breath, on her way out into the vile night.

CHAPTER TWO

— You know, says Lord Rawleigh to Miss Arabella Farthingay, you ought to write a poem about that fellow the Forget-Me-Not.

Your pardon, reader. — We have come upon this interesting exchange, *in medias res*. Much is altered, since our last. The time of year advanced — Our scene removed, from London, to pleasant Somerset-shire. We shall paint the whole canvas, as we proceed — but at present must attend to the *fore-ground*, and principal figures.

— An ode, replies Miss Farthingay, addressed to an humble flower? I should not have suspected your taste to incline towards the pastoral, my lord.

— Flower! — flower, says she! Ha, ha! — Lord Rawleigh casts his look around the immediate company, who join him in dutiful laughter — Ha, ha, ha!

— 'Pon my word, Miss Farthingay, I don't mean any flower. The Forget-Me-Not! That dashing fellow, you know, who goes off to France to rescue gentlemen and ladies from the blood-thirsty mob. What a subject to make a poem of!

Miss Farthingay is mystified by his lordship's allusion. She receives no assistance, from the immediate company. — It consists exclusively of Lord Rawleigh's nearest acquaintances, and his *hangers-on* — the latter not easily distinguished, from the former. They are gathered at my lord's country seat — The antient fiefdom, of the Rawleighs. How Miss Farthingay, who is not one of his lordship's intimates, comes to be present, we shall account for in a page or two. But, like Theseus, we must not lose our thread. — Miss Farthingay has mastered her uncertainty, and speaks again.

— The particular Forget-Me-Not you wish to see celebrated in verse, is a person? How, pray, did this travelling gentleman acquire a name so curious, and so sentimental?

— You amaze one, Miss Farthingay. Not to have heard of the Forget-Me-Not!

The nearest guests signal their astonishment at her ignorance, in the approved manner of the *hanger-on*.

Lord Rawleigh, we ought to mention, is extremely rich.

— I hope you will pardon the lapse, Miss Farthingay says. — My knowledge of affairs in France is unfortunately confined to more prosaic matters, such as the deeds of her legislators, and the general state of her body politic.

— He's the most mysterious fellow alive, I swear, says Lord Rawleigh. Not a soul knows him. — Knows who he is, I mean to say. That's why — you see — every body calls him, the Forget-Me-Not.

— If the gentleman is so desirous not to be forgotten, I should think he would do better going by his own name.

— Hang it, madam, you miss the very point of the thing. If one knew who he was — why, the Frenchies would arrest him, like so. — Lord Rawleigh makes a gesture. — But instead, when they arrive on the scene — Hoping to catch 'em, you see — Some respectable family, it might be, or a poor priest, or whoever falls foul of 'em — Hey, presto! they discover the birds are all flown. All that's left is a little posy of flowers — forget-me-nots, you see. Or it might be a note, signed with a flower — A drawing of a flower. — Demme, it's fearfully aukward explaining it all. I am in the last degree amazed you don't know it already.

Miss Farthingay seems quite unembarrassed. — *Is* quite unembarrassed — for her apparent sensations are often found to be identical, to the actual emotion of her bosom. She is in that regard unfashionable, according to the canons of fashion known to Lord Rawleigh, whose family name is too antient, to permit any dalliance with so *parvenu* a notion, as *sensibility*.

Lord Rawleigh cuts a fine figure. He is not married, nor known to be under any engagement. He is nevertheless counted by no one among the numbers of Miss Farthingay's admirers. The thing is inconceivable. — Handsome and wealthy she may be, but she is of no family at all. — The father, a *tobacco-merchant*. —

Father and mother are both dead, under circumstances which excited the attention of tittle-tattlers, back in the year 'eighty-five. — There are whispers of scandal. Or, of misfortunes — Which, to a name as jealous of its station as *Rawleigh*, are as good as scandal — that is to say, as bad. The mere existence of rumour forbids any interest, on my lord's part. A Rawleigh, is not to be murmured of. His name cannot be passed about by every body, like common currency — &c. —

Still, she's a charming creature, by jingo. — Quite charming!

Miss Farthingay is included among the present gathering, only because she is Lord Rawleigh's neighbour.

Like every other thing in the world, the rules of society are changed, when one goes out from London into the country. In London, proximity is nothing — Mere accident. — One's neighbours might as well be on the moon, unless they are one's sort of people. But, here in Somerset-shire, where the house of Rawleigh has held its seat, since the time of the Conqueror, or of Alfred — or Julius Caesar — of Adam himself — precision would be mere pedantry, in the matter — Here, certain established forms must be observed, among the gentry. Miss Farthingay is the inheritrix of a substantial estate, after the unfortunate demise of her parents — An event, into which it befits not the Rawleighs to enquire, any more than they would be seen turning over a rotten board, to investigate the nest of mice beneath. The Farthingay estate lies in some part adjacent, to the nobler, richer demesne of Lord Rawleigh's father, the Baron of _____.

An invitation must therefore be issued. — One rejoices, that the tobacco-merchant and his wife are deceased! The thought of admitting such people in the present company makes one shudder.

The daughter, at least, is universally agreed to be an ornament. One hears from town that two or three men of no little distinction, have condescended to set their caps at her. — Despite her mean birth — her hot-blooded Whiggish opinions — Her *poetry*.

Miss Farthingay could not decline the invitation, without giving offence — Though we guess it was accepted with as much anguish, as attended its issue.

The entertainment is proving as poor as she anticipated. Lord Rawleigh spends an half-hour correcting her ignorance, on the subject of that gallant British gentleman the Forget-Me-Not, and his exploits in France, on behalf of the persecuted luminaries of the *ancien régime*. — Though there's not a man alive, he says, that knows the whole truth of it — For the Forget-Me-Not works in secret, you know — He's there and gone before the Frenchies know a thing — snap! right under their noses, ha! What a splendid fellow. I hear the Frenchies curse him up and down that Assembly of theirs. Jingo, Miss Farthingay, you really ought to do it in a poem. Every body would read it, I assure you. — The whole world.

Miss Farthingay fears she cannot do justice to the subject, when her whole understanding of it extends no further than the last half-hour's conversation. Perhaps, she ventures to hint, his lordship himself would make the better panegyrist? — considering that he has already dwelt on the man's virtues at length, in prose.

— Quite, quite! Though I never had the trick of poetry — But — wait — Yes — I have it!

He raises an hand, and, making his finger dance to the tune of his verse, like the *maestro* of the Philharmonic Society, declaims —

But WHO is the Forget-Me-Not?
By jingo! no one knows, what, what?

At which the *hangers-on* applaud, and cry acclamation, and repeat the couplet — Until the house rings with it. The wittiest stroke in the world! — One lady, seated at the harpsichord, and eager in pursuit of Lord Rawleigh's interest, sets the lines to music, impromptu — So they may be sung in chorus, by the intire assembly.

Reader, we have hurled you into this country bustle, without a word of warning.

We suspect, had we proceeded in the usual fashion, and favoured you with an invitation — it might have been declined.

Several weeks have passed, since our previous chapter. The London season is finished. — The fashionable world departed, to seek its occupations elsewhere. Of the Monsieur de Charizard, whom we observed with some attention, in our former pages, during the remarkable performance of M Philidor, there is presently no sign. He remains in London. — His pursuit of Miss Farthingay's favour, having met with no success — Despite being conducted with an excess of enthusiasm, that threatened to make *him* the talk of the town — and encouraged *her* to depart from it, as soon as her Somerset estate could be made ready to receive her.

— It is almost enough, says Miss Farthingay to herself, to make the prospect of marriage tolerable. I might accept one of these puppies, if only to put a stop to all the others.

— I will soon be thirty, she thinks, a little mournfully. — Either I must wed, or the world will call me an old maid.

With these and other reflections weighing on her spirits, she has retired to the country.

Some time has elapsed, since she last took up residence at Grandison Hall, the seat of her lamented father. The house brings recollections, not altogether happy, which she prefers to escape, by remaining in town. And what person would not wish to fly the memory of such trials, as Miss Farthingay endured, in the year 'eighty-five, when she was but three-and-twenty? — a tender age, for a feeling heart to receive such wounds — the heart of a poet, no less! which we must suppose more susceptible, than the organ of ordinary men and women. First, her childhood play-mate Miss Clarissa Riddle, her father's ward, turned penniless out of the house, and presumed dead, or condemned to vagrant misery — a doom, compared to which death might be welcome; — then, the partial destruction of Grandison Hall itself, by sudden fire; — and last, to crown all these misfortunes, the loss of her parents, in a single stroke, by strange and horrible accident; — is not this, reader, a series of associations, any body would shun, if they could? — Particularly one, whose temper is naturally ardent and vivacious, and glows, with the Muses' fire.

If, reader, Miss Farthingay knew, what WE know, concerning the events of six years past — If she suspected, what we unwillingly suspect — that Miss Riddle had perhaps some hand in the *second* of the misfortunes, we have just listed — Was, perhaps — *horresco referens* — not intirely innocent, of the *third* — How much more severe, the distress of her recollections!

But Miss Farthingay has been protected, from any such dreadful suspicions, by the tact and care of her friend Mr Thomas Peach. — And, indeed, by the determination of Miss Riddle herself, to avoid her notice — So that Miss Farthingay does not know to this day, whether her father's *quondam* ward is alive or dead — Still less, that Miss Riddle was taken in, as an house-hold servant, by Mr Peach himself.

Forgive us, reader, for indulging again these old miseries. You have not, we trust, forgotten the events, set out in our former volume — Though perhaps, like Miss Farthingay herself, you chuse not to dwell among such dark and dusty shadows.

One assurance we can give you, which may be some comfort. Clarissa Riddle — tormented, unnatural creature! sustained, by unwholesome powers — possessed, by inward darkness — she, is REMOVED from the pages of our history — VANISHED — and therefore cannot obtrude, upon its course — As you will shortly learn for yourself.

But we meant only to account for the fact, that Miss Farthingay is rarely at her late father's country seat, of Grandison Hall. We might also observe, that the calling of the Muses is better answered in London, where the book-sellers are — Along with the majority, of the *book-buyers*. Critics, it is true, are also plentiful there — But the work of critics has been rendered idle, by events of the past two years, for there is now only one rule of literary judgment, which serves in every case — *viz.*, that universal rule, to which we alluded, in our *ouverture*. Miss Farthingay is known to be an adherent of the revolutionary party. Therefore — write what nonsense she may — the liberal journals praise it, to high heaven! — or, were she to pen works of supreme ability and fiery genius — the Tory periodicals will damn them without mercy.

For all these reasons, Miss Farthingay's return to Grandison Hall is a rare and notable occasion, in Somerset society. The Rawleighs cannot ignore it. Hence, the invitation — and hence, in turn, our scene, which now resounds in every corner, with the fresh-minted chorus —

But WHO is the Forget-Me-Not?
By jingo! no one knows, what, what?

So, reader, we explain our scene — And you are satisfied.

The particular *mores* of Somerset-shire, in the year 'ninety-one, require that as well as invitations, there must be *visits*.

Exact mathematical rules govern the proportion, of one to the other — Ratios, and equations, and derivations in algebra — And we know not what. — Nor does any body else, for, unlike the rules of *Newton*, or the constitutions of nations less happy than Britain, these have never been printed, but are known only by instinct, and maintained by tradition. The Rawleighs understand them, better than any other. — Understand them, indeed, better than they understand any thing else.

Therefore it is, that on the day succeeding that of his poetical triumph, Lord Rawleigh must make his visit to Grandison Hall, after breakfast. His carriage arrives at noon exactly, that being the hour signified by *after breakfast*, according to the antient calculations. He is received somewhat reluctantly by Miss Farthingay, who, though she knows the obligation is as fixed as the course of the stars, remains not wholly reconciled to the dictates of fate. She consoles herself with the knowledge, that his lordship considers himself as far above her sphere, as Jupiter above the earth's — and will not therefore take the occasion of his visit, to declare undying devotion — Which, after the ridiculous oppressions of M de Charizard, is no small comfort.

The general progress of his lordship's visit need not detain us. It is undertaken without enthusiasm, by either party — Tedious, to both — And would be to you, were we to dwell on it.

There is, however, one incident of significance, which occurs while Lord Rawleigh is at Grandison Hall. — The arrival of a letter.

This letter, addressed to Miss Farthingay, is brought in by her negro manservant — or steward — The precise station of the man is unclear to Lord Rawleigh, though the fellow seems easy enough about the place, demme! — His lordship knows how servants will get great notions of themselves, when they are left in the house, while their betters are in town.

She ought to be a sight more severe with him, what, what?

The man turns the letter over in his hands once or twice.

— It is sent from France, he says.

— From France! exclaims Miss Farthingay; and —

— From France! exclaims Lord Rawleigh.

The man looks from one to the other without expression. After an interval, which, had it been extended a fraction of a second longer, might have carried the implication of insolence — He repeats — From France — and, bowing, presents the letter to his mistress.

It would never have been done so, in the house of Lord Rawleigh's ancestors. Direct from a servant's hand, to hers! — The letter ought to have been offered upon a salver. The fellow does not even wear gloves. —

But — which is remarkable — Reader, we have already advised you, that the arrival of this letter is an incident of importance — Lord Rawleigh does not so much as raise an eyebrow, at this instance of the manners of tobacco-merchants. He scarcely observes it at all. The information, that the letter is come from France, has aroused in him some strong emotion. He pushes back his chair, and demands the servant tell him, who brought it to the door?

The negro answers, in his habitual measured stile, that the messenger was a country man, who said he was hired for the purpose by a gentleman recently landed at Lyme, with several papers from across the water.

— By jingo! at last! cries Lord Rawleigh. — I must talk to this country fellow — Madam — I beg your pardon — Some minutes only — And, with other remarks equally confused and hasty, he rushes from the room.

The servant directs an enquiring look at Miss Farthingay.

— It is an intire mystery to me, she says, addressing him very familiarly. — Let us however not murmur at being relieved of his lordship's company, if only for *some minutes.*

— You have endured worse, says the servant.

Miss Farthingay sighs. — Indeed I have, Caspar. But I shall seize these minutes, though few, to open my letter. From France! How exciting.

— I will see to my Lord Rawleigh, and do my best to delay his return.

Miss Farthingay casts a look of great tenderness on Caspar. — How I have missed you, she says.

Had my lord been present, to hear such language exchanged, between the lady of the house and a manservant, his eyebrows might have shot upwards with force enough, to lift the wig clean off his head. — Caspar withdraws without another word — Leaving Miss Farthingay to unseal the letter.

She has just finished reading it over, and put it down on the breakfast-table, her eyes full of animation, when Lord Rawleigh returns.

— Hang it — His lordship is out of temper — Hang it, he says, the churl rode away before one could stop him. Would have saddled an horse myself, but all yoked to the carriage — Couldn't find your stables — Footman no use — Hang it all! I wish that man of yours had the wit to keep the fellow at the door, to let one have a word.

— Please accept my apology if Caspar was remiss. In his defence, I suppose he had no grounds to suspect that Lord Rawleigh had urgent business with a messenger sent to Miss Farthingay.

— Urgent? — what, what? — Lord Rawleigh is apparently in some confusion, and attempts to recollect himself. — No urgent matter — Nothing in the least.

— Might I ask Caspar to ride after the man, and bring him back to the house?

— Heavens! no — A trivial business, I assure you, madam — Of no importance. A private matter.

— Naturally, says Miss Farthingay. — I did not mean to allude to any business of my lord Rawleigh's, at all. I only wish the arrival of a letter, brought to me, at my house, had not inconvenienced *him*.

— Oh! not at all — &c. —

Miss Farthingay observes him a few moments, and then ventures —

— You are, my lord, perhaps expecting some communication from France?

At this unexceptionable remark, his lordship leaps almost from the chair — What, what? — none in the world! or upon a small matter only — Lord Rawleigh's face is turning red. — Wine, he says — business of that sort. My vineyards, you know. I entreat you to forget the whole matter. It is not worth speaking of.

— Be easy, sir, she says. — Were I to attempt to speak of it, my invention would be sorely taxed, for I cannot detect any thing that has occurred, except the delivery of this message. For my own part, I must confess the letter is exceedingly interesting. I am invited, it seems, to visit Paris.

— Jingo! by whom, if I may ask?

She picks up the sheet. — The signatory, she says, is a Monsieur Denfert, deputy to the *assemblée législative.*

— Not one of that pack of wolves?

Miss Farthingay cannot refrain from smiling. — You disapprove, my lord, of the representatives the people of France have chosen for themselves? Or is it the act of chusing that excites your contempt?

— My dear madam — we shan't argue. I know you're a great one for *liberté*, and all that. But still you must agree — it's a shameful thing — The king and queen, madam! penned about by a rabble of — fishwives — seamstresses. One can hardly think of it. So divine a lady, brought so low! — Chivalry, Miss Farthingay — chivalry — A queen's honour — You regret it, madam, I'm sure you do, for all your *liberté*, and so forth.

— There are many in France, as in all the world, who endure hardship. I doubt whether the French queen's sufferings be the most pitiable.

— Ha! I hardly think the feelings of royalty are to be compared with any body's! — You are quite paradoxical, madam — But we shan't argue.

Miss Farthingay is in good humour. — And you, my lord, she says, are quite romantic. Like your hero, this Sir Forget-Me-Not.

— What? — Lord Rawleigh colours violently. — I? — Not in the least — Don't know the fellow — Nothing like —

— Have no fear, says she, with a wicked look. — I shall not mention the mysterious gentleman again, and certainly not to this Monsieur Denfert, Deputy to the Assembly. Not even were he minded to ask, though I do not think it likely. His interests incline more towards the arts, to judge by his letter. — Miss Farthingay studies it again — pausing, to lift the paper near her nose — She is suddenly aware of a scent, upon the page. She frowns a moment

— lowers it again, and reads. — Monsieur Denfert, she says, expresses his admiration for Arabella Farthingay, the author of the Poems, Upon the Spirit of Awakened Humanity, and wonders whether she will do the newly constituted assembly the honour of addressing them in person — *in verse or prose*, he writes — To celebrate the amity between our two nations — &c. — Further kind sentiments. — Miss Farthingay puts the letter down. — Nothing at all, she says, of a political nature. Do you know, my lord, I am inclining to accept. An invitation to Paris! Who would refuse the chance to witness in person, the fruits of so momentous a period in the history of the world?

— Momentous, aye, says Lord Rawleigh, darkly. — Momentously bad!

Reader, we need not stay to see, whether his lordship and the poetical lady continue to dispute the question — the great, eternal question, whether this age of the world be the *worst* of times, or the *best*. We dare say, were the argument continued, they would come no nearer solving it. *He*, is one sort of person — *she*, the other. — There is no more to say. Nor, reader, would you benefit from any report of the contest. *Your* opinion is already determined — You are either of his party, or of hers. It is fixed in your nature, as by divine *fiat*. No evidence, no persuasion, can alter your view one whit.

For all our sakes, therefore, we advance our narrative, with a leap of several days.

We have attained the month of October — mists, and mellow fruitfulness.

October, of the year seventeen hundred and ninety-one — Significant month! though for two years and more, significant months are become as regular, as Popish saints'-days. Unprecedented events — unimagined upheavals — Follow one upon the next, like storm-waves battering the shore — each lull, merely prelude to the next crest. Pity the chroniclers! They wear themselves out in writing — yet no sooner is the ink dry, than more news comes from Paris. — Every thing just written, is now superfluous. — The globe of the world is a top, spun by a four-years' child, whose only delight is to make it go faster — FASTER!

On the first day of October, seventeen hundred and ninety-one, the new legislature of France begins. The National Assembly, which for two years has laboured to give birth to a constitution, at last delivers its progeny. — And, according to the unfortunate pattern of nature, expires in the effort — decreeing, that it shall be replaced immediately by the *Legislative Assembly*, whose deputies, all newly elected, are now and for ever to be the first parliament of France.* The long struggle is complete. From every corner of France, the new delegates arrive in the Equestrian Hall, by the Tuileries Garden, prepared to administer a free, just, and prosperous nation.

The ardent heart of Arabella Farthingay glows, at the prospect of visiting Paris, in such a moment!

---

* The progress of the revolution, may be traced in the series of governing bodies, which replaced one another with a rapidity and confusion equalled only by the imperial succession of Rome, in her decline. The Court of Versailles — the Estates-General — Assemblies, *National* and *Legislative* — Committees of This and Committees of That — Directorates — triumvirates — consuls — Buonaparte alone — Reader, you are not required to remember these distinctions, still less to understand them. Only we beg that you do not confuse our present moment, with others past, or yet to come, which may be associated in your imagination with the whole tumultuous era. *There is no Buonaparte* — not yet. There is no *guillotine* — though it draws near. King Louis — King Louis the Sixteenth — is *alive*. You know, that the French revolutionaries executed their king. It is what every body knows. — They threw down the prison of the Bastille, and cut off the king's head, and then old Boney would have conquered the world, if our gallant heroes had not sunk his ships at Trafalgar, and stopped his cannons at Waterloo. — Huzzah! — It is not for us to deepen your understanding. Nevertheless, we must positively insist, that in October of 'ninety-one, though revolution flourishes, there IS NO BONEY, and King Louis is NOT DEAD — No matter how profound your faith, in those two articles of history.

Her preparations are made as swiftly as time allows, though still too slowly for her eager spirit. She will travel with a female friend, a woman in her middle years, whose importance to our tale is infinitesimal, and whom we shall endeavour not to mention again. After much discussion, it is decided the party will make use of a ship at Lyme, which Lord Rawleigh himself is pleased to put at her disposal for the purpose — The captain and crew, as well as the vessel, in some manner belonging to his lordship.

Miss Farthingay sends reply to Monsieur Denfert, author of the letter of invitation, advising that she will arrive in *Cherbourg*, within the fortnight, and will be pleased to await the Monsieur's advice, concerning her onward journey to the capital, in any communication left for her at that port.

There is one visit she wishes to make in Somerset-shire, before she sets sail. —

We say, she *wishes* to. We ought perhaps to have written, she *must*. — But that, too, would slip wide of the truth.

She feels she ought to — Feels, she ought to be glad to — And yet delays the journey, on one cause or another, and, when it can no longer be postponed, rides out with an heavy heart.

There might have been some comfort, in the company of her devoted Caspar. But on *this* visit, he resolutely declines to accompany her. — She knows his reasons, and respects them.

The destination is an obscure and narrow valley, folded away among the hills that rise north-west of Grandison Hall. Only one habitation stands in that dale. — A sturdy old farm-house, named Widdershins Bank — The residence of her friend, Mr Thomas Peach.

And why — you wonder — should Miss Farthingay be so evidently unwilling, to pay a visit to a *friend*?

Reader — in the six years since he and Miss Farthingay first became acquainted, among circumstances to which the word *extraordinary*, does not even the shadow of justice — Mr Tho.s Peach is, we regret to say, sadly decayed.

We too have suffered disappointment, in that interval. — Grievous disappointment. — But we shall not speak of it, in this place. —

The decay of Mr Peach does not confine itself to his person. — But emanates, as it were, into his house — and the valley surrounding. Miss Farthingay feels it, as soon as the road overtops the last rise, and begins its descent towards Widdershins Bank.

The day, already dull, becomes duller. — Its misty hush, heavier — *deathly*, almost. Nothing stirs, amid the oaks and hazels, where the shadows lie thick, nor in the lank verges. At the bottom, willows weep over the hidden stream, dense and still, as though turned to stone.

How changed the scene, reader, since we last came along that stream, and stopped to stand under the willows! — grateful, for their umbrage — For *then*, the summer sun warmed all the valley, whose pleasant verdure luxuriated in its rays. — An English Eden!

What devil crept into that paradise, to work so mortal a transformation?

What but Miss Clarissa Riddle? — It was at that time, when we and you bade farewell to Mr Peach, in the summer of 'eighty-five, that he took her in, as his house-maid — Recognizing a certain kinship, between the dark mystery of her nature, and his own secret practices. And lo! between then and now, the sweet confines of Widdershins Bank are turned — sour — rank, unwholesome, and morbid.

Yet Clary herself, has quit the scene, as you shall soon learn, from Mr Peach's own mouth — Though the gloom and decay remain.

— I mislike the place, says the stable-boy who accompanies Miss Farthingay. His look darts this way and that. — There's some wicked thing about, Lord save us.

Though impatient with his simplicity, Miss Farthingay cannot reprimand him — for her own unease increases, as they near the house.

The best part of a year has come and gone, since her most recent visit to Mr Peach, at Christmas-tide. In those months, the banks of ivy have grown unchecked. The back of the house disappears into them, as though sinking in slow wreck under a dusk-dark sea. What was once the cheery cottage-garden, is now a wilderness of rank weeds. There is no other dwelling within a mile, yet the house appears soot-blackened — its stones, pocked and crumbling — the lath liver-spotted — Its glass, quite lightless.

Miss Farthingay reaches involuntarily towards a locket hanging below her throat, and touches it.

This locket, reader, is also of importance in our story. We are not so poor an artificer, as to interrupt the progress of our narrative, to give its history, and explain its significance. — Not here, when we bend our efforts, to evoking the dismal scene. Attend with care, if you please, when you hear it mentioned again.

There is a modest stable by the road, empty of even the simplest equipage. Last autumn's fallen leaves rot in its recesses, in great heaps. — Miss Farthingay leaves the lad there, with the horses.

No chearful welcome comes from the house, to mark her arrival. Not even a dreary welcome. — The door is shut, and the windows dark.

Another visitor would certainly suspect, that no one was at home. — That the place, indeed, had long since ceased to be home to any body. Miss Farthingay knows better. —

— He has scarcely left the house at all, she thinks, since he confessed at last the loss of his wife.

Reader — you have perhaps forgotten, if you ever knew it, the tragical history of Mrs Eliza Peach. Miss Farthingay uncovered the tale, quite by accident, soon after making Mr Peach's acquaintance. — Though at that time, Mr Peach gave her to understand, that his young bride yet lived — That she was but an invalid, confined to the house. Miss Farthingay learned otherwise — Yet such was her affection for her friend, and her sympathy for his grief, that she consented all too willingly to sustain his consoling fiction.*

In recent years, affection and sympathy have equally lost their place, for Mr Peach no longer pretends to her, that his dear Eliza is still alive. — An alteration, Miss Farthingay can only regret — since her friend, once so amiable, is sunk in idle despair.

— Poor Thomas! she thinks. — What a noble mind is here o'erthrown!†

So miserable is the scene, that she fancies herself come not to an house at all, but a mausoleum, or desolate ruined chantry. — Some place of superstition and faded memory.

She cannot forget that the house, if house it still be, belongs in law to her own estate. — That she gifted the occupancy, to Thomas Peach, out of gratitude for his extraordinary kindnesses, on her behalf.

Those acts of kindness bore witness to a nature abundantly benevolent and humane. Yet, now! — common rumour names her old friend a *magician*, or trafficker in unhallowed arts. — Whose advice, the people say, is sought by desperate and deluded men.

She comes to the door.

— Mr Peach? Thomas? It is I, Arabella Farthingay. — I hope I find you at home?

For good measure, she knocks, though timidly. She fancies she hears abrupt motion within — And, some moments later, Mr Peach opens the house.

---

* We do not mean to imply any deficiency in your understanding, by recalling certain elements of our tale to you. Should these glosses of ours be redundancies — then, good reader, pretend you never saw them — And take no offence.

† We recollect, that when we first introduced Mr Peach to the eyes of the world, several years since, we thought it amusing to fancy a comparison between him, and Prince Hamlet. Fool that we were, and are! — to trifle with such notions, and invoke the art of *Shakespear*, without thought for the consequences!

How she grieves to see him! He has grown more haggard yet, since Christmas. He wears neither wig nor collar. — His hair has not been cut, nor his beard. He carries his dress more like a beggar than a scholar. His cheeks and eyes, equally sunken — each somehow pale and livid at once — As though deriving whatever vitality they possess, from consuming themselves.

— Miss Farthingay, he says, and smiles, beneath the beard.

— Mr Peach — What joy it gives me, to see you again, and what distress also! Are you well? — You cannot be well.

— I am well, he says. — But my dreams are bad.

— May I come in?

Mr Peach hangs his head. — I fear, he says, the house is scarcely presentable.

— However bad your dreams, they cannot have so intirely deranged your wits, that you forget to whom you speak, or how little your devoted Arabella Farthingay troubles herself over a little dust and dirt.

He bows, and opens the door wide.

The interior is not so sadly neglected, as the garden and the environs. Nevertheless, it presents such a scene, as no gentleman ought to permit himself to appear in. Webs decorate the higher corners, and thickets of dust the nether. The fire is not swept, nor the walls washed. In the parlour a pungent odour lingers, which Miss Farthingay, though no apothecary, suspects to be — *laudanum.*

— Dear Mr Peach, says she, looking about the room with a sensation approaching horror. — Do you now live here quite alone?

— Is it so very apparent? I am accustomed to my surroundings, I fear, and forget the impression they must make upon a visitor. Please forgive me, Miss Farthingay. Had I known you were coming I should have done better.

— What has happened to the mysterious house-maid, of whom you always spoke so highly, though you would never permit me to see her? The house seems barely kept at all. Did you put her out, and forget to engage a replacement?

Miss Farthingay's allusion to the maid, is meant a jest. It has long been her pleasure to teaze Mr Peach, on account of his absent-mindedness. — A gentle insinuation, which he was content not to dispute. But on this occasion her remark appears to sting him, though less with indignation, than grief.

— She has vanished, he says.

Miss Farthingay sighs. She sweeps the dust from a chair with her glove, and sits.

— Young women, she says, do not stay young. As the world never ceases to remind them. I suppose some village lad caught her eye, and inspired thoughts of a life spent otherwise than in service. But other girls grow up to replace them. It is the way of nature. Shall I find you one? I can testify to your goodness as an employer. There will certainly be a suitable child among my tenants.

Mr Peach shakes his head.

— She was uniquely situated to her situation, he says. — And as *unsuited* to any other, as I myself.

Thinks Miss Farthingay — You were not always so.

At the corner of her eye there is a stealthy motion, in a dim nook of the room, accompanied by a peculiar momentary noise.

— Have you acquired a cat?

— A cat? No.

Miss Farthingay frowns. — What was it that produced that sound, just now?

A curious expression comes into Mr Peach's eyes. — We might call it a sad mischief, or a melancholy liveliness.

— The isle is full of noises, he says. — But, my dear Arabella, I thought you removed to London in perpetuity. I hope you are not descended to the country only to visit me? That would have been a long journey for so poor a welcome.

— The pleasure of renewing our acquaintance would be sufficient reward for a journey twice as long. But you need not be uneasy. My retirement has a noble cause, and one I am sure you will approve. I have left the town to indulge in a period of reflexion, according to the model of the Latin poets, who rightly advise us that only rural scenes will do for such contemplations.

— May I ask, on what subjects you chuse to reflect?

— Alas, Mr Peach, only the usual ones. Fate, futurity, marriage, and so forth. I wish I had a more original theme.

There is a sudden rapid pattering, on the boards of the ceiling. A sound like a faint moan of wind comes as though from the room above. — That room, Miss Farthingay recalls, with an uneasy sensation, where Mr Peach was wont to pretend his wife lay indisposed, though she knew quite well that poor Mrs Peach was long dead, by her own hand. Miss Farthingay used to grieve that her friend should be driven to such a pretence, in order to allay his sorrow, at the loss of a wife so young. Yet now she heartily wishes he would resume the fiction! — For, ever since he abandoned it, and gave her the locket, which now hangs at her throat — Told her, that it contained his last mementoes of Mrs Peach, and, with tears, bid her keep it safe, but never return it to him, unless in the most dire need — Ever since that day, three winters past, he has been a changed man. His spirits, sinking by degrees. — His kindly quiet nature, turning solitary and chearless. — His appearance, less wholesome with each season. When he surrendered the delusion, that Mrs Peach was yet with him — he seemed to lose at the same time, his own vital force. — All his comfort in, and enjoyment of, existence itself.

— And may I further ask, says Mr Peach, ignoring the brief disturbance above, Whether you have received a proposal? I hope you have not come to ask my advice. I am the worst man in the world to consult on any question of marriage. Or, indeed, of fate, or futurity.

— No, no, no proposal. Or I suppose I have, here and there. A proposal is so common-place an occurrence one hardly notices it. But I would rather tell you about another sort of invitation I have recently had the honour to receive, and which gives me a great deal more pleasure to contemplate. What would you say to the news that your humble Arabella Farthingay is to address the *assemblée législative*?

— I would extend my congratulations, though with more energy, if I knew what the *assemblée législative* signified.

— It is the successor to the *assemblée nationale*, and incorporated within the past two or three weeks, as I understand.

— Ah. And the *assemblée nationale* — ?

— Mr Peach!

He bows apologetically. — You allude, he says, to events in France, I know. I hardly know what passes in Bridgwater.

Miss Farthingay bestows on him a look of playful severity. — You will at least not be surprised to learn, that there has been a *revolution* in France?

He nods, as though she were in earnest. — A bloody and tumultuous one, is it not?

— Bloody? Gracious, Mr Peach! I should not say so. Not in the least bloody. — Not in comparison with the wars and outrages usually attending events of such moment — the contest of arms in our own nation during the last century, or in America. — By every impartial account, the people of France have broken their chains of feudal servitude, and created for themselves a constitution, upon liberal and enlightened principles, all in a spirit of most determined moderation. Some few desperate acts have been committed, no doubt. So great a transformation could never have been atchieved, without instances of energetic struggle, and excess of passion. But, *bloody and tumultuous?* — Certainly not. You have mistaken your bad dreams for the events of actual history.

Mr Peach closes his eyes tight, and rubs his face.

— Very likely, he says.

Miss Farthingay observes him for a while, with unfeigned concern.

— You ought to take walks again. It used to be your great pleasure. Exercise among pleasant prospects might lift your spirits.

— I have not given up the habit, he says.

— Shall we take the air together now? — Miss Farthingay refrains from adding, that there is evidently no refreshment to be had within-doors — that the dismal state of the house oppresses her, and she wishes to escape it — That the peculiar noises, which arise from time to time, in dark corners of the room, make her quite uneasy. It is mice, perhaps, or spiders. — How unfortunate, she thinks, that he should have been so attached to his silly house-maid, as to neglect obtaining another servant!

Mr Peach escorts her out-doors, with attentive care. She feels easier at once — Though the day persists sullen, and the morning's dews seem not to have lifted from the herbage. A gloaming hangs over the valley, as though the autumn dusk were arriving before its proper hour — The whole scene passing from one twilight to another, without the intervening brightness of day.

They link arms and go into the road, leaving the boy at the stable. For a while they walk silently. Miss Farthingay is meditating a proposal, which requires some delicacy, in the choice of words.

— Mr Peach, if I speak what is in my heart, will you promise not to be offended? You cannot doubt, I hope, my sincere concern for your happiness. To disguise my feelings would be to place a limit upon that concern; and your comfort and peace of mind are matters of too much importance, to allow any such restraint.

— Speak freely, Miss Farthingay, answers Mr Peach, as I hope you always will. — Dissembling is not much in your nature, I think.

— Then permit me to ask, my dear friend, whether you have considered changing your habitation? — Miss Farthingay sees that he shakes his head, and presses on, before a definitive refusal can be given aloud. — The house is yours to live in as long as you wish to. That was my decree, and nothing can alter it, except your own request. But you know, my estates are large. Could I but assist you, by putting another house at your disposal — in perpetuity, without condition — I would do it in an instant. It would give me profound pleasure — nay, joy. — Thomas! do not shake your head at me! You shall not be allowed the manners of a bear, because you have adopted the appearance of one.

— Your pardon. I shall listen to your proposal with the respect its generosity deserves.

— That is much better, she says, patting his hand. — But will you not consider it in earnest? Widdershins Bank has been, I know, a place of refuge for you, and for — Miss Farthingay feels a tremor in her voice, and compels herself to speak firmly — And for Mrs Peach. Within its walls are remembrances you would never wish to leave behind. And yet — Miss Farthingay must compose herself once more — And yet, she says, after the loss you have suffered, it is impossible there should not be as much pain in the recollections, as pleasure. To judge only by the appearance of the house, I must think the balance falls to the unhappy side. I speak with candour; if you examine your own heart as impartially as honestly, can you deny it? Are you not very low in spirits, Thomas? And if you are, is it wise to confine yourself among scenes, which every hour present you with reminders of a joy that cannot return, and prompt you again to lament their loss? — when you might be removed to some place perfectly suited to your needs, and chosen by yourself, with no more than a word?

— Every thing you say is as just as generous, Mr Peach replies. — Though I deny, if you will permit me to, that I am *very low*. In our great-grandfathers' day they would have called it a melancholy.

— Call it what you will, I wish with all my heart it did not afflict you. And I fear the clouds cannot lift, as long as you remain here. Look at it, Thomas! — They have walked up to an height, which affords a prospect over the house, and the bottom of the valley beyond. The whole scene is the very picture of neglect and gloom.

Mr Peach sighs. — I would reflect on the proposal with all earnestness, he says, if I could. But I cannot. I must stay here, in the hope that she returns. Were she to come again to the house, and find me gone —

He does not complete his thought. Some reverie has taken hold of him, compounded of regret and longing.

Miss Farthingay hardly dares contemplate his meaning. — Surely, she thinks, he does not persist in imagining, he may regain his dead wife by the mere exercise of imagination!

— Thomas, Thomas, she thinks — Have your wits begun to turn?

The idea is insupportable. —

Mr Peach observes the change in her expression, and guesses her thought.

— Dear Miss Farthingay, he says, I do not refer to Mrs Peach. *That* hope I have intirely and for ever surrendered. She will not come back to me. — I see you still wear the locket.

— I shall never put it off. It might perhaps be a little aukward, if I marry. My husband shall be jealous, no matter how I assure him that it is a woman's hair I keep at my breast, and she, moreover, a woman I never had the honour to meet. But any man who marries me will have to be reconciled to some eccentricity in his wife's behaviour. — Miss Farthingay's natural vivacity is partly restored, by turning a jest. — I must ask, she says — For what woman are you so determined to wait? You cannot mean your absconded house-maid! — Miss Farthingay smiles as she teazes — then sees, that her friend does not smile.

— You do mean the maid! she cries.

Mr Peach does not deny it.

Miss Farthingay is astonished — and as distressed, as she is amazed. — Is *this*, she thinks, the cause of his *melancholy*? Oh, Thomas, Thomas!

Remember, reader, that Miss Farthingay remains quite ignorant, of who it was Mr Peach took into his employ. — The very same Clarissa Riddle, who was once her father's ward, and her own childhood play-mate, before she fell from Mr Farthingay's favour — whom Miss Farthingay has cause to believe mad, or lost, or dead.

She has always held the highest opinion, of her friend's character and judgment. It pierces her to the soul, to see him fallen into the ordinary contemptible silliness of men of middle age, by conceiving an affection for his female servant.

— No wonder, she thinks, the mysterious girl was always kept absent from the house, when I visited. — Oh, Thomas!

— Believe me — he says — if I could explain my reasons, with the frankness your kind behaviour deserves, I would do it. There are things I cannot speak of.

— Even to me, Thomas?

— Alas, Miss Farthingay.

— She won't come back.

He shakes his head. — I much regret, he says, that I alluded to the subject at all.

— Look at me. She *will not*. When a girl of that age follows her fancies, there is no more to be done.

— You think me an old fool.

— My one thought, she says, is that my friend is unhappy — that he makes himself unhappy! — and therefore I wish to alleviate it. As you did, once, when you saw me near insensate with grief.*

— Dear Arabella, he says, and sighs once more.

She sees, he will not be persuaded. In truth, she is not much inclined to try him further. She is grieved for him, as she has been before. — But also — for the first time — she is a little disappointed in him.

The talk turns to other matters. We shall not record them. — It is not an happy scene — Miss Farthingay, whose temper is naturally lively and witty, reduced to gloom — Mr Peach, in his

---

* Miss Farthingay here alludes, to events consequent upon the tragic demise of her parents. — A crisis, in which she had every reason to be grateful for the kind attentions of Mr Peach. We have given the whole history, in our former volume. — Heavens, reader! — we cannot always be interrupting ourselves, to paint *again*, scenes we have already laboured to depict. — You must take matters into your own hands. Seek out the book-sellers and the circulating libraries — hunt high and low — And find that volume for yourself. — *Find* it, and *read* it. We dare say, the effort will reward the toil.

antique melancholy — the valley labouring under skies, that drain colour from each prospect — The house, wherein strange small noises and shadowed motions might still be heard and seen, were any body present —

— Is this — we hear you cry, reader — Is *this* what has become, of Mr Tho.s Peach?

Your pardon. — We had not been certain, whether you knew the gentleman.

We remember, how we laboured to convey certain episodes in the extraordinary life of Thomas Peach, in former years. — How we sat whole days in the dark, straining our necromantic eye, to pierce the veil of the past, and conjure into view events so obscure — so difficult of conception, and yet, if understood, so remarkable in significance!

In that effort we expended much strength. We dare say, we wore out our heart as well as our hand, to bring that TRUE history, before the public. — To expose, what had otherwise been concealed for ever. — To publish revelations, which we dared think any person of discernment must be grateful to read.

And for all this labour, our reward has been — INDIFFERENCE.

— Pish — says the public — We care not for your eyes or your hands — Your heart, is an object of perfect unconcern. — Your tale is one among an hundred — We shall pick it up, or let it drop, at our whim — Perhaps it amused us a little, yester-day, but to-day it bores us. To-morrow we shall try another book. — Next week there will be several more new printed, two or three of which may possibly divert us, for a moment. Thomas Peach, la! he don't seem so much different from the rest. —

Thus is the pain of years, and the fruit of an art whose mysteries are a lifetime in mastering, tossed aside, with no more ceremony than the twisting of waste-paper to light your fire — And we ourselves, ground down and crushed, by the monumental carelessness of the world.

Therefore, reader, we have doubted, whether you were familiar with the earlier history of Mr Peach. — That portion of it, we took such pains to communicate. There have been but a few, who condescended to notice our efforts. —

But perhaps you are one of those rare souls, who remember, how Tho.s Peach was secure, and peaceful, and content, when we left him, six summers ago — And wonder, now — what has reduced him to the state in which Arabella Farthingay finds him, in the early days of October, in the year seventeen hundred and ninety-one?

We cannot tell you every thing that has passed. We have not the strength —

Had we met with even the *smallest* encouragement, in return for our former efforts! —

This much, however, you may be sure of; — that Mr Peach is deprived of the only two companions, of his quotidian existence. A most eccentric pair of companions, certainly — But nevertheless — such props as he had in his solitude, are lost.

For the mysterious Clarissa Riddle, or Clary, who attended Mr Peach in the capacity of house-maid, but whose nature and accomplishments were most certainly not confined within the usual scope of that station, is VANISHED — Without warning — without explanation — without trace.

As for the second companion — Mr Peach has, some two years since, ceased the practice of communicating with the spirit of his murdered bride, an habit once the chief solace of his days — his nights, rather. Indeed, not only has he discontinued the practice, but ensured that it *cannot* be resumed, by sealing the mortal remnants of Mrs Peach — a length of her black hair, and a single tooth, the necessary materials of his nocturnal conjuration — in a locket; and giving that locket to Miss Farthingay, with instructions that she preserve it, but never return it to him, unless at his most dire and urgent request.

If there are further causes, for his decayed condition, we do not at present enquire into them.

We noted the odour of laudanum in the parlour. Whether the drug is obtained as a *cure* for the bad dreams, of which Mr Peach complained — or whether it be their *cause* — We hesitate to decide.

And the sinister noises and motions about the house — We are not so foolish, as to investigate them any more closely than Miss Farthingay did.

For the present — thank Heaven! — the business of our tale is not with Mr Peach, but Miss Farthingay. We shall leave him, sunk in his torpor — and in his laudanum-bottle — Or else our narrative may sink with him. — Whereas the lady invites us, to take flight with her, over the sea — Into the blazing heart of the fire, where deeds that shake the world are daily forged. — To FRANCE!

By day Cochonne works in the fields until she aches like an old man. Gales blow from the sea. The rain is salty and stings her hands. In the evening her stepmother commands her around the house like a slave. Cochonne, clean my sons' boots! Cochonne, scrub the pot! To the mangle, Cochonne, for the linen must be dry by morning. Eh? You are tired? What right have you to be tired? Must your father live in filth because you are a great lazy donkey?

She lies awake while everyone else is asleep and imagines wringing her stepmother's wattled neck.

Her defiance of the Society of Patriots is gossiped all over the town. The young men deny it, naturally. On no account can they admit to being bested by a girl with a rake, even if the girl was Cochonne who has arms like a blacksmith. But everyone believes it and they burn with shame. They dare not provoke her to her face, so they tell stories about her when she is in the fields and are loud in praise of the other village girls if she is in hearing. Isabelle, oh, how delicate and pretty she is! And Jeanette, how soft her nature! Just as a girl should be. — But whose is that strange horse over there across the square? Ah, my eyes deceived me, it is not a horse, but Cochonne. When she goes by at a distance they neigh and whinny, or if they are emboldened by darkness and the distance is great enough, make the noise of an ass, *hee-haw*.

'I also am a prisoner,' she says to Gaspard Lesinge through the aperture in the cell door. 'Condemned to this shit-heap of a town where everyone despises me. I pray it will fall into the sea with every person in it.'

'Not *every* person, I hope?'

'Not you. I do not wish you dead. You alone listen to me.'

Privately, Lesinge thinks he has listened long enough by now. He has heard the girl's complaints a thousand times. They are the complaints of every insignificant country girl in all of France. Her stepmother is cruel, her father drives her like a tyrant, she is not so pretty as Jeanette and Isabella. God give him patience!

But he endures it, for he can imagine no other means of escape. The girl will be brought round. All the girls come round at last under the persuasion of Gaspard. Yet this one comes so infernally slowly! He attributes it to her unnatural size. She is like a ship with three ranks of cannon. To change its course demands tremendous effort.

'My poor Cochonne,' he says. 'But until one is locked in a cell, one does not know the true value of liberty. You think yourself confined here yet you may go anywhere you please. You might be in Coutances tomorrow, and then in Caen in three days, and in Paris in a week. Whereas for me, this miserable room is the entirety of my world.'

'How I wish it were not!' sighs Cochonne.

Lesinge feels a warmth in his fingers. He knows it, this sensation. When he used to stand at the gaming table, the dice in his fist, the eye of every rogue in the room upon him and a purse of coin hanging on the throw, this is what he felt before the winning cast. From his early youth God gifted him a talent to recognise the instant of crisis and to grasp it, like the fisherman answering the flick of his lure.

He makes his voice deep and urgent. 'There is no need to sigh at my fate when one has the power to change it. To change not only my destiny, but your own as well, in the same stroke.'

He stares intently through the aperture and silently urges her. Come, little fish, take my bait! Great fish, I mean. Come, whale! If you were Leviathan himself, I will catch you as soon as you bite.

'My own as well?' she says, with the beginning of a frown.

'Your own as well.'

'How so, sir?'

'Why, here we are, the two of us in confinement, as you say. Might we not both instead be free?'

'I do not understand you.'

Has he misjudged her? It is not the moment for hesitation. The dice are thrown and spin on the boards.

'But it is simple. Only imagine if this door which stands so cruelly between us were unlocked instead of locked. Imagine if someone obtained the key. Then might not Gaspard Lesinge walk away to his liberty? And Cochonne — might she not walk away with him?'

So intent is his regard that he observes the tiniest motions of her face, down to the hairs in her nose. There! He can see it: the inward tremor, the blush beginning to rise.

'Do you mean I might go with you?'

What else could I mean, colossal dolt? 'What else could I mean?' he says, making his most charming smile.

'Oh, sir,' Cochonne says. Her heart feels light as a cloud at dawn. 'Would you really allow me to accompany you?'

Lesinge had expected some hesitation. She is after all only a country girl, with a horizon no more distant than the next market town. Yet she snatches at his hint like a cow at the grass.

'Allow you? But if you set me free, I would beg you to. My liberator, to whom I would owe my life!'

'You would not regret it,' she says. She is full of emotion. 'I am very capable, sir. I can walk as far as any man and labour as hard. I can sew. I am an excellent cook.'

'My Cochonne! Do you imagine Lesinge is swayed by such mean achievements?'

'They are not so mean,' she says, with a suggestion of truculence.

'But of course they are not. I am sure you possess many useful accomplishments. Yet how can I think of them, when to me you would be nothing less than my salvation?'

Damn the girl! She does not simper and swoon. Already he observes a reflex of brutish thought come upon her, weighing down her first flush of elation.

'You must promise,' she says.

'Anything.'

'I could obtain my father's key tonight while he is asleep. I could return here with it. But you must swear on your soul that you will take me away with you.'

He composes himself into the most solemn attitude. 'I do so promise, on the honour of the Lesinges.'

'And on the fate of your immortal soul.'

'And on the fate of my soul, which is identical to my honour.'

Cochonne moves herself closer to the door. She lifts her arms towards the aperture. As if, Lesinge thinks, she would reach through the iron to embrace me!

'Do you see these hands, sir?'

'I do, my saviour!'

'They are large and strong, are they not?'

'They are, my Penthesilea! And so I entrust my whole self to them.'

Cochonne nods with satisfaction.

'If you break your word,' she says, 'I will crush your head between them like a grape. That is *my* promise to *you*.'

A parade of triumph has been forming in the brain of Lesinge, to celebrate his victory over the peasant girl. It scatters all at once as though fleeing a sudden shower.

He preserves his composure only through the most extreme effort of art. 'Alas,' he exclaims, affecting the wounded tones of a tragedian. 'Alas that Cochonne suspects my honesty! Did I not swear upon the honour of my family and on my soul?'

'I do not believe you are a man of faith or that your family is noble.'

The girl is not as dull as she looks, confound her! 'Perhaps not, by the standards of bishops or dukes. But I have a family nevertheless, and a soul as well. A soul filled with the most sincere admiration and gratitude for the one who frees it from unjust degradation!'

'Then,' says she, 'if you wish it to remain inside your body, you will not betray me.'

'Never.'

She lowers the monstrous hands. 'In that case, I will gladly leave behind my cruel father and this whole town which I hate, and be your companion.'

Thank the stars. 'Goddess!' he says. 'It will be this night?'

'Expect me to return after midnight.'

'I cannot tell the hours in this terrible cell. But I will wait for you with such impatience that every hour shall seem a year.'

'The escape will be discovered in the morning. There will be a pursuit. We must walk all night away from the roads.'

Lesinge's triumph reassembles. In his imagination he can already taste his freedom. The clear night air stretching up to Heaven, the grass and mud beneath his boots; how incomparably sweet they will be! And the stars shining above, by God!

'That will be no trial for us,' he says. 'We shall barely touch the earth as we go, for attached to our heels will be wings of love.'

Cochonne has been preparing her departure, arranging her voluminous smock and approaching the lantern to extinguish it for the night. She pauses. She turns again to the cell door.

'Of love?' she says.

'Have I not sworn it?' Lesinge presses his face to the aperture. 'Together we will depart this vile place where no one respects you, and when we are perfectly escaped you shall have my hand, just as I swore.'

Immediately he sees he has made an error. He does not understand what it is but the change in the monstrous girl's manner is unmistakable.

'You swear to marry me?'

Why is the giantess truculent again? Does she wish him to unswear the oath she just now threatened to enforce by violence? 'Of course. My angel, my nymph of Elysium! Can your heart have changed so suddenly?'

'I did not ask for marriage. I only asked that you take me with you.'

'Take you with me, yes, and I shall, my Penthesilea. Are you not ready to be my companion, and cook, and sew, and demonstrate all your other accomplishments?'

'I said nothing about marriage.'

Lesinge's brain spins in confusion. 'But what is it for a woman to escape her home with a man, if not an elopement?'

She approaches the door with heavy steps. 'I thought you sincere, sir,' she says. 'But now I know you are lying, and care only to make me fetch the key.'

'Lying? No, my Cochonne!'

'No one can desire to marry me. I am monstrous. All I asked was to go with you as a companion of the road. I would have been content as your fellow-thief. Do not look so wounded. I know you are a common brigand, no more. And now I also know that you meant only to trifle with my affections and flatter my vanity. You are a fool as well as a liar. Regard me, sir. How can I have vanity? Nature has forbidden it, and also cut me off from the possibility of love.'

'But—'

The aperture in the door has a wooden shutter. She closes it with force and bolts it. He is all at once in complete darkness.

'Count yourself fortunate,' he hears her say, 'that I detected your falsehood now, not after the event. You have at least saved your head from crushing.'

'Cochonne!' he cries. Her hulking tread ascends the tower steps. 'Cochonne, goddess, return!'

But she does not return. When all is finally quiet as well as dark, he understands that he has made his last throw of the dice and lost. Then the rotten air and the damp stones echo with the violent cursing of Gaspard Lesinge.

After he rages, he weeps, though not for long, for even in despair he remains a man. After the weeping he lies down and dreams.

As often during his time of captivity, he dreams of his childhood. He is picking his way between the hop poles. It is summer. Above him soar trellises of toothed leaves and musty flowers, a cathedral of nature. He ought to be running ahead of his sister, dancing as he goes, but his legs are lead; each step is a small nightmare. He regards the child that was himself and thinks: why did I not stay? Why did I run away to fight and steal when I could have lain down in the golden Artois fields and been buried in barley? In the dream the child Lesinge imagines a hangman waiting for him at the end of the nave of hops. It is a scarecrow holding a noose of straw.

'Wake up,' says a voice which belongs to no one.

He flails in the dark. The scent of the hop-flowers evaporates, and the sun of Artois. He is in his cell again, curled on verminous straw. There is a single candle above him, and beyond the candle a shadow which speaks.

'Wake up,' it says again.

Is it Cochonne? It is not Cochonne. The shadow's voice and shape are entirely wrong. No one else can be in the cell with him, and therefore he is still in his nightmare, though he can feel the oozing stone under his hands as he tries to push himself upright.

The shadow dips towards him. It has a human hand, which holds the candle. The hand appears entirely black. Its head is only a dark mass.

Lesinge is excessively frightened, and tries to wake up, as one does when suffering in a nightmare. The effort makes it clear to him that he is already awake. Someone — *something* — has entered his cell while he slept.

Its other hand comes into the light shed by the candle. This hand is also perfectly black. It gleams a little as though it wears satin gloves. Between black fingers it is holding his totem, the ivory knight without eyes.

'Who gave you this?' says the shadow. Its voice is harsh and ugly. He can see no mouth, only folds of darkness.

'Are you Death?' he stammers.

'No.'

Beyond doubt he is awake. A man knows when he is awake. His senses have become attuned to the cell; its stench, its foul air, its dimensions around him. He is imprisoned still.

Then what species of apparition has entered his prison?

Courage, Lesinge! He is in the presence of a demon, quite evidently. If it has come to conduct him to hell he will not whine for mercy. He has lived by setting the world at defiance. It will never be said of Gaspard that he quailed in his last moments.

'Who are you?' he says. It is not what he wanted to say.

'The black queen,' says the hideous voice, 'or the priest-killer, or one of a hundred other cursed names. I answer your question; answer mine. Who gave you this chess-piece?'

His eyes begin to adapt to the candlelight and murk. The apparition's head, he sees, is veiled. It wears black clothes and speaks in an approximation of a woman's voice, though horribly mangled.

'How did you get in here?'

The hand holding the blind cavalier snaps closed and withdraws into darkness. 'Because you do not answer, I take this from you. I have one more question: do you want to live or to be hanged? Fail again to answer and I take your life.'

Lesinge swallows. 'To live,' he says.

'Then listen. On the third night after this one a black carriage will pass along the road between Vire and Mortain, through the wood of Ouigly d'Oeuf. Four black horses draw it, and it will go like the wind. The carriage belongs to a rich man. Intercept it in that wood, rob the man of everything he has, and you will want for nothing for the rest of your life.'

Lesinge blinks.

'Do you understand me?' the demon says.

He scrambles to his feet. The air! It is not the same as it has been. It stirs as he has not felt it stir for long dreary days. The door of the cell has been opened.

'Am I free?' he says.

'You are.'

'The door.' The hint of sweet air almost overpowers him. From somewhere above, outside the old castle tower, he can perceive the sound of rain. 'How is it open?'

'You ask questions when you should only listen. Three nights from now. A black carriage, on the road outside Ouigly d'Oeuf. Remember.' The black hand that held his totem reappears, empty, and pinches the candle flame. He is instantly as blind as his ivory cavalier. He throws out his hand by instinct and cries 'Wait, wait!'

The veiled visitor is certainly no human creature. She moves through the utter darkness as though it were day. Lesinge hears her rustle over stones and up steps. She speaks again from the turn of the stair.

'I give you one opportunity of freedom and one opportunity of riches. Do not waste them, thief.'

He fumbles his way across the cell. 'Come back!' he says, but like Cochonne, the demon does not come back.

Lesinge must crawl, sweeping his arms before him, feeling his way like the lobster over the bed of the sea. He runs fingers through the straw, looking for the cavalier, his companion and only treasure. It is not there. The so-called black queen has robbed him. He would curse her, if she were not a demon and therefore already eternally damned.

So now he has nothing except his mouldy boots and the clothes on his back. Yet because he has his liberty he has everything! With his first breath of open air he almost weeps. The smell of rain and the sensation of a wide sky above overcome him with such elation that he wants to shriek his joy like a maniac.

But now the instant demands silence and concentration. He must forget darkness and discomfort, not to mention the mysterious demon-woman, and attend only to the effort of flight. It is not the first time Lesinge has been required to evade capture. There is an art to it. He studied it as an apprentice brigand, and flatters himself that he has added certain refinements of his own invention.

He does not know the country. The night is pitch black. From conversing with the besotted giantess, however, he knows the castle sits above its town, which sits in turn above a harbour. In this region of Normandy the sea always lies to the west. If he escapes the sea he escapes the town. The wind that buffets him has the smell of salt, and the rain it brings is surely collected from the ocean. Therefore he will put it at his back and let it guide him east, to safety.

How feeble his limbs are! Those fine legs which carried him hundreds of miles across the north of France have suffered from captivity. Nor has he tasted meat for days. The human frame gains no strength from bread and legumes. He encounters a steep rocky pitch beyond the decayed castle wall, and the effort of descending it, sliding on his belly and arse, leaves him drained. At the base is a streamlet which he discovers by its sound. He wades along it, fighting wet bushes and thickets of thorns. Going by water leaves no trail of scent for dogs to pursue but is unkind to his boots and legs. Soon his feet are freezing.

His nose tells him when he passes close to a farmhouse. The dogs there begin barking. Fear inspires him with half an hour of furious exertion, splashing and stumbling and cursing, until all is calm again, except for the relentless rain and the wind shaking trees he cannot see. He crawls into a tangle of roots raised above the mud and discovers he can go no further. There he squats and resolves to wait for dawn.

The next thing he knows is that one side of his face is caked in filth and his whole frame feels cold as death. He can see the shrubbery above him. He fell asleep where he sat and missed the coming of light. He spits out mud and struggles to rouse his limbs.

A minute later he goes perfectly still. There are people nearby.

Over the several years of his unlawful occupation, Lesinge has refined his senses to achieve an exquisite sensitivity to the presence of enemies. The particular cadence of a soldier's tread he knows as well as the musician knows his tune. The gathering of a mob of angry villagers he can detect at a distance of nearly a mile. In the opinion of Lesinge, his former comrades and fellow-brigands did not attend with sufficient diligence to this aspect of their art. They were more interested in learning where to find coin and how most effectually to rob it. Where they studied avarice and violence, Lesinge acquainted himself with the mysteries of stealth and flight; for, he reasoned, the pursuit of wealth was of less fundamental importance than the maintenance of life. Experience has confirmed his philosophy. All his old fellows are captured and hanged. Admittedly he is always poor, where many other brigands are not. But better poor and alive, by God, than rich for a year or two and then extinct!

Some have told him his creed demeans the nobility of an adventurer. Maybe it is so, but those who told him so are now dead by the noose, so they are welcome to their noble opinion of themselves. Gaspard Lesinge has discovered in his wanderings nothing more precious than life. Therefore he will live.

Though the pursuers must be close, or their noise would not have woken him, there is no reason to fear they will discover him if he remains perfectly still. The bushes grow thick by the stream. Even if there is a path immediately adjacent, as he fears there may be, the verdure ought to conceal him, particularly in the weak morning light.

Slow steps scuffle closer. He holds his breath.

There is only one man. It may be nothing but a single peasant trudging wearily to the fields. Lesinge catches a glimpse of a cloaked head and a guttering torch. The steps slow down again. The fellow is investigating the course of the stream, damn him! By the glimpses showing between the concealing leaves he looks tall and sturdy. But if only one man stood between Gaspard and liberty, it would not matter whether he was Hercules himself. Lesinge closes his fists, ready for battle.

The cloaked head passes from sight again. Lesinge lets out a long breath.

'Come out,' calls a familiar voice. 'I can smell you under there.'

Cochonne!

Lesinge is thrown into confusion.

Nearby branches begin to rattle. She is combing through them. 'Come out,' she says. 'I am alone. Your escape is not yet discovered.'

What is the idiot girl doing here?

'You cannot hide from me,' she says. 'The stench is worse than old milk.' Something swipes through the bushes and thuds on the ground. The monster has brought a club.

He composes himself as best he can.

'Cochonne, my angel!' he calls out. 'How I rejoice to hear you.'

'Come out, you villain,' she says. 'Do not call me angel, or anything of the sort, or I vow I will break you in ten pieces.'

He crawls from the bushes. There is a grassy lane beside, running at the bottom of some fields. Cochonne is alone, protected from the dawn chill by a good woollen cloak, carrying a torch in one hand and a long-handled farm implement in the other. She wears stout boots and has a pack on her vast shoulders. Her expression is implacable.

He has never before seen her except through the small aperture in the cell door. Facing her under the open sky, smeared with mud and shivering, he feels infinitely small and feeble. She is twice his stature.

'Come here,' she says.

For a fleeting instant he prepares to assume his former manner: Gaspard the charming, Gaspard the noble, Gaspard the great adventurer. The look on her face immediately cancels that notion. This Cochonne, she is not the stupid romantic child he took her for.

'Eh,' he says, in a resigned tone, 'you are not, after all, an angel, and perhaps I do not entirely rejoice to hear you. But you have the advantage of me, my young lady, and so I shall do as you ask.'

'Hold the torch for a moment,' she says.

When he takes it, she swings up the handle of the farm implement and then plants it in the earth with a tremendous thrust. It quivers as though in fear.

'By God!' he says. 'I was afraid you were going to hit me with it.'

'Attempt to run away and you can be sure I will.'

'Run away? What have I to flee, dear—'

She holds up a single finger in warning.

'Well, then, if not *dear* Cochonne, just Cochonne. I hope I need not think of running from you? You cannot intend to return me to that cell?'

'On the contrary,' she says. 'My only purpose in finding you was to keep my promise.'

'Your promise?'

'You may not care about your word, sworn on your *honour* and your *soul*. But it is otherwise with me.' With those words she reaches out and, though he tries to duck, seizes his head between her hands.

'Ow! What are you doing?'

'Crushing your skull, as I said I would.'

'My young lady,' he says, as well as he can under the powerful compression of his jaw, 'you are unfair to Lesinge.'

The immense hands squeeze harder. 'You ought to consider how you used me before calling me unfair.'

'And how did I use you, that you resent it so violently? Ow!'

'Did you think so little of trifling with my affections, and mocking my trusting heart with false words of love, that you do not even remember it?'

'A condemned man is desperate. His actions must be judged with lenience. Ow, ow, my head! I apologise nonetheless. Please relent, or you will crack my bones.'

'As I swore to do if you broke your promise.'

'What promise did I break? None!'

His head feels like it is being pressed by a millstone. 'That too you have forgotten? Your brains are not worth the effort of spilling them.'

'No! — stop! — listen! My promise was to bring you with me if you released me from prison. Which you did not! — ow, ow, Cochonne, stop, I beg you!'

The pressure relents at last. His brain throbs as though a smith has used it for his anvil.

'Then you do remember.'

'Of course I do. I meant it in good faith. Why do you punish me as if I did not?'

Cochonne takes her hands away. Lesinge drops to his knees, gasping. His head feels like he has spent the whole night drinking wine, not freezing in a ditch.

She pulls an iron key from inside her cloak and holds it up.

'I took this from my father's belt in the night,' she says. 'I came to the castle after midnight, ready to unlock your cell. I came to free you even though I knew you were lying. I knew you would no more marry me than a seal. You are a rogue and a bandit who spent many days trying to ensnare the poor heart of Cochonne, caring nothing what harm you did to it. Despite all that I stole the key, and these boots and this cloak, because I still preferred to escape this town with you. I have no wish for your affections which I know are pretended. I did not even care whether you abandoned me after two days on the road. Cochonne is as desperate for liberty as you, sir, no matter what you think. Tell me, then: do I not have a right to recall you to your promise?'

Lesinge blinks several times. Did he never deceive her at all? It occurs to him that this grotesque Norman farm girl has seen him more clearly than he, Gaspard Lesinge, philosopher and student of the human nature, has seen her.

'Did you truly intend to help me escape?' he says.

She snorts. She waves the key at him. 'Here I stand. Here is the key I stole. You may go back and try it in the lock if you like. You will find it is the correct one.'

'I prefer to accept your assurance than return to the prison, in honesty.'

A glimmer of a smile appears for a moment on her face. It would not be an entirely unhandsome face, Lesinge thinks, if it did not belong to a girl.

'I like you better and am less inclined to crush your head when you are honest.'

'Alas, my young lady, honesty is a luxury for men of my profession. We cannot often afford it.'

'So you admit you are a thief by occupation?'

He climbs back to his feet, shaking the shooting stars from his head. He attempts a ragged bow.

'Well, sir,' she says, 'you had better keep honest in your dealings with Cochonne, or your head will be cracked like an egg. And whether you lied or not when you swore to let me accompany you, you must now keep your word.' She raises her hands again.

'Wait! A moment, in justice! Surely we must agree that because you evidently did *not* liberate me from my cell, whatever bargain we made is rendered null?'

'But,' she says, brandishing the key again, 'it was my intention to liberate you. I have taken irreversible steps. I cannot now go back to my family even if I wanted to, and I would rather die. Therefore it seems to me you are still bound by your oath.'

'Hmm,' says Lesinge, folding his arms and cocking his head in thought. 'From the standpoint of a philosopher it is an interesting paradox. You intended the act, yes. But an intention, in philosophy, is not the same as the act itself.'

'A philosopher may put his head in his own arse,' says Cochonne. 'You ought to consider it from the standpoint of a man whose brains are about to be squeezed from his head.'

'Nevertheless, my young lady, nevertheless. You demanded honesty from me; I demand it from you. Confess that you did not, in fact, open the cell door, which was the condition on which our bargain was agreed. Confess that when you came to the prison after midnight, you found the door already open.'

'I did. How did you escape?'

'A thief must be allowed his secrets,' Lesinge says. 'For that matter, how did you pursue me so easily?'

She wrinkles her nose. 'You stink.'

'Admittedly. But, from your position in the base of the castle tower? On a wet and windy night?'

'The first part was not difficult. I knew you could not have gone far. I went out and heard the dogs barking at widow Bolbasseur's farm. If someone passes there so late, it must be the wretch Lesinge. I found a place where the reeds were trampled. You have left many signs of your passage.'

'Then I had better take to my heels before the alarm is raised in earnest.' Though he knows he cuts a sad figure, scrawny and mud-smeared, he attempts another bow. 'Farewell, Cochonne. May I call you dear Cochonne one last time? I will always remember you with fondness, whether you believe it or not.'

She sweeps the rake up from where it was planted in the ground.

'No, no,' she says. 'You misunderstand. I am coming with you. Resist it, or protest, and you go no further alive.'

He spreads his arms. 'Be reasonable. I am indeed, alas, a rogue and a villain, as you call me. I must live in a manner unsuitable for a young woman. You cannot wish to share such an existence.'

'Try me,' she says, with deadly firmness.

Lesinge is composing further arguments when a sudden clamour of dogs interrupts him.

'Shit of the devil,' says Cochonne, peering across the grey fields. 'I forgot that the house of old farmer Crobatte is just over the hill there. He sleeps with his hounds, but they rise early.'

'They will have the scent!' cries Lesinge in alarm. 'Into the stream, quick!'

After barely a minute of wading in the icy black water he is trembling so violently he can hardly walk at all.

'On my back,' Cochonne says.

'What?'

She lacks the patience to explain herself. Instead she heaves up the shivering brigand and holds him under his legs while he clings to her neck like a child. The torch is discarded. With the handle of the rake she clears a path ahead of them, crashing through shrubs and river weeds. She strides not much less fast than he could run, as though her legs eat the ground.

Still, the dogs are faster. They gain ground by the minute. A man's voice can be heard following and encouraging them, though further behind.

At a place where a huge yellowing willow bends over the stream she stops and puts down her burden.

'Of all God's creatures,' says Lesinge feebly, for the jolting ride has shaken most of the breath from his lungs, 'I despise a dog the most. Worse than the mosquito and the poisonous spider. The dog is the eternal enemy of the adventurer.'

'I myself am fond of animals,' Cochonne says, hefting the rake and planting her feet. The barking is savage now, approaching with tremendous speed. 'I have a loving nature.'

The first hound crashes through the curtain of willow and springs forward, muzzle bared. It is a thick brindled beast, bred from ancestors who fought wolves. Cochonne makes a kind of war cry and brings the handle of the rake down on its head. A second dog dashes behind, only to receive the same treatment. By Saint Michael, the girl wields her farm tool like the musketeers of old! — swish, swish, left and right, too fast for the eye to follow. Before Lesinge can perfectly understand what has happened both animals lie whimpering on the ground. Cochonne fetches one a fierce blow on its jaw, then stamps on its head with her boot for good measure. It twitches and stops moving. Its companion struggles to its legs, whining in terror, and limps away as fast as it can, escaping a fatal parting blow only by the length of its tail.

Lesinge gapes.

'God's blood,' he says. 'If that is how you treat the animals you are fond of, I should like to see you deal with an enemy.'

Cochonne shrugs. She wipes the handle of her rake in the grass.

'Necessity demanded it,' she says. 'Old man Crobatte will give up the chase when he discovers this.' She prods the dead dog with her boot.

Lesinge pulls himself up as straight as he can. He is all shivers and aches from top to toe, but he is a man, and has his dignity.

'I have misjudged you most unfortunately,' he says. 'I extend my deepest apology for daring to practise on you like any village girl. You are evidently a remarkable woman. It will be an honour to have your company on the road of adventure.'

Cochonne blushes with pleasure.

'I am relieved not to have to crush your head,' she says. 'Are you really Gaspard Lesinge?'

'That is indeed my name, and I hope you shall discover why I am not ashamed of it. We must lose no time. We shall walk all day. If I tire, I am not too proud to be carried again.'

'But where are we going?'

Lesinge's brain works as rapidly as his exhausted condition allows. He must not hesitate. The appearance of decisiveness is essential. The Amazon is inclined to follow him, he sees, and what a soldier she may prove to be, if he can at all times present himself as her captain!

'To Ouigly d'Oeuf,' he says. 'I have an appointment there.'

'Where is Ouigly d'Oeuf? I know nothing of the world beyond the dunghill where I was born.'

Lesinge does not know where Ouigly d'Ouef is. Between Vire and Mortain, the demon said. He will find the way.

'To the east,' he says, assuming a confident look. He points that way, to where the autumn sun now rises in earnest, and strides ahead. Within five minutes he is faltering. Cochonne picks him up as though he were a child's doll, and in that manner they go on together.

CHAPTER THREE

FRANCE! — exquisite nation!

The field, where, in antient days, the flower of *romance* scattered its seeds. — Where they took root, and grew to make the gay meadows of the troubadors, and the fine old tree of chivalry — The blossom of courtly manners and noble refinement — that *politesse*, which taught all Europe to bow before it! —

It is something of a disappointment to find, that the sea-gulls shriek the same as their British fellows. Every other thing is so changed, on our arrival. — We hoped to hear the birds speak a tongue of their own, as the people do — To see them wheel and squabble over the harbour, with a touch of *panache* — Cutting more elegant figures than their cousins across the water.

The port of Cherbourg, truth to say, exhibits little of its nation's gaiety. It seems a narrow, dirty, surly spot, that has absorbed the colouring of its antient neighbour the sea, and turned dull grey all over.

Flowers of romance do not thrive, we suppose, in the coastal gales. —

Perhaps we should not have expected a *charmante* French scene. The town is overrun by the English. — As though battalions of misses with umbrellas, and misters with brass buttons, have come to regain by stealth, what the pikes and muskets of Harry the Sixth could not hold by force. Within minutes of their arrival at the *Hôtel Anglais*, Miss Farthingay and her female companion have received several cards, and two invitations, along with an indefinite number of appraising glances.

— Arrived on Rawleigh's ship, says one brass button to another.

Neither, is of the *shiniest*. Each lodges in Cherbourg, to keep out of reach of English creditors and British bailiffs. — A story one would find frequently repeated, if one enquired more closely around the surly grey town, than we intend to.

— Not his concubine, I suppose?

— Lord! how should I know? I heard she's a poet.

— A poet!

The brass buttons laugh, in the manner of men who must persuade one another that they are gay, in order not to admit they are dismal.

— Rawleigh in town himself?

— No sign of him.

The brass buttons are dulled again.

— Spotted that fat old fellow of his. The brandy-factor.

— Dem the fellow.

The presence of Lord Rawleigh's brandy-factor indicates, that my lord does not oversee his business affairs himself, on this occasion. — And therefore, that the dinners he customarily lays on, for the entertainment of the more refined Britons resident at Cherbourg, lie not in prospect. Our two brass buttons count themselves among the refined set — but are, nevertheless, *spongers* — And, to the soul of a sponger, a free dinner denied, is a little death.*

Monsieur Denfert, deputy to the Legislative Assembly in Paris, has left a further letter for Miss Farthingay at the *Hôtel Anglais*. Though fatigued by the crossing, and a little disheartened by the initial impression of awakened France, that she has received from the town of Cherbourg, she unseals the letter with enthusiasm. M Denfert writes in good English — Welcoming her to the liberated soil, of his nation — Advising, that he has, by the authority of the *assemblée législative*, placed a carriage at her disposal, to conduct her to Paris, as soon as she and her companion are prepared to

---

* As the French say, *une petite mort.*

undertake the journey. The coachman is assuredly a master of his trade — Has orders, to facilitate her visit in every detail — Is a man whose probity M Denfert personally guarantees — Will present himself at the *Hôtel Anglais*, on such-and-such a morning — two days hence, Miss Farthingay notes with pleasure. In conclusion, the letter reiterates M Denfert's impatience, to extend from his own hand the hospitality, which Miss Farthingay's declared admiration for France has so notably earned.

— Happy nation! Miss Farthingay exclaims, throwing open the shutters. — Born anew! — Let me gaze on thee in transport!

Opposite the window looms the grey wall of some municipal edifice, overhung by a steep-pitched roof of grey slates, on which a phalanx of grey wood-pigeons sits out of the wind. They regard Miss Farthingay across the street with mournful looks.

She suspects she suffers some lingering depression of her spirits, after her passage. Her soul will be readier for transports, *to-morrow*.

The invitations are declined, and the cards not returned. Miss Farthingay regrets she cannot enjoy the society of Cherbourg, for she intends to change her place for Paris, within days.

— Lord! Paris! how vastly shocking!

— Why so, madam? Is it not an universal ambition, among travellers to France, to see the capital?

— Well, but it's become a frightful place now, don't you know! The women all run about with their hair loose and no shoes. Spitting on decent people.

— I shall remember to walk with an umbrella.

— Oh, *you* may laugh, Miss Farthingay, but it's quite true, the harridans run quite wild. People of quality pass through *nôtre ville* on the way to England. They all say the same, you know.

— It is natural, that those who choose to abandon their own country would spread the blackest report of its condition, if only in order to cover their own reasons with a coat of white-wash.

— La! I declare, Miss Farthingay, I don't hardly follow you. You might not speak so much *poetry*, you know.

Miss Farthingay and her female companion engage a guide, to shew them the sights of the town — Rebuffing several offers from the brass buttons, to perform the same duty *gratis*, and in correct English. She thanks them, but prefers to hear her tales of France, from a native. — The boy hired for the task is energetic and passionate. Between his excitable attempts at the English language — which he has picked up piecemeal from crumbs dropped around the town, by its exiled inhabitants — Between his English, and the somewhat mouldy governess's French of Miss Farthingay's female companion, the parties atchieve a degree of mutual understanding. — Sufficient, at least, for Miss Farthingay to gather, that their guide's notions of history extend no further into the past, than July of the year 'eighty-nine. Every thing antecedent to the revolution, is of no interest. — Those walls, madame? that building? Eh, they have always been there — But regard, mesdames, the break in that window. It was made in the night of fourteen August, two year ago, when the plot of the queen was discovered, to burn all the corn of the people — &c. —

Miss Farthingay herself, we ought to add, knows less French, than is usual among English ladies of her station.

She is not to blame. — It is intirely owing, to a deficiency in her *education*.

We hesitate to draw attention to the matter. It seems ungenerous. — Yet it has relevance, to the course of our narrative. —

In justice to the lady — whom we are inclined to admire, and whose little deficiencies we will therefore always excuse, when we can — Allow us to recall to you, some parts of the history of her family.*

---

* These we have dwelt on, elsewhere — In our previous volume, which, poor offspring of unrewarded toil, and neglected genius! has been universally ignored. — We suppose, you have not yet taken our advice, to seek it out and study it? Of course you have not. — We shall not presume to say, we know *you* — but we know, alas! the world, and its idle frivolous ways.

Miss Farthingay's father, during the period of her youth when the elements of a lady's accomplishments ought to be laid down, was distracted from attending to his daughter's education, by another project. — The education of his female ward, Miss Clarissa Riddle, on which he expended all his enthusiasm — those *paternal* efforts, which ought in justice to have been directed, to his proper child. Her mother had no interest in the liberal arts. — There was a governess, who, discovering herself wholly unsupervised by her employers, became perfectly lazy, and often drunk. Thus young Arabella was left to educate herself — Which she did, by passing silent happy hours, in her father's library, in the company of the Arabian Nights — the fables of Aesop and La Fontaine, in translation — the quaint old English essayists, and the witty and correct new ones — The Roman poets, whom she taught herself to understand, with the help of primer and lexicon.

That library, however, contained no works in *French*.

— Now here, mesdames, is a place most historic.

— The butter-cellar? says Miss Farthingay, who is amused at her young guide's notions. She is, after all, merely passing the day, before the arrival of the coach sent by M Denfert. One chronicle of Cherbourg will do quite as well as another, in the circumstances.

— Indeed yes. In this very butter-cellar, no more time ago than April of this very year, the militia came as close as *this* — The energetic youth holds up finger and thumb, an hair's breadth apart — As close as *this*, to the capture of that treasonous knave called the Forget-Me-Not.

— Oh! exclaims Miss Farthingay's female companion. — The Forget-Me-Not! — She raises the tip of her umbrella, and jogs it up and down in the air, while she chants —

But WHO is the Forget-Me-Not?
By jingo! no one knows, what, what?

The young guide spits. — A miscreant, mesdames, and enemy of the peoples of France. On the April night we speak about, a patriotic milk-maid brings information that the Forget-Me-Not has hidden himself here — In this cellar. — Look through the door — you shall see the very spot, where the boxes are piled. There he is hidden. — *Eh bien!* the guards assemble! They march in secret, to give no warning that they come. They arrive at the door here and surround it, so. — The guide steers the English ladies into their correct positions, and has them hold up their umbrellas like muskets, to enhance the immediacy of his *tableau*. — They call, Come out, villain of England — Pardon, mesdames, but I am obliged to repeat the exact words — Come out, and surrender to the law of France! *Ma foi!* These guards were brave men.

— But, says Miss Farthingay's female companion, the Forget-Me-Not was already escaped, I'm sure?

— On the contrary, madame. You are quite wrong. The villain was caught absolute by surprise. But attend to the history. — At the words of the guards, a man emerges, so. — The young guide now performs the role of the trapped and defeated Englishman, coming out from behind the boxes, and advancing with rueful steps towards the battery of umbrellas, hands aloft in submission. — He is dressed, says the youth, in the clothes of a labourer. It is well known that the Forget-Me-Not, though a *milord*, is a master of the art of disguise. — Says the villain, You have me, messieurs, I am your prisoner. The guards lead him to the Hôtel de Ville, over there. — Is it done then? Has the Englishman of notoriety been taken at last? — The guide looks expectantly at his audience.

— Impossible, says Miss Farthingay's female companion.

— Alas, madame, you are correct. It is all a trick. There were *two* men hidden here in the butter-cellar, behind the boxes. One was a simple dairy-farmer, in his labouring clothes, come to inspect his butter. The *other* man was the Forget-Me-Not, who promised the poor farmer many coins, if he would go out and surrender to the guards, and allow himself to be taken away. And so the *méchant* escapes again, while the guards carry off this other man. Devil of cunning!

Miss Farthingay's female companion claps her hands. — Such daring! such ingenuity!

— But, says Miss Farthingay, lowering her umbrella from its martial position, Surely the captured farmer explained his situation to the guards, who then proceeded to pursue the fugitive?

— Alas no, says the youth, removing his hat and cockade for a moment, and holding it to his chest with a pious expression. — When it was known in the town that the Forget-Me-Not is taken, the people fell upon the Hôtel de Ville and tore the man apart, despite his protestings.

— Frightful! says Miss Farthingay's female companion.

— Come, mesdames, we will proceed to the spot where the dismemberment occurred.

Miss Farthingay taps the tip of her umbrella against her boots, in a manner not sanctioned by any guide to the deportment of elegant ladies.

— The whole burden of this tale, she says, is — That a *dairy-farmer* was apprehended in a *butter-cellar*.

The boy replaces his hat.

— Mesdames, he says, you are female, and English. You do not understand the history.

Miss Farthingay and her companion dine alone. Her first day in rejuvenated France, has not met the hopes she had of it. — To-morrow, she thinks, we shall drive away from the sea, into the true France. There I shall see the people, untainted by the presence of my shabby fellow-countrymen — The common people, at work in field and forge — released from their antient feudal servitude, and rejoicing in the dignity which only LIBERTY bestows.

Glorious prospect! —

Before taking to her bed, she reads again M Denfert's letter, and thrills with visions of Paris. — And so lies down more content, than she has ever been during the day.

The next morning, is that appointed for her onward journey.

In accordance with M Denfert's promise, the coachman is waiting for her, in the common rooms of the Hôtel Anglais. He is a man of an aspect quite funereal — Grave and solemn as a carved angel on a tomb-stone, though much less handsome. He makes an humble approach, and presents the written recommendation of M Denfert. Though he speaks no English at all, he answers every enquiry in French of such Attic simplicity, that no translation is needed.

— When shall we reach Paris?

— *Le jour deuxième, madame.*

— And where are we to stop to-night?

— *Caen, madame.*

— A place is ready to receive us there?

— *Oui, madame.*

At her first sight of the carriage itself, Miss Farthingay's female companion gives an exclamation of surprise.

— Gracious! it looks more like an hearse!

The carriage is intirely black, without any decoration whatsoever, save its brass fittings. A second attendant sits behind four horses. His hat is drawn down over his forehead, and his face is muffled by a scarf, to protect, Miss Farthingay supposes, against the damp autumn air.

— *Le postillon, madame*, says the solemn coachman, indicating his assistant.

The muffled postillion does not acknowledge the ladies, but sits, quite still, holding the reins. — He will not so much as offer to help with the boxes.

— Even the horses are black all over! I declare, I shall think we ought to be in mourning.

— It shows a noble disdain, says Miss Farthingay, for ostentation and frippery.

However melancholy its appearance, the carriage proves both comfortable and rapid. No sooner are boxes and ladies secured, than, ho! with a crack of the whip the four black horses are off, and the cobbles of Cherbourg clatter and spark beneath their hooves.

Like Miss Farthingay's thoughts, the wind hurries south and east, aiding their passage over well-made roads. — Roads, Miss

Farthingay reflects, doubtless created by the loathsome *corvée.*[*]
What further improvements must be anticipated, from the
voluntary efforts of a free people!

The view from the carriage shews much opportunity for
improvement. Though harvest is not yet done, many of the
fields are waste, and few men at work in them. Old women with
bent backs browse by the road, collecting sticks and herbs in
their skirts. They rarely look up, as the conveyance races by —
And on the faces of those that do, Miss Farthingay notices little
evidence of the new dignity of their station. Some, she observes
with horror and compassion, are not old at all, but girls of no
more than twenty, already wrinkled and stooped with constant
toil.

— It is all, she thinks, so very *new*. — A land cannot be reborn
in an instant, from the corpse of its decayed parent. When the
snake sheds its old skin, the sloughed-off remnant does not vanish.

The metaphor seems eminently poetic. — She slips into a
reverie of rhymes and numbers.

Her female companion falls alseep. —

At a filthy hostelry the horses are changed, and some refreshment
taken. The muffled postillion remains in his seat, his hat still low,
while the lugubrious coachman attends the ladies. It is a curiosity,
that all four of the animals newly yoked to the carriage, are also
perfectly black.

— *C'est la façon du pays, madame.*

— Miss Farthingay has not heard of these famous black
Norman horses. — But she is no *connoisseuse* of horse-flesh.

As they prepare to resume their places, the clatter of another
rider is heard on the road, approaching in haste.

---

[*] A notorious tax of the *ancien régime*, collected in the form of forced
labour. Reader, you may shudder to think, that a form of *slavery* was
imposed on the people of a cultivated nation, in the previous century! —
Close your eyes, and offer once again your orisons, that you were born
British.

— *Diable!* cries the muffled postillion, from under his low hat. It is the first sign of animation Miss Farthingay has detected in the man. — He is suddenly very much agitated.

— *Veuillez entrer, mesdames*, the coachman says, opening the door.

— Mercy! says Miss Farthingay's female companion, alarmed at the sudden commotion. — What is happening?

— *Rien, madame.*

— Is it brigands?

Perhaps the gloomy fellow does not know the word. — He does not answer, but attempts to shepherd the ladies into the conveyance, with some urgency.

Miss Farthingay follows her companion within. — The coachman mounts, with surprizing agility — The whip cracks — Off they go — Though not before Miss Farthingay has glimpsed through the window, the rider whose arrival inspired her conductors with such alarm. She sees him only for a moment, before the dust flies up to obscure the window, and the carriage speeds away. Nevertheless, her single glance suggests he is no brigand. The rider is a comely young man, well-dressed, with remarkable golden hair, reminiscent of the cavalier youths flattered by the brush of *Van Dyck* — Though the face of this boy renders flattery redundant.

— Where have I seen such a face before? thinks Miss Farthingay. — Such beauty is not easily forgotten. — Ah! — The recollection comes to her. — That rider could be the twin of the libertine de Charizard's valet! — what was his name — des Sables.

— What a narrow escape we had there! exclaims her female companion, adjusting her bonnet. — I shall not be content until we are safely arrived at Paris.

— I doubt there was any danger, says Miss Farthingay. — It was but one young man, and his appearance not very *brigandly*.

— You ought not have let him see you, my dear. Whatever will become of us if such people know we are but two women, travelling alone?

Miss Farthingay lets her old friend rattle on, like the carriage. She is contented with the distraction — For the recollection of the libertine and his valet, has necessarily brought with it other memories, she is glad to have left behind across the sea. — How unpleasant the man's attentions were! and how tiresomely sustained!

— The petty nobles of the *ancien régime*, she thinks, were proverbial for immorality, in affairs of love. What a blessing that their time has passed — never to return!

The day turns mild and yellow. Though the country continues rougher than Miss Farthingay is used to, the air might have come with her, from dear old Somerset-shire. — It is hazy, and soft — glistening in certain corners, as though preparing to transmute itself to gold. The sun is a brilliant smudge, which appears to race through the tree-tops beside the road.

Miss Farthingay observes the picturesque effect for some time, and then frowns.

— We are driving south, she says.

Her companion has fallen asleep again. — Arabella?

— Look, there is the sun, to the right of the road. It has been visible on that side for the past hour.

Her companion looks dutifully through the window. — Very fine, she says.

— The road from Normandy to Paris runs east.

— Perhaps it is all arranged differently in France. I have heard a mile here is not the same as at home.

Miss Farthingay sighs.

She remembers the maps nevertheless. — How eagerly she studied them, in her father's library! Caen, she recalls, is all but directly east of Cherbourg. — If they are to pass the night in that town, as the coachman said, the descending sun ought to be *behind* them on their way. — Yet it remains resolutely beside. — Indeed, the road from time to time bends towards it.

Reason and inference agree, that the direction of their journey has certainly been south and west, since they left the hostelry.

— I shall enquire, she says, and raps the roof of the carriage with her umbrella — Shouts through the narrow window, which permits communication with the driver — Excuse me — Stop — *Arrêtez* — Be so good as to stop at once!

There is no response. Her indignation begins to rise.

— I insist, she cries, with a vehemence that startles her female companion, That you stop the carriage immediately.

Some words are exchanged between the coachman and the muffled postillion, and, to Miss Farthingay's satisfaction, she feels their motion relent, and draw at last to an halt.

The road is as deserted, as it has appeared all day. — For France, as befits a kingdom that has recently suffered a fatal shock, has very little *circulation.** The face of the country has turned pleasantly hilly, variegated by little woods.

Miss Farthingay taps at the window, to signify she wishes some conversation with the driver. — Though it is now the muffled fellow, and not his melancholy associate, who descends to the road, and approaches the door.

Miss Farthingay turns to her female companion, whose knowledge of French is, as we have already mentioned, rather the better. — You must talk to him, she says. — Ask, whether he is certain we are on the right road to Caen, and if he insists we are, how he accounts for the position of the sun.

— Gracious! Arabella! had not you better talk to the man?

— I shall perhaps not understand all his answer, if he speaks rapidly, as natives do.

The postillion opens the door, bows, with no little grace, and converses a few sentences in French, with Miss Farthingay's female companion. His voice is more elegantly tuned, than the gloomy coachman's — He seems polite and complaisant — Though he does not raise his hat, or remove the scarf, which conceals the greater part of his face. He extends an hand, inviting the elder of the ladies to descend from the carriage. —

* *vide* Young's *Travels*, &c.

— He says he will show me the mistake regarding the position of the sun, says Miss Farthingay's female companion.

— There cannot possibly be any mistake, says Miss Farthingay.

Miss Farthingay's female companion takes the offered hand and steps down into the road. —

How glad we shall be, no more to have to force our pen through this aukward nomenclature! — Perhaps we were wrong, not to give the poor woman's name, several pages past. It would have tried our patience less, to call her Mrs____, And, we fear, yours also.

And yet — To name her, would have been to invite a certain sympathy — a concern with her history, and her fate — Which, when we consider the next events in our narrative, might have caused you some anxiety.

Your peace of mind, reader, is a thing we hold precious. If we must trouble it, from time to time — *when* we must — We take great care, that the cause is justified.

Miss Farthingay's female companion goes to the margin of the road, and peers up towards the after-noon sun, following the postillion's gesture.

The muffled man, in that instant —

SPRINGS! with the suddenness, and the precision, of a fencing-master, or an accomplished cat — to the carriage door —

Whisks from a pocket, a small bundle wrapped in purple velvet — which he presents to the startled Miss Farthingay — his eyes flashing with mysterious animation and purpose, under his hat — And then —

Shuts the door, with a rude *bang* —

LOCKS it! —

All this, in less time than is required to pen the words, *Miss Farthingay's female companion* —

And, leaps again! into the seat of the carriage — with a cry of triumph. The whip snaps — the four black horses whinny, and strain in their traces —

At once the vehicle is in motion! — speeding away along the road. — *Leaving* the poor English lady, whose name our tale no longer requires us to know, quite abandoned — *alone* in the road!

Her situation is pitiful indeed. — And yet not to be compared, with the evident catastrophe, which has overtaken Miss Farthingay herself.

Beyond doubt, our admirable heroine is ABDUCTED. — Shamelessly, foully!

She expends several minutes, in shouts, and threats, and shaking of the door. To no avail. — The carriage flies on, in the direction her wicked captors have chosen, without regard for her protests — without hesitation — without mercy.

Her state of mind, is indescribable. Rage — terror — The dread, colder and more insidious, of what may come.

No — We cannot linger over her distresses — as though exerting ourselves, to move your pity. If such an effort was wanted, in *this* moment, why — You, reader, would be a beast — and we no better than a keeper of beasts, in vile compact with our brute performers.

With trembling fingers, Miss Farthingay unwraps the small velvet bundle, handed to her by the masked villain.

Within its soft enclosure are two chess-pieces, carved with marvellous delicacy, one in ivory, the other in some dark polished stone. — A *white queen*, and a *black king*. The two have been tied together, by a slender cord of red silk, sealed with a bow.

It is undoubtedly a kind of card, announcing the author of this unforgivable act. — A *signature*, to his creed of libertine villainy.

— De Charizard! cries Miss Farthingay, as enraged as terrified.

The rider, who came up behind the carriage at the hostelry, was indeed the wicked man's valet! — Ordered, no doubt, to ride behind at a distance, so that Miss Farthingay would not see him and know him. — And the postillion, who crouched in silence, and hid his face, from the very beginning of the journey, is — the villainous *seigneur* himself! — *He* it is, who has arranged the whole of this desperate and criminal proceeding, to have by force, what he could not come near attaining, with all his polite attentions and assiduous flatteries. — *He*, aficionado of the game of chess — who imagines himself the sable king, to be paired at his wish, with the spotless virtuous queen!

The carriage door is bolted fast. —

Miss Farthingay reproaches herself in the most bitter terms, for entertaining no suspicions, of the postillion who hid his features — For entering upon this whole venture so lightly, in a spirit of such innocence — As though no evil thing could befall her, in a nation renewed on principles of reason, virtue, and justice.

Why is it, reader, that women will always be blaming *themselves*, for the cruelties practised upon them, by the male sex?

This world of ours is most barbarously made. —

She thinks of her female companion, cast aside in the road like a dog. — Perhaps the valet who follows the carriage will ensure no harm comes to her?

Noble soul! to call to mind another's distress, when her own is so pressing, and so dreadful!

When her first tide of amazement and horror recedes, she addresses herself to the small aperture in the forward part of the carriage, which permits communication with her abductor. She demands explanations — Issues the most impassioned reproaches — Appeals to the honour of one who dares call himself a gentleman — to the mere humanity, of any man, conscious of the wrong he does. — All expressed with the force and eloquence, natural to her poetic spirit. The reply she receives is only —

— An hundred thousand pardons, most exquisite lady. — I must attend to the road, to ensure that a place of comfort is reached before the night. Once you are accommodated as befits one whose beauty and virtue are to the rest of her sex, as silver to lead — Then I hope to beg permission to appear before you, and account for these actions, which must not alarm you in the least — for they arise from, and are impelled in every moment by, the most pure and ardent sentiments of admiration. For the present — I must drive — Ho! — The despicable Monsieur cracks his whip again, and the carriage rattles ever faster.

Miss Farthingay replies to this speech, with all the contempt it deserves. — But so furious is the racket of wheels and hooves, that she doubts she has made herself heard at all. She turns her anger, upon the token the villain saw fit to present to her. The ribbon of red silk, that ties the two chess-pieces together, has been pulled very tight. — Very well. — She tears at the knot with her finger-nails — teeth — Until, to her satisfaction, it is pulled apart, and black king and white queen are no longer bound together. The pieces themselves she attacks with the heel of her shoe, hoping to break off their heads, but they resist the assault. — She attempts to hurl them from the conveyance, by means of the window in the door, but the latch that opens it has also been bolted, from without.

By now, the sun — mute sentinel! which gave warning of the crime, yet presents so tranquil and serene a front, that Miss Farthingay never thought to take alarm — Has descended low, and frequently disappears, behind the hills to the west, or the yellowing woods that line the road.

The hours of darkness approach. —

We cannot bear to remain in the lady's company. We, too, are driven far from our own country, and the springs of our powers. We can do nothing to assist her — Nothing! Shall we then linger, in spectral horror, to witness whatever may now transpire? — to make a *record*, of acts so infamous?

NEVER.

Would to God, we had stayed in Britain. — Heaven preserve her!

It is the afternoon of the third day since Gaspard Lesinge escaped his prison.

In Paris all is ferment. Each hour of every day, the deputies in the new assembly make speeches and laws; all through the night they make factions and enemies. Many priests and nobles flee across the borders of France: to the Rhineland, the Papal States, the Austrian Netherlands, and across the Sleeve to proud rapacious Britain. Which of them go to join hostile armies? Which conspire with the king's escaped brothers or conduct secret correspondence with the queen? Does it matter? Surely all of them are traitors to France, or why so eager to desert her? The deputies argue whether to confiscate their lands or their heads.

Meanwhile the people are hungry, for the harvest is very bad. When the commoners of Paris cannot have bread at the price they wish their rulers tremble, whoever they are.

Some hundred miles to the west, among the hills which once separated the kingdoms of France and Brittany, the fires and furies of Paris are not felt. The weeds decay, the pears turn soft, the sun cools and the mists return as they always do in this season. Here too the people are famished, and the baker will not sell his loaf for less than half a day's wages; but these people have always been poor. Their misery is as eternal as the mists. They shrug their shoulders and call it the will of God.

In the village church of Ouigly d'Oeuf Cochonne kneels in prayer.

The preceding days weigh on her conscience. Since she first took the sacrament she has gained comfort from unburdening her soul of its sins and cancelling them in penitence. But those were the sins of a farmer's girl: an envious thought here, an unkind word there. Now she has run away from her father, which is breaking one of the commandments. Can she confess such a deed? Or others since then? She does not know how to tell a priest that — for example — she and Lesinge filled their bellies last night at an inn, and then Lesinge started a fire in the kitchen so that in the confusion they could leave without paying for what they ate. Or that she stood in the streets of Villedieu-les-Pôeles and watched her brigand companion take scraps of food and a few coins from the bowl of a blind beggar. Would she not be damned on the spot?

Lesinge says confession is mere superstition. 'If one truly desires to lay one's soul before God,' he told her, 'one has no need of a priest. God must know our hearts, or He is not God. Therefore one must implore His forgiveness directly, as the Protestants say.'

'But the Protestants will all burn eternally in hellfire.'

'Bah! If hell is the punishment for our sins we shall certainly all roast there together, Catholic and Protestant and Jew. I have seen the world. It is nothing but wickedness in every quarter. You and I, Cochonne, we are good people; but see the things we are compelled to do, just to eat and walk at liberty!'

He promises they will soon be rich. Cochonne prays he is not lying. She had not expected the life of a brigand to be so mean. On the first day, when Lesinge was still too weak to walk, she refused to help him rob farmers and poor travellers. But on the second day she was desperate with hunger herself. She is larger than other people and must eat more, as a dog must eat more than a mouse.

'A conscience,' Lesinge said, 'like a carriage, is for people who can afford to keep one. Which makes those people greatly worse than us; for they have the luxury of choosing their actions but still choose to be greedy and selfish. The richest men of France want for nothing but are the most avaricious and lustful. A brigand, on the other hand, is like a natural creature. He merely does what he must to sustain his existence. The fox is not wicked because it kills the chicken.'

Never in her life has Cochonne heard one who talks like Lesinge. In her soul she knows his philosophy is sinful, but it entrances her while they walk. And the roads! Every hour brings new scenes to wonder at. She had not known there were such mountains in creation as these hills overlooking the village of Ouigly d'Oeuf. Lesinge says they are to the mountains of the far south as the ripple in a stream to the wave of the sea.

'Take me to see those mountains,' she said, 'when we are rich.'

She cannot regret what she has done.

The church door creaks open. Cochonne remains in prayer. A man clears his throat.

'Welcome to the house of God, traveller. Whatever comfort I can offer is yours, in the name of Jesus.'

She looks up and sees it is the curate, a youthful man with a heavy build.

'Pardon me, sir,' he says. 'I should not have disturbed your devotions.'

It is dim in the old village church. Cochonne's heart sinks a little. She is reminded why she must not be in love.

She remembers her purpose in coming here. Her conscience retreats to its usual place.

'Good day, father,' she says.

The curate peers and discovers that the giant form kneeling in his church belongs to a woman. He is mortified. While he offers his apologies Cochonne looks over his shoulder and sees Lesinge slip stealthily through the door. He puts a finger to his lips and winks at her.

'I have not seen you before, young woman,' says the curate. 'What brings you to this village and this house of grace? Have you perhaps a poor widowed aunt or a cousin whom you visit?'

Cochonne says she has come from the coast, having heard that the church is a place of pilgrimage.

'A pilgrim! Then you know of the blessed egg of Ouigly d'Oeuf.'

Lesinge moves noiselessly behind the curate, past the worn tableaux of the Stations of the Cross, towards the bell-tower.

'Please, my father, tell the miraculous tale in your own words.'

The priest is delighted to repeat it, though Cochonne knows it already from travellers at the inn. One day long ago a chicken of the village laid an egg on whose shell appeared the face of Our Lady. The holy egg then saved the village from plague and destruction by war, and performed many other miracles which the priest relates at her request. Meanwhile Lesinge enters the door in the belfry wall, silent as a ghost, and ascends the tower. A few moments later she sees the rope that swings the bell ascending too, pulled up by his invisible hand.

'I thank the good Lord,' the curate says to Cochonne, 'that in these times there are still such simple pious souls as yours. What is your name, my daughter?'

'Marie,' says Cochonne.

'You are named for Our Lady herself.'

'Yes, my father.'

The rope has vanished completely. How Lesinge has managed to bring it up to the height of the tower without disturbing the bell at all, she cannot imagine.

'In my village near the coast,' she says, 'there some who say that the priests are not the friends of the people. Can that be true, good father?'

'It cannot be.' The priest looks at Cochonne very earnestly, while behind his back Lesinge reappears, with the rope now coiled around his shoulders. In perfect silence he offers her a merry salute. The curate has begun a lengthy explanation of the superiority of religion to all earthly authority. She attends to it long enough for Lesinge to leave the church and then interrupts by standing up. She looms over the stocky curate.

'But are all priests not required to take an oath of loyalty to the new constitution?'

'My daughter, the Bible, which is the word of God himself, tells us that—'

'I suppose you have refused to swear that oath,' Cochonne says.

The young priest is furtive and embarrassed.

'I shall mention it,' she says, 'when I return to my village. Certain men there will be interested to know.' She leaves the priest mumbling in confusion and strides out of the village, to where Lesinge has established their camp in the woods.

While setting the kitchen of the inn on fire he also had the presence of mind to steal an iron pot. With its help he is cooking mushrooms over a fire of sticks and moss. He is in high good humour, whistling and singing his favourite song —

Who passes by this way so late?
Companions of the marjoram!

'A fine strong length of cord!' he says to Cochonne, brandishing the stolen rope. 'It will serve our purpose very well. The bell-ringer of Ouigly d'Oeuf knows his tools, by God!'

Cochonne cannot share his glee. 'I do not like to steal from a church,' she says.

'None of us *like* to steal at all, my dear. Myself, I would much prefer to possess everything I need, and be free of the trouble of obtaining it. But in order to attain that happy state we must exercise our wits a while longer, like it or no.'

'You appear content enough,' she says.

He inhales with relish. 'I have the forest air. I have these excellent mushrooms, which you and I will shortly enjoy together, before our evening's work. I have the best of companions.' He winks at her. 'Why should I not be happy?'

She pulls her woollen cape around her and sits, looking sulky. The day has been fine, but already its warmth fades.

'Guilt and fear,' says Lesinge, gesturing with one end of the rope as if it were a scholar's cane, 'belong to past and future. You and I must live exclusively in the present moment. The wise men of the East, the Chinese and Indians, say that past and future do not exist. Well then! In this moment I find fire and food and liberty. Therefore I whistle and sing like the thrush.'

'You sing more like the crow.'

He bows. 'As you say. But, my dear, shall we both be crows this evening? The sable bird loves to swoop on fallen prey.' He holds up the rope. 'We shall imitate his example.'

Despite herself the giantess is intrigued. Lesinge sees it in her eye. By Saint Christopher, but this one was born to be an adventurer of the roads! His former allies would have roared with laughter at the notion of a female brigand. But Gaspard, he is a man of the modern age. He knows how to see what is in front of his nose. He discards prejudice. Three days have demonstrated to him that the colossal Norman girl is resourceful and uncomplaining, as well as owning the strength of an ox. Also she will not get drunk or throw away all her caution out of lust for a passing milkmaid, which are failings that between them have destroyed the career of many a thief.

'When will you tell me about this mysterious appointment of yours? Will it come tonight?'

'It will,' he says.

'And it will make us rich?'

Lesinge has not told her about the demon or the promise it made. It lurks in his mind like an old bad dream. Sometimes as he walks he berates himself for remembering it at all. A black carriage and four black horses? A nobleman to be robbed, and all the wealth he could desire? Gaspard, Gaspard, are you a child, to be deluded by this species of nonsense? But then he reminds himself that the demon opened his cell. God knows his freedom is not a delusion. Since this demon called the black queen performed one miracle, why doubt that she can do another?

Also he must show no uncertainty before Cochonne.

'Before dark,' he says, leaning over the fire to stir the pot, 'a carriage will come along the road down there. In that carriage will be a very rich man. We will stop him and appropriate his coin to ourselves. And there! — we change places: he becomes the poor one, you and I the rich.'

'How can you know all this?'

'As we know anything, my dear. No man anticipates the future with certainty. We must all proceed with the knowledge we are given. The information I have is that this carriage drives towards Ouigly d'Oeuf this evening, and that it is all black and pulled by black horses. Regard.' He gestures through the trees, across the valley. 'From here it is possible to see a section of the road on the other side. When we hear a vehicle approach we will observe whether it fits the description. If so—' He snaps his fingers. 'My information is correct, and we hasten to the road below and execute our ambush.'

Oh, Cochonne, what a glorious brigand you will be! Though her eyes narrow as if she mistrusts him, he detects in them the light of adventure. She cannot help herself. Her soul is forged from the true steel, and sparks fly from it at his words.

'How shall we, who are only two people, stop a nobleman's carriage?'

'Come with me,' he says.

They go down through the wood to the place he has chosen. There he makes the first preparations, securing one end of the rope around the trunk of a tree and laying the length of it across the road to the other side, where he loops it carefully around boles and branches. He extracts a skin of oil from his coat. He begins applying the oil to the hemp by means of a rag. It is no more than three minutes' work to ensure a good coating, and in that time he explains to Cochonne what must be done when the time comes.

'Remember,' he says in conclusion, 'that the essential advantages are surprise and speed. Allow the enemy time to gather his wits, and he may load his pistols, and recognise that nothing confronts him but an unarmed man and a girl with a stable implement. Should that happen we must instantly bend every effort to flight. But as long as we exploit the very first moments, they will be in total confusion, and easily rendered helpless.'

'Pistols?' says Cochonne, wrinkling her large eyebrows.

Lesinge shrugs. 'A nobleman usually carries a pair. Slow weapons, difficult to control. Most likely he will have them in a box of ivory and pearl and velvet, where they will remain useless.'

Cochonne flexes her fingers on the handle of her rake. 'I do not like the nobles,' she says. 'They are the cause of the poor people's unhappiness.'

'Nor I,' he says. 'Let us see which of us can overpower him first. A wager of honour.'

'What do you mean, *overpower*?'

'Just what I say.' His eyes widen as he understands her meaning. 'By God, Cochonne, we are not required to knock out his brains!'

'Why not?'

'Why not? Because that is murder!'

She snorts. 'So you have discovered your conscience now.'

'Every brigand knows it is better not to kill the rich men. They do not enjoy being robbed, but they have infinite wealth, and in time they forget the offence if they cannot apprehend the offenders at once. But they most certainly will not forgive being murdered. Then the pursuit is relentless and eternal. A brigand who murders cannot escape the noose for long.'

Cochonne sweeps the rake low over the road. 'I shall aim for his legs,' she says.

She has no fear at all. He has heard that in Paris the common women are ten times more fierce in the cause of revolution than their sons and husbands. Some call this unnatural: but what is Cochonne except a pure child of nature, uncorrupted by education, acting entirely in accord with her native character?

A drover comes by with a dog and a few goats. He stops to ask what Lesinge and Cochonne are doing, rubbing a rag over a rope lying across the road. But the Norman peasants are proverbial for incuriosity, and after a few words of conversation he follows his animals in the direction of the village, shaking his head. A poor man has his own troubles without concerning himself with enormous women and ropes. He ought to have been summoned home an hour before now, but the church bell did not sound to warn him of the hour. Why did the bell not ring? His ears are not yet so feeble that he cannot hear it up in his pasture. That bell-ringer, he is lazy as a cat. The drover hopes he will be fined. He complains of it to Lesinge, and to Cochonne, and to his dog, and continues muttering his disgust as he trudges out of sight.

The mushrooms make a fine dinner for a pair of brigands who have only to watch, while the shadows lengthen on the hilltops and the lower slopes of the valley turn dim and cool.

They hear the carriage long before they see it.

'What clamour!' Lesinge exclaims. 'This nobleman drives as though the devil pursues him.'

Cochonne gets to her feet and stretches her enormous frame.

'Is it him?'

'Certainly,' says Lesinge, with more confidence than he feels. He is trusting in the promise of a supernatural creature, and no doubt a cursed one at that. But did the black queen not say a carriage would come along this very road at this very hour? And here is the sound of wheels and beating hooves. 'Quick now. We must raise the rope as tight as we can.'

'I thought you meant to watch first.'

'There is no time. Listen how fast this carriage comes! If the horses do not take fright our plan is undone.'

Being much the superior in strength, the task of securing the rope is entrusted to Cochonne. She pulls it taut across the road and begins tying its loops fast between branches. Meanwhile Lesinge works at his tinderbox in feverish hurry.

'Did you also steal that oil from the church?' Cochonne says.

'Now is not the time.'

'I hope you have not angered God.'

'I shall make him a generous gift as soon as I am rich. Not so low! And tighter, tighter! The rope must take the horses just below the knee, or they may break straight through.' The carriage is coming on at an infernal rate. Its noise is like a waterfall of metal. Lesinge looks across the valley and glimpses it for an instant, a racing shadow, sparks shooting beneath.

His hands are unsteady. It has been more than a year since he last robbed a vehicle in the roads. Have his days of imprisonment weakened him? Is his resolve less than it was?

The rope jerks before his eyes and then strains, quivering under the stress. Sainted Jesus, she has made it tight as a bar of iron! He renews his own efforts and at last raises a small flame. He applies it to the oiled rope, blocking the wind with his body as best he can. Patience, Lesinge, patience! — though the carriage approaches as if drawn by the four horsemen of doom.

'They have crossed the bridge,' Cochonne calls. 'They will be here in instants.'

He ignores her. The head of a brigand must be cool or it will not long remain attached to its neck. He coaxes the flame with tiny breaths, as when he blew the seeds from the dandelion's head when he was a boy. He cannot think which saint he should pray to for fire, so he prays to the demon. Creature of temptation, he murmurs, black queen, send the everlasting flame of your own regions to my aid!

The rope hisses and smoulders and begins to glow.

Lesinge dives for the trees beside the road. He quickly adjusts the scarf that conceals his face. The carriage is thundering up from the valley bottom. He can hear the driver's shouts: 'Ho! Ha! On!' A lick of flame travels along the rope. Suddenly the whole length of it burns bright. Catching the odour of smoke, the horses whinny, and the beat of their hooves loses its ferocious rhythm. But it is too late for them to stop. Their own haste condemns them. The vehicle hurtles into view, confronting the line of fire across the road, and the horses panic, shying and rearing. With a terrible noise one of them falls, tangling in the traces, and the carriage is overturned, throwing coachman and postillion into the road. Cochonne and Lesinge rush out together, one from each side.

The coachman, a tall fellow, has fallen hard enough to knock his head on the stones. Cochonne steps over him towards the postillion, who exclaims in pain and rage — 'Devil! Brigands!'

— and is attempting to regain his feet. She looms over him, raising the handle of the rake. 'Do not dare touch me, filth!' he cries. This postillion is brave, for a servant! He fumbles inside his coat as if seeking for a knife. The weapon is no more use to him than the bravery; Cochonne brings her stout implement down on his skull.

Lesinge meanwhile has danced around the thrashing horses to where the carriage lies on its side, two wheels spinning in air. The door now lies on its upward surface. He must not hesitate. The nobleman inside, and whatever attendants travel with him, are certainly stunned and thrown in a heap. This is the moment to assault them, unarmed though he is. His decisiveness will make them cower.

The door is locked. He considers breaking the glass. Then he notices that the bolts are on the outside. Eccentric arrangement!

'Surrender!' he cries, throwing back the bolts, 'for you are overwhelmed! Whoever resists will die!'

But there is only one person within, sprawled and still, and that person, to judge by the dress, is a woman.

Cochonne has found the coachman's knife and is attempting to free the struggling horses. Lesinge curses.

'Come here, imbecile! Did I not say a sudden attack was essential?'

'I do not like to see these animals suffer. One has broken its leg, poor creature.'

Where is the nobleman? Where are the riches? Several ordinary travelling boxes have spilled from the back of the carriage. Two are broken in the crash and disgorge their contents across the road; not coins and jewels and silver, but articles of clothing.

'Are the people in the carriage insensible?' Cochonne asks.

'No thanks to you.' After the thrill of the ambush a returning tide of irritability has come over him. He surveys the wreck. There is no nobleman. There are no riches. Is it the wrong carriage? But no, the vehicle is completely black, and the four horses are like night as well, exactly as the demon foretold.

Has he been played for a fool?

His heart sinks. Gaspard, he thinks, are you a halfwit, to have placed your trust in the promise of a supernatural apparition?

He jumps down into the road and begins turning over the boxes with some savagery. It is to no avail. He finds nothing but the ordinary cargo of a travelling townswoman. There are wrapped petticoats and hats in boxes of their own. The clothes might fetch a price, if he had the least understanding of what such things were worth, and knew where to sell them. But he has enough wit to know these are not riches, let alone a treasure great enough to secure him from want eternally.

Cochonne joins him. She removes the covering that concealed her face.

'What is this?'

'A lady's baggage. The lady you may see for yourself, inside the carriage.'

'Where is the gentleman?'

'There is no gentleman.'

'I do not understand.'

'What of the servants?'

'Both dead,' she says. 'One broke his head on the road, the other on the handle of my rake.'

'Poor devils.' Lesinge shrugs. 'They have died for nothing, I fear.'

'Then where is the treasure?'

Lesinge is too downcast to care about the rising anger in her voice. 'Come. What is done is done. We shall take whatever we can find from these' — he kicks at the baggage spread over the road — 'and be on our way before this sorry scene is discovered.'

'Do you tell me,' she says slowly, 'that we are not rich?'

Lesinge begins sifting through the boxes. 'I have been duped. It is a hazard among thieves. Still, these are the belongings of a respectable woman. There may be rings and other jewellery. Help me look.'

By now a certain stillness has descended. Three of the horses have been freed, and having galloped to the middle distance now stand uncertainly, not knowing what is required of them. Their wounded colleague lies in the road, struggling and making grunts of protest. Some interested crows have gathered to give their opinions from the trees. Otherwise the peace of the wood reigns again. In that tranquillity the brigands hear a feeble groan from the carriage.

'God! I thought she was killed as well,' Lesinge says. He climbs back onto the side of the vehicle. It creaks alarmingly when Cochonne joins him.

In the overturned compartment the lady has raised her head and is groping in confusion. She mumbles nonsense sounds.

'We ought to assist her,' Cochonne says.

'A handsome woman!' says Lesinge.

She turns towards them. Her look becomes incoherent, and she faints.

'She is stunned,' says Cochonne. 'Let us bring her out into the air.'

'She is alive at least, in which case we leave her in a better condition than her poor attendants. The rest is not our concern.'

'To abandon a woman in such a state is inhuman.'

'We are robbers, my young lady, not doctors.'

'You cannot call yourself a robber when you have nothing to rob. We might as well be doctors. I will not leave the lady to die.'

'You would kill a lady's servants, rouse her until you allow her a plain view of your face, and then help her live to tell the tale? You will not be a robber for long if you practise such methods.'

The argument seems likely to continue, for Cochonne is as stubborn as Lesinge is insistent. It is broken off, however, by a new noise. Across the valley iron clatters on stone again. Another traveller is riding down towards the bridge, and at speed.

'Curse it! To the woods, quick!'

Cochonne's reluctance does not last long. A glance at the scene of catastrophe impresses on her the wisdom of not being discovered. But when Lesinge tries to drag her on into the depths of the wood she plants her tremendous legs and will not go.

'At least I shall watch from here,' she says, 'to be sure the traveller discovers the lady's plight.'

'Your tender heart will be the death of us both,' Lesinge whispers, but since he cannot move her and dare not leave her, he crouches also in the shadows. The two of them go behind a fallen trunk from where they can watch the road unobserved.

The single rider crosses the bridge, comes around the corner in haste, and pulls up his horse with exclamations of astonishment. He dismounts.

His voice and manner mark him as a young man. The horse he rides is very fine, the brass of its equipage shining brilliantly. He wears a travelling cape of good material. When he pushes back the hood to survey the scene of disaster, his golden hair spills out like a second sunset.

Lesinge's heart quickens.

'The nobleman!' he whispers to Cochonne. 'He must have ridden behind the lady's carriage. Perhaps it is required by chivalry.'

The youth hurries to the carriage. Beneath his cape his dress shines with the watery glimmer of patterned silk. His face is elegant and beautiful. Its perfection bespeaks a lineage of ancient superiority.

Lesinge rises from his crouch.

'Remember,' he murmurs, as Cochonne raises herself beside him, 'even if he has pistols he will not have time to prepare them. Charge him at once and he is but a single man.'

The poor youth is hardly even that much, in truth. When the brigands come screaming out of the woods he freezes in terror like a child of eight, then falls on his knees, crying 'Oh, mercy! Do not hurt me, I beg you!'

Lesinge leaps forward and seizes him by the nose. He pulls and shakes his head most fiercely. 'Wretch!' he cries. 'Surrender!'

'Ow! I do surrender! Oh, my nose!'

'You shall have worse to complain of than this nose' — Lesinge gives it a savage tweak, at which the beautiful youth howls — 'if you do not submit instantly.'

'I have already said that I submit. Ow! Mercy, kind sir! I have an old mother who depends entirely on the pittance I send her. I am young, with all my life ahead of me. I wish no harm to any man. Oww!'

'Enough of your prating. Give up your pistols at once!'

'Pistols? Sir, I have no—'

'At once, I said, you dog. Cochonne, pick him up by his legs.'

The youth's nose is released, but his relief lasts only a moment, for Cochonne grips the ankles of his boots and lifts him in the air. He hangs upside-down, wailing.

'Be quiet! Cochonne, shake him. We shall see what the sir has concealed about his noble person.'

'I am not — Ah! Oh!' Thrown from side to side in the air, poor des Sables cannot speak in any language beyond groans of terror.

No pistols come loose from his person, though a purse on a ribbon is shaken out. Lesinge snatches it up with an exclamation of triumph. But his expert hand knows at once that it is light. It holds only a few pennies. He throws it down in disgust.

'Bah. Where is your treasure, my lord? Eh?' He gives the young man a buffet with his boot, setting him swinging and howling. 'By God, if you do not show us your riches instantly, your life is not worth one of these pennies.'

Des Sables begins to weep. Further kicks from the boot of Lesinge interrupt him as he tries to answer. 'I — ow! — I beg you, sir — ah! — let me down.'

'My arms become fatigued,' says Cochonne.

'If he will not tell us where he hides his money, it would be simpler to break his neck and be on our way.'

Des Sables moans more pitifully still.

'I advise letting him to the ground,' Cochonne says. 'He appears a puny boy, no danger to us. He may be more inclined to speak with his head above his heels.'

'Very well,' says Lesinge, with bad grace.

Des Sables is set down in the road, where he sits shivering and wiping his tender nose.

'Thank you, good sir and good young lady,' he says. 'Oh, my poor head!'

'He speaks prettily,' Cochonne says.

'They always do,' says Lesinge. 'The better to tell their lies. Accursed nobility!' He kicks the boy again, who cringes and turns his tear-stained face to his tormentor.

'You have utterly mistaken me, sir. I am not a nobleman, but merely the valet. My master—' He looks around. 'Where is my master?'

'You see?' says Lesinge, preparing another kick. 'Lies, lies and more lies!'

'By my grandfather's soul I swear it! My master — ah!' He has seen the figure of the postillion, laid out in the shadows at the edge of the road, leaking blood from his head. 'Master!'

Lesinge frowns.

'You have killed him!' des Sables exclaims.

'Enough of this pantomime. Your treasures at once, sir, or you follow these poor devils to hell.'

'I have no treasure!' Des Sables spreads his hands. 'You may strip me naked and search every corner of my clothes. You will find nothing. That man lying there is my master, the Sir de Charizard, travelling in disguise. Rob his corpse if you seek wealth, not mine.'

'In disguise? What is this species of nonsense?'

Explanations tumble from Des Sables as freely as tears. 'No nonsense, sir, but plain truth. I am only the humble and much-abused servant of that wicked man, and poor as a mouse despite these good clothes, for the little wages I am allowed for myself I send to my old mother who is blind and cannot walk. Everything you see of mine is only lent to me at the whim of my master, who is — who was! — as miserly as heartless. Ah, what will you do, mother, now my master is killed, and your Valentin will not longer have his pittance? You may as well kill me too, sir, for that would at least break the good old widow's heart, and spare her the descent into unrelieved poverty.'

Cochonne blinks away a tear.

'Let us investigate that one,' she says, indicating the man whose head she broke open. 'It is not worth tormenting the boy any more. Look at him.' And indeed des Sables is a most pathetic spectacle, squatting in the road and blubbering.

'We shall see,' Lesinge says darkly. The situation has begun to cause him a painful confusion. He feels certain he has been cheated, but the trick is shrouded in fog; he cannot see it clearly. It sours his temper.

Nevertheless, to his surprise, the crumpled corpse of the postillion, beneath its plain outer dress, is clothed in a silk shirt of rare quality, and black stockings without a hole to be seen in them. On further inspection his cloak proves to conceal a pair of pistols, a purse of gold and silver coins, and a black velvet bag.

'God's blood,' he murmurs. 'Is the boy telling the truth after all?'

Cochonne looks in the purse. She has never seen so much money in the whole of her life.

'The pistols and the coins,' she says. 'This was the nobleman after all. And I have killed him.'

Despite all the warnings he gave her before the ambush, Lesinge now seems to consider the murder as a point of no importance. He prods around the cloak with his foot. 'If this is the nobleman, where are his riches?'

Cochonne tosses the purse in her hand.

'That?' says Lesinge, with a tremendously dismissive look. 'A good purse, but not the millionth part of the wealth of any fine lord.'

'What is in the velvet bag?' says Cochonne.

Des Sables has wiped his eyes and is watching his assailants from his place in the road. He gestures in alarm.

'Sir!' he exclaims. 'I implore you, do not on any account open that bag.'

'Aha!' Lesinge nods. He holds the soft black bag before his eyes. There is a single object within, the size of his fist; he can feel it.

'So this is what you hoped to keep for yourself, is it?' If it is a precious stone, as he guesses it must be, it is huge: twenty times bigger than the biggest jewel he ever set eyes on, which was an emerald itself worth a thousand pounds. 'Sly rogue!'

'No, I swear! The stone in that bag is more wicked even than the man you have taken it from. I would not touch it for all the wealth in the world.'

'I knew it was a stone,' Lesinge says to Cochonne. 'I have the instinct for it. Here is the wealth I was promised.'

'Let me see,' she says. Lesinge loosens the cord of the bag.

'Ah, do not!' cries des Sables, but his plea is ineffectual in the face of the instinct of Lesinge. The thief takes out the stone and holds it up in the fast-fading twilight.

'It does not look very precious,' Cochonne says.

She is right. It is dull and uncut, a lump of rock, with here and there some hints of translucence reminiscent of a dirty glass window.

'Put it away, sir,' des Sables says, struggling to his feet. 'That is the summoning-stone of the de Charizards, sometimes called the demonoscope, and a most evil thing!'

'Whether evil or good I do not give a fig,' says Lesinge. If it is a jewel, it is the ugliest he has ever seen, as well as the biggest. He has heard that diamonds when taken from the earth look like dirty pebbles. 'But is it of great value?'

'Hide it from the light, I beg you, or you may rue the consequences. Unholy powers use that stone to pass from the infernal regions into this world.'

'They must be very small unholy powers,' says Lesinge, turning it this way and that.

Des Sables brings his hands together in supplication. 'I have no reason to lie to you, sir. My life is in your hands, and my future, if I have one, is in ruins. I advise you sincerely and impartially. Like all his ancestors before him, the Sir de Charizard dedicated himself to the Devil and trafficked with imps and spirits. That stone, the demonoscope, he called the greatest treasure of his family and swore he would conjure fiends with it. Perhaps even now they approach to conduct him to eternal punishment!'

As though in answer to the unfortunate youth's words, a spectral groan floats across the scene.

'The lady stirs again,' says Cochonne, recognising the source of the noise. She is not easily frightened, even by talk of imps and fiends.

Lesinge puts the stone back in the bag and pockets it. 'Who is this woman,' he says to the youth, 'whom your master was driving in such a madness of haste, and disguised?'

'You ask whether des Sables was entrusted with his master's confidence, sir.' With the removal of the cursed stone from view, the valet has regained some of his self-possession. 'I know nothing of the business. Some poor lady, I guess, upon whom the reprobate intended to practise the arts of the libertine. I only had orders to follow all the way to Castle Charizard, though it required me to ride night and day with barely time for a morsel of bread to sustain me. But fate has at last punished the reprobate Sir for his many crimes.'

'Castle Charizard, you say? Where is that? I have not heard of any such place.'

'It is many miles to the west, on a bare bluff of rock in the middle of a haunted forest. Ah, sir, though your intentions were criminal, you have done me an inexpressible favour by terminating my master's journey, and his life also. A thief you may be, but I will never condemn you.'

'Criminal? Thief?' Lesinge rounds on the youth in indignant anger. He cuffs his pretty head on one side, and then back in the opposite direction for good measure. 'Do you dare insult me?'

The altercation is interrupted by the reappearance of Cochonne, who has lifted the lady from the interior of the carriage with her bare arms, and now carries her down to the road even more easily than she carried Lesinge.

The lady moves her head and mouth a little, emitting peculiar sounds, like words in a foreign language. Her eyes flicker sometimes but do not open.

'The shock of the crash perhaps disarranged her wits,' says Lesinge, studying her more closely.

Des Sables comes up beside him. 'Is that—' he begins.

'Out of the way, boy!' Lesinge elbows him back. 'I will not have you obstructing the light.' The lady wears no ring or brooch. There is, however, a little whisper of silver at her neck. A less practised eye might not have seen it. With expert fingers Lesinge moves the high collar of her dress aside and finds a chain, to which a small locket is attached.

'You will excuse me, madam, for relieving you of this,' he tells the insensible lady. He works the tiny catch with ease and in moments has locket and chain stowed in his pockets along with the nobleman's purse and ugly gemstone.

'You take advantage of her,' Cochonne says sternly. 'It is base.'

'If what the blubbering boy says is true, you and I have saved this woman from eternal dishonour,' he says. 'In the circumstances, I do not think she would begrudge us a reward. It is a poor enough one compared to the service we do her.'

'I will take her to the village,' says Cochonne. 'Someone there will help her. The curate perhaps.'

'Are you mad? You have just murdered a titled lord. Do you think you can now walk into Ouigly d'Oeuf there as if you had not a care in the world? You might as well take his pistol and shoot yourself in the head.'

Cochonne looks downcast.

'I cannot leave her to die,' she says.

But now torchlight flickers through the trees in the direction of the village, and there is a distant murmur of voices.

'Well,' Lesinge says, 'you need not be concerned about that. The alarm is raised, it seems. We must depart the scene immediately. They will find the lady. How fortunate for her she did not awake and see our faces.'

'Ah!' des Sables exclaims. 'We will all be arrested!' He looks for his horse, which has wandered to the edge of the road to crop grass.

Cochonne lays her unconscious burden down as gently as if she deposited an infant in its crib. As she does so, a small white object dislodges from the hem of the lady's petticoats, where it had been tangled in imbrications of lace, and rolls in the road.

Lesinge snatches it up.

'Mother of God,' he murmurs.

'What is it?' says Cochonne.

The wood is very dusky now, dim enough to impede des Sables's search for his horse, which like its fellows in the stable of the Sir de Charizard is perfectly black, well disguised in the shadows. For a moment Lesinge doubts his own eyes.

'A chess-piece,' he says.

'A what?'

His brain races. (How dare the whimpering snivelling boy call him a mere thief! He is to brigandry as Molière was to comedians, or the Pompadour to whores.) In his hands he holds a white queen. He thinks at once of his lost companion and totem the white knight, stolen from him by the demon who released him from prison and led him to this ambush. She called herself the black queen, did she not?

Is this the treasure he was promised? His fingers work over the queen's tiny pointed crown, feeling for precious stones. His brain works too. What does it mean, this conjunction of chess-pieces? He does not respond to Cochonne. There is no time to explain himself to heavy-witted peasants. Think, Gaspard, think!

But now the mumble of the villagers is becoming distinct. The direction of the road towards Ouigly d'Oeuf glimmers with torchlight like a second sunset.

'Bah,' he says, stowing the white queen inside his coat alongside the silver locket, the nobleman's purse and the so-called demonoscope in its bag. The time for thinking will come later. Now is the time for taking to one's heels. 'To our camp, Cochonne. We must extinguish our fire. Then we slip away like creatures of the night.'

'What about him?' she says, nodding towards des Sables.

The valet! Absorbed by the mystery of the white queen, Lesinge had forgotten.

'I think he is attempting to ride away,' Cochonne says.

'To run to the guards and lay murder to our accounts? Prevent him, quickly.'

Des Sables has found his horse and is busy trying to persuade it back into the road. Cochonne is on him in five of her giant strides. She plucks him up by his collar so that his legs kick in the air.

'It would be best to kill him too,' Lesinge says.

'No! Mercy!'

Cochonne shakes her head. 'He is almost a child. Also his nature seems good.'

'It is! A thousand blessings on you for saying so. I am gentle and peaceful and wish no harm to any creature!'

'Hush!' Lesinge exclaims. 'If you wail like a cat these oafs who approach from the village will hear.'

'Do not kill me, good sir,' des Sables says, lowering his voice. 'It would be contrary to both reason and nature. I have done no injury to you.'

'You do not understand the laws of brigands,' Lesinge says. 'Among the first of them is: Leave no witness alive.'

Des Sables whimpers and closes his eyes.

'No,' Cochonne says. 'I have assisted you in burning an inn and robbing a church, but I will not allow cold-blooded murder.'

Lesinge sighs. If he gives the command and she refuses, that would be insubordination. He cannot countenance it. There is no time to argue the point.

'To say the truth, I have little inclination for it myself. A brigand is not a monster. Nevertheless, we cannot let him ride away. Bring him with us.'

'Oh, thank you, good sir, thank you!'

'Do not thank me yet. We shall decide what is to be done with you in the morning. And stop your snivelling! Not another word, or Cochonne will silence you with her fists. Away!' He darts away from the scene of wreckage and is in a moment vanished.

Cochonne swings poor des Sables in the air and tucks him under her arm. She looks back with regret at the handsome lady lying defenceless in the road. It pains her heart to leave a solitary woman in such a condition. The stocky curate will see she is well looked after, Cochonne hopes. He seemed a pious man. She regrets the deceptions she practised on him. She regrets many things! — yet as soon as she thinks of her stepmother and her stepbrothers, and the unending taunts and insults she suffered, she cannot prevent herself rejoicing at her new existence. She will never return to her village, never.

Carrying des Sables like a sack of flour, she follows Lesinge into the deep shadows.

Much later, deep in the night, a new shadow moves along the road. A little moonlight, veiled by gusting clouds, creeps down between the trees. The shadow is nevertheless almost invisible. It is a single woman dressed all in black, like the night itself in human form. Her boots click softly on the road as she walks, *tap*, *tap*.

The villagers have come and gone, returned again with carts and coffins, and gone again. The bodies, living and dead, have been removed to Ouigly d'Oeuf. The lamed horse has struggled away. Wild dogs will claim it soon. Only the overturned carriage remains at the scene. That at least, the villagers said to one another, can wait until daylight. It is miserable enough work for one night to carry away two corpses and a foreign woman.

And who is she, this woman who is not French, travelling alone, in a carriage without heraldry; travelling in haste and in secret, by night? Who is she, this fine foreign lady, who but for the unlucky accident of her carriage being overturned and her two attendants killed in their fall, might have escaped to the coast and even now be aboard some ship, bound — no doubt! — for hated England?

That she is some aristocrat is quite certain. She has the hands of one who has never toiled and the face of one to whom rich men pay court. Oh, her clothes are plainer than a fine lady's, but that is all part of her disguise. Such a woman would never travel with only two attendants if she were not going in secrecy; fleeing her country like a traitor!

She has taken a blow to the head and only wakes for a few moments at a time. In those moments she looks around uncomprehendingly and mumbles words which are not French.

No one knows who whispers it first. It might be the carpenter's wife, whose husband goes as far as Vire sometimes, and comes back with the news; it might be the innkeeper, who has heard from travellers many stories of the great people and their treasonous plots; it might even be mad old Binacle the goatherd, who has some tale of conspirators gathering in the road above the village, though no one listens to him since he is mad. Someone begins the whisper, it does not matter who. But once begun it multiplies by its own power until everyone has heard it from everyone else. This female aristocrat who goes in disguise in her black carriage, hastening in secret to escape the country; is she not the very same fine foreign lady who attempted only a few months ago to flee the bosom of her nation? — the *queen of France*?

The shadow approaches the ruined vehicle. *Tap, tap*; stop. It halts there, inspecting.

Most certainly it cannot be surveying the wreckage using the ordinary power of sight. The keenest eyes in Normandy would struggle to see anything more than masses of blackness, heaped in mysterious confusion. Nevertheless, the shadow walks around the carriage slowly, attentively. At its rear the shadow stops again and suddenly crouches to pick up an object from the road.

The frame of the vehicle is cracked in this corner and split open a finger's width. Out of this crack some very small thing has fallen. The shadow raises it to her veiled eyes.

It too is black. No human eyes could make out such a thing in this scene of darkness. It is very small, no longer or thicker than a man's finger.

The shadow traces its shape with gloved hands. It is another chess-piece: the black king.

The shadow holds the chess-piece close to its head, hidden behind black lace and crêpe. It speaks.

Even in a murmur its voice is harsh and ugly. It speaks four syllables only. They are not French. Some demonic incantation; a black vow or a curse.

'*Come, Thomas Peach.*'

CHAPTER FOUR

Where are the *churches*? — Venerable square towers, sturdy and honest as the Saxon hands that raised them? — which rise o'er hill and vale, to shew the way to the village — Beckoning parishioners to their beds — Travellers, to the village inn — the Old Duke's Arms, where our ruddy-cheeked hostess, in her neat apron, keeps a chair and a kind welcome for all — The Old Duke's Arms, with glass in the windows, and oak blazing merrily in the hearth! Why, even if the church tower was out of sight, any labourer would direct you there. — The Old Duke, ma'am? bless me, who don't know the road to the Old Duke? You may be there in ten minutes straight, and have a dish of mutton from Bessy in another ten. God keep you, ma'am, and grant you good journey — Nay, ma'am, nay, keep your coin, I'll not take charity for doing as any fellow would. A farmer has his honour as a lady does. — Are we not all one in this good commonwealth of Britain, rich and poor together?

God save the king! —

Where are the neat hedge-rows? that guide us through the lanes, as the banks of a river keep our sweet streams in their allotted course?

Here, are only dismal wet fields — And, dismal wet woods — succeeding one another, without sense or order. — And, dismal wet hamlets of hovels and tumbled byres. — Look! there is one stone barn, topped with a dreary squat steeple, from which, at mournful intervals, an instrument clangs in disconsolate lament over its surroundings — *That* is what they call a village church, in *France*!

And, the people! — hunger-bitten — sour-faced — God help them, half go with wooden shoes — half the remainder, with no shoes at all. They trudge in the distance, as though oppressed by the waste around them — Fleeing from sight — hurrying away, if one threatens to approach, to ask *where one may be* — where an inn is to be found, or any shelter whatsoever, from this unhomely land.

We shall not voluntarily transgress the limits of our native island, ever again. We vow it before you, reader — You may hold us to it.

If only Arabella Farthingay had sworn the same!

Her female companion —

A thousand curses on our head, that we never took pains to record her name! Each time we think we are done with her, she obtrudes on our page once more.

Whatever mastery we once had in this trade of ours, we fear it is decayed. Disappointment — and, a wounded heart — These are deep mines, that undo the firmest foundations —

We must not speak of our own griefs, when our tale requires us, to attend to another's.

Miss Farthingay's female companion has been rescued from the indignity of abandonment in the road, by a travelling merchant and his wife, who came upon the scene some few minutes after her expulsion from the carriage, and, expressing astonishment and sorrow at her plight, conducted her to the nearest town, on the back of their cart.

There she rouses the mayor from his after-noon slumbers, to give an account of her circumstances, and, with trembling accents, to reveal the still more dreadful situation, of her abducted friend, Miss Farthingay.

— Alas — says monsieur the mayor — these *seigneurs*!

The lady demands immediate recourse to the police — the militia — the army — notaries, magistrates, and judges — Every apparatus of authority must be exerted, for the sake of Miss Farthingay, to prevent that lady from succumbing to — No

— her *quondam* female companion cannot bear to pronounce the word.

We understand only parcels of the conversation, and must glean what we can, from the English lady's expressions of outrage. — Monstrous! — barbarous! — The mayor shrugs, and pulls his moustaches, and indicates in every motion of his features and his deportment, that there is nothing to be done. — Most particularly, that there is nothing to be done, *by him.* The times are uncertain. His predecessor — a cousin of sorts — was, alas, a man who would always be doing. Decisions — proclamations — Enacting this decree, or that — investigating one fellow or the next. *Ma foi!* — where does it lead? Inevitably the day came, when this cousin did *the wrong thing.* It might have been the right thing, one week previously — might perhaps have also been correct, another week after — But was, in the particular instant, a grievous error, amounting almost to a crime. He was denounced — Interrogated, by a committee of patriots — Imprisoned — Replaced, by monsieur the present mayor, who pursues the politic course, of total inaction. *Ah, madame!* One regrets exceedingly the outrage upon your companion. These noblemen and noblewomen, it is how they conduct themselves since always. They have been abducting one another, during the time immemorial. Among them it is a kind of sport. — Once more he shrugs. — Honest patriots, madame, had best have nothing to do with their affairs. You have friends in England perhaps? It would be my honour to furnish you with the means to write a letter.

She writes several, inspired by such force of indignation that her pen is broken twice. Only one concerns us. — It is directed to certain persons in Cherbourg — *British* persons — who are entreated, in the most urgent language, to ensure that the inclosed paper crosses the sea with all swiftness, and makes its way to — *Lord Rawleigh.*

How happy we would be, to pursue the course of that letter at once — And so return ourselves, to good old BRITAIN! — the mown stubble of her fields glowing gold, in her autumn sun, while honest John Bull takes his well-earned ease, after the exertions of harvest, and gathers in charity with his neighbours, to sing decent hymns, under the benevolent gaze of the parish priest — The very picture of peace and contentment!

We cannot drive these visions from our thoughts.

They never appeared in our imagination, before we went *abroad*. —

Though we long to fly the scene, and retrieve our native shore, as the swallow is impelled by unconquerable instinct to return each summer to her proper home — we cannot abandon our heroine, Miss Farthingay.

Thank Heaven! she is delivered, from the despicable machinations of the libertine de Charizard.

How she is delivered, we cannot say with precision. — Our gaze was averted — And her own recollections are confused, in consequence of a severe blow to the skull. Do not be alarmed, reader — There has been no lasting injury — she is under the care of a doctor — Her present situation, is quite comfortable.

The carriage, it seems, met with an accident in the road, in the course of which Miss Farthingay struck her head against some unyielding part of the vehicle, with enough violence to render her temporarily insensible. — Horrors! — and yet we thank Heaven nevertheless — For, in the same accident, Monsieur de Charizard and his grim-faced coachman were each thrown from the seat — hurled, we suppose, into the rough wild country, beside the road — Rendered insensible, perhaps — we cannot say. — Yet we *do* know, with certainty, that neither of the villains returned, to inflict further oppression upon our heroine.

We shall suppose them to have slunk away. — Cowardly dogs!

Miss Farthingay appears to have been taken in, by the people of a nearby village, whose attentions, though doubtless well-meant, were rough and crude — So that she could not be certain, whether she was their guest, or their hostage. — Her senses remained disordered for a time — No body in the village, knew a word of

English — All was confusion and obscurity, until the doctor arrived — Sent for, we suppose, from the nearest town of significance.

Forgive us, reader, that we cannot lay out the narrative, as we are wont to. France herself baffles us. — A nation, in chaos — Revolution, plot, and betrayal, in every direction, from Alp to sea — and all of it conducted, in *French* —

The doctor, we are pleased to say, is as humane and intelligent, as we would wish every member of that profession to be. Furthermore, he speaks tolerable English. — And can therefore attempt to satisfy Miss Farthingay, on those matters of most concern to her — Which are, principally, the fate of those who drove the carriage — for she dreads the reappearance of her devious tormentor! — and, the prospects of her return to her own country. Regarding the first of these, the good doctor gives some reassurance. He has not heard of any others, who escaped the accident. — The conveyance, madame, must have been driving at a most excessive speed — We are fortunate that your own injury is merely superficial, and will give you no trouble after four more days, or perhaps five — The head-ache, madame, will certainly subside — You have only to rest. — Miss Farthingay thanks the gentleman — And thanks Heaven as well, though silently, that the monster de Charizard has not been heard of, and cannot know where she is taken. — Prays, indeed, that the seducer suffered some such injury as her own — a blow to the brains, sufficient to efface every thought of his vile scheme, and its innocent object. She offers this latter prayer, with no more hesitation than we ourselves, despite its unchristian spirit.

If one cannot sincerely wish such people to the Devil — What use are our notions of justice, at all?

On the other subject of immediate concern to Miss Farthingay — that is, her wish to return home, as soon as possible, and put this whole misadventure behind her — The doctor is of less assistance. The duty of his profession, is to care for her injury — of his humanity, to see her properly accommodated while she recovers, which he is kind enough to ensure, by offering the use of his own house. Any thing beyond, lies out of his sphere. The civil authorities must be consulted. The mayor has been notified, and will interview madame, when the doctor deems her sufficiently recovered — The day after to-morrow, very likely. — Madame may demand of *monsieur le maire*, whatever she wishes to know.

Poor Miss Farthingay — Injured, though not, we fervently hope, to a degree that might cause serious alarm — Unaccompanied, in a land where she is a stranger — yet attended, with a certain courtesy —

Our heroine is better situated — infinitely better! — than we feared to find her. — We think we may take our leave of her again, for a day or two, until she is permitted to speak to the mayor. There can be no danger.

In the interval, we change our scene — with inward rejoicing — to our own country of BRITAIN.

The letter intended for Lord Rawleigh, makes its way with remarkable expedition, as far as the port of Cherbourg. Miss Farthingay's *quondam* female companion has ensured its swift passage, by berating the post-master, and the commissioner of roads, and every other person of authority unfortunate enough to come within her purview, with such bull-dog persistence, that they are compelled to submit, for the sake of their own peace of mind. — *Ces Anglaises!* Always busy and interfering! —

It is, they all agree, why the nation of England has commerce, but no culture.

In Cherbourg, certain British gentlemen read the letter. They are highly entertained at the account, penned by Miss Farthingay's friend. — How amusing, the situation of the old lady! — expelled from a carriage, and left squawking alone in the road like an hen, ha! ha! — A fine jest — to be told, with successive elaborations, over several dinners. Two of them despatch themselves, to rescue the old pullet, and fetch her back to Cherbourg. They name one another Lancelot and Galahad, knights-errant — ha, ha! It will all be vastly amusing — so long as the shadow of sobriety never falls upon the adventure — A risk they take pains to avert.

The inclosed papers, which the author of the letter insists must be communicated to Lord Rawleigh, with all possible haste, are sent at once across the sea, by fast packet.

The noble lord — for reasons quite obscure to us — continues to anticipate with feverish enthusiasm, the arrival of papers from France. He is always at Lyme, riding the hill-tops that overlook the Channel, with a brass telescope in his pocket — when it is not clapped to his eye, surveying the maritime traffic. The news-papers from Bristol and London are ordered to be brought to him each day, as soon as they arrive. If his man brings them when he is out upon the hills, he reads them *en plein air*, rain or shine — Scanning the columns for information from Paris — most particularly, any thing touching the fate of the queen.

— That rabble of democrat dogs — he curses — If they offend so much as an hair of her head — He will — He swears he will — He growls, and grinds his teeth. — Tears of passion form in the corners of his eyes.

He spies the Cherbourg packet, as soon as it crests the horizon, and is on the harbour quay an hour before it comes to land — Urging it on, as though he possessed the bag of Æolus, to command the winds.

At the news of a letter sent to him from France, his heart gives a mighty leap.

— So, he thinks, it begins! —

But, no — The letter is in *English* — Author and hand, equally unknown to him.

Dashed and broken hopes! —

He is on the point of hurling the paper into the sea, where crabs and eels may read it at their leisure, if they care to — when, the name of *Miss Arabella Farthingay* catches his eye. — It is twice under-lined.

He scans the letter cursorily — Then, once more, with attention.
By thunder!
Miss Farthingay — IN DANGER!

The author appeals to him, to exert every possible influence, which a nobleman of distinction commands. — To speak of Miss Farthingay's plight, in the House of Lords, or among ministers of state — perhaps, in the *royal ear itself*. — To address severe protests, to the powers which now govern France. — Or to do, whatever Lord Rawleigh deems best, to protect so honourable a lady, from so dreadful a plot.

Lord Rawleigh permits himself a smile, as he re-peruses the pleas of Miss Farthingay's female companion. The author is not to be blamed — She cannot know, good woman! that in addressing herself to *him*, she renders every other course of action unnecessary — That the rescue of Miss Farthingay need not be entrusted to parliament, nor to ambassadors — To any body, except the very person addressed in the letter.

No — she cannot know — NO ONE knows, the secret of Lord Rawleigh!

— By jingo, Rawleigh, he says to himself — What a fellow you are, hey? — And at once he proceeds home, to make his preparations.

Thus we have planted one foot of our narrative — if the metaphor may be allowed — on BRITISH soil — While the other, remains in France.

We shall bestride the two nations like a colossus, as Buonaparte dreamt he might. — Though, we confess, we lean with more favour, upon our northward limb. —

Let us return to Miss Farthingay, now we have determined her rescue is in train. Or, we suppose it is. — Lord Rawleigh's intentions remain at present somewhat cloudy. Besides, we know, as his lordship cannot, that our heroine is *already rescued* — if not from France, then at least from the vile scheme of Monsieur de Charizard. — Thanks to the injurious, yet fortunate, accident in the road.

Our *one* leg, remains to a degree ignorant of the circumstances attending the *other*. — We shall manage the situation as best we can.

The doctor having pronounced her head sufficiently restored, Miss Farthingay is attended by the mayor of the town.

This official, is one of the *new men* of France. It is his determination, to sweep away the rubbish of the old regime, with the most vigorous of brooms. — Nevertheless, though notable for zealotry, he is also a gallant fellow, and not cold-hearted. His first business is to enquire whether Miss Farthingay be accommodated to her perfect satisfaction — To assure her of the hospitality of the town, in every particular which accords with the doctor's directions. Necessary articles shall be provided, or sent for if they cannot be obtained at once — For Miss Farthingay is at present possessed of nothing beyond the clothes she sits in, and those already much the worse for her recent misadventures.

Nevertheless — although the mayor pronounces himself the lady's servant, in every matter pertaining to her comfort and peace of mind — He will not instantly accord with her stated desire, to be conveyed as soon as possible to Cherbourg, whence she hopes to proceed with equally little delay, across the sea. Alas, he cannot but wonder — nay, it is his duty as a patriot, to wonder — what the Englishwoman is doing, travelling unaccompanied in this region of France. Her story of abduction and accident appears fanciful — a *romantic* adventure, such as the novelists invent, for the entertainment of women and fools. It is known the English have spies in every place. Their fingers are inky, with plots against the constitution. — And is the whole of Normandy not plagued by that perfidious Briton the *Forget-Me-Not*, the friend of nobles and priests, and abetter of traitors?

He will get to the bottom of the matter. He will discover who this lady is, and what brought her to his city, for the sake of the security of France! — And until he is satisfied on those matters, though he will shew her every courtesy, the lady shall remain — for all his courteous protestations — his *prisoner*.

— My obligation, mademoiselle, is above every thing, to my nation.

He will place a commodious house at her disposal, and a good servant, and every convenience. — It will be a matter of some days only, while he makes certain enquiries. He is desolated. — To give offence, is a mortification — Yet his duty, and the state of the nation, stand above all. — A thousand pardons, mademoiselle — I entreat your patience — &c.

Has Miss Farthingay then exchanged one form of captivity, for another? — Is she now detained, not at the pleasure of an heartless libertine, but of the very nation of France, in the person of this its appointed representative?

She sits in the window of the apartment prepared for her, looking out over the smoke and mud — Hearing the mingled cries of the streets — cats, birds, and people, equally incomprehensible to her — And reflects on her situation. Quite alone — Penniless, for her purse has been taken, perhaps by one of the ruffian villagers — she cannot remember — Utterly at the mercy of strangers.

Her hand goes often to her breast, where for three years and more Mr Peach's locket hung. She feels its loss more keenly than the theft of her monies. It cannot be replaced. — She swore to look after it always, and is pierced to the heart, that her oath is broken.

— My dear Thomas, she murmurs — How shall I ever face you again? If, indeed, I ever return to Somerset-shire. —

She sighs often, and deeply.

Every poetic fancy, is quite banished from her brain.

There is but one recourse left to her. She contemplates it with reluctance — For, when she recollects the circumstances which brought her to France, she doubts whether it is quite safe, and worthy of her trust. It is — to invoke the name of *Monsieur Denfert*, deputy to the Assembly.

She fears this Denfert may be no more than a phantom, conjured by the malevolent pen of the libertine, for the purpose of enticing her across the sea, and into his black carriage. The letter of invitation, purporting to have come from the deputy, might have been fraudulent. — Authored, by de Charizard himself — A cog, or spring, in the infernal device, by which he meant to capture her. — The name, *Denfert* — she reflects — Is it not as much as to say, *d'enfer* — which is, *of hell*? — The loathsome de Charizard may have intended a joke, by assuming so apt a name, to lay his diabolical snare.

— Wicked man! You will be well paid for your joke — For if there is a place, of everlasting torment, you shall certainly find yourself there, when your time is come!

— And yet, she thinks, as the shadows lengthen in the room — which is plain and scantily furnished, though decent, and free of cobwebs — And yet, the letters I had from Monsieur Denfert had the stamp of authenticity.

— What other course of action is open to me? she thinks, as she lies in the wooden bed, listening to the parliament of owls in the belfry. — We beg their pardon — The owls of France, we suppose, gather in *assembly*, not *parliament* —

— What other course of action, except to wait within the town walls, which the patriotic mayor will not permit me to pass, until my friends in England can procure my liberty? — A prospect which hope may anticipate within a few days, but which reason must admit, might not be encompassed for several weeks — If at all.

The next day, Miss Farthingay requests the honour of a further interview with the mayor, and any other dignitaries of the town, who may be competent to determine her fate. The request is granted at once. — She is conducted to the Hôtel de Ville, escorted by a mob of urchins, of unimaginable filthiness. *L'Anglaise mystérieuse* has become a person of notoriety. — Several citizens aver, that their prisoner is certainly the queen herself, apprehended in another attempt to flee from France. They hiss as she passes. — They would throw handfuls of filth from the gutters, but for the admonishments of Captain Cramorant, whose company of guards have assumed responsibility for the Englishwoman's safety.

Captain Cramorant has conceived *une tendresse* for Miss Farthingay. — How, you ask, and why? — Reader, it is because — he is French.

She appears before the mayor, and three further officials, of mysterious function and capacity. A commissioner of something — A delegate, of some body — A judge, perhaps, though in what court, and enforcing which laws, no one knows. The nation is but a few weeks old — Its limbs, and eyes, and brains, still in their infant confusion.

Under examination by these worthies, Miss Farthingay invites them to assure themselves of the perfect innocence of her purposes, by making application to Monsieur Denfert, deputy to the *assemblée législative*, who will vouch for her.

— Denfert! exclaims the mayor, turning pale.

He confers with his fellows, in rapid anxious whispers.

Miss Farthingay senses, she has gained an advantage. —

The name of Denfert has inspired the town officials with the deepest awe — Not to say, terror. — All at once they are profuse in apology. They regret mademoiselle did not declare, that she was the guest of that noted patriot! Many inconveniences might have been avoided — Inconveniences they cannot sufficiently deplore. They will send word to Paris without delay. — Ah! how unfortunate a series of misprisions! Whatever they can do in recompense will be done. They beg an hundred pardons — a thousand. —

Miss Farthingay is as delighted as surprised, by the perfect efficacy of this recourse, to which she had turned so reluctantly. She concludes, that M Denfert had no part at all, in the conspiracy. — That his invitation, was after all quite genuine. — She supposes de Charizard learned of it, from some other source, and laid his plot accordingly — perhaps bribing the coachman at Cherbourg.

— The villains were frustrated, by a mere accident — Caused, indeed, by their own guilty haste, which made them drive the carriage at a reckless pace. — It is as fine an instance as one could imagine, of *natural justice*.

For the first time in many days, some apposite lines of verse occur to her.

We too, reader, are pleased at this turn of events. It is not often in our power, in the course of a single chapter, to raise an heroine from danger and injury, to perfect comfort, with every prospect of the complete restoration of her fortunes.

We shall not be altogether content, until Miss Farthingay be safely disembarked, on a British shore. — But — for the moment — We are satisfied.

How different her situation must appear, to her friends in England! — who know nothing of these latest events, but believe her, on the evidence of the letter penned by her female companion, at the mercy of an unprincipled black-hearted villain!

The news has come at last, to Grandison Hall.

Horror consumes the house, high and low. Miss Farthingay is well-loved by her servants. — By none more, than Caspar, steward of her estate, and of —

It is not for us to say, which of Miss Farthingay's other properties Caspar holds in care. On such matters, when we cannot speak with exactness, we prefer not to speak at all.[*]

The poor man is in agonies. He rides out in search of further news, and meets only with rumour and confusion. Some say Miss Farthingay is taken by the Paris mob. — Others, that she is imprisoned in a private dungeon — not the Bastille, for that is destroyed, as every body knows, but another one — They are found on every street-corner, in France.

Another report has her sold into slavery, to the *sooltan* of the Turks.

Some say she is lost at sea —

All Caspar knows for certain, is that no letter has come from her hand, since her first landing in Cherbourg, though she

---

[*] A philosophy we hope to see adopted, by all our fellow-creatures. — Although, alas, we do not *expect* it.

promised to write from every town along the way, and most of all from Paris. — And, that her female companion is reliably reported in Cherbourg, alone, and appealing for her friend's rescue.

He would ride to France himself that very day — were there not a body of water interposed.

Yet what can he do? He is but one man, and no more than a servant, in the eyes of the world.

There is one thing he is able to do, and must do. He acknowledges it with the greatest reluctance. He is sworn by a great oath, never to do it — Never to take the road, he must now take, nor visit the house he must now visit. The oath was confirmed before his sacred ancestors. — They slumber, perhaps, here in the white sheepfold of England — But abide nevertheless, and will not forget, if he offends them.

To spare Miss Farthingay dishonour and injury, he will pay any price. He will expose his spirit to the ire of the antient ones, if he must.

It is resolved. — He will seek out *the magician*.

With an oppressed heart, he makes the necessary arrangements at Grandison Hall, in case he *never returns*! — and rides out, alone, towards — Widdershins Bank, the home of — MR THOMAS PEACH.

How strange is the force, that compels our narrative!

We have come a good distance already, and might almost have persuaded ourselves that the gentleman was to play no great part in this tale. — That the power we invoked before his tomb, to bring his remarkable history to life again, had assumed an holiday mood, and released us from its native darkness and mystery, to dance our pen over foreign fields, in the gay and delightful company of Miss Arabella Farthingay.

It cannot be. We have made our bargain, and shall not be free, until the tale have done with us. —

Since the journey cannot be avoided — no more by ourselves, than by Caspar — Let us run ahead of him, and discover Mr Peach, before the amiable negro can.

But ah! how we shudder to enter the confines of that valley, hidden away among hills so sweet! — For miles around, the beeches are decked in copper and bronze, and on the open ridges peaceful flocks graze, while kites and crows toy with the gentle air. Yet within the bounds of Widdershins Bank, nature herself seems sickened. — By the stream, the willows droop, as though feeble with age. Choking weeds wind through meadow and hedge. Nothing stirs. — In all the landskip, there is no vital spark felt. — It is as though the whole valley, were consecrated as a place of burial — Mournful and forbidding.

The country people do not pass this way. It is agreed among them. — They knew Mr Peach was a bad man. — Didn't I say so from the first? — Aye — So you did — So we all said — A bad house, and an evil man!

In the house Mr Peach lies dreaming.

He sits in his parlour, and his eyes are open, but in a dream he must be, for he flies or floats through vast ruins, their gloom relieved only by fires burning in fathomless depths. — They were once cathedrals, built by titans — The procession of their colossal arches, infinite, like reflections in opposed mirrors — Their vaults, invisibly lofty — Their stones carved into leaves, and beasts, and angels, and devils, all fixed, monumental, silent in their writhings, like the marble serpents of the Laocöon. — Each ruin, though inconceivably huge, lies inclosed within the bounds of a far greater one. — And the whole infinite series, contained within the skull of Mr Peach, so that he drifts through the solemn wreckage of his own brain, like a speck of phosphorescence, in sunken *Atlantis*.

A sly scraping voice whispers in his ear.

— Art called for, Tom. Art summoned by enchantment.

Mr Peach's lips move to speak. — Leave me be.

The voice chitters its laughter.

— I shall never, it says. — Thy death shall not divide us. Is it to-day, Tom? Hast had thy fill? Art ready to die?

Mr Peach makes no answer, but the Olympian darkness of his vision begins to fade — surrendering to the parlour, and the laudanum-bottle on the table, and the chearless foggy noon.

— Shalt not escape so easy, says the whispering voice, which belongs to no one, unless the dust and shadows of the room have gained a tongue.

The change in Mr Peach's appearance, since he gave up the practice of communing with poor murdered Mrs Peach, is scarcely credible. He was used to be a man of neat and sober habits. — Respectable in his appearance, though quite without foppery. Were he to appear in company now, he would be scorned as a maniac. His dress is shabby and dirty — his beard unchecked — His hair long, and threaded through with grey and white. — His complexion, that of one who has long shunned the day. He moves without vigour or resolve, as though still in his dream — Speaks, when he speaks, to no body.

— Called? he says, going distractedly about the parlour. — Summoned? — Call how you may — It shall be the last pleasure of my existence, to deny you — Ha —

It is inexpressibly painful to us, to see such a man, reduced to such a state.

As the negro rides into the valley, his horse slows, and grows skittish — Doubts, evidently, whether to go on at all.

Caspar himself is not much less reluctant. He dismounts, observing the dull diminished light ahead.

He takes the reins, and leads the horse by hand. — Let us proceed together, he says, patting its muzzle. — Necessity compels us both. — I, for, Arabella's sake, and you, because you are a beast of burden, and wear an harness.

The animal grunts and whinnies. — We are no expert in the management of horses, but we guess, it is not persuaded by his reasons.

— I understand you, my friend, Caspar says, continuing to stroke the anxious creature, as he guides it on into the gloom. — It is an unhappy thing to be a slave, whether of tyranny, or of love.

The road descends. The air itself, begins to feel weighty, as though its essence were admixed with lead. No birds sing — None appears, even, on bush or bough, or in the open air above. The soaring creation, that feels not the taint of earth, shuns Widdershins Bank!

— I ought to have warned our mistress not to treat with this magician, Caspar says to the horse, in the manner of one who sustains his talk, to quiet his own nerves. — Men of power must be shunned. But I could not so advise her, for I swore never to speak of him at all.

When they come in sight of the house, the animal draws up, and positively refuses to continue.

— I shall have to tie you here, Caspar says, and leave you on your own. Is that what you prefer?

The horse stares at him with a single eye, very wide and white.

— True, true, says Caspar, knotting the reins on a willow bough, which is scabbed all over with grey mosses. — You are a slave, denied the expression of your preference. I shall come back as soon as I can. You have my word.

Caspar has not set eyes on Thomas Peach, since the very last page, of our former volume. — A span of six years and an half, as the chronicle measures it. The dirty unkempt fellow, whom he sees in the door, he takes for some vagrant labourer. — Perhaps this is the man employed to work the garden, and keep the exterior of the house, for both tasks have evidently been neglected, and this fellow looks correspondingly incapable of any work whatsoever. But when the man steps forward, to greet the visitor, certain tricks of his gait awaken Caspar's recognition, along with a peculiar glitter in his eye.

— I know you, says Mr Peach. — You came once, bearing a gift I treasure greatly, and then I spoke to you another time in chains.[*] You are Miss Farthingay's man.

---

[*] Further allusions, to events formerly recounted. — As, reader, we need not explain, for you have by now procured your own copy of the volume, and read it from beginning to end — Have you not?

Caspar observes with relief that the mad magician has forgotten his name, and inwardly resolves not to speak it, so it cannot be conjured with, or laid under any curse.

He bows low. — I come to you, sir, in the extremity of need. No lighter reason could have made me disturb your peace.

— My peace? says Mr Peach, with a rueful look.

— Your trouble, then, or your despair. It is not for me to name it. I ought to shun whatever belongs to you, good or ill, as a thing far removed from my humble sphere. Yet here I stand. Hear my reasons and you may forgive me.

Mr Peach studies his visitor with interest for a long while. Nothing stirs, but the withered head of a tall sun-flower, which shakes regretfully from side to side.

— I recall, he says at last, that I could not determine whether you were the wisest man in the county, or the most deluded.

— Do not think of me at all. I have come to speak only of Miss Farthingay.

— Dear Arabella. She is gone to France, is she not?

— She is, great sir, and may not return, without your aid.

Mr Peach blinks.

Caspar continues. — For several weeks past, in London, Miss Farthingay suffered the attentions of an egregiously odious suitor; a petty *seigneur* of France, living in exile. Unable to reconcile himself to my lady's refusals, he has criminally waylaid her upon the French roads. The event is confirmed by a direct witness.

Mr Peach frowns, drawing his unkempt eyebrows into a single mass. — She has been robbed?

— She has been taken captive. The *seigneur* bears the character of a notorious libertine. Many say he has renounced the Christian god, and devoted himself to His infernal antagonist. I shudder to contemplate the intentions of the Monsieur de Charizard, now that —

— Excuse me, Mr Peach says. — De Charizard, did you say?

— I did.

— I have heard the name.

Caspar forces patience upon himself, while the madman attempts to collect his thoughts.

— He wrote a letter. I recall the signature now, though not the contents. Was he not a gentleman amateur, in some obscure branch of knowledge?

— I cannot answer. I know with certainty only as much as my mistress told, which was to complain of his manners, and his wearying persistence; and, alas for her, I know the reputation he has acquired.

— He is among the *émigrés* in London, is he not? He hoped to meet me there, I now recall.

— He is.

— But Miss Farthingay went to France.

Caspar clenches his left thumb in its fist. He presses the nail hard against the palm, so that the sharp pain will occupy some of his attention, and prevent him from crying out in impatience.

— Monsieur de Charizard may be supposed to have pursued her across the sea.

— And what is he supposed to have done there?

Caspar descends on one knee, with so marked a grace that the gesture is altogether without meanness or servility. He bows his head, and addresses the earth between Mr Peach's feet. — Great sir — Question me not — I have said only what I have heard. What I know beyond doubt, is that Miss Farthingay has sent no communication, since the day she disembarked. That some dreadful event has occurred, which prevents her from writing, is beyond doubt. According to the letter of Monsieur Denfert, which my lady was pleased to shew me, she ought to have reached Paris several —

— Denfert! exclaims Mr Peach, with sudden animation, as though lightning-struck.

Caspar does not raise his head. He feels the change, in Mr Peach's manner. The ways of a man of power — a cursed and haunted man — Are not to be studied closely — or watched, at all. — Not to be spoken of, when silence is possible. The magician seems moved, by strong inward emotion. — Caspar has done all he can, and must now let that emotion work — And hope, that it works for weal, not for woe.

— I must go to France at once, Mr Peach says.

Caspar intones an inward prayer of gratitude, to whatever spirits congregate in this place, foul though they be.

— How may I get to France?

Emboldened, Caspar rises to his feet. — I understand, he says, there is a ship to depart within two days, from Lyme. It is my Lord Rawleigh's vessel.

— Lyme? What is Lyme?

Mr Peach appears distracted. His eyes move rapidly about, as though following the motion of invisible sparrows, flitting about the decayed garden.

— The port of Lyme, in Dorset-shire. It lies some thirty miles to the south.

— Thirty miles from this house? This valley? I cannot depart them. I cannot. If Clary returned, to find me gone —

He is certainly mad, thinks Caspar, and therefore I am also mad, to appeal to a lunatic for Arabella's rescue. — Yet the powers this madman commands touch the very doors of life and death.

— You must do as you will, great sir. I have spoken all I dare.

— But, says Mr Peach, as Caspar turns to go, Is it quite certain, that Arabella went to France at the behest of Madame Denfert?

Caspar cannot guess why Monsieur Denfert has been replaced by his wife, in the corrupted imagination of Thomas Peach. It is not for him to correct the error.

— Perfectly certain, he says. — I saw the letter myself, and took note of the name subscribed.

To Caspar's amazement, Mr Peach smiles.

— Then I am summoned indeed, he says. — Sir — my thanks to you. — I have forgotten your name. — Go, I pray, without ceremony. This is no place to linger.

For an instant, Caspar wonders whether to express his gratitude — To wish Mr Peach success — To entreat his haste, and impress upon him, that Miss Farthingay's honour and happiness are in his hands — Her very life, perhaps. — To offer his eternal fealty, if Mr Peach will only bring her back, safe and inviolate. He thrusts the nail into the soft flesh of his hand, with extreme force. — And leaves without another word.

The great tempest brews.

West of Paris, in the fields of Maine, a wet summer has rotted the wheat where it grew. From the millstones trickled meagre grey dust. When the carts of flour arrive at the city gates, guardsmen punch a sack with their bayonets and discover the mouldy grain mixed with sawdust from the windmill floor. The carters are turned over to the mob.

To the north, in fertile Picardy, the corn has been withered by weevil-blight. Refractory priests declare it the judgment of God.

All over France the harvest has failed. Like the whirlpool, Paris opens its hungry maw wider, wider, sucking the country barren for a hundred miles around. Bread, the insatiable maelstrom roars, give us bread! The rats skulk in catacombs and sewers, afraid to dare the streets where dull-eyed children wait for them with sharpened sticks. Day by day the sun's warmth shrivels. Cold, twin sister of starvation, begins to close her fist.

It is a whisper at first, heard among the rustle of windblown pamphlets in the avenues and the scratch of rain on the slates, and the slither of the swelling Seine. Then it is the universal murmur; and then an angry cry leaping like fire from one window to the next; and then it is the furious chorus of all the common people. *Where is our revolution?*

The delegates of the new Assembly are so busy making noise of their own they cannot hear the storm. Their hall rings with oration and response, motion and counter-motion. They indulge in feasts of language. Their brothers and sisters of the empty bellies cannot live on such fare. Who, the people wonder, will stop talking, and start doing? The king and queen in their palace, the counts and viscounts and marquises in their mansions and perfumed gardens: *they* have bread, for themselves and their children and their footmen and their actress whores. Somewhere in France are stores of grain! The people break open the houses of merchants, and descend upon the properties of well-off farmers — or farmers they believe to be well-off, and houses someone says belong to corn-merchants.

Outside the chamber of the deputies, a few of their number turn their ear to the angry wind, and sense what gathers in the distance.

They recognise one another, these few. Ah, you too, citizen? Then join us, after sunset, at the old convent of the Jacobins. That is where we meet to discuss what must be done.

The hungry people love them, this determined fraternity of the Jacobins. They gather at door and window to overhear the discussions. The words they hear are relayed all across the city, tinder-sparks to its combustible kindling. Confiscation of the wealth of priests; sentences of death upon emigrant nobles; denunciation of wavering deputies; and *war*, war against each enemy of France, inside her borders or beyond. No more pamphlets and speeches, no more votes and constitutions: instead of air and paper, blood and destruction. Since there is no bread the people feed their hearts instead of their stomachs, with promises of slaughter. Now this, citizen brother, citizen sister, *this* has the taste of revolution!

Every night, under the roof that once housed the Jacobin convent, Denfert is in attendance.

He is not the warmest in ardour or the bloodiest in argument. The people do not cry his name as they proclaim their heroes, Barnave, Pétion, Marat. He does not stand on tables to receive their adulation. He listens and he watches; a private conversation here, a word or two at your elbow there. He whispers. He suggests. He encourages.

When he makes a speech the Parisians are puzzled, for it consists exclusively of condemnations of religion. He says the churches ought all to be pulled down, their altars desecrated with blood and dung, and the crosses and madonnas hacked apart, then burnt and the ashes poured into the sewers. The hungry people know that the priests are fat rogues whose talk of obedience is superstitious oppression. But let their just rage be vented on the rich before it is directed against the God of their mothers and grandfathers, surely? The violence of Denfert might stir them more readily if communicated with more fire. He is a curious-looking man. Like Robespierre he is pale and small, but he is also delicate, with fine sharp features that remind one of the fox. Though diminutive, Robespierre seems to wear a mantle of authority. Conviction bursts from him. He makes one see what is true as if dispelling an enchantment from the brain. Denfert has no such grandeur. One might easily overlook him. His presence makes one nervous. One feels he might bite when you turn your back. His voice is soft and high-pitched, almost sweet. It is not the voice of a commander of men.

Who is Denfert?

The lists of deputies are contradictory. He was elected, it appears, by a commune high in the Pyrenees; or was it the Jura? Or the marshes of Gascony? The contradictions go unnoticed. He is influential, in ways that surprise even those who are influenced. He is the centre of no cabal, yet every cabal finds him an indispensable ally, without being certain why or how; as long as that particular cabal is devoted without restraint to the furtherance of revolution. Do more, Denfert whispers. Be bolder. Banish hesitation! If a little blood must spill, let it spill. Some are reluctant? They prefer not to move? Then break them and cast them aside. It is what the people want; and what are we, my deputies, but servants of the people?

Denfert makes one anxious but he also charms.

He has modest lodgings in the east of the city. No one visits. He is not sociable. One cannot quite feel oneself at ease in the company of Denfert.

It is very late when he comes home each day; after midnight, no matter what the weather. He has been meeting someone privately, to reassure him there are others of like mind. Do not hesitate in advancing your proposal, Denfert murmurs, though some might call it fanciful or extreme. Denfert listens to the hungry people and knows they are waiting to follow just such a leader. Or perhaps he has made a late visit to the workshop of Dr Guillotin, whose most recent invention he quietly promises to patronise and help perfect.

Such is the day's and evening's work of deputy Denfert.

His night's work no one knows at all.

The upper floor of his lodging projects above the surrounding roofs. This is old Paris, where the buildings are heaped against one another, wall fitting to wall however it may. Cries of starving cats and infants rise from below.

Denfert closes the shutters against the sullen moonlight.

'Minion,' he says, 'appear.'

Parts of the boards underfoot are charred black as if by fire. These parts form approximate squares of similar size, touching one another at the corners, so that in the faint nocturnal radiance the floor appears chequered sable and argent like a chess-board.

Abruptly, there is another person in the room. Only the shadows can say whether she was there a moment before. She is dressed like a mourner, head to foot in black, veiled. She stands on one of the charred squares, into whose darkness her feet seem to melt.

'Where have you been roaming, my pretty imp?' says Denfert.

'Here and there,' the veiled one says, in graceless and clumsy accents.

'And what have you done here and there, my priest-killer? You earn your sobriquet, I hope?'

The mourner sighs a little. 'I passed an old Sister of Charity drawing water from a well. I pushed her in.'

The poetry of the French language is a mystery to her. She speaks it like a Dutchwoman or, in her very worst moments, as the English do.

'And?'

'She broke her neck, I estimate. Or drowned. Or both.'

Denfert waves a delicate hand dismissively. 'I was not asking about the precise fate of the old sow. What else have you done, slave?'

She sighs more distinctly. 'Many things of that sort,' she says. 'I do not want to enumerate them. I am tired.'

'Tired? What is this? Who gives you permission to be tired?'

The veiled one bows but does not reply.

'Tell me this,' Denfert says, beginning to pace the room. 'In the north, the common herd: do they learn to forget God? Do they begin to despise Him? Are His temples of stone empty, and ready to crumble or burn?'

Her answer carries a hint of petulance. 'I do not know the minds of the common people. They are imbeciles who disgust me.'

Denfert stops his pacing. He stares at her. He takes two swift menacing steps until he stands on the adjoining square of undamaged wood, where the little moonlight entering the room falls in a dim silvery pool. He spreads the fingers of one hand and lays it on the veiled woman's head.

She gasps in pain, buckling at the knees.

'When you cease to be of use to me,' he says, 'you become nothing.'

'Forgive me, mistress.'

'Master!'

'Master. Forgive me, master!'

Denfert withdraws his hand.

'The common people of the north,' the woman says, shuddering as if emerging from a cave of ice, 'are certainly sinners. All their thoughts are lust and brutality when they are young, envy and spite when they are old.'

'Good,' Denfert says, relenting. 'Good. And they curse the name of God?'

The mourner hesitates.

'I am sure I have heard some of them do so,' she says. 'I believe they do in their hearts.'

Denfert considers whether he is satisfied with this answer. After some moments he retreats to a desk at the side of the room, where several opened letters lie in disorder. His minion lets out her breath in relief.

He picks up a letter and brandishes it. 'Perhaps I shall have the chance to investigate the north myself,' he says. 'At last there is news of the Farthingay. She is at Fougères.'

The veiled one is suddenly very still.

'How or why, these are mysteries. The mayor writes some nonsense I do not care to untangle. It seems—' Denfert flicks rapidly through the pages, though there is no candle to read by. 'The carriage was intercepted by — Robbers?' He puts the letter aside impatiently. 'No matter. We have her again, and to make sure there is no second mistake I will go myself.'

The woman replies anxiously, if any shade of emotion can be detected amid the clattering gourds of her consonants and the squeezed bladders of her vowels. 'Master — are you sure? Ought not so mean a task be given to your slave?'

'Of course,' Denfert says. 'However, I have a fancy to see for myself this soul that is owed in exchange for the demonoscope.'

'I have seen her. She is nothing of note.'

'She *was* nothing of note,' Denfert corrects. 'But now she is part of my triumph. In return for the Farthingay, the fool de Charizard gives me the demonoscope, and once the stone is mine I may call forth my legions. And then this whole earth will—' He stops himself and laughs. Oh, it is entirely charming, the laughter of Denfert! Yet everyone who hears it frowns or shudders, and wishes the joke had not been made. 'No,' he says. 'In front of a thing such as you I do not say what is to come. Yet the Farthingay is a species of key, which opens the door through which my victory enters the world. I think I should like to appraise so significant an object.'

'What will you do with her?'

'Impudence!' Denfert's eye flashes despite the gloom. 'Ask only what *you* are to do.'

'Send me ahead of you,' she says. 'I will learn what has happened and prevent any other accident. I will ensure the Englishwoman is given over to de Charizard.'

Denfert ponders. His boot taps the floor.

He picks up the letter again. 'The Farthingay is distressed, writes this mayor of Fougères, and requests assistance in returning to England. I shall send letters to them both approving the plan. There must be some conveniently situated closed house where she shall be invited to rest in safety while arrangements are made. Yes, that will do. Some convent or the like. We will shut her up like a recalcitrant daughter. Once there, she must not leave the place until I come.' He waves carelessly towards the veiled woman. 'Perhaps you may go before me after all. You are to ensure everything proceeds without interruption. There are three or four matters I must complete in Paris before taking any journey.'

'Send me at once,' she says. 'I long to do as you instruct.'

'Did I not hear my pretty blackbird chirp that she is tired? Poor blackbird. Had she not better lie down in her nest?' Denfert's careless wave turns into a purposeful gesture, pointing at her, then closing the fist.

'No,' she says, 'not tired at all.' But her voice already slurs. In three seconds she has fallen, curled on her side on the charred wood. She is fast asleep.

Such is the night's work of Denfert, which nobody knows.

That same night, far to the west, a malicious wind lashes the heaths and woods, hurling fistfuls of rain in every direction. This was once the beginning of the kingdom of Brittany, where the France of vines and orchards and meadows ends, to be replaced by another more inhospitable country, a sea-girt realm of moors and rocks and moss. The Breton folk know its evil winds well. They make their windows narrow and deep to frustrate its assault.

But on the very worst nights the rain has the devil's own cunning and comes at their poor huddled houses from the side instead of from above, sending in the rain by every window at once. There is nothing to be done but put on one's coat and sit in front of the fire, if it has not blown out, and curse the weather.

Lesinge, Cochonne and des Sables have no windows. They have found — to be precise, Lesinge has found, for he leads the bedraggled company, though like the king in Paris his authority rests on sand — some abandoned Breton wreck to shelter in. It might have been a woodsman's hut once, or the refuge of a hunter. Now it is only four crumbling walls that sprout weeds, and a roof as much ivy as beams and shingles. Here, miserable as it is, they rest while the gales blow. It is the best shelter they have had since fleeing Ouigly d'Oeuf.

They have made a fire on the bare ground within. There is no hearth or chimney. They trust there are enough holes in what remains of the roof to vent the smoke. Because the rain drives sideways the holes are less inconvenient than they might otherwise be on so foul a day. Lesinge warned against making a fire, but Cochonne and des Sables declare they would rather choke to death than remain cold and wet. If he forbids the fire they will kill him. He laughs at such a threat from the beardless infant des Sables, who could not vanquish a mouse. At Cochonne he dares not even smile. Days of walking at twilight and making camp in the woods, wary of pursuit and avoiding all human comforts, have stretched her patience thin.

'Eh, then,' he says, and shrugs. 'Make your fire, and do not blame me if we are all dead by nightfall.' But secretly he is as glad of it as they are.

Like the rest of France, they are tired, hungry and displeased with one another. Lesinge blames Cochonne for murdering the nobleman. Did he not tell her, in language plain enough for the stupidest peasant to understand, that it was the one thing she must not do? It is only because of her that they have to skulk in the freezing woods and walk all day, keeping far from inns and towns where questions might be asked. It is also entirely the fault of the idiot girl that he is now burdened with des Sables. This gentleman's valet, dressed in silk and velvet! — who cannot walk a mile without complaining that his feet hurt, and is afraid of the dark, bah! Several times in the past days Lesinge has been ready to knock his head against a tree and leave him for crows. Cochonne forbids it. Perhaps her heart goes soft at the sight of a pretty boy. As if a pretty boy would have anything to do with her, great ogress that she is!

He should not have admitted her to his company. A peasant girl for a brigand? What were you thinking, Gaspard?

Seeing that his life was in danger, des Sables fell to his knees and promised a reward for keeping him alive. Oh, sir, now that you have slain my wicked master, do you not want to make yourself master of his treasures? 'His treasures?' Very valuable treasures, which he accumulated at the Castle Charizard. 'Pah! You said yourself the castle is neglected and unfashionable and at the ends of the earth.' It is, sir, but that is why my master kept certain treasures there which he wanted to conceal from the fashionable world. Things strange and rare and immensely valuable, hidden in a secret crypt which none but I know how to enter, now that he is dead.

Ridiculous lies! But where else can Lesinge go in search of the riches promised by the demon? He is enraged at the valet for attempting to sway him with such absurdities, and even more enraged at himself for allowing himself to be swayed. Where is this Castle Charizard, then? In Brittany, sir, the valet said, in the far west. I can lead you there, if you spare my life. Do not kill me, but let me join your company, and I will show you the way to treasures that will make you rich for ever.

Rich for ever? It is precisely what his demon the black queen promised when she freed him from the dungeon. Was this her meaning? Must he endure this blubbering boy with his lilywhite hands in order to attain his reward?

He begins to think he would rather be poor.

Des Sables, meanwhile, wonders if he would rather be dead. The spiteful old thief makes him walk, walk, walk, though his shoes pinch unmercifully and the ground is nothing but mud and rotting leaves and roots that trip him up every third step. Their companion the giantess is perpetually surly. Also she smells of the pigsty. They sleep each night under bushes where he cannot close his eyes for terror of wolves and snakes and lice crawling in his hair. For the first days he told himself anything was better than the service of his accursed master. Now he doubts it. He would run away in the night while Lesinge and Cochonne snore, except it is too dark and his shoes hurt too much. In the day he cannot escape. Like a fool and a coward he promised the avaricious brigand to take them to his master's castle, and now Lesinge reminds him every hour of the promise. 'These rare strange things collected by your master, they had better be worth the journey, eh, boy? Or by Saint Christopher, I swear I will throw you from the roof of the Castle Charizard myself.'

Des Sables does not even know the way to the castle. What will they do when he admits it? Kill him, most certainly. Although he suspects he would rather be dead than endure this horrible cold wet journey, he is still afraid to die.

Therefore he leads them westward, into Brittany, where the people are fish-eating savages, and despises himself.

Cochonne regrets ever feeling sorry for the boy. He whines intolerably about his feet. Every morning when she shakes him awake he complains he has not rested enough. She would happily leave him behind, if only he did not know what she has done. In her dreams the ghost of the nobleman comes before her, white as a cloth and spotted with blood, promising revenge. In vain she explains that she thought he was the postillion, and anyway she would not have struck his head so hard if he had not first insulted her and then reached for his pistols. *God condemns you, Cochonne!* She does not believe the ghost, who is angry and trying to frighten her. Many nobles have been killed, she has heard; if it were absolutely forbidden God would not let it happen so often.

But Lesinge will not let her go near a church to seek confession and absolution. He says they must not be seen until they are many miles from the place of her crime.

Her crime! She did not know it was a nobleman. He was in disguise!

Lesinge says he is leading them on an adventure in search of great wealth. But Cochonne knows all he is doing is running away because he is nothing but a petty brigand who will hang as soon as the soldiers lay hands on him. She tells him as much. He tells her to go home to her farm and dig shit all day. Do not squabble, cries des Sables, this journey is miserable enough already without your sulking. My sulking, says Cochonne? And who is it who will not stop talking about his aching feet? We would not have to listen to his complaints of his feet, says Lesinge, if you had permitted me to kill him, as we should have done days ago. And then who would lead you to your precious treasure, says Cochonne? Can you find your own way to this castle?

So the mutual displeasure goes round and round, until they are all as tired of themselves for repeating the same arguments as they are of each other.

The fire is made in silence. They sit staring at the flames while the demented wind whistles through cracks in the walls and toys with the smoke.

Deep in his heart Lesinge knows he has been deceived. If he were able to look just a little deeper he would find he has deceived himself, but this is not to be confessed. He broods, turning the chess-piece in his fingers.

These things taken from the ambush: his little ivory queen, the purse, the locket, the lump of stone in its velvet bag. Can they be all the treasure the demon promised? — sufficient riches that he will want for nothing for the remainder of his life?

Impossible. Lesinge has been tricked. The demon used him for some purpose of her own. Unless, unless. Could there be some significance in the strange adventure which has eluded him; some meaning in the peculiar selection of objects, which will make him rich as a lord if only he can unriddle it? Can it be mere coincidence that he found an ivory chess-piece so closely matching his old friend the blind knight? If it was only coincidence, why did the demon name herself the black queen as if she too was a piece from the game of chess?

He remembers how he came by the knight, his companion and talisman of so many fortunate years. Now *those* were the good days; *that* was the real France!

It was before the revolution, in Picardy, when the land was green and well-ordered, and the estates of the nobles ruled over every plain, and their money went back and forth on the roads like flocks of fat ducks begging to be put in the bag. Another life! He and his company of that time were spending their winnings in a tavern. Ah, the wine and the laughter, the easy careless adventurer's existence! One of their number overheard some travelling fellow at the next table boasting of his good fortune. He was a collector of rarities, he said, whom everyone laughed at for being a poor old dusty scholar; well, let them laugh now, for he has found a mad nobleman in Paris who will pay him five hundred pounds for — this!

Lesinge slipped through the drunken crowd and saw the scholar showing off the thing that was going to make him rich, waving it before the crowd. It was a little white horse's head with tiny eyes of jet. Five hundred pounds, for one chess-piece? Everyone jeered. You are the mad one, old man! The scholar grew angry. No, he insisted, it was true, he would be a rich man as soon as he reached Paris, ten times as rich as all of them put together; they could all continue to drink in their dirty tavern for the rest of their lives while he would have wine in silver cups before bedding down with the most lustful actresses of the French Comedy.

Ha, old man, you will be as satisfied by your dreams as the Paris whores would be with your tiny wizened staff!

Only Lesinge did not laugh. Something in the proud curve of the little horse's neck caught his eye. He returned to his brother brigands and told the story. Five hundred pounds? — said his captain, with a glint in his eye. When the old scholar left the tavern in rage they followed him outside, going along a little way behind until the road was quiet, and then robbed him as easily as stealing from a baby. Unfortunately he resisted a little and called the captain certain insulting names, which earned him a knock on the head that killed him. Even more unfortunately, the fatal blow was given before the poor fellow had the chance to name the nobleman in Paris who supposedly offered five hundred pounds for the white cavalier. The whole enterprise was therefore profitless. The robber brethren dismissed it as a drunken evening's entertainment, not the worst of its kind. They would laugh heartily at it until they were all hanged for it; all but Lesinge, who felt the way the wind was blowing. In the meantime the captain prised out the two little stones of jet and threw the blinded knight aside in a ditch. No one saw Lesinge rescue it. He wrapped it in a rag and kept it in his boot.

It became his best companion of the roads. He would apostrophise it: My friend, you were made with no legs to go on, and have cruelly been made blind. I will be your eyes and legs, and in return you will be my luck.

And good fortune he has enjoyed ever since, by a brigand's standards, for is he not still alive, when so many others rot?

Now a demon has stolen his talisman. His luck is lost, and for what? A promise that turned out to be a lie. He should not have listened to the demon at all. He should have dismissed her as one dismisses a dream by waking up. Only one more hour waiting in his cell and the giantess would have come to release him. Then he would have been truly free! No carriage, no ambush, no flight westwards into the Breton wind and rain. He would have gone to Paris, where the world is turned upside down every day. A man of skill and spirit could have risen God knows how high there. Instead of which he is crouching in a shack shunned even by the forest animals, and for what?

He lays out his paltry treasure again: the white queen, the locket, the velvet bag. He takes the ugly stone from the bag and inspects it gloomily. Des Sables has closed his eyes and slumped by the fire, which is good; the whining boy retains a mortal terror of this dull piece of rock which he calls *demonoscope*, and would begin new choruses of complaint if he saw it in Lesinge's hand.

Lesinge holds it closer to the fire to see whether any part of it will gleam like a gem. But no, it cannot be of any value. It is a thing the foot of a donkey might have kicked loose from the road. The boy is a superstitious imbecile. A piece of rock that can summon infernal spirits from hell? Is Gaspard Lesinge a drooling peasant, to believe such nonsense? Most probably des Sables's tales of the castle's secret riches are also absurdities. No. Lesinge has endured these charades long enough. It has been four days, going as fast as the necessity of concealment and the incapacity of the milk-white valet permit. They must be thirty or forty miles from Ouigly d'Oeuf, out of reach of search or pursuit. Tomorrow he will leave these useless companions who shame the honour of brigandry. He will make his own way to Paris. As for the girl who looks like a man and the boy who looks like a girl, let them care for themselves. What are such people to Gaspard except encumbrances?

Cochonne has her broad back to him. For a moment he feels a pang. She was a good companion before she turned sulky. In a strange way she is not ugly, though monstrous in size. One day she might have made him a wife. Imagine the sons she would have given him! But she is a woman nevertheless, hardly more than a girl in years despite her stature, and a woman cannot be an adventurer. Nature and reason forbid it. Her sulkiness is no doubt caused by the mysterious fluctuations of the female body. How it would torment him if each month the performance was repeated!

He gathers up the pathetic hoard, ready to store the items in his coat again. They will fetch something in Paris; not much, but something, and something is a good deal better than nothing.

He takes the chess-piece and the silver locket in his left hand and casts one more long glance at the lump of stone in his right, hoping against hope that the firelight will make it sparkle deep within.

Wait — what is that gleam?

There! A flicker of radiance, in the heart of the stone!

Lesinge twists it from side to side, trying to coax the subtle glimmer into brilliance. Subtle it may be, but there is no doubt; the stone somehow reflects the firelight, with flashes of deep inward colour.

Then it *is* a gem, and of unparalleled, perhaps unprecedented, size! More importantly still, Gaspard Lesinge has not after all been deceived!

The radiance inside the rough gem takes on a shape. Lesinge holds it close before his eyes. His right hand is suddenly very cold. Perhaps in his excitement all the blood rushes to his brain.

Now the whole stone has suddenly turned crystalline. It is like looking through a cloudy window tinged with the colour of the fire. There is a tiny figure made of light within. It seems to grow bigger, like a bright fish swimming up from the depths of a flaming sea.

Lesinge cries out in pain and drops the stone. God! — colder than ice! His right hand is in agony.

Des Sables starts awake. He sees the demonoscope lying on the earth by the fire, glowing now like the heart of a forge, and turns white with horror. Cochonne too has roused herself and lumbers to her feet.

'What are you doing?' she says.

'Put it away!' des Sables cries. His voice is like a frightened girl's. 'Put it away!'

'You may try if you like,' says Lesinge. 'It is like touching Death himself.'

The brightness of the stone intensifies, going from red to yellow to the white of the summer sun at noon. All three of them must throw their hands in front of their eyes or be struck blind. 'Oh,' des Sables weeps, 'we are doomed!' There is a silent explosion of white radiance from which they each recoil. When they can look again, the fire has gone out and the ruin around them is dark, full of the noise of the wind.

The stone lies where it was, pulsing like a living heart with soft ember-light.

In the air above it a phantom has appeared.

'Mother of God,' Cochonne whispers, and drops to her knees, making a spray of wet earth.

The phantom is a woman made of glimmering mist. Her features are mild and pleasing. Being approximately transparent, her complexion and colouring are mysterious, but it seems to Lesinge and Cochonne that her hair would be long and dark if it were not so ghostly, and her skin not the fairest. Des Sables has covered his eyes with his fingers and therefore has no opinion.

Indistinct drapery clothes the phantom's body. Her ghostly head turns from Lesinge to Cochonne and back again, as if she is perfectly conscious of their presence before her.

'What witchcraft is this?' Lesinge mutters.

'I told you!' Des Sables still cannot bear to look, but cringes and cowers as though he expects at any moment to be struck dead. 'Did I not warn you never to touch that accursed stone? Now we are all certainly haunted for all eternity.'

'Be quiet,' Cochonne says, 'or I will kick you senseless.'

If it were not for the fact of being a ghost, the apparition would not be at all alarming. She stands quite calmly, or rather floats, for the region where her feet might be consists only of the faintest and most indistinct mist, without contact with the filthy earth or the gleaming stone that lies there.

She fastens her phantom gaze upon Lesinge. Her lips open and move.

'She is speaking!' he says.

'She is beautiful,' Cochonne whispers.

'Hold your tongue, woman. The spirit has a message for Gaspard. I cannot make it out over your noise.' There are words, he thinks, but so faint! They blend with the constant moan of the wind.

'Oh, her message is for you? Only for you?'

'Quiet!'

'Make it go,' des Sables pleads. 'Cover the stone again!'

'By God, if you will not be quiet, I shall—'

The ghost appears to make an effort to speak more distinctly, and for a moment Lesinge is certain he hears its language. But the sounds are all confused.

'What is your message?' he says. 'Speak again, vision, I command you!'

Cochonne snorts.

'Ah, do not invite it to speak, if you value your soul!'

Lesinge ignores the wailing boy. His heart is beating fast enough to burst but he will not be afraid. He must know more. 'What is your name, spirit?' he says.

The ghost once again looks between him and Cochonne, and also at des Sables, who watches between his fingers, too frightened to turn his head away or close his eyes. Her lips part a third time. Impossible to be sure whether those bodiless sounds are the speech of the phantom, or merely surges of the wind! — but no, Lesinge feels certain there are distinct words. Yet they are nonsense, meaningless syllables; except perhaps the last of them, which the ghost seems to repeat, with urgency. The light of the stone is fading. Its eerie heartbeat slows. The apparition dissolves also, as a morning mist thins out to nothing.

'Stay!' Lesinge commands, to no effect. 'What did you say? *West?*'

West, the ghost seems to echo, unless it is only the noise of air whistling between the stones of the ruined shelter. *West*.

The stone goes quite dark. All within the ruin is suddenly obscure: no phantom, no fire. Cochonne, kneeling, has begun to recite her *Ave Maria*. She feels neither cold nor fear. She is filled with wonder. Like Sainte Jeanne of old, she — she, the monster whom everyone despises — has been granted a vision of the Virgin.

CHAPTER FIVE

— Beg pardon, your lordship.

— Come in, Spott, come in. By jingo, it's a foul night, what?

Behold Lord Rawleigh, set sail from Lyme. — He sits in the aft cabin, at the captain's table, where a chart is pinned under the lamp. — Lamp, chart, table, and cabin, all sway, and shudder, and pitch alarmingly, in the manner of an elderly drunkard making his way home — if, that is, the inebriated gentleman were escorted, by a pack of lamenting fiends — For the ship's timbers groan at every surge of the sea, and spray hisses furiously at the glass.

His lordship's invitation to cross such unsteady ground, is not easily obeyed. Mr Spott nevertheless rises to the challenge. — He is a neat, capable-looking fellow, with the hardy look of an experienced mariner. We guess, it will take more than a little wind and rain, to *ruffle his feathers*.

— A little inclement, to be sure, says he.

— Rum, Spott?

Bolted to the table is a cup in a gimbal, designed to hold a single bottle perpendicular to the plane of the earth's surface, no matter what other angles be assumed by the rest of his lordship's vessel the *Marie-Antoinette*. The bottle presently *in situ*, its neck steadfastly pointed to the heavens, is, Mr Spott observes, half emptied. The cabin smells liquorish.

— Not for me, my lord. Much obliged.

— You're a dry old dog, Spott. — Lord Rawleigh seizes the bottle. — Your health! and to the bottom of hell with this d—nable wind!

— My lord, the steersman asks permission to run in the lee of Jersey. — Mr Spott places a finger on the map. — And then make for harbour here, at Saint-Malo. — The finger slides southwards, to touch the coast of France.

Lord Rawleigh squints at the chart. — Hardly the proper direction, what?

— I particularly requested the winds to send us towards Finisterre. But they are of another mind.

— Ha! Very good, Spott. — Lord Rawleigh attempts to steer the neck of the bottle towards his lips.

— If my opinion were asked, your lordship, I'd say there's no profit setting the *Marie* westward. Best drive for what shelter there is and see how the wind blows to-morrow. The mariners know their business, and say the same.

— They do know it, Spott. Hearts of oak, eh? Never failed us yet.

— Malo's a fine harbour, sir. A little breeze like this won't trouble our *Marie* — Mr Spott claps the beams above his head, with affectionate familiarity — But if there's a canvas torn here, or a seam splintered there, Malo'll keep us good and snug while we repair them.

Lord Rawleigh replaces the bottle in its housing. He is suddenly solemn.

— No time to be lost, Spott.

— As you say.

— Dark matters, this time. We ought to make the devil's own hurry. The stakes — Never higher — A *lady's honour.*

Mr Spott bows acknowledgment.

— Your lordship, he says, might consider going westward from Malo by land, if the winds continue to make difficulties. I could procure a cart.

Lord Rawleigh makes a shew of examining his maps. — Though he has difficulty fixing his eyes on any single point. Every thing sways, under his sight, because of the sea — and also, because of the rum.

— Very well then, he says. — Tell the steersman to do as he thinks best.

— Thank you, my lord.

Mr Spott makes as though to leave, and then pauses.

— If I may, sir — There is another consideration.

— Hey?

— The passenger.

Lord Rawleigh sighs.

— You know how seamen are, Mr Spott continues. — Hearts of oak, but they stick to their superstitions like old women. They say the passenger brought bad weather and bad luck. They'll have him disembarked at the first opportunity, or I wouldn't answer for them. Half the men are for making landfall at Sark in the dead of night to see him off the *Marie* at once.

— By God — Lord Rawleigh plants his fists on the table. — I hope the crew don't turn mutinous.

— It's the grumbling of sailors, sir, no worse. But they'll be a sight more tractable if we land our guest at Malo.

— Where's the old fellow now?

— Fast in his cabin still. No one's so much as seen the door open, day or night.

— Keeps himself out of the way, what? Thought the mariners liked that in a passenger, hey?

Mr Spott shakes his head. — They've took against him. Who knows why? Sailors, your lordship. No more reason to them than women.

— Ha! — Lord Rawleigh attempts to wink.

— One of the men has a cousin up-country. Says this Peach is a notorious cursed man. Sold to the Devil, they say in Somerset-shire.

— Balderdash!

— Doubtless. But the worse the weather, the more they'll talk so. They remember the clouds came over and turned black as soon as the passenger stepped aboard. Which I can't deny, from my own recollection.

— I say, Spott. No more of this nonsense. We shall need our heads clear, for the adventure to come. — Lord Rawleigh aims a decisive stab of his finger, at a certain spot on the map, in the west of Brittany. — Deep in the lion's den, what?

Lord Rawleigh is not perfectly clear in his own mind, how his passenger came to be aboard. It cannot — he thinks — It was surely not his intention, to spare a berth on the *Marie-Antoinette*, on *this* passage — On a voyage so significant, whose purpose is so secret, and freighted with peril! — None but his trusty companions at his side, led by the inestimable Spott — Several barrels in the hold, cunningly concealed, and packed with — *pistols* — and powder — and *disguises*. — And yet the old fellow appeared at the quay, and made his request, in the name of Miss Farthingay — as though he had somehow divined the secret purpose of their expedition. — And Lord Rawleigh invited him aboard, without, now he thinks of it, quite knowing what he did — Or, why he did it.

To the eye of reason, Mr Peach has been no trouble. He takes his rations alone, in his cabin, and does not come out, as most passengers will, when the seas are heavy, to annoy the men with a landsman's questions — When shall we come to harbour? How long will the wind blow? — Is the ship sound?

Perhaps the sailors would view him less suspiciously, if he *had*.

That Mr Thomas Peach was, in his younger days, as accustomed to the sea as any man not enjoined to the mariner's profession, they are not to know. — In those years he sailed as far north, as the extremity of the *Bothnic* Gulf — Voyaged from one end to the other, of that inland sea, whose waters sustained the first stirrings of civilization, and art, and philosophy — antient *Egypt*, where writing began — the Holy Land — Greece, and Rome, and the lands of the wise and noble Moors. To the oldest places of the world he has been, in search of mysteries. — Ah, reader! what stories we could tell of his travels, could we

call back yesterday, bid time return

— and restore Tho.s Peach, to the vigour of his early manhood!

But it is not given to us, to stray so far from the all-receiving grave — The fast anchor, of every human life. —

From the time of his ill-fated marriage, Mr Peach did not once leave land — Until this our present chapter. An interval of nigh ten years, might be enough for a man to lose his *sea-legs*. — Yet he seems content to remain in his berth, enduring the tumult of wind and wave with equanimity. — Unnatural equanimity, the sailors mutter. — What *land-lubber* could sleep, through such a night at sea?

Mr Peach is not quite asleep — Nor yet, quite awake.

He lies in an *hammock*, that rolls side to side, like a pendulum. Secured nearby is an apothecary's box, with his bottle of laudanum — diminished by several drops, from the quantity it held, when he came aboard.

Inside the fluttering lids of his eyes, storm-clouds pile high, making and unmaking phantastical shapes, of colossal dimensions. Winds proclaim great speeches in his ears, in an hundred hollow voices together. — Whither goest thou, Thomas Peach? —

— To France, he says.

They echo him in manifold triumph. — The word *France*, becomes the sea-spray's hiss, and the whistle of the wind.

— Then thou yieldest at last to thy master-mistress.

— I do not, he says. His voice is a speck of flotsome, in the universal storm.

In his reverie, he thinks of the night, two years past, when his existence began its last fall towards the abyss. — He remembers the voice, speaking to him in his wife's place — her beloved gentle spirit, supplanted by some infernal presence — Mocking him in the dark — Commanding him, to go and serve his master-mistress, in France. — The invocation issuing from within his own house, declaring him enfeoffed to inexorable powers, and contracted to obey. — *The hour comes nigh. — In France, the great victory is destined, and beginneth.* — Strange, troubling dreams! Mr Peach denied obedience, and refused the summons — Since when, gloom has gathered around him. His one living companion, his house-maid Clary, linked to his fate by mysterious sympathy, vanished from the house, the next day. — All the comforts of his existence, began to leave him — Replaced by tormenting visitations, that tell him he is lost — D——ned —

The grandeur and misery of these waking visions, we cannot adequately express. — Our pen was made, for lighter purposes.

When the *Marie-Antoinette* passes the Saint Catherine light-house, and places the island of Jersey between herself and the wind's quarter, Mr Peach's hammock sways more gently, and he sleeps at last. — True sleep — Not the opiate reverie, sipped from the druggist's bottle, but that rest, apostrophized by Shakespear in his Macbeth, in language too familiar to repeat, though too beautiful ever to be forgotten.

The tempestuous night relents.

Whether Mr Peach sleeps, because wind and rain grow calmer — Or, whether wind and rain grow calmer, *because Mr Peach sleeps* — is not for us, to decide.

In either case, we are grateful. — These storms, and these tenebrous visions, sap our strength. Into what confusion is our narrative hurled, amid all this crossing and re-crossing, between Britain and France! — Here is Mr Peach — our hero — We think him our hero — Hastening, we suppose, to aid Miss Farthingay, in consequence of Caspar's plea. — But *here*, not twenty miles distant, is that very lady — No longer in need, of his assistance, or any rescue at all — Making her own way *back to England*, with the assistance of M Denfert, who has promised that every courtesy shall be extended to her, on behalf of the nation, in recompense for the much-regretted accident she has endured.

We must endeavour to write, at *crossed purposes*.

All our false steps, and diversions, have come since we first set sail for France.

France! — a pot at the boil — where every thing that enters, is dissolved, or mangled, or tossed asunder with heat and violent motion. — An alchemical fire, which nothing touches, but it is utterly transformed.

— For the better! cries one half of the world.

— For the worse! cries the other. —

The effect produced upon our narrative, we must leave you to judge for yourself, good reader.

Miss Farthingay, as we just now mentioned, has received a lengthy and attentive communication from her friend in Paris, the amiable deputy Denfert. He professes himself shocked beyond measure, to hear of the trials she has undergone — Though relieved in equal degree, to know her unharmed. The disappearance of the carriage on the road to Caen, gave him the most excessive alarm. He fears his coachman was bribed. — Monsieur Denfert is desolate — had thought the man incorruptible — Will see him punished, with the strictest severity of the law. He regrets most deeply, that Miss Farthingay will not come to Paris, to address the Assembly, as was his eager hope — But, respects her desire, to return home as soon as is practicable. He takes it upon himself, to make every arrangement for her return to Cherbourg, and her passage thence by sea. Affairs in Paris, alas, forbid his personal attendance, but he has already given directions — which he expects will be effected, within a few days. In the interval, he invites her to repair to the house of the Poor Sisters of Mercy, near Domfront, where she may be accommodated in perfect comfort and security, until every thing necessary is done. — All this, expressed in such delicate and chivalrous terms, as quite disarm any hesitation.

— And, thinks Miss Farthingay, reading the letter over again, There are some in England, who declare that courtesy has been banished from France, by the revolution!

On her journey from Fougères to Domfront, she is attended by that military captain Cramorant, to whom we have already alluded. It is as well. — For the rumour every where, is that the detested *queen* has made a second attempt to escape France, and was intercepted at Ouigly d'Oeuf, and held at Fougères. The people are inspired to paroxysms of patriotic fury, or ecstasies of sympathy — the one, or the other, according to the universal division of mankind. In either case, their feelings run very warm — Even according to the measures of temperature, appropriate to the French — which scale heights, and plumb depths, far beyond our British *thermo-meters*. — We shudder to imagine, what forms the expression of those sentiments might have taken, among those who notice Miss Farthingay ride by — Were it not for the gallant captain, and his armed men.

The journey passes without incident, until its conclusion, where, with splendid ceremony, the captain assumes a kneeling posture, and announces, in passable English, his eternal and absolute enslavement to the divine lady — &c. — We shall not linger over this episode. The protestations of romance have, we confess, lost much of their freshness and perfume, to our senses — Ever since — but, no — We are not to speak of it. — We must not try your patience, reader, with the recitation of *our* woes, though they rise before us each dawn, and come thronging at night, as we pull the curtains close. — Miss Farthingay listens to the performance with what patience she can muster, and then attempts to end it, by declaring she is already engaged. — A poetic fiction — or bare lie, if you will. — And not to the purpose either, for the captain, being French, cannot comprehend what obstacle her engagement is supposed to present, in an affair of gallantry.

With what relief she presents her letter of introduction, into a society where the male sex is forbidden!

It is, she reflects, another instance of the tact and gentility of Monsieur Denfert. — A temporary accommodation, better suited to her present state of mind, he could not have chosen.

The house of the Poor Sisters of Mercy is modest, and has seen better days. Since the Mother Superior took the oath, swearing obedience to the civil constitution, not a few of the sisters have abandoned it, in defiance of their own vows.

Reader — it is a curious thing. — This French business of oath-making, and swearing.

We happy inhabitants of these enlightened islands, have long understood, that oaths are merely *serviceable words*. — To be spoken as required, and then decently forgotten, while the necessary business of *lying*, without which neither commerce, nor society, nor domestic existence, would be tolerable — possible, indeed — Continues its course. Why our neighbours across the water set such store by their vows, we cannot say. — Or, why they used to. — By this our own day, we hope, they have learned their lesson, as we learned from our own civil disputes, tyrannies, and regicide, two hundred year ago — And are become thoroughly modern in their mendacity, like any advanced nation.

To our purpose. —

Miss Farthingay is received with the greatest politeness. The Mother of the foundation was born among the nobility, though in questionable circumstances. Before she was dismissed to a cloistered existence, she obtained certain accomplishments — Among them, a respectable command of English. She welcomes Miss Farthingay like a sister — Invites her, to enjoy the intire liberty of the house — which is not much, but comprises some pleasant walks, among the kitchen-gardens, as well as chapels, places of private contemplation, &c. The guest may take her wholesome meals alone, or in company, just as she prefers. Ease without obligation — Tranquillity, without the oppressions of solitude — In short, all is exactly as Miss Farthingay would desire. Only she is advised, that she should not stray beyond the house, without an attendant, and that her cell will be locked at night. — The times, alas! says the Mother Superior, in her charming accents. — The whole France, she is greatly enervated. But we pray, that Peace soon comes, following her sister Justice. —

Miss Farthingay suspects there is a sonnet to be made, from the Mother's conceit.

Monsieur Denfert's letter suggests, that the duration of her stay among the Poor Sisters of Mercy, will not amount to more than three days. The first of these she passes to her perfect satisfaction.

Late in the second evening — the opening quatrain of the sonnet laid down, though not yet polished to the standard of Miss

Farthingay's exacting muse — She is attended, in the cell where she is accommodated, by a silent young novice. That is, Miss Farthingay supposes the visitor to be a novice — as do we, reader — For, unlike the other sisters, she wears a veil, which conceals her features altogether, and her garb is black. Though her face cannot be seen, her youth is unmistakable. The slightness of her figure bespeaks it — and a certain impatience, in her deportment.

She has brought a jar of well-water, freshened with some leaves of mint. This she places on the table, and then stands before Miss Farthingay — Staring, we suppose, from behind her veil — as though expecting thanks, or some further instruction.

She cannot be waiting for an *emolument*, surely?

— *Merci*, Miss Farthingay says, wondering how to dismiss the girl. — *Vous êtes très gentille.*

The veiled novice trembles, as though this unremarkable compliment had inspired her with deep emotion.

Miss Farthingay begins to feel aukward. — It is a strange thing, to be watched with silent attention, by an invisible face.

— *Et bonne nuit*, she says.

The girl bows rapidly — a convulsion, almost, like the nod of a bird — But shews no sign of withdrawing.

— Heaven help me, thinks Miss Farthingay. — I trust this is not yet another person, who believes themselves enamoured?

— *Comment vous appelez-vous, mademoiselle?* she says — for want of anything better. — Miss Farthingay's French is, as we have mentioned already, confined to rudiments.

— *Soeur Maledicta*, replies the novice, in a whisper barely audible. Miss Farthingay starts at it nevertheless — for the voice, though so quiet, that one might imagine it fearful of being heard, lacks any of the sweetness of youth, but scrapes, like metal against stone.

— *Maledicta?* she says.

The strange novice bobs her head.

— *Ça veut dire* — Miss Farthingay struggles to recall her vocabulary — *Maudite?*

With animal swiftness, the young sister kneels, takes Miss Farthingay's hand, and presses it to her lips, behind the veil. Her grip is unexpectedly firm and decisive. — Just as rapidly, she rises — Turns — and flees the cell, the lock grinding closed at her back — Leaving our heroine in such astonishment, at the peculiar adventure, that all she can do is shake her head, and laugh — And resume contemplating the second quatrain, of her intended sonnet.

The next day she observes the sisters of the house, as they go about their work — Watching for the passionate young novice, whose behaviour has left an impression upon her.

A convent, is not the place one expects to find a curiosity. —

But the veiled girl is not seen — Unless she has dispensed with her veil, and changed her black habit, and — inverting the very notion, of disguise! — conceals herself, by shewing her face like all the others.

The after-noon is blustery. Flocks of dead leaves fly before the wind, lifting and swooping together like starlings. Miss Farthingay desires to take a walk, among the orchards outside the house. Since she is not permitted to pass the gate alone, the Mother Superior consents to accompany her.*

They stroll for a while, in pleasant but inconsequential talk, until Miss Farthingay is reminded to ask the Mother, about the curious Sister Maledicta.

---

* We are not certain, whether we bestow on the holy woman, her proper title. The apparatus of Papism is a mystery to us. — We understand, that in France, in the last century, there were monks who were noblemen, and priests who were politicians, rich as Croesus. — That certain nuns went about the country like ordinary women. — That there were orders open, and closed. – Foundations religious, but belonging to the king, and little different in their nature from courts. Had bluff King Henry not abolished all these subtleties from our nation, long ago, we should have understood them better. The furthest we are able to deduce, is: that in France, in the reign of the sixteenth Louis, a person is a monk, or a nun, if — they say they are.

— Good Heaven! exclaims the Mother, with a delicate pout, and crosses herself. — Such a name! No bride of Jesus will think to take it.

— Perhaps I misheard, says Miss Farthingay. — The girl murmured barely above a whisper.

— But most certainly you misheard.

— She wore the veil also, which is, I think, not the *habit* of your order? — Miss Farthingay is inwardly pleased with her witticism.

— Madam, there is none in the veil here. You have probably been visited by a dream. It is common among those who endure recent surprize and suffering, to dream extravagantly.

— The girl brought a jug of water, which stands even now in my room. That would have been an extravagant phantasy indeed, to be endowed with solid arms.

The Mother looks perturbed. — I send no one to you with water the last night, she says.

— Might the girl not have taken it upon herself to bring refreshment?

— But your door, was it not locked? Madam, it is of the biggest importance that the door is locked, after the evening prayer.

— Perhaps the mysterious sister availed herself of the key.

The Mother takes Miss Farthingay's arm in her own, and turns back in the direction of the gate. — This wind, oh! how cold it is, she says. — It is too cold for the walking. Come, we shall go back.

Miss Farthingay is enjoying the prospects across the landskip, and hopes they may walk in the open air a while longer.

— No — no — we must return within the gate. — The Mother propels Miss Farthingay along vigorously, her own arm locked in that of her guest.

— Excuse me, says Miss Farthingay. — I hope you have not conceived some anxiety regarding this girl, who was charitable enough to bring me a jug of water? She behaved with nothing but kindness.

— Come — please — It is not safe.

— Not safe?

— The times, madam! Alas, these times! It is better you remain within the house, until I have word from the good Monsieur Denfert.

— Honoured Mother — I am sensible of the obligation I owe you, as your guest. It is as a guest that I am here, I hope? — not a sister, bound by vows of obedience? — or, a *prisoner?*

— Ten thousand pardons, madam. — The commands of Monsieur Denfert are most explicit.

— And what commands can that gentleman have conveyed to you, that are not also included in his letter to me?

— But all is only for your safety, madam. Monsieur Denfert has the biggest concern that no accident will occur to you. I am most severely enjoined to hold you safe in the walls of this holy house.

— To *hold* me, Madame? says Miss Farthingay, with no little indignation.

— One hundred thousand pardons. — To protect you, as the shepherd his flock.

— Am I to understand Monsieur Denfert writes to you, that I am a sheep?

The Mother has turned quite red with embarrassment — But continues to urge Miss Farthingay, towards the gate. — An effort which also contributes, to her heightened colour.

— I must demand, says Miss Farthingay, that you explain this treatment.

The Mother's apologies redouble, like the heads of Hydra, yet she does not relent. — She is concerned, she says, by this account of the mysterious novice in the veil, whose appearance and behaviour correspond to none of her sorority. She has a great fear, that Miss Farthingay was visited by a person of evil intent, in a disguise. Miss Farthingay must understand — All Normandy lives in terror of an ingenious villain, who goes about the country, wreaking harm on those who love France, and calls himself — how is it said in English — *Ne m'oubliez pas?*

Miss Farthingay bursts into laughter. — The Forget-Me-Not?

— But it is no jest, madam! — The Mother is greatly shocked.

Miss Farthingay composes herself, though she cannot forbear smiling. — And what terrors are there in the name of this Forget-Me-Not, that the mere thought of it compels us to hide within-doors, in the middle of the day?

— Excuse me, madam — You are quite ignorant of the affairs. The only desire of the Forget-Me-Not is to assist the enemies of France, and he is a fiend of infinite schemes and tricks. A clever devil, absolutely a devil!

— You quite astonish me, Mother, says Miss Farthingay, her good humour restored. — This silly fellow, who flatters his vanity with his absurd *incognito*, and fancies himself a knight-errant in the service of royalty, is to my nearly certain knowledge merely an English peer of no great wit or ingenuity. His reputation outshines his deeds as the sun the moon. The girl who came to my room in the evening was no more Lord — was no more the Forget-Me-Not in disguise, than the Empress of Russia.

The Mother is not to be persuaded. She takes the evening meal with Miss Farthingay, in her own handsomely appointed rooms, and entertains her guest with several tales of that master of disguises, the accursed Forget-Me-Not. — To which our heroine listens patiently, for she expects to leave the house of the Poor Sisters of Mercy the next day, or the day after, and feels she ought not to resent the hospitality extended to her in the interval. Her thoughts drift to her sonnet. —

What a comfort is the poetical imagination, when conversation is tedious, and society irksome!

Returning to her appointed cell, she crosses the court-yard of the house — the next couplet complete in her mind, and ready to be committed to paper. — She notices, that the convent gate is shut, though the evening prayer is not yet sung — shut, and *barred*. — And that two hard-eyed sisters sit beside it, and watch her go past, with faces like stone.

'It was a vision of the Virgin,' says Cochonne.

'It was an unquiet spirit,' says des Sables.

'It was not.'

'I know that stone. It calls the dead from hell.'

'She was not from hell. She was solemn and beautiful like the Madonna.'

'She was white, luminous and transparent. That is the appearance of a ghost.'

'How do you know? You were on the ground with your head in your hands, filling your breeches with piss.'

'I was not! Do you deny that the apparition was white, luminous and transparent?'

Cochonne growls.

'I saw her face,' she says, stubbornly. 'It was the face of Our Lady.'

'How do you know? Have you met her?'

'I know in my heart.'

'Then your heart is in a state of confusion.'

'You do not understand the heart of devotion. You are the servant of an evil man, you said it yourself. You do not love God.'

'He was an evil man, and that stone was his most treasured possession. Nothing good can come of it.'

'With God anything is possible. The Bible says so.'

'SILENCE!' roars Lesinge.

The weather has relented. He has led his company back onto the roads, for they are now several days distant from Ouigly d'Oeuf and he judges it no longer necessary to avoid all notice. All would be well, except for the simmering theological dispute between his companions.

He refuses to produce the stone again. It stays in its velvet bag inside his coat and will remain there as long as Cochonne and des Sables continue to squabble. They drive him to distraction. It is plain as day that the apparition in the stone was neither the Madonna nor a ghost from hell, but a spirit sent to him, Gaspard Lesinge, with a message. Has he not already had an unearthly visitor, in his prison? That some great destiny has been bestowed on him is not surprising. Gaspard is not like other men; this he has known all his life. The exact nature of the message is obscure at present but he does not doubt he proceeds as he ought, for the black queen's instructions seem to have pointed him towards the Castle Charizard, and the phantom woman also said *west, west*. Further revelations will come in their time. If only des Sables and Cochonne would hold their tongues!

Sometimes they appeal to him to judge their dispute. He strides ahead, ignoring them both, and sings.

> *Who passes by this way so late?*
> *Companions of the marjoram!*

When des Sables is not arguing with Cochonne he complains about his feet. A morning comes when they break out in blisters and he refuses to go on. Cochonne says she will not carry him until he admits that the vision they saw was the Queen of Heaven. Des Sables says he would endure any agony before telling a superstitious lie.

'Walk on, then,' says Lesinge, 'and endure the agonies of your feet. Today you will suffer miserably, and then your soles will grow callouses all over like an honest man's.'

'I cannot!' Des Sables tries a few steps. He emits a note of pain with each strike of his foot against the ground, like a human harpsichord. 'If you are such a great thief, why have you not stolen horses for us?'

Lesinge turns quiet. 'Steal horses?' he says, in a dangerous tone.

Des Sables snivels and sits down in the road. 'It would facilitate our journey,' he says.

Lesinge crouches next to him.

'Let me enlighten one corner of the great cavern of your ignorance. There is no crime so universally reviled as horse-thieving. A thief of horses is less than a dog. When a man's horse is stolen, be he as great as an abbot or the poorest of poor farmers, every one of his neighbours joins him in pursuit of the culprit. Each man for miles around, even if they live in mutual detestation, will take up his pistols or his pitchfork or even the leg of a chair, and go without rest until the thief is found, whereupon he is shot or beaten to death upon the spot.'

'You exaggerate,' says Cochonne. 'It is what you said about murdering nobles.'

'I do not exaggerate. I shall explain the reason why this crime excites a universal revulsion. It is because the people reason that if their neighbour's horse is stolen, their own will be next. Suppose the neighbour's gold robbed or his daughter violated. "Eh," people say to themselves, "old Bouffalant ought to take care of his money and his family, like I do." But the horse!' Lesinge claps des Sables on the shoulder for emphasis, producing another gasp of pain. 'It is intolerable.'

'It seems to me,' Cochonne says slowly, 'that whenever there is a thing it would be useful to do, you find a reason why it cannot be done. Is your philosophy only good for robbing ladies in carriages?'

Lesinge walks off along the road without another word.

Cochonne looks at des Sables, who has thrown his shoes into a ditch and sits rubbing his bare feet.

'I ought to leave you there,' she says. 'You are useless and have no faith.'

Des Sables gestures towards the back of Lesinge. 'Yet you follow him willingly, even though he has no more religion than I do, and keeps you poor and sleeping under hedges.'

'True,' says Cochonne.

'I suppose,' des Sables says, 'it is not altogether impossible that the apparition was something other than an evil ghost.'

Cochonne raises one of her enormous eyebrows.

'My master's family was under a curse,' he continues. 'Since he had no children, and the line is therefore extinguished, perhaps the curse is finished and the stone of the de Charizards no longer entirely evil.'

'Do you want me to carry you?'

Des Sables gives her a smile of such beauty it would melt ice.

She sighs and heaves him up onto her back.

The tenderness of her heart is a mystery even to herself. But, she thinks, it is an act of charity, and what the Virgin would want.

Towards the end of the day they arrive at a draughty spider-infested inn. With the Sir de Charizard's coin in his purse and no guards known to be in pursuit of him, Lesinge agrees that they can rest tonight under a roof.

Cochonne throws herself onto the bed, which creaks in terror at the tremendous weight.

'I cannot carry him another day,' she says.

'Boy!' says Lesinge. 'How much further to the Castle Charizard?'

'Several days,' says des Sables, to be safe.

'Then we must obtain a pair of proper boots for you. At this pace we will not get there before the snows arrive.'

He leaves his companions to their squabbles and installs himself in the public room. As a brigand should, he listens and observes. There are only four other travellers. He studies their legs and feet and forms a plan.

When he returns to his followers to explain what he intends, he is amazed to hear des Sables — the lilywhite valet, who starts at his own shadow! — volunteer to do the deed in his place.

'You?' Lesinge scoffs. 'What do you know about the art of the brigand?'

'The other travellers have not seen me,' says des Sables. 'The imposition will be more plausible. And I have a face formed to give the impression of innocence.'

'That is true,' Cochonne says.

'You both call me useless,' des Sables says, 'but you have not taken into account the fact that I am unused to this life, and tired, and my feet hurt. Give me this opportunity to prove myself and you will see that I am very capable.'

Cochonne rolls over in the bed, making it shiver and groan. She is exhausted. 'If the boy wants to be something more than an encumbrance,' she says, 'let him try.'

Lesinge considers it.

'Well,' he says, 'you may try then. But if you end up beaten for a rogue and driven from the door we shall not help you. Nothing keeps me from pillow and blanket tonight.'

'I will surprise you, my captain,' says des Sables, 'and you, my lady.'

Both Cochonne and Lesinge love to be addressed like this, though neither admits it.

A little later, des Sables knocks on the door of another patron of the inn, a small black-bearded fellow as crabbed and bitter as the Breton heather.

'Go away!' the sulky man shouts.

Des Sables adopts a honeyed tone. 'It is I, sir, the boot-boy.'

'I want no boot-boy. Be off with you.'

'The master of the inn commands me to clean the boots of all his guests tonight.'

'Tell the interfering old miser I am quite able to clean my own boots. Also that his wine is despicable.'

'There is no fee,' des Sables says.

A pause, and the door swings open.

'No fee?'

Des Sables, who is holding a candle in the exact position to best illuminate his features from below, inclines his head humbly. 'Certainly not, sir. It is a part of my apprenticeship. My master wishes me to learn all the ways of adding to the convenience of the patrons.'

The black-bearded man glares. 'The boy of the house, eh?'

'Yes, sir.'

'You look like a girl.'

Des Sables holds out a hand. 'Your boots, if you please. So as not to disturb your rest I will leave them here outside your door, ready for the morning.'

'And no fee?'

'None at all.'

'You had better not expect any gratuity. I have better uses for my coin.'

Des Sables looks shocked. 'If sir was to offer any such thing I would return it to him instantly. I am only the boot-boy, and the sum of my desire is to serve every guest to the best of my abilities, and to give satisfaction in the greatest measure.'

The swarthy man considers the matter for some moments.

'I wager your master sends you to *serve* his guests,' he says, with an unpleasant leer, 'and loves the coin they give for your *service*. I am not that sort of man.'

'I do not understand you, sir.'

'You understand me perfectly. Tell that rogue the innkeeper I have no interest in his boy-whore. My boots, however, you may indeed clean.' He retrieves them from within the room and thrusts them into des Sables's hand. 'For nothing.'

Des Sables bows again. Years of service have taught him how to do so with ideal grace. 'It will be my most exquisite pleasure,' he says.

The man cries after him. 'Not a speck of mud left on them, do you hear?'

Des Sables returns to the room he shares with his companions. Though his feet are raw as butchered flesh he tries on the boots and finds they fit perfectly. His captain's judgment, he must admit, is perfect.

'Hmph,' says Lesinge. 'It was a simple enough task.' But secretly he is impressed.

The theft requires them to leave the inn well before anyone else is awake. By fitful moonlight they turn aside from the road to throw off any pursuit, and discover a westward track. Des Sables walks when he can without complaint. When he begins to flag, Cochonne carries him. They are much more content with one another than they have been for days. The stone and its apparition are not mentioned.

Day arrives. They follow the track across scrub and moor until around noon, when they come across an elderly woman who has driven her cart into a ditch.

One wheel is stuck deep in swampy earth. The donkey in the traces twists and brays. The poor old woman sometimes fusses with the animal, trying to calm it, and sometimes lifts her arms to Heaven, imploring Jesus and his blessed Lady for help. A small load of sticks has spilled beside the road. Her clothes are filthy and fraying. Her face is deeply marked by age and toil.

It is impossible for Cochonne not to be touched by her plight. She puts des Sables down and hurries to assist.

'Who is there?' cries the fearful widow as Cochonne looms before her. Her eyes have a milky cast, clouded by age and disease. 'Jesus preserve me!'

'Do not be afraid, good mother,' Cochonne says. 'I and my companions happened to be passing this way. I shall push your cart from the mud.'

The aged woman peers uncertainly at Cochonne's enormous form. Evidently she is nearly blind.

'Ah, sir,' she says, 'if that is true, the good God has heard my prayers. I am old, you see, and my eyes are not as strong as they were. I rely on Him entirely.'

'It fills me with pity,' Cochonne says, 'that one so old and pious should drive her cart alone across this moor.'

'But how else am I to gather sticks for my fire? My husband is dead and my daughters live far away. I must find wood myself or I go without fire, and then, sir, I would die of cold.'

Cochonne inspects the pitiful cargo remaining in the cart. It is barely two handfuls of sticks so thin that even des Sables could carry them all day without complaint.

'Is your home far from here?'

'We set out in the morning,' says the poor old woman, 'and return at dusk. How far we go I do not know.'

'Surely you cannot drive your cart all day long when you are almost blind and do not know where you are going!'

'Ah, sir, Broubrou knows the way.' The donkey's long ears swivel backwards at the sound of his name. 'He leads me out and home again. I do not know why today he walked into a ditch. Wicked, wicked Broubrou! A devil must have entered him. If God sees us safely home I will send for the good priest tomorrow to drive the devil out.'

'You will go home tonight,' says Cochonne, setting herself to the stuck wheel, 'and with a load of good thick branches for your fire, I promise.'

Tears trickle from the old woman's failing eyes. 'Heaven bless you, sir. You are an angel — oh! — Who is there?'

'That is only my two companions, good mother.'

The widow has not noticed Lesinge and des Sables until they are nearly on top of her. Lesinge, who has been watching with amusement, turns thoughtful as he surveys the tangled traces and the skittish donkey. He goes to the side of the road and begins scooping up handfuls of weeds and thistles, leaving des Sables to suffer the old woman's squinting inspection.

'Is this your daughter, sir?'

Cochonne rolls her eyes. She heaves against the wheel. It is very deeply mired. It resists her efforts obstinately.

The old woman blinks at des Sables, reaching a feeble hand to touch his long golden tresses. 'Her hair is so beautiful!'

'Thank you, grandmother,' des Sables pipes.

Her breath stinks of fish and clammy rot. She pinches his cheeks. 'Pretty one! You are also an angel. God has sent two angels to save me.'

Lesinge has gone to stand by the donkey, to feed him thistles and weeds and stroke his long nose. 'Eh, old mother,' he calls out, 'you should be careful what you say. In this new France we do not care for talk of angels and devils.'

The old woman turns her head from side to side. 'Who is that?'

'Only my hired man,' Cochonne says, through gritted teeth. For a moment the wheel lifts and moves a few inches. Then the mud sucks it down again. 'An impious villain. Come here, rogue, and help me push.'

Grinning, Lesinge shakes his head at Cochonne. He begins loosening the knotted traces.

'If he is impious,' the old woman says, 'I will ask the good priest to pray for his soul.' She pats des Sables around the shoulders as if she cannot bear to remove her bony withered hands from one so beautiful. 'You are a good girl I hope, who believes in God and His saints?'

'Yes, grandmother,' des Sables pipes again.

'What is your name, sweet beautiful child?'

'Marie, grandmother.'

Lesinge makes a violent snort of laughter. Already he has untwisted the traces and freed the donkey from the cart. He holds it by its halter while he continues to feed it and caress its nose.

'What are you doing, rogue?' Cochonne would like to release the wheel, pick up her rake and smash it against his head. But if she gives up the effort now the cart will sink all the way back and she will have to start from the beginning. She makes an angry face at Lesinge. In return, he winks.

'I am attending to the donkey, master,' Lesinge says loudly. 'The poor Broubrou is caught in the traces. I shall have him free in moments. — There — it is done — Oh! He is running away! No, Broubrou, no! Come back!' He has the donkey securely by the halter and begins leading it away from the road in the direction of a tempting patch of thistle.

'What is happening?' cries the old woman, peering helplessly towards the commotion.

'The beast has run off,' Lesinge exclaims, in a voice of woe. 'Broubrou! Return at once to your mistress, disobedient donkey!'

The old woman wrings her hands. 'Broubrou is a good donkey. He would never abandon me.'

'Alas,' Lesinge says, 'you were right, old mother. A devil must have possessed him. Look at him run! Already he is almost out of sight over the hill.'

The terror on the widow's face is pitiable. 'Help!' she cries. 'My Broubrou!'

Hearing its name spoken by its mistress, the donkey emits a deafening bray.

'He is there!'

'Unfortunately not,' Lesinge says, stroking the beast's muzzle again to quieten it. 'That bray was my own voice. I hoped Broubrou might answer a call in his own language, since he ignores every other plea. But no, he has run away.'

'Villain!' Cochonne exclaims. But now the wheel is beginning to move and all her strength is required to prevent it sinking back. She has no more breath to curse Lesinge's trickery. She braces her Olympian calves on solid earth and heaves.

'Hee-haw!' cries Lesinge, leading Broubrou rapidly away from the scene. 'Hee-haw!'

'But I certainly heard Broubrou,' the old woman insists. 'Please tell me what is happening! God preserve me, I cannot see well any more.'

Des Sables takes gentle hold of her shoulders.

'Grandmother,' he says, pitching his voice as high as he can, 'we must resign ourselves to the will of Heaven.'

'What? What?'

'All will be as the good Lord intends it.'

With a tremendous clatter the cart at last comes free. It is propelled by the force of Cochonne's effort up the angle of the ditch and onto the track, where it comes to rest.

'Do not be angry, master,' Lesinge calls out, from where he and Broubrou now stand some distance apart. The donkey tears contentedly at a bunch of thistles. 'I shall pursue the devil-haunted animal and expend every effort to recapture it.' He directs another magnificent wink at Cochonne.

Out of breath, she can do no more than wave a fist.

'What has happened?' the old woman repeats, turning this way and that in blind bewilderment.

Des Sables speaks soothingly, like a devoted child. 'Your cart is recovered, grandmother, but your donkey is lost.'

'Lost? Ah, no. What will I do? How will I live without Broubrou to pull my cart?'

Cochonne is tired of the cruel sport. She beckons des Sables close and in a whisper instructs him to go to Lesinge and demand the return of the donkey. While the boy limps away she addresses some gentle words of her own to the poor widow, then sets about gathering up the tumbled sticks.

Des Sables exchanges a few words with Lesinge and limps back alone. He draws Cochonne aside.

'Our captain says we will travel three times faster with a donkey for me to sit on. He recommends that if you care so much for the old woman you pull her cart yourself.'

Cochonne spits. 'I will crush his head for this.'

'Setting aside his rude joke, what he says has merit.'

'What?' Cochonne is astonished. The boy is less than half her size. She had not thought him possessed of enough spirit to argue with her.

'We have miles still to go. The donkey will be very convenient.'

'And what about this poor pious widow? Do we rob her of her only living companion and leave her to fend for herself?'

'One cannot save every religious old woman in France. Her remaining days are short. Ours, it is to be hoped, are long.'

Cochonne glares. 'You have no heart at all.'

'One tries to consider the issue rationally. What is the advantage to the widow of going out every day with her donkey to collect a bundle which any person might gather in ten minutes outside their own house? Remember also that she speaks of a good priest. Since she is so pious, this priest will undoubtedly ensure she receives all necessary charity. It is logic.'

'What is happening now?' wails the woman, flapping her arms as the hen flaps her wings. 'Where have you gone, sir?'

Cochonne shakes her head at des Sables. 'Your logic is also no more than excuses to do what you want.' She raises her voice. 'One moment, mother. I am fetching the last of your sticks.'

'God in Heaven bless you!'

'The pain in my feet is intolerable,' des Sables murmurs. 'Do you want to carry me all the way to the Castle Charizard?'

'I do not want to carry you another step. I want to leave you here and never see you again.'

'I understand. But our captain will not allow it. I must be your guide to the Castle.'

'Anyway,' Cochonne says, frowning, 'the villain said he would never steal a horse.'

'I addressed that very point to him,' des Sables says. 'You may guess his answer.'

'That a donkey is not a horse.'

'Exactly. He also mentioned that a brigand is often required to adjust his philosophy according to circumstance.'

Cochonne straightens, flexing her hands.

'I should crush both your heads. One in the left fist, one in the right. Pop, pop. Then where would his philosophy and your logic be?'

Des Sables favours her with his most angelic smile. 'But, Cochonne, we three love one another, is it not so?'

Cochonne growls at him like a bear.

Her heart will not allow her to abandon the widow. She hitches the pole of the cart under her arm and pulls it along the track herself, while des Sables and the old woman sit on the back, dangling their legs.

It is only half a mile to the patched hovel which serves the poor creature for a house. She is astonished to arrive home so quickly. She weeps with gratitude at the kindness of her saviours, though a portion of her tears are shed in grief for lost Broubrou.

'When I was young and beautiful like you,' she says to des Sables, 'I was very wicked. See how the good God now punishes me for those sins.'

'I am sure you were not wicked, grandmother,' des Sables says.

'Very wicked! There was a devil in my loins. My child, do not surrender your virtue as lightly as I did! God will not forgive. It is a precious jewel, never found again when it is lost.'

'Like Broubrou,' des Sables says, with a sigh.

'Ah, Broubrou! Ah, my wickedness! Dear Marie, you would marvel to hear the things the devil in my loins made me do. I was as beautiful as you then. Every man wished to rob me of my jewel.'

Cochonne beats her head silently against the low beams.

The old woman fumbles for des Sables's hands and takes them into her leathery grasp. 'I was only thirteen when Jean the wood-cutter—'

'Come, Marie,' Cochonne says loudly. 'We must be on our way.'

'Yes, father,' des Sables pipes.

'But no!' the old woman exclaims. 'You must stay and share my pottage in return for your goodness.'

'We cannot,' Cochonne says, and indeed the stench of the hovel is almost intolerable to her, farmer's daughter though she is. 'But I will fetch the priest for you if you tell me where he is to be found.'

She leaves des Sables with instructions to gather as much wood as he can from the windblown scrub surrounding the house, and goes in search of the curate. Outside she discovers Lesinge waiting further along the track with the donkey. He waves her towards him. She answers with an insulting gesture, at which he seems highly amused.

Heartless rogue! She will not go a step further with him until she has found someone to care for the poor widow.

The priest has no church. He is one of those who refused to swear the oath to the civil constitution. Forbidden the open practice of his calling, he has become a hero to the women of the parish, young and old, who do not care about the turmoils of the state but only want to worship God in the manner they always have. He roams the parish giving comfort and blessing where it is needed. The women would never tell a strange man where to find him, but another woman is a different matter, and when Cochonne explains her reasons they are happy to direct her to the sheepfold where he administers the sacraments in secret.

She finds him at prayer. Autumnal sunlight has broken through the fast-running clouds. Beams of radiance enter the humble building through gaps in the walls. With his bare feet and head and plain robe, and the light of Heaven embracing him in golden fingers, the priest looks like a saint. He is remarkably handsome.

At Cochonne's entry he opens his eyes and arms together though he remains kneeling. 'Welcome, dear one,' he says. His accent sounds peculiar to Cochonne but the voice is warm and strong.

For a moment she fears a devil has entered her own loins. From below her stomach a great upwelling warmth rises at the sight of his well-shaped arms. Then she realises that the sensation is in fact the love of God, rekindled deep in her body by the presence of the holy man. She desires God with a sudden and immense passion. She aches for Him.

'What brings you to me, my child?' says the priest, smiling.

Cochonne cannot think about the old widow and her wicked loins. It is too disgusting. There is a far higher purpose in her which she knows she must entrust to the handsome man of God.

'Father,' she says. Her deep voice trembles. Heavenly adoration burns her cheeks. 'I have seen the Virgin in a vision.'

The priest's expression does not change. With his hands he beckons her into the rear of the sheepfold where the ground is swept. There are a few rushes, a trencher and an earthenware pot. A simple crucifix hangs from an old nail.

'Come in,' he says. 'Kneel beside me. Tell me your vision.'

Cochonne feels faint with the excess of devotion. When she kneels close to the priest it is as if he radiates the fire of divine love.

'Three nights ago,' she says, 'I was sitting alone by the fire and the Madonna appeared before me in ghostly form as plainly as I see you beside me.' There is no need to mention her companions who are impious people, or the business with the stone and its supposed curse. God does not want to hear such things. 'She was grave and beautiful and looked kindly on us — on me. At once my heart knew it was Our Lady.'

'This is remarkable, my child. Tell me, what did the blessed Madonna tell you to do? What was Her message?'

'Nothing, father. She just stood there.'

She has said the wrong thing. She glances at him and sees his small frown.

'If the vision had no message for you it cannot have been a true visitation. Whenever Our Lady has appeared on Earth, it has always been because She wishes to make known to us the will of Heaven.'

'I did see Her lips move,' Cochonne says.

'Then She did speak.'

'Yes, father. She did. It is only that the night was very windy and there was noise in the roof, so it was a little hard to hear the words.'

The priest takes one of her hands in his. God's love erupts in Cochonne's loins like a sunrise.

'Think carefully, child. Did She not tell you that She instructs all Christian people to hold fast to their faith, and to resist the heretic philosophers and atheists who seek to turn France into the empire of Satan?'

'Yes,' Cochonne says. 'I think that is exactly what She said.'

'And was not Her instruction to you to go out among the poor people and testify that She appeared to you, to strengthen them in resistance to the godless revolutionaries?'

Though this feels as if it must be true, since the inward flame still warms her, it is so distant from her recollection of the scene that she hesitates.

'But, father, why would Our Lady give a task like that to me? I am only a farmer's girl. Perhaps those were not Her exact instructions.'

'Because, my child, in these times when the great deny God and France is at the mercy of Heaven's enemies, it is among the poor and humble that her salvation will be found. Remember how Jesus came to live among fishermen and beggars and sinful women. You may be a farmer's girl but God has given you the figure and frame of a warrior. You are to be His soldier.'

'But what can I do?'

'Bear witness to the favour Heaven has granted you. You have been granted a miracle, child. Tell all people of good faith that Our Lady has appeared among us to lead the cause. You will do that, I trust? Everywhere you go?' His hands tighten on hers. They are warm, strong and earnest.

'Yes, father,' she says.

'That is good,' he says. He smiles. 'Will you now pray with me?'

They kneel side by side under the crucifix. While her lids are closed God sends her another beautiful vision, in which the priest is indeed a saint: her favourite, Saint Sebastian, naked and bound to a tree, pierced with arrows. She would like to tell him about this second vision so he knows he too is favoured by Heaven. However, his prayers are so fervent and continuous, and so long, that it is impossible for her to speak until she joins him in the Lord's Prayer, which they say together in conclusion.

She leaves the sheepfold full of joy. She does not remember the old woman until she has descended all the way to where the track crosses the heath and sees des Sables and Lesinge waiting for her. Des Sables is sitting astride the donkey Broubrou, who appears to accept his new employment with equanimity.

'At last,' Lesinge says. 'I thought you only went to deliver a message, not to attend mass and listen to a sermon.'

Cochonne's rapture leaves her at a stroke.

'Do not mock me,' she says. 'I am not in the mood for it.'

'Very well, my fair Penthesilea.' Lesinge himself is in high good humour. 'But is your duty to the old blind mother done? Are we free to proceed on our way?'

'Hee-haw!' cries Broubrou sarcastically, as though he sees into Cochonne's shamed soul.

'Go on then,' she mutters, picking up her rake. The priest, she thinks, was a liar anyway. The Madonna did not say any of those things about atheists and philosophers.

'Excellent!' Lesinge will not let her sulks ruin his mood. A good pair of boots and an excellent donkey in a single day! It is a tolerable achievement in the circumstances. And miracle of miracles, the lilywhite boy demonstrates a little spirit after all. He points towards the declining sun with a flourish. 'Onwards and westwards, to the Castle Charizard!'

CHAPTER SIX

Reader — We are severely embarrassed.

Our narrative has a second time contrived, to lead Miss Arabella Farthingay into a state of — Captivity.

Mortifying! — yet the facts cannot be gainsaid — Not in a tale such as ours, with its scrupulous regard for historical veracity, in every detail.

An *heroine*, reader, is an odd creature indeed. —

An *hero*, may strive against fate and circumstance. An *hero*, cuts his own path through the world — Chusing his way, and atchieving his end —

> *He'll labour night and day*
> *To be a pilgrim!*

But, study the heroines, who adorn the great tales of the last century, in which our humble narrative also passes — your Pamelas, and Evelinas; your Cecilias, and Belindas — study, if you can, the subtle and inward creations of Miss *Austen*, whom no one knows, though they deserve better than the eternal obscurity into which they are sunk. — Examine these women, with scientific rigour, and you will discover them perpetually hedged about, and bundled hither and yon, by powers quite beyond their controul. Inheritances — codicils — guardians — masters, barely distinct from *owners* — tyrannical aunts, and importunate cousins — suitors — Nay, even manners and fashions, to contravene which is a kind of death. And all these perils must be negotiated, only in order to arrive at the acquisition of an *husband*! — whom our heroine is then engaged to *obey*, by custom, law, and her own voluntary oath, given at the altar.

What is a poor heroine to *do* — When she is immovably fated, to be *done unto?*

Consider the case of our Miss Farthingay. — Knocked from pillar to post, since her first arrival in France, as though she had no will of her own. — Abducted — Liberated, after a fashion — Viewed with suspicion, by her rescuers — Kept under supervision — escorted — proposed to! — And taken at last, to a place of refuge, which — she is not permitted to leave.

The letter from Monsieur Denfert, with instructions for her onward journey, does not arrive. — Meanwhile — The gate of the Poor Sisters of Mercy is kept shut, and presided over, by a pair of harridans in holy orders — and Miss Farthingay is not permitted, to pass out of it.

To all her protests the Mother Superior answers imperturbably. — It is for madam's own safety. — Monsieur Denfert is quite insistent — And, until his letter arrives, she shall remain a *guest* of the house.

Miss Farthingay writes her own letter to M Denfert. — A brief missive, breathing in every line a spirit of noble indignation.

— Alas — says the Mother, with a rueful pout, which is her habitual expression, to signify the unfortunate necessities that constrain all private choice — A gesture, whose eloquent meaning is that *nothing can be done* — ever — by any body — You have perhaps seen it, reader, on the face of certain French *concierges* and waiters. — Alas, says she, all Paris is in the turmoil. — Such times! — Who can say when monsieur the deputy may have leisure to attend to his correspondence?

But, FEAR NOT, Miss Farthingay! — for *rescue* is at hand —

Or, if not precisely at hand, it approaches in great haste —

Our narrative has been compelled, these last two or three chapters, to peer in several directions at once.

The sensation is, we confess, not altogether comfortable. — Nevertheless — it permits us to observe, that rescue is on the way! — Though still some miles distant, and taking a somewhat hap-hazard course.

Is it *Mr Thomas Peach*, who rides to relieve his friend, patroness, and benefactrix?

It is not. —

Mr Peach is landed at the picturesque old port of Saint-Malo, on the coast of Brittany. He disembarks the *Marie-Antoinette* without ceremony — ignoring the sailors, who look at him askance — Explaining to the customs-men and the harbour-master, that he is an English traveller and antiquarian, come to inspect the famous druidic monuments of that region.*

Has he letters of introduction?

He has not.

The harbour-master and the customs-men frown, and look uncertain. — Well then, Monsieur Peach — they say — Pin the cockade in your hat, and be on your way. — And off he goes, into the town. They wonder after-wards, why they let him pass, when he had no letters. Was that not cause for suspicion? — But now it is too late to delay the journey of this unknown Monsieur Peach. For no sooner did he enter the walls, than he bought a saddle, and an old mule, and rode out of them again — who knows where.

Monsieur Peach hardly knows as much himself. —

He takes the horse-ferry across the gorge of the Rance, in a kind of waking stupor. Memories come and go, alternately vivid and remote. He recalls how he rode across France, alone, in the days of his early manhood. He feels, he lives those days again

---

* Such as the remarkable stones, at *Karnack*. Have you seen them, reader? — They stand in long straight rows, like soldiers on the parade-ground. An impressive spectacle — yet lacking the pleasing circular forms, of our British monuments, such as the *Stone-henge*. Why the French druids were unable to discover the principle of the *curved line*, which came so naturally to their British cousins, we cannot guess — Unless it be ascribed to some antient deficiency, in the national character.

— Yet with an acute sensation, of the great gulph separating that time from this — an abyss, in which lie tragedy, defeat, and despair —

He is, in short, partly delirious.

The laudanum is to blame, we fear. —

Amid reverie and phantasy, he knows he seeks Miss Farthingay — his old friend! if not his *only* friend, in his reduced state, now Clary is gone — Clary, and dear Liza too — He seeks her in the Chateau Charizard, to the west.

— Little lady Farthingay? says an invisible voice, which seems to wind about his shoulder, and flutter like a moth in his ear — Though its actual situation, must be within his own brain, for Mr Peach travels alone — Does he not?

— You ride away from her, not towards. — The voice seems to laugh, with malevolent satisfaction.

Mr Peach ignores it. It is, after all, only a phantastical impression, produced by his troubled mind — Is it not?

So he goes on, west-wards, across Brittany — AWAY from Miss Farthingay! in the house of the Poor Sisters of Mercy, near Domfront, in Normandy — Though he cannot know his mistake.

We shall return to mark his progress, when we can. We are solicitous for his safety. — He has not the appearance of a man well-suited to any solitary adventure, and least of all, in a land riven by suspicion, faction, and violence. — Although we observe with relief, that those three hand-maidens of revolution seem very distant, from the bleak silent Breton wastes, where for the most part Mr Peach and his mule trudge along, with no body to disturb them — except a few bent-backed old women, scouring the gorse and ling at the edge of the road, for sticks to feed their fires.

But we see you grow impatient, reader. The promised RESCUE of our heroine, is all you wish to hear of.

Very well. —

Cast your eye, then, over this sturdy merchant's cart, drawn by a pair of sweating horses — Driving at furious pace, across the wide tedious plain, in that elbow of land where Brittany and Normandy meet.

The driver — Flicking the reins, and urging the animals on, in more than passable French — Do you recognize him? Look closely —

It is indeed Mr Spott! — whom we last encountered, in the heaving cabin of the *Marie-Antoinette*. You did not know him at once — for his dress is altered, from head to toe. He now presents the appearance, of an ordinary French countryman. — A farmer of middling prosperity, perhaps, or a modest provincial tradesman.

Crouched in the cart, among tight-lashed barrels and crates, are four other men, similarly attired. The clothes they wore, when they left Britain, are concealed at the bottom of the barrels.

— Can ye make 'em go no faster, Spott? cries a familiar voice — My lord Rawleigh, who gazes along the straight flat road ahead, with evident impatience — As though he regrets he cannot sprout wings, and outpace the straining animals by a wish.

Now — before we proceed — We must account for the fact, that Lord Rawleigh and his faithful companions, are hastening *east-wards*, from Saint-Malo — When our best guess at their purpose, on being compelled to land in that harbour, was that they meant to go *west* — as Mr Tho.s Peach does, this very same hour — In order to liberate Miss Farthingay, from the libertine de Charizard, in his remote and ill-omened château.

Reader — we think you will do better to submit to the confusions, like an *heroine*, and allow yourself to be carried on the cross-currents of our tale — Instead of endeavouring to hack your way through them, like an hero.

We shall be as brief as we can.

In sum — No sooner had Lord Rawleigh, and Mr Spott, and their companions in adventure, come to land at Saint-Malo, and assured the harbour-master and customs-men, that their purpose was only to visit his lordship's orchards — than they heard the common rumour about the town, that *the queen* had essayed

flight from Paris — was apprehended, at Fougères, and taken —
To prison, said some — To the old conventual house near
Domfront, said others — to hell! cried not a few.

This intelligence descended on Lord Rawleigh, like the
thunderbolt of Jove.

— Hell and d——nation! exclaimed he, to the loyal Spott —
Her majesty has acted upon our plan too soon! — Lord Rawleigh
gnashes his teeth and paces in a circle. — Why did we never have
her letters? he says — We were assured they would arrive with an
old abbot — Weeks ago! — Had I known, her majesty was
preparing to leave — I would have flown — Flown, demme, Spott,
d'ye hear? — To any town in this d——nable country — Sword
drawn — To receive her, and protect her, and spirit her away to
dear old England. A thousand curses on the d——d abbott that
should have brought her letter — I will find the villain and cut his
hands from his wrists. — And now, her majesty is captured again
— D——n them — D——n them all —

— My lord, says Spott — These are only rumours.

— Rumour be d——d! — We must go — at once — there is not
an instant to lose —

— Very well, my lord; but where must we go?

A fair question — But to Lord Rawleigh, a tormenting one. —
Where have they taken the queen, the idol of his chaste and
honourable passions? If only he can learn the place, he will ride
there at once, and surrender his life, if necessary, in the cause of
the royal lady. — He pursues the rumour about the quaint streets
and cramped inns of the old town — aided by Mr Spott, who is
rather more familiar with the French language, than his master
— Until they come across an old fellow, who has spoken to one,
whose sister's father-in-law in La Bouëxière saw with his own eyes
the queen, under armed escort, and was told by the guards, that
their destination was a certain convent, in the hills around
Domfront.

— What of Miss Farthingay? says Spott.

— D——n Miss Farthingay!

We are very sorry to report such language, in the mouth of a British peer. One cause alone can excuse it — The fervour of Lord Rawleigh's devotion, to the beautiful and noble queen of France. — A lady, we must confess, his lordship has himself not once set eyes on — which is not the case, with Miss Arabella Farthingay.

We suppose my lord to be inspired, by *chivalry*. — An ideal too lofty and refined, to be understood by those not noble born.

Thus it is, reader, that the daring Englishmen, drive their cart towards the convent, where poor Miss Farthingay is shut up like a prisoner — intending RESCUE!

If you have maintained your equilibrium, among all these rumours, and changes of course, in the warring currents of our narrative — for which we congratulate you — You will have remarked, that the RESCUE Lord Rawleigh intends, does not, speaking strictly, have Miss Farthingay as its object.

Nevertheless — To those of us, whose interest in the welfare of the amiable poetess, is sincere, and felt in the heart, an accidental or erroneous rescue, will certainly be preferable to *no rescue at all*.

Therefore — God-speed, Lord Rawleigh!

Or shall we say — God-speed, FORGET-ME-NOT? — for it is surely in the character of that daring *master of disguise*, that we must now salute his lordship. — That defender of the privileges and virtues, of antient nobility — that scourge of revolution!

How feeble and insignificant is the plodding progress of Thomas Peach, in comparison! —

We are amazed that Caspar addressed his plea, for the recovery of his honoured mistress, to the latter — Not to his chivalrous lordship. Who, when haste and vigour are called for, appeals to the *tortoise*, instead of the *hare*?

Well, reader — if the antient fable be true, the choice was perhaps less unwise, than it first appear. *Finem lauda*, as the proverb is — that is to say, The end crowns all. — We shall reserve judgment, until we have seen the event.

Miss Farthingay's indignation at her treatment, grows warmer by the day. No reply comes from Monsieur Denfert in Paris. Her repeated insistence, that she be set at liberty immediately — that no law of God or man justifies what is done — that *arbitrary imprisonment* is a vestige of tyranny, she thought banished from France for ever — &c. — are all met by shrugs, and silence. — Madam — says the Mother Superior — we must await the deputy's further commands — His letter will certainly arrive *to-morrow*. — Be patient, madam — It is a Christian virtue.

Miss Farthingay composes a series of satirical couplets, upon Popish superstition, after the manner of Dean Swift.

No letter comes *to-morrow*, or the next day.

Miss Farthingay feigns illness. — I am in agonies! cries she, from her bed. — I must be taken to a doctor — an experienced doctor. — Send for Monsieur_____ at Fougères.

— We shall pray, say the sisters who attend her. — The good Lord will be your comfort.

Miss Farthingay redoubles her pretended symptoms. Shrieks and groans emanate from her cell at night. — A doctor is called from the nearby town. — There is no danger, this *savant* of the healing arts declares. — The English madame is quite well.

— We rejoice that you are recovered, say the sisters, in mirthless tones.

During the day, when she has the liberty of the house, Miss Farthingay goes to the chapel. She throws herself down before the altar, and complains loudly of her treatment, in eloquent English, to God. Among her favourite volumes, in her youth, when she had the freedom of her father's library, were the Olney hymns of Mr Newton. Many of those good sturdy Wesleyan songs she has by heart. She makes the nuns' chapel ring with them. — Her voice is not the most sweetly-tuned of instruments, but what it lacks in accomplishment, it gains by loudness. — The sisters attempt to remove her. — Is this not an house of worship? she says, and throws off their efforts with disdainful force, and resumes her hymn, louder than before — Until she unfortunately runs hoarse.

— Finds, she can no longer speak at all — and must submit to be escorted to her own cell, raging inwardly at her defeat.

— Calm yourself, we implore you, madame, say the sisters. — Letters from Paris will surely come, *to-morrow*.

Meanwhile — The cart has crossed the plains — sparks shoot from the iron of its wheels, as they fly over the road! — and turned to face the higher ground, where French castles once stood, to discourage Breton invaders, before the two kingdoms became one. — If the patriotic militias are encountered, or the National Guard, their enquiries are satisfied — for Lord Rawleigh possesses several documents, obtained expressly for that purpose, and Mr Spott speaks persuasively in French — it being the native language of his mother, though the good woman has long been settled, in Dorset-shire. — The cart races on, into the fertile Norman valleys — And at last atchieves the region of wet and fallow fields, interspersed with woods of beech and ash, where lies the obscure convent of the Poor Sisters of Mercy.

Now the cart slows — Plods along, so as not to excite the interest of the peasantry, in whose dull unchanging existences any new or rapid event is as marvellous, as the appearance of a comet — Comes finally to an halt, concealed in a woodland path, within a mile of the convent.

Its driver and passengers arm themselves — pistols and powder hidden, beneath their plain farmer's weeds — And spread around the vicinity, in various directions. Lord Rawleigh puts a scythe over his shoulders. — The season for reaping is past, but his lordship has traditional notions, of the proper accoutrements of an agricultural man — Among several other notions equally traditional, some of which we have remarked heretofore. He makes his way along country paths, until he comes to a vantage-point, from which the house of the Poor Sisters may be surveyed — Its walls, windows, and means of ingress and egress — The nature and number of those who go in and out — &c. — His heart quickens, when he observes that the gate remains perpetually closed, except to admit two or three sisters, with business in the orchards, or among the bee-hives. — By jingo — thinks he — The place is kept d——d closely shut up — She must still be here — I am not too late!

Mr Spott goes about the nearest town, striking up conversation, in casual fashion. — When the time is right, he asks whether any fine lady is recently admitted to the convent? — perhaps arriving under an escort of guardsmen? — The good Normans shrug. — Perhaps, they say — Perhaps not — One cannot say for sure. Maybe some say it is true — Others, maybe, say it is not. For myself, monsieur, I would not like to declare, one way or the other. Good-day, monsieur. — Mr Spott enters a tavern, hoping to loosen tongues, by the application of the fruit of the vine. — Ah, says a farmer, whom wine and a friendly nature have rendered particularly susceptible, to the society of the newcomer — It could be, that a great lady came, with armed men from Fougères, five or six days past — Or it could be, that she did not. I myself, monsieur, do not know, and therefore cannot say with certainty. Your health, my good friend! And long live the revolution! Or, the king! — whichever you prefer — Oneself, one admits either possibility — Who can declare for sure, which is correct?

No such equivocation afflicts the judgment of the passionate lord. In his imagination, there is not an hour to be wasted. The vision of that exquisite beauty — for so Lord Rawleigh imagines the queen — immured in confines so dirty and ignoble, is intolerable torment. He pictures her astonishment, when he steals to her place of confinement — her modest yet effusive gratitude, as the royal heart fills with the prospect of deliverance — crystal tears, and a palpitating bosom — Her awe, at the inspired boldness, of the FORGET-ME-NOT — that mysterious prince among men!

— A convent, eh? he says to Spott, when the company is gathered again, in the wood where the cart lies hidden. — Shall we obtain nuns' disguises? They'd be the very thing.

Mr Spott pauses a moment or two before answering. — An excellent thought, my lord, he says, but even if we could get them, our proportions might arouse suspicion. — He nods towards one of their fellow-adventurers, a fair-faced broad-shouldered fellow near six foot high. — Also, one lifted veil would scupper us.

— True, Spott, true.

— If I might suggest — ?

— Speak free, Spott, old fellow. All in the business together, hey? — master and man both, what?

— The conventual orders of France are often charitable foundations, as much as religious. An appeal to charity might have those gates there open, to my way of thinking.

— By jingo! I forget you're half a Frenchman yourself. Know your way around the nuns, do you, ha, ha?

The companions laugh dutifully.

— Well — the noble lord continues — the plan has merit. I shall think it over an hour or two. — He reaches for a bottle of brandy.

The next day, five men approach the convent gate. One is carried in a sling, by two of his fellows. Another limps behind with the aid of a crutch. The invalid in the sling twists about, and groans — *oh! ah! quelle maladie!* He is comforted, poor man, by the leader of the small band, who advises him to be patient, for the destined help is near. — Arriving at the gate, he raps against it, and cries for aid and mercy.

The wicket remains closed, but a barred window opens, and a sour face looks out — *Qui est là?*

Mr Spott's eloquence in his mother's tongue exceeds, alas, our power to record it. We suppose he pleads for the sick man to be allowed entry, to receive the sisters' care. — His accents are piteous, as he indicates his groaning companion. He appeals, certainly, to the divine virtue of charity, for we discern several religious terms in his homily. — All this is accompanied by the most tragic exhibition, on the part of Lord Rawleigh, who takes the role of the afflicted unfortunate — and many sighs, from the other companions.

— There is a doctor in Domfront, says the sister — we translate for your benefit, reader. — The window slams shut.

Mr Spott knocks again.

— Go away, is the reply.

Baffled and chastened, the five bold companions are forced to retreat to their camp, in the brown decaying wood.

— D——n the miserable witches! — Lord Rawleigh rages — There's for your charity, Spott — d——n Frenchies — not a drop of religion in 'em — He heaps further imprecations on the Poor Sisters of Mercy, until Mr Spott judges the tide of his passion to be ebbing, and observes, that the frustration of his lordship's plan is at least a strong indication, that some person of great consequence is held within the convent. — Why else would the gate be closed to the simplest exercise of charity?

Lord Rawleigh declares, he had the very same thought. —

Over the course of the day, a second stratagem is formed. This, is to be executed *nocturnally*. — It will be an assault by stealth, upon the walls. The expeditionary force may be small in number, and lack any siege equipment, but the place is hardly a castle. — Surely its modest architecture offers ledges, and other protuberances of stone or iron, by which a daring fellow might ascend to the roof, and let down a rope? Lord Rawleigh suggests Mr Spott for the fellow in question. — His own daring is better expressed in more gentlemanly feats, such as swordsmanship, and pistol-work. He is not too proud to allow his loyal Spott a share, in the atchievements of the FORGET-ME-NOT — For all degrees of rank and station ought to be united, in the cause of honour, king, and country.

Miss Farthingay, meanwhile, sits at the table in her appointed cell, and pens another letter to Monsieur Denfert, in Paris. — All unknowing, that her rescuers lurk less than a mile off, cleaning pistols, and making shades for their lanterns, and greasing the cart-wheels with tallow, so that when the time comes it will go silent as ever it may.

The loss of her voice is a great annoyance to our heroine. She cannot upbraid her captors. — Cannot even annoy them, by shouting demands from behind the door of her cell, which is once again locked, after provision of the evening meal. Her tongue — her sole weapon — is blunted.

An heavy gloom overtakes her.

She recalls how her heart stirred with emotion, at the first view of awakened France. — France, now proven to be a land of tyranny still!

She sinks her head on the paper, and despairs.

When she retires to her bed at last, sleep eludes her.

In the early hours of the night, her unhappy meditations are interrupted, by the turning of the lock. Candle-light warms a portion of the dark.

Miss Farthingay sits up in alarm, and attempts to cry, Who is there? — but produces only a grating whisper. — Her voice has still not recovered, from its vigorous rendition of Mr Newton's hymns.

Her alarm turns to surprize, as the person with the taper enters. It is — the mysterious veiled sister!

— Dress yourself, says the young nun, in English, without the slightest colouring of a French accent. — As quickly as you can.

— What is the meaning of this? Miss Farthingay croaks.

The nun presses her taper into Miss Farthingay's hand. — Go to the gate at once, she says. — You will find it open. There will be men there to take you to safety.

Miss Farthingay takes the candle. She is too bewildered to do otherwise. Her head spins. — An hundred doubts and questions clamour within her — all, fruitlessly! for the secret novice is already stolen away, in perfect darkness, without another word.

Can she be dreaming? — The scene just passed, has the flavour of phantasy. — Not least, because the nun spoke in English, and in a voice, which to Miss Farthingay seemed in some degree familiar — as, in dreams, things strange and nonsensical often appear natural, and provoke no surprize.

She goes to the door of the cell, and finds it — open.

This at least, is no dream! Her prison is unlocked. It is deep night, when all the convent is at rest. — She needs no further invitation, to dress in all haste, and gather up two or three necessary items, and leave the room.

In one hand she holds the taper. — In the other, her boots, so that she goes on stockinged feet, and makes no sound. She halts at every corner, and each turn of the stair, to observe whether the way ahead lies clear. —

Miss Farthingay would do well for the heroine of a *Gothick* tale — were she unfortunate enough, to find herself in a narrative so ludicrous and implausible. *That* indignity, at least, we promise she shall never endure.

Where is she to go? —

Where else, but towards the gate, as her mysterious visitor instructed?

She steals noislessly along the inner cloister, and then to the small court, at the entrance of the house. With breathless anxiety, she peers at the lantern by the gate, where the two harridans have sat, hour upon hour, forbidding any approach.

The harridans she does not at first see — Then, notices where they lie, upon the ground. — Notices, rather, their shoes, and a portion of their ankles, and a length of the hems of their habits. It appears they have fallen in the bushes either side of the gate, where they rest, quite motionless — Their legs sticking out.

The wicket gate is wide open. Beyond it, a rectangle of mere darkness — The most welcome *nothing*, Miss Farthingay has ever set eyes on.

She looks left, and right, and behind. None stirs — No one watches.

She steps noislessly on. — As though recalling the froth of a dream, she remembers that the nun said there would be men, to take her to safety.

In the instant — conjured, seemingly, by her thought — She hears a murmur of *English* surprize, outside the gate —

— By jingo! the door's open!

Out she hastens, to freedom — And, at the very exit, comes face to face with — LORD RAWLEIGH — pistol in his hand — cloathed in a strange imitation of an humble labourer's garb — With several other men behind, similarly attired, and also wearing, like his lordship, expressions of severe astonishment.

— Miss Farthingay? says Lord Rawleigh.

— Lord Rawleigh!

— Hush! his lordship says, in sudden alarm — I am not Lord Rawleigh — You are quite mistaken.

Miss Farthingay falls to her knees. — For God's sake, sir, get me away from this place!

Lord Rawleigh is in the last degree of confusion. He appears incapable of motion at all — let alone the decisive action, which Miss Farthingay urges on him. — But — he says — the *queen* —

— I entreat you, Miss Farthingay says — They may awaken at any moment —

— Have no fear, ma'am, says Mr Spott, stepping forward to take her arm, with unaffected solicitude, and raise her to her feet. — You're safe as the king's jewels now. Come, sir — the cart.

— Why, yes, says Lord Rawleigh, attempting to compose himself, as Mr Spott begins leading our poor heroine away from the convent, shielding the candle-flame from the pranks of the breeze. — Yes indeed — to the cart, and away we go! — Hang it — I must leave a *flower* — Have you the flowers, Jenkins?

One of the men produces an handful of papers from within his garments. On each sheet a five-petalled flower is drawn in ink, and below it inscribed the famous couplet —

But WHO is the Forget-Me-Not?
By jingo! no one knows, what, what?

Now Lord Rawleigh must search for some means, to pin one of the papers to the gate. — He finds none. The lantern is retreating towards the cart, in the company of Spott and Miss Farthingay — leaving him to stumble, in the shadows — d——n this dark!

— He locates at last a stone, whose weight he uses to fix the paper to the ground, just within the convent. As he places it, he notices the two nuns, laid out quite motionless in the bushes to either side. — Quite *dead*. — He wonders, who shot them — whether it was him.

Reader, you must understand — My lord's state of mind is utter perplexity. — Caused, we suppose, by the appearance of Miss Farthingay, in place of the anticipated *queen of France* — and, we also guess, by certain guilty sensations, associated with his disappointment.

His lordship's perturbations need not delay us. Our RESCUE is accomplished! — and all without the need for climbing walls, or breaking windows, or letting down ropes, or storming an house of prayer with pistols drawn.

Indeed, the contribution of the dashing FORGET-ME-NOT, to the relief of Miss Farthingay, amounts, we suppose, to —

But it would be churlish to keep accounts, like an officious clerk, in such a noble enterprize. What matters, who opened the gate, and rendered its pair of female Arguses insensible? The deeds were done. — We ask no more — but rejoice merely, in the deliverance of our heroine. Any lingering mystery, attaching to the expedition, only adds to the legend of the Forget-Me-Not!

How the new authorities of France gnash their teeth, at reports of his exploits, and unleash an hundred curses on his name! Every mischance is attributed, to his endeavours. — Every distinguished *émigré*, that escapes across the sea to Britain, is agreed to have been spirited away, by the English devil. —

It is the nature of a *legend*, we suppose, to exceed historical truth. — And to do so, by a wide margin. Else what distinguishes it, from mere happenstance?

Had you, reader, been eye-witness to the siege of Troy, you would doubtless have found it tedious. — An indecisive protracted affair — all carping quarrel, and muddy skirmish — Ten years of back-and-forth over the plain. No person of sense wishes to know the *truth* of the matter, when they can open their Homer instead.

Lo! we have accidentally invited a comparison, between Lord Rawleigh, and *Achilles*, or *Hector*. — A sign, that we ought to lay aside our pen. We leave Miss Farthingay rattling along in the cart, by lantern-light, and what radiance the wintry night affords — Accompanied, if not by heroes, then at least by well-wishing friends, who may surely lead her safe to England, and Grandison Hall — And so, with relief, we close our chapter.

Each morning the grass is tipped with frost. Lesinge, when he wakes, cannot feel his fingers or toes. Castle Charizard remains far to the west. How far exactly des Sables does not say. 'Find me a civilised place,' he declares, 'and I will tell you where we are, and how long is the road ahead.' He gestures at the brown heath and the bittergreen and yellow of gorse. 'What is this? This is nowhere.'

Cochonne loses patience. She wishes to see the Virgin again. She sits in the road and refuses to continue until the stone is produced.

On all sides Lesinge feels his authority challenged, as if he was King Louis himself. It is time for firmness.

'Come, des Sables, Broubrou. We will leave her here.' He wags a finger at Cochonne. 'You begged to follow me. If you have thought better of it—' He shrugs. 'You may please yourself.'

Cochonne lays her rake across her knees and says nothing.

'The aroma of shit will guide you home,' Lesinge says.

'I saved your life,' she mutters.

Lesinge bows. 'For which Gaspard thanks you, noble Penthesilea. Alas, he is no knight of romance but a modern brigand, and does not consider himself eternally bound to your service.'

'Go then,' she says, staring at the stones between her boots. 'You will be back within an hour.'

It is less than half that time before he and des Sables return. He cannot do without her. These are wild roads, no doubt infested with smugglers and Breton bandits, to say nothing of wild boars and packs of famished dogs. With Cochonne he fears nothing. Without her who will protect his flesh and his purse, lean as both are growing? Des Sables? The best he could hope for would be to throw the boy to his attackers and hope to flee while they feast on him.

'Well,' he says to Cochonne, 'stand up, after all. We are companions, and ought to stick by one another.'

'The stone,' she says, putting out her enormous blacksmith's hand.

She is like stone herself, by God! A woman's stubbornness ought to be like a mule's; one overcomes it by beating. But he cannot beat this living boulder.

He examines the impasse with philosophical precision, then gives her the velvet bag. Gaspard Lesinge knows when he is defeated. Is it not his supreme virtue as a brigand chief? His old captains used to fight against impossible odds, despising the name of surrender. They are all hung or broken on the wheel. He lives to struggle on. He recoils, as the proverb has it, to better leap forward.

Cochonne takes the strange old stone from the bag. She whispers to it, holds it to her eye, cradles it in her hands and prays. Nothing happens. It remains an ugly grey lump.

She looks up to see Lesinge and des Sables grinning at one another.

'Do not say anything,' she says, taking hold of her rake, 'or your heads will suffer.'

No vision appears from the stone, but rumours sprout in their wake as they travel the westward roads. Old women gathering sticks among the gorse straighten their bent backs and squint across the heath to watch the little band pass: the bearded man leading the donkey, the beautiful youth astride it, the imposing woman walking behind. If their sight is particularly poor they say, 'Ah, look there, it is the Holy Family!'

This is not the France of observation and measurement and reason. There is one France, yes, one equal nation under the new constitution, but there are also a thousand Frances, scattered beside one another like pieces of a mosaic floor. The single France is an idea whose head and heart both lie in Paris. It is a beautiful thought: the whole unified country, its parts assigned into equal departments, all subject to the same law, without privilege or distinction. And then there are the thousand tiny Frances, jealous of their borders, where no one eats or speaks or thinks like the Frenchmen next door, nor wishes to; whose roots lie in earth the revolution has not turned over. The France Lesinge and his company now pass through is a land of superstition and miracle. It is tenaciously ignorant of the name of progress. It holds the other nine-hundred and ninety-nine in contempt. Let those other fools think what they wish. The old women know what they saw.

There are whispers that the Madonna has revealed herself to a simple farmer's girl, as Jesus once spoke to Saint Jeanne. A good priest bears witness to it. God willing, the king will soon be back on his throne and all the good priests in their churches. Who will imprison one for saying so when one is only a poor old woman?

The feet of des Sables are armoured now with callouses as well as good boots. He can walk almost as fast as the others. However the sight of him mounted on Broubrou has a marvellous effect on the peasants of this France. Therefore Lesinge insists that he rides. All the grandmothers declare he is the picture of Jesus himself. They are Bretons and speak no French at all, but their reverence is plain. They offer the companions bread and onions and invite them to rest in their byres. Their decrepit husbands and brawny sons grumble, for bread is scarce enough without sharing it with vagabonds, and they resent the effeminate loveliness of des Sables. But they are ruled by the women as they always have been. Many of the thousand Frances are secret matriarchies.

No one had heard of Castle Charizard. In the west, say some few who can converse in French? Do not go to the west. Over that way they are all barbarians who eat butter without salt and venerate the Devil. Their babies are born with fur. Their churches are built of human skulls. The western forests are haunted by pagan spirits. At night drowned bells ring from under the sea.

'God preserve us,' says Lesinge, and looks pious.

The nearest great town? It is Dinan, to the north. The women also advise against going there. The towns have turned godless and are full of men making laws against religion and hoarding bread. Everyone knows someone whose cousin or nephew has been arrested. At this the menfolk growl and clench their fists. In their eyes are violence and revenge. Lesinge knows this look intimately, as a father knows the face of his child. There will be other revolutions here, he thinks. Not one great one as in Paris, but many small ones. Soon the one France and the thousand Frances will be at war with one another.

The prospect contents him. When people fight themselves they are too busy to pursue thieves.

Des Sables declares he knows the road from Dinan to Castle Charizard. He does not, in fact; he has never heard of Dinan. The provincial towns of France were of as little concern to his late master as the nobodies inhabiting them. But he is tired of making camp under hedges and in farm buildings. He dreams of rooms with wooden floors and stone fireplaces and people who do not stare as though he had descended from the moon.

He has also discovered that he is an excellent liar.

North, then, to Dinan! And out of one France, into a different nation. Approaching the fine old town, which nestles high above the Rance, and gathers its walls tightly around itself like the cities seen in the distance in sacred paintings, Lesinge and his company reattach their cockades, and hum patriotic songs in time to the beat of the donkey's walk. Of all Frenchmen the burghers of the towns have gained most from revolution. They profit from the destruction of their ancient enemies in the bishops' palaces, the monks' estates, the castles of barons and marquises and viscounts. The burghers of the towns are in fact at this moment the revolution incarnate. They have elected themselves to fill the new Assembly. They steer the ship of state, in place of those discredited navigators the king and his court.

This is no place for old women's superstitions. Des Sables dismounts from the donkey.

A steep lane ascends from the bridge to the city gate, lined for half its length with teetering houses which seem to cling together to prevent them all tumbling down the gorge. Curious faces come to the windows and watch the little procession. A knot of urchins forms behind the donkey to call out the usual insults. One boy dares to mock Cochonne directly, at which she halts and gestures with the rake so fiercely the children scatter.

The gate is watched by a detachment of the national guard.

'Oho!' says one to another. 'Regard these comical vagabonds.'

'My faith! Are they escaped from an exhibition of monstrosities? Hey, you there!' They shuffle lazily to their feet, leaving aside cups and dice. They address themselves to Lesinge. 'Your name and business, old fellow!'

'I am Fraternité-Voltaire de la Nation,' says Lesinge, 'and these are my wife and my orphaned nephew, whom we conduct across Brittany to be married.'

'Your wife! Ho, ho!' All the guardsmen snigger.

'Do you have no children of your own?' asks one, with a smirk.

Lesinge looks mournful. 'Alas, no, though we pray Nature will one day bless us with a son.'

'I doubt your little worm can find its way in so big a hole,' the smirking soldier says. His colleagues hoot with laughter. 'Poor little worm.' He holds up his small finger and makes it into a crook. 'Madam cannot feel it when it goes within.'

'Unlucky madam!' exclaims one of the others, to further peals of amusement.

'Ho,' says the first, winking at his fellow soldiers to prepare them for another demonstration of his wit. 'This wedding of your nephew. Is he to be the groom? Or — the bride?'

Encouraged by the action of their seniors, the urchins take up a chorus of mockery as well. Cochonne's face is scarlet thunder.

'Bravo, sir, bravo,' Lesinge says, mustering his dignity. 'You do credit to your duty and your uniforms by making sport of loyal

Frenchmen. You exhibit the patriotic virtue of brotherhood, for which I myself, though a poor and ridiculous man, have at least the honour of being named.'

'What did you say your name was?'

'Fraternité-Voltaire de la Nation, sirs, and a proud citizen of France.'

'If his flesh was as big as his name,' the witty soldier says, 'Madame de la Nation would not look so discontented.'

Cochonne grips her rake and takes a stride forward.

'Come, wife,' Lesinge says, hastily. 'These men are servants of our country. We must allow them entertainment even at our expense, for they are the sabres and cuirasses of France. They deserve from us nothing but gratitude.'

Cochonne is still fuming as they pass into the city streets.

'You should not have stopped me cracking their heads,' she growls to Lesinge. 'Tonight I will go back and lay them out in the dirt one by one. Shit-mouthed dogs.'

'And what then? Languish in prison until you are hanged? That is not so satisfying a prospect, I assure you.'

'Insults should be repaid.'

'Let me explain a thing to you.' He slips his lean arm in Cochonne's brawny one, for all the world as if they are indeed husband and wife. She has never known him make such a gesture before. It startles her with unexpected delight. 'Do you know how we entered this town without having to answer more questions, even though we are' — he looks left and right — 'brigands? Because, my dear Cochonne, a man with authority does not care about the one he makes fun of. People like those soldiers, they are grateful for victims to mock and bully. If they think of us again it will be with a kind of satisfaction because we gave them amusement. Were they to search the city for a band of thieves, we three would be the very last to be enquired after. Do you see?'

Des Sables, who has hidden his hair and visage under a hood, comes to Cochonne's other side and takes the other arm in his.

'Our captain is wiser than he looks, my lady,' he says. The sight of men selling sausage and pickled onions and the smell of wine billowing from lamp-lit corner houses fill him with good spirits. His old master is safely tucked away in hell, and his new companions, he thinks, are not the worst one could wish for.

'Bof,' says Cochonne dismissively. But she has never before had one gallant on her arm, let alone two. Her angry mood blows away like the October leaves.

It is the anniversary of something, or it could be the feast-day dedicated to one patriotic virtue or another, or perhaps there is simply news from Paris to be celebrated, true or false. At dusk torches are lit. Up and down the streets go children banging pans with spoons, upbraiding any citizen who has not joined the parade. In the cramped and dirty public squares Liberty Trees are decorated with ribbons and lanterns though their natural branches died months ago. They resemble skeletons dressed for the fair. People sing and dance and brawl.

Lesinge has a jug of wine. Though it is thin and bitter as ashes it is cheap, and the innkeeper filled it to the brim. The first draught makes him wrinkle his nose and rub his beard. By the third his blood is warm and his spirits exultant. His little company, his brigand band, is in perfect amity, the squabbles of the road forgotten. For this he gives himself the credit. Gaspard Lesinge, leader of men! Or of a freakish man-woman and a milk-white girl-boy; but have they not proved themselves, under his tutelage? He pulls off his boots and rests his feet in the window where the winter air carries away their stink. Noises of revelry rise from below.

The imposture of him and Cochonne as man and wife simmers in his blood. By God, he has not had a woman for an age! He would roam the town for whores except that his boots are off, and Cochonne and des Sables would laugh at him, which would reduce his authority. If the boy were not present he would board her, to the devil with the size of her! A giant she may be, but still a woman, and a young one too. Perhaps he will wait until des Sables is snoring and then steal under her blanket. She will welcome it. The country girl has not yet been born who can resist the charm of Lesinge. Wife, he will whisper in her ear, do your duty to your husband. She will laugh, and then cry tears of delight.

Unknown to Lesinge, Cochonne's blood is beating equally hot. She has not often had wine before. It makes her head dance and her belly throb. Her virginity was lost to her stepbrothers years ago but since she grew able to protect herself she has been chaste as a saint. Now she shares a room with two men, like any slattern. Exactly what does a slattern do, she wonders, in such a situation? Her hands have a curious desire of their own to move to a certain part of her body where it seems the answer lies. She tells them to wait until late in the night, when neither God nor any person will be watching.

Des Sables is the most drunk of the three. Also he is the happiest. The treatment he was for years subjected to by his master and his master's libertine associates has left him with an unbreakable aversion to all the so-called pleasures of the flesh. He cannot even contemplate the private regions of his body without revulsion. Therefore he enjoys the delights of drunkenness without feeling its sting. The wine he used to steal from his master's stores was the best, and this vile western piss must surely be the worst, but he does not care. He is a revolutionary youth: a thousand times better to be free and drinking piss than a nobleman's pampered slave with a bottle of the Champagne vintage. He would go down to the street and join the celebrating patriots, except he knows they would lay hands on him and force him to perform those acts he cannot bear to think of. It is the curse of beauty. But how fortunate he is to have come under the protection of Cochonne, who has the strength of three men and the unnatural desires of none!

He wonders whether he is in love with her, not with filthy corrupted human love but as an angel might love a mortal.

'So, boy,' says Lesinge, stretching his legs in the open window. 'We are here, in Dinan. Thanks to me.' He raises his cup as if to drink to the city's health. 'How much further is it to this castle of your master and all its riches?'

Des Sables thinks the number ought to be quite large, to allow room for error, but not so large as to be discouraging. 'Four days,' he says. 'Perhaps five. Six, at most.'

'That does not sound like the answer of someone who knows his way.'

'My master travelled only in his black carriage, drawn always by four black horses at the speed of the wind. To estimate the same journey by foot is a puzzle. One must approximate.'

'Oh, you are a mathematician now? You are Laplace? Look, Cochonne, here is the great Laplace, disguised as a mermaid. But excuse me, Cochonne. You know as much of mathematics as of mermaids.'

'I do not care how many days we have to walk,' Cochonne says. 'I will walk them all better than both of you.'

'Granted.' Lesinge will neither give nor take offence. He is wit and good-fellowship from top to bottom. 'Your health, and the health of your splendid legs! I also do not care how long the journey is, so long as we know the way. You do know the way from here, boy?'

'Certainly.' Des Sables is not troubled by his lie. He will find out if he can, and if he cannot he will simply continue to lead them west, for he is sure the grim old castle of his master lies near the end of the earth.

'Tell me about these treasures,' says Lesinge.

'Which treasures, my captain?'

'The treasures we will find when we get there, of course! What others concern us?'

Des Sables hiccups. 'Old books. Pictures. Cups and bells in which devils' voices are heard. Many wicked things. The Sir de Charizard scoured all France for such valuable antiquities.'

Lesinge frowns. 'Pictures? Cups? I thought you said you would lead us to great riches.'

'The master wasted the fortunes of his estate on purchasing those things. For one single book I heard him offer a thousand pounds.'

'But are there also jewels and objects of silver and gold?'

'Assuredly,' des Sables says. 'All noble families have many objects like that.'

'By God, boy! We are not walking half the width of France to prove a hypothesis. Have you seen objects of silver and gold with your own eyes? Do you know for certain where they are hidden?'

'I know how to enter the secret crypt of the de Charizards. There are perhaps only three others who can say as much.'

'More mathematics! But good sir Laplace, I would rather know what is *in* the secret crypt.' Lesinge stabs the air with his finger. 'Number coins for me, not people.'

'Thousands, no doubt.'

'No doubt? What is this *no doubt?*'

Des Sables shrugs. 'The crypt would not be secret if one knew precisely what it contained.'

'So. You do not know at all.'

'The master bound my eyes with velvet before he led me there, each time.'

'Ha!' Lesinge's stabbing finger folds into a fist. 'You have never seen it! What if it is a catacomb filled with nothing but bones and dust?'

'It cannot be. The things I have seen—'

'But you were blindfolded. With your own eyes you have seen no treasure at all. Can you deny it?'

'That is not—'

'You had better hope your master's crypt overflows with jewels, for if we walk another week across these Breton heaths in the rain only to have a heap of bones for our reward, I will shut you up alive in the secret vault of the Castle Charizard and leave you there until you are dust yourself.'

'He will not,' says Cochonne sleepily. 'I will prevent it.'

'My captain,' des Sables says, adopting his most soothing manner. 'Do not agitate yourself. Look, you have already a tiny portion of the treasures my master accumulated in his short and profligate existence. The demonoscope of the de Charizards and the piece of the chess-set—'

'What? That worthless lump? And a little piece of ivory? Do you promise me more such trash?'

Des Sables is too drunk and too contented to defend himself with vehemence. 'Your little white queen may be more than she seems. Do not dismiss her as a piece of ivory quite yet, if you will take my advice.'

'Pah. It looks like a piece of ivory to me.' Lesinge fumbles in his coat for the chess-piece, but it is tangled in the chain of the silver locket. His fingers are clumsy with the wine.

'Once,' des Sables says, leaning forward, 'I myself witnessed one of master's chess-pieces come alive.'

'I suppose this was while you were wearing a blindfold?'

'It is the truth. I swear it on my mother's life. It was the black queen. She knocked at the house. These very hands' — des Sables holds up his delicate fingers — 'opened the door to admit her. She was a spirit dressed all in black and veiled, reeking of sulphur and brimstone, with a voice like iron. The master, may his soul be eternally tormented, had commanded me to lay out the chess-table and—'

Lesinge stands up abruptly and puts his hand on his head. 'Silence!' he says.

Cochonne, who has almost fallen asleep, lulled by the quarrelling of her companions, rolls over and stares in surprise.

Lesinge fixes his look on des Sables, who is equally startled. 'Did you say a spirit in black clothes? Wearing a veil? And speaking harshly?'

'Precisely,' des Sables says.

Lesinge twists his hands in his greasy hair. 'The black queen!' he says.

'It is better not to speak the names of such evil spirits. One does not know whether they are listening and will come at the—'

'SILENCE!' Lesinge roars, making the boy flinch. An angry murmur breaks out in the street below; some revellers have perhaps taken the cry as an insult against their patriotic singing. Lesinge does not care. He rubs his head in furious thought.

'My demon, my demon,' he mutters. 'What does this all mean?'

Cochonne shakes des Sables's shoulder. 'We should put him to bed,' she says. 'He is drunk and babbling.'

'Babbling?' Lesinge strikes a fist in his palm. 'There is more meaning in one word uttered by Gaspard Lesinge than in everything you have ever said.'

'Babbling and boasting,' Cochonne says. 'My father was the same when the wine got in his brain.'

'Tell me this, farmer's daughter. Who released me from the prison where you first found me? If you are the clever one, explain that.'

Cochonne's brow wrinkles in a sleepy frown.

'I came with the key,' she says.

'And found the door already open. So then, who opened it? You do not know. Gaspard has never told the world his secret. Well, now I tell you: I was freed by a spirit in the form of a woman, all in black, with a voice like stones grinding together. She called herself the black queen.'

Des Sables cannot be sure if it is his head spinning or the room where they sit. 'Is this true?' he asks Cochonne.

'Why ask me?'

'Oh, no,' Lesinge says. 'No, it is all lies. The truth is that I escaped prison by wearing the lock away with my teeth. Or was it a trick of magnetism? I cannot remember. Imbecile! Of course it is true. Why must I waste my speech on you?'

Cochonne pushes herself into a sitting posture, accompanied by desperate noises of protest from the bed. 'Does he mean,' she says to des Sables, 'that he was released from that dungeon by an evil spirit?'

'Evil?' Lesinge has begun to pace the room in agitation. 'No, she cannot have been evil. All was exactly as she said it would be. The carriage, the four horses, the day and the hour. Where then is the treasure?'

'My captain—'

'Be quiet, or go away! Your captain attempts to think. Chesspieces, chess-pieces . . .' He fumbles again inside his coat.

Des Sables turns to Cochonne. 'If this whole adventure was some device of the black queen, we ought to abandon it without delay.'

Cochonne yawns. 'I would rather sleep.'

'Ah!' des Sables exclaims in sudden alarm. The velvet bag has tumbled loose from Cochonne's voluminous clothes while she sat up. 'At least put that away!'

'What — my stone?' A comforting thought comes to her. 'My stone, blessed by Our Lady.' She picks up the bag.

'You are mad,' Des Sables says, 'if you imagine there is any blessing in that terrible thing.'

'The good priest assured me my vision was from Heaven.'

'Please, dear Cochonne, put it away. This priest of yours knows nothing of the demonoscope's nature. It will summon all the legions of hell to this earth.'

Cochonne smiles at him, turning the bag in her hands. 'It is you who know nothing, little boy. You are without faith.'

'Not this again!' Lesinge shouts. 'I forbid it!'

Another angry murmur comes from below the window. Oh, one forbids us? Who dares?

Des Sables throws up his hands. 'I only try to save you both from yourselves. But no one ever listens to me. Good night, my senseless companions.'

Lesinge has at last extracted the white queen from the recesses of his coat, though it is still all tangled in the chain of the locket. With clumsy fingers he tries to unpick the fine silver knots. Meanwhile Cochonne opens the velvet bag. Tonight she does not care about her temperamental companions. They have both had too much wine. She forgives them. She is full of warmth and favoured by Saint Mary herself. 'Blessed Virgin,' she murmurs to the stone. 'Teach these impious men to love you as I do.' She hears des Sables snort as he lies down.

She takes the stone from the bag and gives a great gasp of shock. It is colder than ice in her hands.

She drops it on the floor. The light of the candle sparkles for an instant over its rough surfaces and then is extinguished.

In the next instant there is a fourth person in the room, though it is a person made of shadow and glimmering mist. She stands, or floats, between the three brigands, each of whom has fallen back in amazement. She turns her spectral head one way and another as if her sudden appearance is just as surprising to her.

It is the same ghost as before, with long hair that seems dark, and interesting eyes, and a mild quizzical expression. Her ghost-clothing might be a plain dress with long sleeves.

'Madonna,' Cochonne says, under her breath.

'White queen?' Lesinge says, tugging his beard.

Des Sables says nothing, but squeezes his eyes shut and hopes that this episode will soon prove to have been no more than a delusion of wine.

As she did before, the ghost parts her fleshless lips. 'Hush,' Cochonne and Lesinge hiss, in the same moment. 'She speaks!' But it is quite impossible to distinguish words. There is some commotion on the stair of the inn beyond their door.

'Tell me what I must do, holy Virgin,' Cochonne says.

'Tell me where I must go, spirit,' Lesinge says. 'Still west?'

The ghost smiles. It is so tender an expression it makes Cochonne's eyes fill with tears. The lips move again, whispering.

'What the devil is that noise outside?' Lesinge exclaims. 'Curse them! I cannot hear her.'

Though her soul is overwhelmed with divine love, Cochonne is also becoming irritated at the tramping and knocking and shouting on the stairs. She clambers to her feet and picks up her rake. 'Excuse me, blessed Lady,' she says. 'I shall go and deal with this interruption.'

By now a small mob of insulted citizens has reached the door of the brigand's room. They have forced their way through the inn to the upper floor, seeking the contemptible reactionary who dared to cry for silence from his window while they were singing the famous chorus, *Oh! It will go, it will go!* There is only one room in the inn which overlooks that street, and now they have found it.

Just as their leader sets his shoulder to break it down, Cochonne flings it open, and the mob tumbles into the room, waving fists and sticks and falling over one another.

Then it is all flailing limbs and cries of fury and pain. Des Sables dives under the bed. As Cochonne sets about the intruders with her rake, Lesinge and the ghost look at one another. Her fascinating exotic eyes widen a little as though in amusement. He shrugs. Someone's foot kicks the stone under the bed where des Sables is; he squeaks in terror and throws a blanket on top of it. Immediately the ghost begins to fade, though already she had been hard to see among the mass of bodies succumbing to Cochonne's rage. What a theatre of chaos is this new France! — thinks Lesinge, while the assault of the patriots crumbles into bloodied retreat. Yet in the midst of it some higher power has chosen Gaspard to receive miracles and riches. He saw it clearly in her tranquil yet earnest face. His queen, he thinks, the fumes in his brain robing the thought in splendour: his white queen. Lesinge may only be her blinded knight, stumbling through the chaos, but he will follow her command. *West!*

'Are they gone?' says des Sables from under the bed, when the melee is over.

'Is she gone?' says Cochonne.

Lesinge sighs. It is a hard task, to be a leader of men.

CHAPTER SEVEN

Meanwhile —

We shall need the heads of *Hydra*, to continue our tale! — A single one will not do. All this wild roving, across the map of France! — and much of it, in contrary directions —

With one eye — the dexter — We must follow Miss Farthingay, bounced and rattled along the roads, as her rescuers race for an house of safety, on the Norman coast. — A place belonging to Lord Rawleigh, where the daring Forget-Me-Not has often retreated, to elude the jealous minions of France, and plan his adventures in secret. — God-speed!

Our sinister eye, separates itself, and turns west — Searching out Mr Tho.s Peach, whose progress we ought also to observe.

Some infection clouds it. — Or, some marsh-mists arise, that catch peculiar lights, and make the eye doubt the shapes it perceives. We know not what to make of the things we report. — Is that a bird, that appears to perch on Mr Peach's shoulder, and sometimes atop his hat? A black and crooked shape — A jackdaw, perhaps, that its cruel fellows have pecked and plucked — with twisted legs — But what bird ever had such *eyes*? — Like tiny coals ablaze —

What bird was ever gifted, since the long-spent age of hero and legend, with the power of speech?

Reader — if you are prompted to think of the *parrot* — You had better turn to the next chapter. There will be nothing here, to suit your sensibilities. — We offer the advice, in a friendly spirit.

Perhaps we linger yet, in the penumbra of Mr Peach's opiate visions. We could swear, the bird — the perching black thing, with its eyes of minuscule flame — Puts its beak at his ear from time to time, and croaks a few dark words.

To the west, where they ride, the sky is stormy. Thunders echo in the upper air.

— Thy master-mistress bids thee welcome — says the bird.

Mr Peach answers not — But rides on.

— Behold — says the bird, two or three miles further along the road — Here is one who may direct thee.

Mr Peach has come to an hollow, where the road dips between hills, overlooked by an huge twisted willow. Here is erected a simple frame of wood, to which is fastened the broken corpse of some poor villain, victim of peremptory justice, or feud, or revenge. — It matters not which — not to us, nor, any longer, to him. His head hangs limp and sodden, from his neck — His jaw, in turn, hangs half loose from his head.

Grisly spectacle! Though not unknown, in the wilder regions of France. — A barbaric practice, you may say. — Though, reader, you may pause to recollect the gibbets that decorated our British high-ways, and the gates of certain cities, not so very long ago.

Mr Peach's unwanted companion hops and flaps to the frame of wood, and fastens its beak in the dead man's hair — Hauling up the head, so that its ghastly sightless eyes seem to regard the traveller — Making it nod, as though in welcome.

The dangling jaw quivers, and begins to work —

We tell you no more than what we witness ourselves. Who will accuse us, of dreaming such a sight? — We have not the capacity for it. If we did, we would *never sleep* —

The corpse addresses Mr Peach, in rustic English, hoarse and strained. — Where bound, traveller?

— The Château Charizard, in the west, replies he, quite unmoved by the state of the questioner.

— At whose behest?

— At my own.

A death-rattle escapes the corpse's withered lips. Its hands and feet twitch.

— Speak true or get no answer. At whose behest?

Mr Peach sighs a little, as though the conversation were no worse than an inconvenience. — I am engaged to relieve an oppressed lady, by one who has devoted his heart to her, and desires her brought safely back to him.

The corpse screeches. — A sound we hope never to hear again, dream or no dream.

— Love? it says. — Devotion? Lies! You attend the summons of the Prince below. You are called by the Enemy Perpetual. Dread Satan commands, and you obey. Confess it! — The rotting head waggles furiously, shaken by the black bird's mouth.

Says Mr Peach — Is this charade quite necessary?

— Confess! repeats the corpse.

— Very well. — He shrugs. One day only in France, and already Mr Peach has adopted the shrug! — We guess, he is one of those travellers, peculiarly sensitive to local custom and habit, who absorbs the manners of the country without deliberate effort, as though by mesmerism. — Very well, he says. — It so happens that I go where your mistress desires me to go. Though I assure you the compliance is mere accident.

— My mistress? Your mistress, and your master!

Mr Peach bows.

— There is no accident, says the corpse. — All is fated.

Mr Peach thinks no reply necessary.

— Never will you find your lady, it says, with as much of a sneer, as an inanimate and partly decayed face may be imagined to assume.

Mr Peach closes his eyes. — Say your piece, he says, or do not. I shall ride on in a few moments. This pantomime is no more than indulgence on your part. It interests me very little.

— Seek the old forest called Huelgoat, the dead man says. — Find the cliff of granite at its heart.

Mr Peach tips his hat.

— When the Prince below has the stone, then the legions of hell will rise, and claim the lesser creation.

— No doubt, says Mr Peach. — Good-day to you.

He rides on, humming a tune. — *Lillabulero*, unless our ears deceive us —

Reader —

This scene just passed — And other scenes, shortly to come —

Perhaps even now, some querulous inward voice accompanies your perusal, of this second volume, in our partial history of Tho.s Peach, Esquire — which persists in saying — These grotesque fancies — Can such things have occurred, in plain material fact? — They cannot have — No — they cannot — &c.

Have you not yet understood, reader, that Mr Peach was a man, of *another time?* — And, we dare say, the *last* such man, there ever was, or will be — for one time is ended now, and another begun.

Lo! in plain words we have thus laid the secret of our tale before you — Yet, in passing only. It is to be grasped, by instinct — in a momentary flash — Or, not at all. — Reflexion avails you not, nor reason. Attempt to apply them, and you will discover — behold — our story dissolves, and becomes, *only a book*.

No — You must see, if you see at all, in the stroke of lightning. Brighter than day — and then — gone —

Says Mr Peach — I may just as easily enquire at the next town. And receive better directions in fewer words, I'm sure.

His dark crooked familiar has vanished from sight. There comes, nevertheless, an angry hiss in answer, emanating from the air. — Akin to those bodiless murmurs and exclamations, which troubled Miss Farthingay, on her visit to Widdershins Bank, in our former chapter.

— Indeed, Mr Peach continues, spying a pall of smoke over the next rise in the road, and two or three wet roofs, I shall employ that very course. Look, here is the town.

If we ever learn the name of the place, we do not intend to record it. — It is low, and dirty, like so many we have seen, since we crossed the water. That modest pride, which the English burgher and his goodwife take, in the impression their property leaves by its appearance, on neighbour and visitor alike, is a virtue not cultivated in France. All the town is the colour of mud and heavy clouds — as though it wished to hide itself for shame, among the bare fields, and under the dull sky.

It boasts, nevertheless, the two ornaments Mr Peach requires. — An inn, and a church.

The inn, he seeks for the usual reasons. — The church, from considerations quite peculiar and private.

Having established himself at the one, he makes his way in the direction of the other, as the bell begins to toll for evening prayer. Invisible whispers circle his head in agitation — Drawing no more notice, from the sullen townspeople, than Mr Peach already attracts in his mere person, for a traveller is no common sight here — Still more so, when his dress and bearing bespeak a degree of cultivation, quite foreign to so poor and backward a place. If odd noise emanates from his hat — bah! who knows what is to be expected, from strangers of that sort?

The noises cease as soon as Mr Peach comes under the shelter of the porch, and trouble him no more. — *This* is the reason, for his attendance at church — A practice he is known to shun, at home. His phantastical attendant cannot tolerate an house of worship. — Is compelled, to leave him in peace, for as long as he chuses to stay.

He takes a seat within, among old women with chickens, and those reduced to infirmity by a life of miserable labour. He watches the mumblings, and shufflings, and brandishings of this object or that, which together constitute a form of divine service — Ignoring the scowls, of the devoted — the squawks, of the chickens.

His eye is drawn to a figure of a death's-head, cowled, with a scythe in its bony grasp, all carved in a pillar of the church. — An unusual ornament, he thinks, in such a place. He goes to examine it — Provoking further baleful looks, to which he remains quite indifferent.

Once the lame curate has finished ministering to his ailing flock, he comes to greet the visitor. He is delighted to discover an

Englishman, for a pair of reasons. — First, because he knows the language, after a fashion. It is many years since he has been presented with the opportunity, to demonstrate his knowledge. — But also, because he feared that his evidently impious visitor, wearing the dress of a *bourgeois*, and having about him the air of the *philosophe*, might be some emissary of the new authorities. — This priest is one of the so-called *refractories* — those, who refused the oath of obedience to the civil constitution. He has been protected from any consequences, by the obscurity of his parish — but lives in daily expectation of arrest, or the confiscation of his office. He is therefore much relieved, to find the interloper in his church a mere Englishman. — Welcome at the house of God, milord, he says. The English, he remembers, are all lords, after some fashion. — For what reason is bring you between us?

Some polite conversation ensues. The exchange is immaterial. — Mr Peach's only concern, is to remain on holy ground, for some while longer, as, in times of old, the distressed and the hunted would claim sanctuary within consecrated walls.

He is, however, pleased to have the priest's explanation of the carved death's-head. He learns — and we learn with him — that the figure is named *Onkou*, and can be found, in several of the old churches of Brittany. According to the priest, the skeleton Onkou was placed there, by the antient architects, as a pious *memento mori* — though Mr Peach, observing the hollow eyes and grinning jaw, silently begs to differ. — He detects no orthodox feeling, in the image, but is reminded of those mysterious heads so often hiding in our English churches, whose mouths and ears sprout leaves — Relics, of *druidical* worship.

The good opinion of the priest, regarding his visitor, is unfortunately not shared, by civil society.

At the inn, the same prejudice takes general hold, to which we alluded a moment ago. — *viz.*, that the traveller must surely be a representative, of the new authorities — sent by some director, or intendant, or observer, in one of the great towns — Most probably for the purpose of raising new taxes, and arresting the good old priest.

The men of the town do not particularly care for either the king, or the revolution. All that is as it may be, and far away. They are Bretons. — They wish to lead Breton existences, without interference. That the *seigneurs* are cast down, is well and good, for the *seigneurs* were dogs of Parisians. But they will have no new *seigneurs*, of whatever sort.

They turn their backs on Mr Peach, in the ordinary of the inn. His wine is served without a word. — His room, that most favoured by the spiders of the house.

He decides he will not, after all, ask to be directed to the Château Charizard.

The hostility of the townspeople is otherwise of no concern. A few curmudgeonly looks, and some instances of rudeness, from perfect strangers, are nothing, compared to the oppressions which throng upon him, in the privacy of his own brain. — Regrets, and torments — omens of dark futurity — His constant companions, since he was compelled to give up his nightly transaction, with the unquiet spirit of Mrs Peach. For alleviation of his inward sufferings, the only recourse is laudanum — Which, when it does not render him as insensate as stone, has at least the power, to invest his mental turmoil with visionary grandeur. While the spiders and lice bustle about his bed, he dreams of storms in the west — Crags and battlements of sable cloud, riven with thunders — Into which he flies, like a wandering sea-bird snatched by an *hurricane*, and overwhelmed, though never destroyed — A perpetual subjugation, without final defeat. *Behold*, cries the thunder, *what awaits thee eternally!*

While he lies prey to these visions, the men of the town decide, in conference, that it will be best to deal with the unwelcome emissary, while he is but one man.

Home they go, and gather cudgels, and ropes, and the planks and nails required, to construct a simple frame of wood.

In the morning Mr Peach pays his bill without complaint, though it is as naked an act of robbery, as was ever committed — Remounts the mule, which has enjoyed rather better hospitality — And rides on, the ascending sun at his back, pulling his travelling cloak tight against a cold wind.

Some half an hour after his departure, the men of the town assemble. — Or, certain representatives of their number — their deputies, one might say, selected as those most suited, to carry out the will of the majority. The principal consideration for selection, is brutishness — Which quality the assembled men possess in abundance, to judge by appearances. They have also included among their party, a carpenter, to construct the simple frame of wood.

They ride after Mr Peach, at first at a walking pace — Then, as the poor farm-land and stunted orchards give way to heath and gorse, with more haste.

There is a particular place — wild, and far from the sight of man — where they intend to overtake the stranger.

Dark clouds roil in the west. — More than once, muffled thunder erupts — Louder, we fancy, than it did yester-day. Mr Peach's mule plods on, heedless of these omens, until it approaches the appointed place — By which time, the sounds of pursuit are unmistakable.

Mr Peach draws the animal to a stop, and turns in the saddle.

Some six or eight villains ride into view. — An excessive number, we think, for the murder of one Englishman, and he quite unarmed, and entered upon his middle years. Why does Mr Peach not set his heels to the mule, urging it to flight? — He must yet be under the influence of his stupefying draughts. No expression of terror appears on his face. He is just as he has been, each time our narrative has attended him, in this second volume of ours. — Sunk in strange lassitude — like a ship becalmed, in an immense ocean — As though the world, and all its concerns, were infinitely distant. — Resigned, we would say, to his fate — whatever it may be.

There seems little doubt on that score, in the present instance. What hope has one defenceless Englishman, against six or eight French blackguards with knives and cudgels, bent on his murder?

You, reader, who feel by *tact* the deep order of our narrative — You know otherwise. We need hardly assure *you*, that Mr Peach's fate is not to be determined, by a gang of vicious peasants. You have stood at his grave, and seen inscribed, in unalterable stone, the year of his death — Two decades and more beyond the year 'ninety-one.

The would-be murderers slow their pace as they come nearer. They leer, and grin, and exchange laughing words, which we are pleased to say we cannot understand. There will not be the smallest shew of questioning their victim — No pretence of justice, however perfunctory. — No — Remember, this is France — founded for centuries upon arbitrary tyranny, and, at the time of our tale, shortly to embark on an exercise of *judicial* slaughter, beyond the dreams of any tyrant.

Murder is, in effect, the custom of the land. —

Mr Peach lifts his hat.

The men of the town smirk, and raise their cudgels, and unwrap their lengths of rope.

Now — reader — We shall tell you, as exactly as we are able, what you would see and hear, were you present at the scene in your own person. — Has that not been our constant purpose? and is it not the mere duty, of the historian?

There comes a scream, from the empty air. — Something between a scream, and the rending of wood, or the breaking of a colossal wave, upon an high cliff.

In the next instant Mr Peach is enveloped by — *wings* — A pair, or perhaps several pairs, of coal-black wings, vaster than the eagle's, and beating in phrenzied motion. From amid this instantaneous apparition of roaring shadows, an head appears, of similarly gigantic proportions — With a snapping beak, and a pair of eyes that burn with infernal flame. The dreadful phantom lunges towards the six or eight men, trumpeting its horrific cry.

We need hardly say, that the murderous brutes turn tail as one, dropping ropes and cudgels in the road, and galloping back to town with all possible expedition. No spurs are needed, to propel their horses to so desperate a pace — for the animals are quite as witless with terror, as their riders.

So much for them. — We are sorry we allowed such a pack of villains even these few pages' attendance in our narrative, and are as pleased as Mr Peach himself, to see them dismissed from it. — We do not enquire too deeply, into the *method* of their banishment. They deserve no better. — Their future course lies, thank Heaven! outside the sphere of our concern. — Though it pleases us to picture them all killing one another, in the civil broils to come.

A voice murmurs in Mr Peach's ear — or, in his waking dream —

— Thus all mortals will quail in your presence, when great Satan rules this world, and raises you vice-regent.

— That will be very inconvenient, says Mr Peach, to the maintenance of wholesome society.

— Didst not thrill to it?

He coughs. — I am certainly grateful for the demonstration, he says, in this instance, but I cannot in candour say it gave any pleasure.

Again the distant thunder beckons. — He resumes his journey, in sturdy silence.

We must leave him to enjoy — or, to endure — his progress, unobserved. There are things, unfit for the eye of our narrative — even its *sinister* eye.

Only one other incident we cannot forbear noting. It is of a certain historical — perhaps, prophetic — interest. —

On another barren length of road, amid country so poor and unmanageable, that it is deserted even by the old women gathering sticks, Mr Peach is surprized, by a rare occurrence. — Another traveller — mounted on an horse, and coming in the opposite direction.

The traveller is cloaked, and hooded, and bears a reaper's scythe, with a long-crooked handle, which he carries with the curve of its blade resting at his back. His horse, when it approaches near enough to be closely observed, is a thing so gaunt and grey, that Mr Peach is astonished it walks at all. It is caparisoned in tattered rags, which seem equally composed of shadow and cloth. — The horse's own substance, as much sinew and bone as flesh.

As Mr Peach passes, the rider raises his head under his hood, and nods courteously. It is a *death's-head* — A fleshless and eyeless skull, upon a neck of bones. The hand that holds the scythe, and the other, which commands the reins of the cadaverous beast, are likewise those of a skeleton, from which the living substance has long rotted away.

Mr Peach touches his hat.

— Monsieur *Onkou*, I presume? says he.

— The very same, says the skeletal rider.

— What brings you out on the public road, if I may be so bold as to enquire?

— I ride to Paris, says the other. — They will soon have need of me there.

— Then I wish you a good journey, monsieur, says Mr Peach, bowing politely.

— And I also, monsieur, the death's-head answers. — The exchange of civilities is complete — They pass one another by.

'Escaped?'

Deputy Denfert unsheathes the word like an assassin's knife.

It is after midnight. Rain clatters the high room of his lodgings. All the day Paris has been under assault; hail and bitter winds, downpours to make the Seine foam. People hold pamphlets over their heads as they come and go. The streets are veined with dissolving ink.

Though publications still pour from the cellars of the city no one now reads. The time for words is over. Paper may sustain a fire for a few minutes, or resist the rain for less time. Otherwise there is no use for it. A new revolution is preparing, one with less declaiming of speeches and more chopping of heads.

The people slink about the palace of the Tuileries, staring at the royal apartments like hungry jackals.

Denfert loves this hunger, this rage. He is less often seen in the chamber of the deputies, and heard there not at all. One finds him instead on the streets. He appears at the shoulder of those who stare. He nods towards the windows of the mansions where firelight gleams against glass. Those ones, they are still warm, he murmurs in that thin voice of his, like a woman's voice. They still have bread, while your little ones starve. How much longer, citizen?

Denfert is discreet and insinuating like the serpent in Eden. Like the serpent, he prepares catastrophe.

This night, though, he is as furious as the weather.

'How, escaped?'

In the high room with the chequerboard floor there is no candle. Moon and stars are obliterated by cloud; in any case the shutters are closed. But the darkness is not quite complete. A barely perceptible glow emanates from somewhere, like embers. It may be that the charred squares of the floor are about to burn again, for what light there is seems to arise from below, like deep-buried volcanic flames glimpsed through fissures in black rock.

The minion of Denfert crouches on a burnt square. As before she is all shadow, and veiled. She cowers as though threatened by a crushing weight.

'It was the Forget-Me-Not,' she says, in her grotesque parody of French speech.

'What?' Denfert stands somewhere by the window, cloaked in darkness.

'The Forget-Me-Not. An infamous Englishman who adopts disguises and rescues priests and nobles. You must have heard the stories, mistress.'

'Master!'

'Master.'

'He rescues priests, did you say?'

'Yes.'

'And why, worm, does he do that?'

'I do not know.'

'Is it because he is a man of religion? A slave of God?'

'I do not know. No one knows who he is. He is always disguised.'

'If he is a slave of God, should you not have destroyed him long before now? Or have you been allowing the slaves of God to go free in the north all this time, while I thought you served me? You, my priest-killer?'

'If I could find him, master, I would have destroyed him in an instant. But he has a thousand faces. He is everywhere and nowhere — Ah!' The veiled woman cries out in pain. She has felt the weight descend on her.

'I do not wish,' Denfert says, while his minion draws breath through clenched teeth, 'to hear the praises of this lackey of the old tyrant.'

The cowering woman gasps an apology.

'He serves priests and nobles, is it so?'

'Master — please—'

'Priests and nobles?'

'Yes!' shrieks the minion, as though the confession had been forced from her by torture.

'Then, my ill-omened blackbird, answer this: what had he to do with the Farthingay, who is neither priest nor noble?'

The woman shudders and gathers herself. The weight has relented for a moment.

'Answer well,' Denfert adds, 'for I am displeased with you. Your existence is only at my pleasure. It hangs now by a thread.'

The black-garbed woman speaks slowly, choosing her words with care, or perhaps with fear.

'It is possible that the Forget-Me-Not was acquainted with this Farthingay in England. He is known to be a gallant of that country. I suppose he learned she was in distress and went to relieve it.'

'And who says the Farthingay was in distress? My explicit command was that she be attended to with every comfort. Water and food and a bed to sleep in. Things of that nature. I most sincerely hope my instructions were followed precisely, or it will not only be you who endures my anger.'

'Master.' The minion hesitates to answer. Denfert, however, waits silently, and she must continue. 'I observed the convent where you sent her, exactly as you told me to. It is possible . . . I had a certain impression . . . that Bella — that Miss Farthingay — might perhaps have resented the confinement.'

Now Denfert's tone is indignant as well as enraged. 'I informed her in my letter that she need only wait there a few days. I gave exact commands. Was the letter not delivered? Did she omit to read it?'

'Perhaps,' says the minion in a whisper, 'she misunderstood? Her temper appears wilful—'

'Disobedience!' Denfert roars, though his voice is not formed for roaring. 'I will not have it!'

'No, master.'

'You. You!' The mysterious radiance burns hotter, as if one had breathed on the embers. 'Your task was to attend the Farthingay. The bargain I made for the demonoscope was to be impeded and delayed no more. In that single task you have utterly failed.'

'I know it,' she says.

'Do you understand what it means to oppose my will?'

'Yes,' she croaks.

'For you it is annihilation. It is effacement. You will be unwritten. You will become nothing. A page without words. You will not even be given the mercy of eternal fire. You will cease on the instant to exist at all. There will not even be regret, perpetual pain and hopelessness. There will be *nothing*. You will *not be*.'

There is a long silence.

'How dreadful,' the woman says at last. She sounds more composed. 'The threat appals me. Spare me that fate, I beg you.'

'Then explain to my satisfaction how you let the Farthingay escape a second time.'

'Forgive me, mistress — Master! I went to her cell myself, more than one night, to confirm that she was secure under lock and key. I went also to the gate of the convent and ensured it was barred and watched. Then I went to rest. You know I must sometimes sleep. I have a mortal body. While I was asleep the Forget-Me-Not entered the place in disguise, by some trickery, obtained the key, and stole her away.'

Denfert says nothing. The rain drums, *rat-a-tat*.

'All across the north,' the woman says nervously, 'one hears such stories. His cunning is legendary. If I had known he was coming for Bella — for Miss Farthingay — I would not have slept, but watched day and night. Even then he might have defeated my vigilance. They say his disguises can deceive a man's own mother. He has the stealth and speed of the panther. Many people say his powers have a supernatural — Ah!'

Denfert slams his fist on the table, scattering flocks of paper. Once more his minion writhes in invisible pain.

'Find him!' screams the deputy. The room is suddenly hot as a fire. Papers smoulder and smoke. 'Find him and have him hanged!'

'Mercy, omnipotent one!'

'I leave tomorrow for the north,' Denfert says, tight with fury. 'This slave of God is to be in chains and condemned by the time I arrive. Condemned or already killed. Or else you are eternally undone.'

'Dread prince—'

The woman rises to stand, although unwillingly. Unseen hands have laid hold of her and lifted her up. She goes on rising. Her feet lift from the smoking floor. She is suspended in the air.

'Go now. You have two days.'

'Return already? I am tired, master, so tired — ah!'

Her form begins to dissolve.

'Back to the north. I send you now. Begone.'

'No!' she cries as she fades. The encroaching shadows torment her. 'I must — I must—'

'You,' Denfert hisses, 'must only *obey*.'

She is vanished. The subterranean fires fade; the room is dark.

In the old towns of France one is never far from a house of worship. The inn at Dinan where Lesinge and his company passed a turbulent night stands straight across the square from the imposing church of Basilique Saint Sauveur. Contemplating the view from the window, des Sables has an inspiration.

'I will prove to you,' he says to Cochonne, 'that the apparition was not the Madonna.'

'It was the Madonna,' she says.

Lesinge covers his throbbing head and moans.

Des Sables's former master used to mock him for his lack of education. My eyes are tired tonight, boy, he would say, reclining in a brocade chair with some depraved book. Read this passage to me, will you? 'Sir, you know very well your servant reads with great difficulty.' Well, but my eyes are so very sore. And des Sables would be compelled to stumble over the words while the Sir sniggered and rolled his eyes, and the text would always be some lewdness which the Sir would delight in forcing him to repeat. Did you not learn this word from the old village dame, des Sables? Devil! — how ignorant you are!

But des Sables is not stupid. He has seen much of the world, much more than his companions who mock him for being a rich man's slave. At his old master's side he was admitted to the great salons of Paris and listened to the conversation of people notorious for their wit. He has seen London, in England, where even common people sometimes go in carriages and every house has glass in the windows and poor children wear shoes. Des Sables is no bumpkin, raised in sheds and fields like a cow.

His opinion is for Paris. He is resolute and also logical. If this whole project of their captain's was concocted by an infernal spirit, as Lesinge now concedes, self-evidently it ought to be abandoned. Instead they should make their way to the capital, the centre of France and the world, where the revolution is. This revolution, his master used to say: people write that it will make the servants into masters and the masters servants. Would you like that? Would you be pleased to dress me in a velvet blindfold and use me as a man uses a woman? Oh, how he laughed at his chattel des Sables! And now he is dead in a ditch while des Sables lives free. Evidently the revolution is working. In Paris, he urges his companions, they will no longer be peasants and thieves. The changing of France will lift them up among the great.

Cochonne remains obstinate. In the frame of a hero she has the soul of a superstitious old woman. The priest she went to see has turned her head. Cochonne says the revolution is impious and the blessed Virgin has returned to keep people in the path of their old faith. She will not hear of Paris.

Des Sables says that if it is a time of wickedness, does that not make it more certain that the vision emanating from his master's stone is a demon?

Cochonne says that it is in times of wickedness that saints and angels appear to show the true path.

Des Sables says that if that is so, hell, being the most wicked place, ought to be full of saints and angels, which is contradictory in logic.

Cochonne tells him to put his logic in his arse.

Lesinge, whose head feels like a log of wood being sawn in two, puts his hands over his ears and wishes them both in hell, or up their arses, or anywhere but arguing noisily in his room.

Then des Sables's eye falls on the porch of Saint Saviour and inspiration strikes him.

'Come,' he says, 'both of you. I will prove it.'

He leads them across the square, filthy with the remnants of last night's revels, and under the porch, where a painted sign is suspended between the crowned heads of two ancient kings of Israel, reading REASON — JUSTICE — LIBERTY.

Inside, a great tricolour hangs in the nave. A few old people shuffle about. They stop to stare at des Sables as everyone does everywhere. He ignores it. He goes up and down the aisles until he finds the chapel he seeks. A number of candles are lit there, assisting his purpose. The illumination is poor, but not so bad that the painting above the little altar cannot be seen.

Cochonne gawks. Poor simple child, des Sables thinks, she has not often seen such a place. To him, who has visited the temples of Paris, it is nothing. Even Lesinge looks at the painting without understanding its significance. The captain boasts of his wit, but, des Sables reminds himself, he is a common thief, who has lived by roaming from wild to wild in the manner of unwanted dogs.

'That is a picture of the Madonna,' des Sables says. 'Every church of significance has a chapel with such a picture.'

Cochonne frowns.

'How do you know?'

He sighs a little. 'See how she holds the infant Jesus on her lap, and her head is circled with light to show that she is a saint. Ask the priest if you have any doubt.'

'We are not fools,' Lesinge grumbles, still rubbing his head. 'Of course that is a picture of Saint Mary.'

'Well then. As you observe, she is quite plainly fair-haired with a white complexion and a smiling well-fleshed face, and wears old drapery of a blue colour. I have seen many similar pictures in the Paris churches. They are incomparably more fine there of course, but they all agree. Saint Mary was a blonde woman with the features of a beautiful French girl.'

Cochonne looks crestfallen. She can see as clearly as her companions that the painting is nothing at all like the apparition in the stone.

'Consider another point,' des Sables says, in a kindly manner, for he is fond of Cochonne and regrets having to disappoint her. 'It is plain from the Bible that the Virgin spoke French. Everyone knows the words she exchanged with the angel. But we are all agreed that the demon in the stone does not speak French. You, captain, have tried twice to understand its instructions and concede that you cannot.'

Cochonne is terribly disheartened. She goes to the priest and asks whether it is true that the picture des Sables shows them is really the Madonna. She would tell him about her vision but she does not warm to him. He is not like the handsome curate in the sheepfold, so passionate in faith! This one stands like a particularly unctuous innkeeper, holding his hands together while he explains that Mary represents the domestic and feminine virtues such as calmness of temper, obedience, and the maintenance of a good household, as well as being the paragon of motherhood, which is the first and greatest civic duty of a woman. He addresses them all as *citizen*.

Soon they are forced to leave the church. Too many urchins approach des Sables and ask if he is Jesus. Cochonne trudges unhappily across the square.

'I will not go to Paris,' she says, 'no matter what. And in my heart I still believe.'

'To believe contrary to the evidence of your eyes cannot be true faith,' des Sables says, 'or why did Jesus demonstrate miracles? It is logic.'

'I will still not go to Paris.'

'It need not be Paris at first. Any good city would do for people such as us. One with distinguished houses and good inns.' He wrinkles his nose at the square: its spilled filth, its debris of paper streamers and flowers trampled in the cobbles, the six or seven men still asleep in their coats under the sky, too drunk to move from where they fell over. 'The great city of Brittany is called Rennes, and lies not far away.' Des Sables has never set eyes on Rennes. He has no idea where Rennes is. 'We could go that way initially.'

Cochonne looks at Lesinge.

'What do you say? You are not usually so quiet. Or are you still drunk?'

Lesinge is not drunk. His head may beat like the gongs of the Asiatic emperors, but it takes more than a pitcher of bad wine to impair the genius of Gaspard. Drunk? To the contrary. His self-possession is remarkable. All morning he has listened while Cochonne and des Sables parlay back and forth. A general must be sensitive to the tides of influence. Let the subordinates express their thoughts while it does not matter. When the time arrives that they exhaust themselves and turn to him, that is when the leader of men stands and is decisive.

He clears his throat, *pfah*.

'What do I say, my friends? I say it is time to fetch Broubrou and make our way out of this town, before any friends of the wretches you chased from our room in the night take it upon themselves to expel us.'

'But which way shall we go?' says des Sables. 'To Rennes, or perhaps to Paris herself?'

'Never,' Cochonne says.

Lesinge stretches his back. 'You were not persuaded by the boy's demonstration, my dear Cochonne?'

Cochonne mumbles something inaudible.

'My demonstration was unarguable,' des Sables says. 'The apparition cannot be Saint Mary. Therefore we should ignore it and put the demonoscope away as an evil relic, as I have said many times.'

'Hum,' Lesinge says, stroking his beard. 'Unarguable? Those painters who decorated the church there, in days past; who were they, I wonder?'

Cochonne and des Sables look at one another.

'Old artisans of the town,' Lesinge says, 'with their smocks and brushes. Honest Bretons! Masters, one imagines, in some famous school of painters. I envisage the mayor of this town in those days, with his soft velvet hat and chain of office. He writes to the famous school: Sirs, we in Dinan beg you send us a great man of your guild to paint our church of Saint Saviour, for we desire a picture of the Madonna that will make the people of the next town bitter with envy. Ah, worthy old official!'

'Drunk after all,' Cochonne says, with a shake of her mighty head.

Lesinge snaps his fingers to compel their attention. 'Tell me, des Sables, since you are so fond of logic. Did that painter ever set eyes on Mary, who lived in the Holy Land, one thousand seven hundred and ninety-one years ago? Well? Did he? No, my friend, logic tells us he did not.'

Des Sables looks as though he might be about to protest. Lesinge sweeps his arm for attention as the masters of rhetoric do.

'Someone says to this painter, Give me a Madonna! What does he do? Does he go to the Virgin and ask her to sit before his easel? No. He tells himself, I shall copy the most beautiful image of motherhood that exists in my imagination. So he paints a fair smiling girl with rosy cheeks, because that is the beauty he has seen in the pretty young wives of Lille or Dieppe, and he dresses her in a blue robe, to prevent her from looking too like just such a girl. There! That is their Madonna.'

Cochonne begins to nod. She is slow as a river of shit, Lesinge has observed, but she gets where she is going.

'Here is some more logic for you,' he says. 'Mary herself was a Jew.'

Cochonne gapes.

Lesinge smirks at her. 'You imagine she was a Christian? But how can she have been, when she was born before Christ?'

'Our Lady is not a Jew,' Cochonne says, flexing her fingers.

'Let us put it differently,' says Lesinge, who like every good general knows when he must adjust his course a little. 'Let us agree what is unarguable, which is that Mary the mother of Jesus lived one thousand eight hundred years ago in the Holy Land, which is adjacent to Jerusalem where the Jews and paynims are, and very far indeed from France.'

He allows them both a moment to dispute if they can. It is of course impossible.

'Therefore, whatever the true face of the Madonna — and neither you, nor I, nor the old painters ever set eyes on her — it was not the face of a pretty French girl.'

His meaning is at last descending on Cochonne.

'The Madonna was dark like a Jew,' she says. 'Though not a Jew.'

'Precisely.'

'But—' des Sables begins.

'One final point of logic,' Lesinge says. He is enjoying himself. The boy thinks he is so clever. As if a child with a girl's hands could alter the course of Gaspard Lesinge, leader of men! 'Though the Bible is written in French, it comes to us translated by various wise old scholars. If they do not even speak French in England, or Austria, or the Low Countries, which are all adjacent to France, do you imagine it is the language of the Holy Land, which is far away beyond mountains and seas and deserts?'

'Hah!' Cochonne exclaims. 'Only an idiot would think so!'

It is des Sables's turn to be downcast.

'My dear child,' Lesinge says to him. He puts an arm around the boy's drooping shoulders. 'Your demonstration was ingenious but faulty. You are young. It is excusable.'

'My heart always knew it was the Virgin I saw,' Cochonne says.

Lesinge wags a finger at her. 'I, your captain, do not say that. Nothing is yet certain. I have in mind certain experiments which may determine further. But in the meantime: we continue west.'

Though he was born in the gutter and raised to nothing better than dirt, Gaspard Lesinge is a man of the new age.

He has been freed from imprisonment and certain hanging by a demon, in the form of a woman dressed all in black? Very well. He does not surrender his reason or go running to the priests or say the Lord's Prayer backwards. He reflects on the event, as the men of today do.

He has twice seen a ghostly woman appear out of a crystal of dubious provenance? If he has, he has. His eyes have witnessed many things during his eventful existence. This one, like those, is neither to be feared nor worshipped, but merely to be considered as an event in the course of things.

There are magic chess-pieces in the world? It surprises him, admittedly. But if it is true, it is true. Some say that chess is a game of reason and rules; others, that it has occult significance. If at this moment the world is poised between superstition and enlightenment, then Gaspard will balance with it, and look both ways when he must.

Above all he remains calm.

They leave the town without incident. There will be questions about the riot at the inn, but not until everyone involved has recovered. By that time Lesinge and his companions are long gone.

Over the next two days he makes various attempts to produce the phantom from the stone. By the systematic application of trial and experiment he discovers the conditions which must be met before the ghost will appear. There must be the light of flame — candle, lantern or fire — to fall on the stone and arouse its inner luminescence. Also — an unexpected curiosity, but proved by the scientific method — the silver locket, purloined from the woman in the carriage, must be in his hand. He had assumed the locket was a trifle. It contains only a length of black hair and a single tooth; most probably, Lesinge thinks, mementos of a dead child. But the apparition will not come without it.

By the end of the second day Lesinge can bring the ghost before them as easily as calling the donkey. He teaches his companions to be quiet when she comes so he can strain to hear her whisperings. Cochonne kneels before her. The joy that comes over her in those moments is indescribable.

Des Sables has to concede that the ghost is gentle, with an appearance and manner in no point demonic.

Perhaps, he thinks, it is really true that the character of the stone has changed now his evil master is dead.

The legend of the family de Charizard tells how they were bound to Satan for all their generations in perpetuity. But the late Sir de Charizard has no children, or at least none that he acknowledges or bears his name. It occurs to des Sables that the family line may be formally extinguished and the curse therefore ended, in which case the demonoscope may have lost its infernal character.

The speculation is logical. It pleases him.

He is partly reconciled to the westward journey. His demeanour improves.

I have managed the boy with genius, thinks Lesinge.

There is one curiosity that continues to puzzle des Sables, though he keeps it to himself. He does not want to be schooled again and have his ignorance mocked.

It is nevertheless a matter of simple fact that he has been to London and his captain has not. Listening to the obscure rustle of the apparition's whispers, des Sables cannot rid himself of a suspicion that the words the ghost attempts are . . . *English?*

CHAPTER EIGHT

Lord Rawleigh is — we must have remarked it before now — a very rich man.

For generations, the first-born Rawleighs have been diligent in acquiring wealth, and more wealth. Not for them, dissolution and indulgence! — nor the pursuit, of vain and uncertain *preferment* — that insubstantial phantasm, subject to the whims of monarchs, and the quicksands of fortune. — No — They have always been country men, attached to the good old earth of England, and other solid possessions. — Things measured by number and dimension — which increase in plain fashion, like quantities in arithmetic. One purchases an estate, or comes into it, by a well-judged marriage, and lo! there is *more* land, counted in honest acres, and *more* income, received in coin of the realm. One incloses — improves — puts up the rent — sells the fruits of the earth, at an higher price — And so it goes on, in happy perpetuity, while other noble families dance to the uncertain tune of fashion and fame.

The Rawleighs are not spoken of, as those families are. They will not be raised to dukedoms. Some whisper, they are *rustic* fellows. —

But what is true nobility, if not *magnificence*? And what is magnificent, except visible splendour? — a finer house, than other houses — more acreage of wheat and pasture, than other estates — more men, to toil on the said acreage. Better equipage — more plate, and silver, and china — Overabundance, every where. — An happy profusion of those things, which money may buy, in

contradistinction to mere fame, which is a property too nebulous
to be safely purchased, counted, and sold.

On coming into his inheritance, at an unexpectedly tender age
— barely arrived at his majority — The present Lord Rawleigh
turned his eyes to France — A nation for which he had long
nurtured certain attachments, quite romantic in character. His
agents purchased an estate, in the northern regions of the country,
convenient to crossings by sea from those shires, where the
Rawleighs have been established since antient times — And two
or three properties besides, suited to the private pleasures of a
gentleman.

Among these latter acquisitions is a provincial mansion, in the
classical French stile, built originally by the Comte de____ as a
retreat from Paris, at the time when that distinguished nobleman
was advised by his doctors, to take up natural bathing.

Other mansions have been raised nearby, on this part of the
Norman coast. — The doctor, we suppose, had become
fashionable at court.

In our present season, when autumn and winter mingle, and
not even Hippocrates or Galen could persuade a man of leisure,
to try cold-water bathing, the houses are left to their keepers, to
chase away owls and children, and scrape salt drops from the
windows.

One of these keepers sits by the gate at the road, as the early
dusk draws on.

He is a long-limbed fellow, with more than a little of the
scarecrow about his appearance. He goes by the name of Vieux
Bidouphe. — Though he cannot be above five-and-thirty — which
perhaps marks him as one who was always called *Old*, even when
young, in consequence of a chearless or lugubrious character.

We do not know for certain. We are not privy to the man's
history. — We merely amuse ourselves, in speculation. — It is a
dull evening.

The road is quite deserted. The man sits. — We must take our
amusements, where we find them.

As to *why* Old Bidouphe sits there, with a single lamp hanging from an iron hook at the gate, though there is nothing to watch by its light except dead leaves hurrying before the wind — reader, only one explanation can be imagined — He has been commanded to.

No one, however chearless, would take up such a station voluntarily, when they might instead be within-doors, by the fire.

He grumbles, and shivers, and sips from a bottle.

It is, to his disgust, the only bottle he is provisioned with. — Otherwise, *ma foi!* he would not content himself, with *sipping.* Milord keeps the key to the cellar himself. Old Bidouphe has not yet discovered a means to open the door, or otherwise approach the mansion's hoard of wine and brandy, without it — Though not for want of trying.

It follows, that the unwilling watchman is not drunk. — And therefore, has no reason to doubt his eyes, when a most unlikely traveller comes into view, emerging from the deep shadows under the poplar-trees.

The wanderer appears to be a solitary woman, of some elegance, in deep mourning. This Old Bidouphe deduces from her deportment, which is upright and deliberate, like that of the *bourgeoises*, and her dress, which is black in every particular, a veil included. — So thoroughly black, that the lady's approach was quite invisible to him in the murk, until she came to a point only a few yards along the road to the south.

She has neither horse, nor companion, nor any attendant, but merely walks along in the dirt, quite alone. She has not even a light.

It is several miles to town, and the road will soon be dark. — Any man of charity, would interest himself in the predicament of such a traveller. — Would he not?

Old Bidouphe sits and stares without a word — Wishing the woman, and every body else, to the Devil. He is commanded to watch. Therefore he will watch — and, only watch. Milord gave no instruction, what he is to watch *for* — Nor what he is to do, should he see it. The whole of his duty is circumscribed, in the act of sitting in his wooden chair, at the gate, without falling asleep. Every thing else — To the Devil with it!

The *bourgeoise* in her mourning dress comes across the road, and, without the least acknowledgment of Old Bidouphe, peers between the bars of the gate, as though to inspect the drive, and look for the mansion beyond, though the house is concealed from the road by trees. — She appears as indifferent to his existence, as he wishes he could be to hers — though her bold approach to the very limit of the property, has unfortunately now rendered it impossible to ignore her.

He growls some few words, in what the French call a *patois*, or rustic dialect, impenetrable to us. We think we detect some reference, to a *private estate*. — The meaning of his rough gesture, indicating the north-ward road, cannot be missed — *There lies your way, madame — Be off with you.*

— Have you seen a cart pass this way? the woman asks — without introduction, or any preface whatsoever. — Perhaps she is determined to be Old Bidouphe's equal, in abruptness. Her language we decipher without difficulty, for her French is almost as plain and clumsy, as our own.

This mourning woman must be a foreigner — as well as travelling alone in the road, afoot, at dusk. — Curious specimen!

Old Bidouphe spits in the road and shakes his head.

— A cart, the woman continues, carrying several men, and one woman.

Says the ill-tempered watchman — I have seen nothing at all.

The woman points inside the gate, to where a cart is visible, drawn up beside an handsome brick stable. On her hand she wears a black velvet glove.

— A cart, she says, very like that one there.

Old Bidouphe straightens his back, and makes a show of turning to look at the cart, before resuming his station facing the road. He speaks slowly and loudly, for the benefit of the intrusive foreigner — thereby permitting us, reader, to render the whole exchange in translation, for your benefit — We supply certain flourishes of our own, when necessary, but assure you, that every significant point is recorded with intire precision.

— No, he says, I have seen no such thing.

The woman continues to stare in the gate, as though it were broad daylight, and she the mistress of the property.

— Whose house is this?

— Not yours, says Old Bidouphe. — Yours must be further along the road. You should keep walking until you reach it.

The veiled head for the first time turns towards him directly. He can see nothing of the visage behind. — He feels it is a carved figure that addresses him — one of the church statues, with their antient faces worn blank. A chill runs through him.

— I have heard, the sinister woman says, that one of these houses belongs to a milord of England.

— What you have heard is no concern of mine.

— I have heard he does not pay his servants as well as good servants should be paid.

Old Bidouphe is silent.

— They say, she continues, in her ugly voice, That this milord is also not generous with his wine.

Old Bidouphe looks at the single bottle near his feet. Whether the woman also observed it, he cannot say. It is impossible to know where her eyes are directed — Or even — the thought comes unbidden, and makes him shudder — Whether she possesses eyes, at all.

Already the evening is on the verge of night.

— Is it true? the woman asks.

He shrugs.

— My husband is dead, says the strange mourner. — I inherit his house, which is nearby, and has three cellars, each with an hundred bottles.

— May he rest in peace, says Old Bidouphe.

— Myself, I do not like wine.

Not a speck of natural flesh shows anywhere on the figure before Old Bidouphe. All is pitch-black cloth, velvet, and lace — Now barely distinct, from the night air.

— I have need of a new house-keeper, she says. — On winter evenings such as this one, he would be required to sit by the fire and drink the stores of wine, until they are all used up.

Old Bidouphe does not know what to say.

— Which is the house of the English milord? I wish to go there and look for a servant who is in need of a better master.

Old Bidouphe is suffering a strange burning sensation, in his mouth and heart. — A sudden intensity of desire, for wine — A species of *intellectual* longing, astonishing to him, whose whole inward life has for years consisted merely of general and settled resentment.

— It may be, he says, that this is the milord's house.

The woman watches unmoving for several moments. — Then produces a coin, from within the black drapery, and holds it out to shine under the lantern.

— I wish you a good-night, she says, and drops it in his hand. He squints at it — looks up again — She is gone, vanished in the shadows on the road, as though she never was.

What valuables does the house possess, whose entrance is thus guarded, though the hour is late, and the situation remote? — beyond the contents, of its cellar?

Nothing, we hope, of great price — Or else, a better watchman would be required.

It is a melancholy place — As any dwelling is, when seldom occupied. Life and society are to an house, as youth to the human frame. They give it animation — beauty — freshness — In their absence, a pall settles, and signs of decay impress the senses. — One cannot help but think, of the eventual ruin.

Though the furniture is elegant, each piece is draped in coarse cloth. The hangings are taken down from window and wall, and wrapped, and stored in closets of cedar-wood, to discourage moths. Great branched candlesticks stand, with only two or three pillars of wax alight and guttering, where there ought to be twenty. The fire-places are shut up with boards. Bats clatter up and down the cold chimneys — Mice, to and fro across cold floors.

Here Miss Farthingay, our unwilling heroine, lies awake, in a room prepared for her use with much haste, and correspondingly little ceremony or care.

Unwilling, we insist — for, she had never the least desire to act the protagonist, in so turbulent a series of adventures. At the mere hint of any adventure at all, she would have stayed at home.* Nor, reader, we assure you in all candour, did we expect our tale to follow such a course. We thought, we were merely to conduct her to Paris. — It is the narrative of that extraordinary man *Thomas Peach*, along with the secret significance of those famous events, that unfolded in France, in the last years of the previous century, we intended to tell. — Instead of which, here we find ourselves, in this dreary mansion, by the cold sea, in the company of the unhappy Miss Farthingay.

We cannot in good conscience abandon her. You, reader, would not permit it — you *could* not.

We know you. Your heart beats, in sympathy with ours.

Would we could say the same of *another*, who gave us cause to believe it!

To our purpose —

We are pleased to say this much at least, that Miss Farthingay is not, at present, in captivity. Old Bidouphe is not set at the gate, to bar her passage out of it.

Yet what use is liberty to her, when she has no where to go? — nor knows, except in general and imprecise terms, where she is?

---

* We dismiss any imputation, that Miss Farthingay lacks spirit. — That she remains unmarried, at her age, and in possession of her fortune and personal charms, is sufficient confirmation of an independent temper. — No. — Her aversion to turmoil, and her preference for a well-managed existence, are easily accounted for, by the upheavals she has suffered already — Which will be familiar, to those who have studied our former volume.

She is profoundly exhausted. All the previous day, the cart rattled and jounced, until she felt the teeth might come loose from her head. Though she has now some semblance of proper accommodation, she is dusty — uncomfortable — Has gone many days, without the assistance of a maid — And, which impresses her most deeply, is quite lost and powerless, amid the buffetings of fate.

Her rescuers advise her, that their ship will be brought, in two or three days, to the small coastal town nearby — which vessel, as soon as it arrives, she may board, and be conveyed in safety to the port of Lyme. Until then she has only to wait. — They regret the lack of society, congenial to a female guest. They must leave her for the most part to her own entertainments, though the house is perfectly safe — The entrance watched, at all times, by the most faithful of retainers — One at least of their own number, will remain constantly within-doors, and is sworn to lay down his life, to prevent further insult to the person or honour of Miss Farthingay. As for the rest — They declare, the work of the FORGET-ME-NOT is never done. While Miss Farthingay waits, for the *Marie-Antoinette* to be sailed from Saint-Malo, that daring man and his brave companions have other business — whose nature they hint at, in solemn and mysterious terms — But which Miss Farthingay herself thinks cannot be so very taxing, since she hears them drinking and gaming down-stairs, late into the night, while she wrestles with the angel of sleep, in the draughty room above.

She feels obliged to sustain the fiction, that the identity of her rescuer is unknown to her. It is expected. — She thinks it would be gross ingratitude in her, not to acknowledge the expectation. Nevertheless, the ridiculous imposture adds to the weight on her spirits. At home — in beloved Somerset-shire — she would smile at the comedy, and make a mock-heroic ode upon the subject — to be distributed only among friends. — But for the present, she can find no amusement, in the eccentric vanity of Lord Rawleigh — Nor, alas, in any thing.

It is only justice to remark, that Lord Rawleigh finds himself almost as discomposed by Miss Farthingay's presence abovestairs, as she by his below.

He has sent the ever-faithful Mr Spott, to ride post-haste to Malo, with the order to bring the *Marie-Antoinette*. Now, he also has nothing to do — despite the hints offered to Miss Farthingay, by his companions, that further daring adventures are in train. — Nothing to do, but await the vessel, and pass the intervening days, in such gentlemanly amusements as can be extracted from the surrounding country — which extend no further, than the shooting of partridges in the fields, and ducks by the shore.

He is greatly troubled by the suspicion, that Miss Farthingay *knew him* — Despite his disguise!

She had always the reputation of a keen intelligence, for a woman. — It is one of the reasons Lord Rawleigh did not embrace her society, though their estates be neighbours.

The Rawleighs, as we remarked at the head of our chapter, have always been country folk — With deep respect, for the opinion of established tradition, on many subjects — including, the suitability of *clever women*, for the company of a gentleman.

But — Hang it all — thinks his lordship, as he stalks the shore in the company of one of his tall brave fellows, wreaking bloody havoc among the ducks — She's devilish handsome, when you look at it square — And rich as the old Persian fellow — and the land is adjoining. — It's almost an invitation, to enlarge one's property — and if the woman must be had along with the land — Heigh ho! a wife was always to be got, one day.

— Besides — if she's uncovered my *secret* — ha — What else is there to do, but marry her?

— No doubt she was used to think me a plain old stick — hem — A fellow of no interest. — But knowing me the Forget-Me-Not himself! why, her opinion shan't be the same at all — She'd think me vastly dashing, and all that.

His companion, when Lord Rawleigh voices these thoughts aloud, is all encouragement.

— Saved her life, what? says the fellow. — Irresistible — Obliged to you, for ever — D——n good thing, in wives, if a fellow must have 'em.

Lord Rawleigh is resolved. — Or, very nearly resolved. He will pay his address, in his own person, and make his proposal — *to-morrow*.

Poor Miss Farthingay!

Not for an instant do we doubt, that she has the wit to refuse a *booby* — And, indeed, the grace to do so, in a manner that acknowledges her recent obligation to his lordship, while remaining quite decisive.* But his proposal, and her immovable opposition to it, will be a trial to her — Another trial — At a time, when her spirits can ill bear it.

And yet, this particular oppression, she is fated *not* to endure.

An extraordinary event now draws near. — So strange and surprizing, that its shadow falls ahead upon our page. We glimpse it already — in dark outline —

Miss Farthingay passes a tedious day — Long, though she rises late, in consequence of the little rest she enjoyed during the night, and though the dusk comes early; long, for a day without occupation or society cannot be otherwise, no matter how few its hours, measured by the indifferent clock. There are no books in the house — No walks, in the grounds. Had she pencil and note-book, she might record her musings, or lighten the dismal *reality* of her situation, with the unfailing gleams of *imagination*. But, she has neither — nor possesses the poetic temper, in her present state. Impatient, yet dull — Distracted, yet weary — She eats little, and talks less, and watches the sun from the windows, as it descends over the sea to the west — Wishing its progress quicker.

---

* Although our progress into a new chapter, with the consequent opportunity for reflexion, has done nothing to quell our doubts, concerning Lord Rawleigh's contribution to the rescue of Miss Farthingay. *Who* opened the convent gate, and disposed of those set to watch it? – not the FORGET-ME-NOT, not any of his band.

The noises of drinking and gaming begin to rise, from other rooms. With as little ceremony as possible, she announces, that she will retire for the night — Proceeds to the apartment above-stairs, having derived one solitary satisfaction from the whole of the day, which is — that it is done.

She enters the room, with its grand French bed, that smells of slow decay — closes the door at her back — Lights two candles — and — GASPS — dropping the taper to the floor.

A sable and silent apparition stands at the window. — Its veiled gaze, fixed upon her.

You, reader, have met this sinister presence, only a few pages past. But to Miss Farthingay — who thought herself quite alone — Who, indeed, has every reason to suppose, that the house is empty of all save herself and the men below — the shock is considerable. In the gloomy bed-chamber — its unadorned windows, shewing mere darkness — the candles moving uneasily, in wintry draughts — The motionless intruder, clothed head to toe in black, seems in the first instance, more *phantom* than living creature — A spectre, summoned from the very shadows!

Miss Farthingay recovers her composure with commendable speed.

— Excuse me, madame, she says, in French. — Are you the house-keeper?

— Miss Farthingay, says a female voice from behind the veil, in English. — We must leave this house at once.

Miss Farthingay is almost as surprized to hear the native accents of her country, as she was upon discovering the unnannounced intruder, in her bed-room. She collects one of the candles and brings it towards the window.

— The house-keeper, she says, I suppose you are not.

— There is little time, says the other.

— On what possible account have you entered my room? I must insist that you remove yourself, whoever you are, and do not disturb my rest again. I am very tired.

— Miss Farthingay, this house will soon be attacked by armed men, and everyone within killed or made prisoner. I am here to take you away before they come. It will be within minutes.

Miss Farthingay comes a little nearer the ominous apparition, raising the candle. Her visitor seems to shrink from inspection.

— I know your voice. You are the nun.

— Come, says the intruder. — The soldiers approach along the road. The side door of the house will be out of their view. We may use the servants' stair.

— No, says Miss Farthingay. — I shall not.

— You must.

— I say, I shall not. I am tired, and intend only to sleep. — Miss Farthingay places the candle upon a night-stand, and sits herself on the bed. — Who are you, she says, to pronounce with such confidence, what I *must* do? And why is it, that for a second time, and in a new disguise, you presume to come in upon me, with your face concealed, and demand that I remove myself, who knows where? Whatever amusement you derive from these mysterious appearances, I assure you I do not share in the least. It is cold. I am quite out of patience with nocturnal journeys. Go by what stairs and doors you please, but you shall go alone.

— Bella — says the mysterious apparition — Please.

We mentioned, we think, that when the veiled nun came to Miss Farthingay, in the house of the Poor Sisters of Mercy, our heroine was momentarily struck by the impression, that she *knew her voice* — But, we suppose, dismissed the thought, as a trick of the brain — and, harried about with matters of more immediate import, forgot it.

The same impression now returns with overwhelming force. — Prompted by that one word, *Bella* — the form of her name, used only by her most intimate acquaintances, and the companions of her childhood.

The intruder has conquered her hesitation — approaches the bed, with three or four rapid steps — and — Raises her veil.

— Bella — she says again, extending a gloved hand — which trembles —

Miss Farthingay KNOWS THE FACE. —

She also does not know it — *Cannot* — For it is perhaps the very last face in all the world, she expected to see again. — Cannot, for until this moment she believed it lost for ever — entombed among past events, she will not voluntarily recall, so heavily grief weighs on them —

And yet, she knows it *instantly*. — As every one must recognize, without thought, by a pure motion of the heart, the face of one familiar from daily intercourse — in that tender time of youth, when impressions are made, which no length of time can efface. —

— CLARY?

Reader — we cannot guess, whether you have anticipated this moment.

We ourselves, are quite astonished. — And yet feel, in the very same breath, that we ought not to be — that nothing is *less* surprizing, than to discover the *quondam* ward of Mr Farthingay, and house-maid to Mr Peach, making her entrance in our narrative, at this moment. — Her acknowledged entrance, we ought to say — For there is no doubt at all, that the very same Miss Clarissa Riddle, was hidden behind the disguise of the so-called *Sister Maledicta*, who came to Miss Farthingay in the convent cell, urging escape.

How well-chosen the name, she used to disguise herself! —

It is certainly she. The years, since we made her ill-starred acquaintance, in our former volume, have not visibly touched her at all. It is the same dark-eyed angry face — Grown, if any change may be detected at all, still more fierce, as though perpetually conscious of an inward struggle, or affliction, without respite.

CLARY! — but how comes she here? — in *France*?

— Speak again, says Miss Farthingay. — Tell me it is you.

— It is I, Bella, says Clary. The natural pitch of her voice is harsh, and its tone unyielding. — Yet in the present moment it trembles with emotion.

— How can this be? I thought you —

Dead, Miss Farthingay meant to say, but she cannot.

Clary lifts Miss Farthingay's hands in her own — which, though small, and sheathed in fine black velvet, possess extraordinary strength and firmness — And draws her to her feet.

— I will explain every thing, she says, if I am allowed time. — But we must depart the house at once.

— Clary — let me go — I cannot. — I would endure any thing, rather than being thrown in the road again. Stay — let us talk —

— The soldiers are nearly upon the house. Do not, Bella, force me to compel you!

— Soldiers? — Miss Farthingay pulls her hands from Clary's grasp, and goes to the window, which reveals nothing at all — An acreage of mere dark. — Only the ghostly doubles of Miss Farthingay and Clary appear in the glass, conjured by the candle-light within.

— There are no soldiers! — She gestures at the empty night. — No one is there.

— These windows look towards the sea. The militia approach from the other side. They will surround the house soon.

— How can you know —

Clary's interruption is impassioned. — Because it was I who fetched them, Bella! Now — follow! — And she grasps her childhood companion once more, with importunate firmness, and pulls her, by force, to the door.

— Violence, Clary? to me?

Miss Farthingay has been overwhelmed under a tide of memories. Days and years long forgotten, rush in on her, in so confused a mass, as to be indistinguishable. But she thinks now of the last year of Clarissa Riddle's residence at Grandison Hall, before her father's poor young ward was turned away. — The sulks, and defiance, and ungovernable rages — outbursts of such furious truculence, that two servants were required, to controul her. Though Clary's anger was not once turned on Arabella, the friendship between them, formerly so free and unreserved, could not but cool. — The fondness Miss Farthingay felt, could not but be tainted by reserve — even, by fear.

— I do not say, forgive me, Clary replies, while continuing to direct Miss Farthingay from the room. — I am past all forgiveness. But the violence of the soldiers will be worse, when they enter the house. I have informed them this is the lair of the Forget-Me-Not — A name inexorably hated in this region.

— You? — stop, Clary, stop! I must fetch my papers — some other articles —

— Too late, Bella. — Clary opens the door with one hand, keeping hold of Miss Farthingay in the other.

— I will raise the house. I will scream!

— I think you will not, says Clary, drawing her into the adjacent room, where utter darkness reigns.

— I cannot see! —

— I will guide you. — Here is another door — Now, the passage — And here the stair. — In this wise Clary leads Miss Farthingay down through lightless quarters of the dismal house, without the smallest hesitation. Our heroine can only follow — first, because she is compelled, by the strong grasp of her guide — And second, because she can see nothing, and therefore could not chuse another way.

The revels of Lord Rawleigh and his companions echo through the house, as she descends the wooden stair.

— If you will compel me so cruelly, says Miss Farthingay, when she can speak, for all her wits are required, to prevent herself falling in the dark — Tell me at least where you are taking me — Why — How you are here!

— It is all for your sake.

— Were you the nun who visited me before?

— I was. I could not leave you shut up in that house, any more than I can leave you in this.

— But how did you know of that — of this —

— Hush. Here is the door.

A lock turns. — The air of night rushes in, and the noise of the sea. Miss Farthingay is not dressed against the chill. No glimmer relieves the utter dark.

— This is madness, she says. — You cannot mean to go out.

— Darkness means nothing to me, Clary says. She is no more than an invisible voice, and a firm hand on Miss Farthingay's arm. — I am taking you to a safe place — I swear it, Bella.

— No — I cannot — Miss Farthingay attempts to pull away from the hand.

— Look.

A spot of fire-light has appeared beyond the house, bobbing among black shadows of trees.

— The soldiers are here, Clary says, whispering close by Miss Farthingay's ear. — We have not a moment to waste.

Further torches come into view beside the first. Three — five — then ten, and more — Too many to count. Miss Farthingay detects the murmur of masculine voices.

— This way, Clary says, drawing her out onto a path Miss Farthingay cannot see.

— Which way? Have you no light?

— The men would see any light. Come now.

Only the sight of the torches prevents Miss Farthingay from resisting. Flashes of metal catch the light — muskets raised — bayonets fitted. — The soldiers creep stealthily towards their prey. Despite the dark, she lets herself be guided along — trusting, though reluctantly, in the strong grip that directs her — She has no choice.

— You are much changed, she says.

— More than you know.

— I feel I am in a dream. — A night-mare — Can it really be you? — my sister?

— We were never sisters, Bella. That was the dream, not this. — Step carefully here — the path turns left, and is a little overgrown.

The soldiers' torches and weapons have been sighted, from within the house. Muffled exclamations can be heard — Then, the breaking of glass — a roar of command — Furious oaths, English and French — And, in moments, some form of *melée* is under way.

We shall not divert our narrative, to describe its progress. As battles go, it is brief, and the outcome quite decisive. — It serves us, as it serves Clary and Miss Farthingay, as a *diversion*, allowing us to proceed in haste through the neglected grounds, to a door at the margin of the property, that opens west-ward, towards the coast. Here again a lock is heard to turn, and the two women pass through. — And pause, listening to the clamour behind. — Cries — shots —

— Heavens! exclaims Miss Farthingay, alarmed at the violence of the commotion. — Lord Rawleigh! What will become of him?

— Had we delayed any longer, you would have seen the answer yourself, and met the same fate.

— Horrible!

— Do not think of it, Bella.

— Why did you bring the militia here? — Miss Farthingay emits a small cry, as the report of a musket cracks the air. — They will all be killed!

— Their danger is nothing, compared to that which threatens you.

A tinder strikes. — By some alchemy too swift to observe, Clary has set alight the wick of a candle, which burns straight and steady in her grasp, despite the gusting breeze. — At last, Miss Farthingay can see a little of the world about her. — Some shadowy intimations, of a sandy path, and tall grasses — the unrelieved night beyond.

Clary relaxes the hold on her arm.

The colour of the candle-flame is strange — As though it were not good homely wax providing the fuel, but another substance, burning with a reddish cast. — The movement of air, disturbs it not in the least.

Miss Farthingay is again overcome by the conviction that a dream embroils her. — Wonder — terror — confusion — so intirely blended, that each seems an aspect of the others.

— Even now, Clary says, there is little time. Walk beside me, Bella. The exercise will warm you.

'Cries of alarm and fear rise from the house behind, and further shots. Miss Farthingay knows, she cannot turn back — yet to press on, seems impossible.

— Where are we to go? I have studied this shore from the window of the bed-room. It is all desart.

— A short distance only. Then you will be out of the night, and far from those who pursue you.

— Pursue *me*? Who —

Clary interrupts with strange urgency. — You are bargained for, Bella, and promised to destruction, as I have been. For me it is too late. — But you may escape yet — you shall escape — I have sworn it. I will make this my one good deed, to cancel an hundred vile ones, before my end!

The confused and sudden retreat from the house, added to the astonishing reappearance of her childhood play-mate, have for the past minutes as it were suspended Miss Farthingay's faculties, and carried her along like a marionette. But now, her reason begins to reassert itself. — She knows, this is no dream, though it is as strange as any phantasy of the night, and threatens to be as fearful.

The suspicion comes over her, that Clary is quite mad.

— Do you intend me some harm, Clary?

— Never!

— You had some cause to resent me, I know. I was always sorry for it.

Clary shakes her head. — All that is long past.

— It is. — Yet you have disguised yourself, and followed me all over France, though I myself scarce know where I have been. — Where will you take me? It is so cold — I cannot go much further, in the dead of night. — And what light is that? — Miss Farthingay is seized with strange horror, as she watches the candle, its flame stretched tall and still, as though it burned in the absolute stillness of a tomb. — Clary — if any remnant of fondness for me remains in your heart, explain yourself, I beg you. You say we were never sisters — Yet I often wished we were, for I had no other!

The faint light dances. — Not because the flame has stirred — no — It is the hand holding it, that trembles. — In the next instant Miss Farthingay finds herself in a fierce embrace. — Arms of black silk tight about her, and the folds of the veil against her cheek.

The flesh within, communicates no warmth at all.

— Clary! — you are quite cold!

Clary releases her — And wipes away a tear.

— Walk close beside me, she says. — It is not very far.

— Will you still not tell me —

Clary interrupts more savagely. — Walk, or be left alone in the dark.

Miss Farthingay is pierced to the heart. — Her tide of affectionate remembrance breaks, and flows back, as though it had met a sea-wall. She follows the retreating candle — Wrapping her arms about herself against the chill wind, and stumbling on uneven ground. The clamour behind is quieting. — The brief contest of arms, has been settled. A few cries come from the house, growing fainter, while the perpetual moan of the waves becomes more distinct ahead.

Miss Farthingay navigates an universe of sound, like the sightless bat.

— Bella, Clary says. — I did not mean to speak harshly. I have forgotten the use of kind words. — She pauses, and offers her arm.

Miss Farthingay takes it — Though it is cold! but strong, with masculine firmness.

— I am sorry, says Miss Farthingay, that you have not met with kindness. — Where have you been, all these years? — where lived? And how? has no one cared for you, since Papa —

— Do not speak of him.

Miss Farthingay feels the rebuke. — She reveres the memory of a parent, from whom so many blessings and advantages were inherited, and whose fond indulgence inspired in her every sense of obligation and duty. Yet, on occasions when she permitted herself to reflect on the household at Grandison Hall, with disinterested candour, she has sometimes thought, that her father's experiment in philosophical benevolence, of which Clary was the innocent object, had, perhaps, certain flaws. — Perhaps fell a little short, of the philanthropic spirit, in which it was conceived. — And that Clary's resentment, which grew to so tempestuous an excess, was, though very wilfully and wickedly expressed, perhaps not wholly unforgiveable.

— I met with kindness, Clary says, after some moments of silence, From one soul.* It would have been enough. I asked no more. But even so small a share of contentment is forbidden me. The peace I found was not permitted to last.

— You are all mystery, Clary. Mystery and — forgive me — misery! How I wish you had come back to me in some kindly moment. — At some hour, in some place, where I might embrace you, and sit in comfort with you while you told me all your trials — Where I might have leisure to consider how to relieve them.

We have remarked on several occasions, that Clary's voice has no natural softness nor grace. Time has no more altered it, than changed her visible form. It remains an instrument of iron, suited only to the funeral dirge. Yet her answer is pronounced with the nearest approximation to tenderness, that voice can atchieve.

— Dearest Bella. — I share that wish, with whatever remains of my heart.

— Then let us go now — Let us escape this dreadful night, and rest. We shall talk as we used to. Do you remember? — by the swing, under the copper beech-tree? You shall unburden yourself of this unhappiness, into the loving bosom of your Bella.

---

* She refers, surely, to her former employer, Mr Tho.s Peach. — But appears reluctant to name him before Miss Farthingay. Recall, reader, that our heroine remains quite ignorant of any connexion, between her friend Mr Peach, and her old play-mate Miss Clarissa Riddle — for, as we mentioned in an earlier chapter, Mr Peach's house-maid was always sure to be out of the house, if ever Miss Farthingay came visiting.

— We have only the present dark hour, Clary says, in tones of grim resignation. — There will not be another. Even what I do now is forbidden to me. I will suffer for it.

— Forbidden? By whom? How strange is every thing you say!

— Have you not also suffered strange afflictions these past days, Bella, since you rashly accepted the invitation of Denfert? Do you not feel yourself oppressed by an hateful and determined power?

— You know of Monsieur Denfert! cries Miss Farthingay.

Clary gives a bitter laugh. — Too much of him, she says, or of her. — That one is neither man nor woman, or is both.

— What in heaven's name do you mean?

— I shall say no more. The French have a proverb, that when you speak of that one you shall soon see his horns.

Miss Farthingay's head is a-whirl. — We do not like to say it. It has somewhat the savour, of an *heroine's* behaviour — all fluttering confusion — oh! what am I to do? who shall preserve me? &c. — But in the present circumstances, we think it admissible. At language, such as this of Clary's — at the inference, such language invites! — any person, might be utterly bewildered.

Miss Farthingay nevertheless wavers, in her former suspicion, that the friend of her childhood has lost her wits. The allusion to M Denfert indicates, that Clary has *some* rational understanding of events. — Some knowledge of truth. *How* her old play-mate knows of Denfert — of her own adventures, in France — is an impossible puzzle — A riddle so complete, it cannot even be thought of. Yet in every word of Clary's there is a force, that is its own persuasion. Her language is like a request for surrender, made by the general who has already won the field. — One may wish it were not so — may still consider the request, an outrageous imposition — Yet the fact of it can no more be refuted, than the swelling of tides.

The track turns between two hills of darkness, and comes out to the beach. Here the shore is long and flat. An expanse of wet sand stretches away, to the greater expanse of the sea. Some fraction of moonlight descends from among the clouds, and allows the liquid element to glisten — Very faint — Yet when the night is so absolute, the eye is grateful for any hint of radiance.

— It is but a mile or two along the shore, Clary says. — This hard sand is easier to walk on. Take my arm. I will sustain you.

— To where?

— The place I will make you safe.

— Another unknown house? More doors and locks? Speak plainly, Clary, I entreat you. You are so strange and gloomy — I dread what you may intend!

— I cannot tell you, Clary says, turning now to walk with the sea to their right, and the invisible land to the left. — But I would never harm you, nor allow any harm to come to you, as far as it is in my power. I thought I loved nothing in my accursed existence. But as soon as I knew of the danger to *you*, I resolved to prevent it. Believe me — or do not, as you chuse. I wish you would think kindly of me, as I of you, but soon I will be gone, and neither of our sentiments will matter a jot.

— I would think kindly, if I knew what to think at all! — Who wishes me harm? — What offence have I given, to any body?

— None, Bella, none! There is no justice in this world, or the next. When we are chosen for destruction, it is waste of breath to complain. All that remains is defiance — To resist. — These last words Clary pronounces, with furious emphasis.

A musket-shot again pierces the dark. Miss Farthingay's nerves are in a tender state. — It would be remarkable, were it otherwise. She starts at the noise, and presses close against Clary.

Another single shot — another —

— Are they still fighting? God preserve them!

— Those are the sounds of execution, Clary says.

Miss Farthingay cannot restrain a cry of horror.

— Lord Rawleigh? — shot?

— He and all his men. The soldiers are informed he is the Forget-Me-Not. They have no inclination to wait for prisons and judges. — A fourth shot comes, and then a fifth. — There, Clary says, with horrible satisfaction. — That is the last of them.

Miss Farthingay withdraws her arm.

— So cold in the face of murder? What are you become?

Clary stops also.

— What I was intended from my birth to be. A thing inhuman. Never forget, Bella — it was your father who began the work, which other powers perfected. I was denatured from the day I was born.

Miss Farthingay wishes to rise to the defence of her parent. — His intention, noble — his motive, benevolent. — But she cannot put these opinions to Clary.

— Murder is the currency of this land, Clary continues. — Soon — very soon — it will be paid to all, high and low. Then war will come and men will die in thousands. Do not weep for an handful of fools, Bella.

— But did you truly lead the soldiers to the house?

— I did.

— Why? Why invite this assault, knowing it would end in murder? If you only wish to keep me safe, why did you not leave myself and those poor men alone?

Clary's voice rises with passion. — Because I am compelled to. Because the one who commands your destruction also commanded theirs. But I will not beg your pardon for what I am. Come — follow —

The light goes with her, and Miss Farthingay must walk after it.

— What is it, Clary, that you are? she says, speaking small. — The child I loved as a sister is long dead, I see. Even the angry girl, who turned aside from that love — Even she was not as I see you now.

Miss Farthingay fears another outburst, but Clary's answer, when it comes, is quite without anger.

— What am I? I have met no other like me, and so cannot be sure how to answer. Am I perhaps a witch? I think I must be.

— Do not trifle with me. I am near enough my wits' end already.

— Look at the candle, Bella. Do you know why the wind does not blow out the flame? It is because I expend a portion of myself to make it so.

Miss Farthingay thinks — Then she is mad, after all. Poor Clary!

Perhaps you, reader, have the very same thought — In the weak and superficial sphere of the brain, that conceives only what it is used to conceive. But you, like our bewildered and benighted heroine, can see the unbending candle-flame. — There is precious little else in our scene to be observed at all.

— If you prefer another word, Clary says, you may suggest one. I have also been called *démone*. — She uses the French word. — With your pardon, we decline to translate.

— A little distance from here, she continues, lies one of the antient druidic stones, abundant in these regions of France. When we reach it, I shall expend a far greater portion of myself to convey you far from here. The evidence of your own eyes will confirm it to-morrow. Then you may remember me in any language you please. Take my arm again. You look as though you might fall in a faint.

Miss Farthingay obeys, though hardly knowing what she does. — Is it then a dream, after all? she thinks.

— Should you receive further letters from Denfert, continues Clary, encouraging her companion to go at a brisker pace, Burn them unsealed. Do not read a line. It would be best not even to touch the paper. Should there be any communication which purports to come from that one, by any method at all, refuse it, or if you cannot, do the opposite of whatever it instructs. Do you hear, Bella? If you heed nothing else, heed this: Denfert is not your friend, but your most determined and malicious foe. You were betrayed to the fool de Charizard, and will be betrayed again, if you again put your trust in Denfert.

— Do you know every thing that has passed? — my whole miserable history, in this miserable nation?

— I have watched for you whenever I could.

— Then if you are indeed not my dear beloved Clary, but the oracle of all this mystery and horror — explain to me, why Monsieur Denfert, of whom I was intirely ignorant, before I had his letter — how I, as innocent as ignorant, have earned his enmity?

— There is a thing Denfert must have. An object of power and influence, to further that one's purpose in these turmoils. The object belonged to Monsieur de Charizard by antient inviolable right. Therefore it could not be stolen, but must be bought or bargained for. You, Bella, are the price to be paid. Had the fool's lustful eye alighted on any other woman in the world, I would have done nothing. What do I care, if the world is overcome by fire and drowned in blood? But when I heard him name *you* —

Some emotion takes hold of Clary, which prevents her saying more. It is this very outburst of feeling, which touches Miss Farthingay, and gives her some impression, that Clary must be sincere. — Deranged, yet sincere.

We ourselves do not know what to think. — There is something in Clary's manner, that forbids doubt. — And yet the plain meaning of her speech, is evident absurdity — is it not? — Our poor heroine, the subject of some malign and unnatural transaction?

We are loath to entertain any such theory — And yet — might it perhaps account, for the extraordinary ill-luck, which has attended her, since her departure from Cherbourg?

That de Charizard might have bargained with wicked powers, as the magicians of less enlightened times were said to do, is not wholly impossible to credit. The *libertines* of the Old Regime, were men who sneered at conscience, and declared themselves at odds with every principle of virtue and morality. — Have you ever looked into the writings of the *Marquis de Sade?*

Let us attend to our tale. —

— De Charizard no longer pursues me, Miss Farthingay says. — There was an accident.

— It was not an accident. The robbery of his carriage was my own contrivance. I dared not openly interfere with the machinations of Denfert, but persuaded another to the act. Yet though the fool is gone, the bargain remains. You are still the price of the summoning-stone, and you must still be paid to de Charizard before Denfert may have it. Therefore you must be sent to join him, where he is.

— Where he is? Where is that?

— In hell.

Miss Farthingay walks on beside Clary for several steps, and then — laughs.

We think it much to her credit. —

— Whatever you have done for me, dearest Clary, since this dreadful voyage overtook me, I am sincerely grateful for. And, to see you again — to renew so fond an acquaintance, which I had never dreamed of resuming — Gives me a joy equally sincere. But, my love, I fear your mind has suffered some terrible derangement, in the years of your life that passed unknown to me. — Do not be angry — Pray, let me speak a little more — I wish only to say, that whatever to-morrow brings, and all the days thereafter, I intend — as long as it is within my power — to keep you with me. — To preserve you, as you say you have preserved me. Whatever you have suffered — whatever you are become — however clouded your thoughts — I love you still. I shall not let you be lost again. — There — now, rage as you please. I have said all I mean to say.

Clary stops.

Miss Farthingay must perforce stop also, since the two are attached arm in arm. She looks at her companion's face, framed by the veil, and the high neck of black lace, and is amazed to see the gleam of a tear.

She is once more embraced, with a force near painful.

— I am not at all angry that you think me mad, says Clary. — To have heard you speak those other words — to know myself cared for, and loved, even for a single night — is — Bella —

But Clary is unable to say, what the knowledge signifies.

Perhaps the words elude her, in the excess of emotion. — Or, perhaps — dreadful thought! — it is not permitted to her tongue, to express a sentiment so noble and pure.

Miss Farthingay speaks again, with gentleness — It is not only for a single night, my dear. Did you not hear me promise to care for you always? We will not go to Grandison Hall. I know you could not bear that. I have other places —

— Bella.

— What is it?

— You will not see me again, after to-night.

There is a fearful finality in Clary's pronouncement. — The unswerving conviction, which often attends lunacy.

— Can you intend to leave me? Miss Farthingay says. — Though you are only just returned, and after so long an interval?

— If I could chuse not to leave you, I would not. These visions you conjure — You and I reunited, never to part — oh! — But it cannot be. There will be a reckoning for what I have done here. I dare not say more. — You will not see me again, nor will any body.

— Clary! cries Miss Farthingay — greatly alarmed, that her dear friend intends to do herself some harm.

— Do not speak of it. We have not much farther to walk. Our time draws to an end. — Let us not waste it in grief and complaint.

— But, my dear, you have said you are determined to watch over me. Do you mean to abandon me to these imagined dangers?

— I have delayed them, but I cannot end them. I am Denfert's slave — hell's slave. When it is known what I have done — Clary draws in a sudden breath. Her frame stiffens with resolution — No matter, she says. There is one person who may have the power to break the bargain and protect you. I must entrust you to him — and hope — hope! — that my trust is not misplaced.

— Who — begins Miss Farthingay, much alarmed at this new trick of Clary's phrenzy, for the very last thing she desires, is to be led to some other stranger — Some person perhaps equally ensnared, in these wild delusions.

— Thomas Peach, says Clary.

Miss Farthingay forgets that she is cold — that it is a winter night — that she is being dragged along a beach, in France, by a lunatic — Forgets all these things, in her absolute and universal surprize.

To hear THAT name! — pronounced, by *Clary*! —

— Mr Peach! What can you know of Mr Peach?

— I leave it to him, to explain the history of our connexion, if he chuses to. He may be glad to hear news of me. — I hope he will be glad. You may tell him also that I am lost for ever and will not be seen again. — That I regret it — that I am grateful —

Inward emotion once more prevents her from speaking. — Her heart, thinks Miss Farthingay, is as wild as her brain. These phrenzies ride her unmercifully — poor, wounded child! —

She speaks gently again. — My old friend Thomas Peach is in England, far from here. It will be some time, I fear, before I am able —

— He is in France, says Clary.

— Do you watch *his* every motion, as you say you have watched mine?

— He came across the water, seeking you. But he is looking in the wrong place. — My last act will be to correct his error. It is all I can do. Then you will come under his protection, I hope. — Were there any power to pray to, I would pray that Tom will see what must be done.

Clary is greatly agitated. — She scarcely hears me at all, Miss Farthingay thinks. — She cannot attend to any thing, beyond the whirling phantasies of her diseased imagination.

— Shall we rest a moment? You must be very tired, dearest Clary.

— Exhausted beyond description. But I will be at rest soon. Keep walking, Bella. — Talk to me of other things. Remind me of how we used to play together. I would remember that I was once happy.

Miss Farthingay thinks it wise, to humour her. — And, in truth, it gives her some comfort also, to cast her mind back to the sun-shine and verdant gardens of Grandison Hall — To dismiss, as far as possible, this endless drear night, and conjure instead the innocent past-times of youth. No brother or sister of hers survived its infancy. Her father's ward, though several years her junior, was her best companion. — Sweet-tempered then, and docile, and eloquent even in her playful prattle — How delightful a friend, despite the difference in their age and station! An hundred remembrances come upon Miss Farthingay, and she revives them with pleasure, and wonders how she ever forgot them.

No on-looker can derive the same pleasure, from such fond recollections, as those who share them. We shall not transcribe this part of their talk — but allow the reunited friends to walk on, in something like contentment, like two shades, bound by lost affection, whispering as they wander the fields of the dead — the waters of Styx murmuring ghostly accompaniment — Until they come to a place, where Clary halts.

— What is it, my love? says Miss Farthingay.

— Here we leave the shore, says Clary. — It is just a little way inland. Come.

— Might we not permit ourselves a little rest? Or, perhaps, seek some refuge? There are other houses along this coast, I think. — Their keepers will surely admit us out of charity.

Clary sighs deeply.

— Yes, Bella, she says, in the tone of one, who placates a querulous child. — Now we shall find refuge, and rest also.

Miss Farthingay presses close on her companion's arm — which is still strangely cold. — I could not go much farther, she says. — What a night this has been! Yet I shall always remember it with joy, because it brought you back to me.

— Stay close beside, Clary says. — The path is wet and narrow.

Miss Farthingay looks ahead, hoping to see some light — a fire in a window, or a lamp at a gate — Any sign, that they approach a place of shelter. There is nothing — only dripping fronds, that pluck unseen at her sleeve, and stones underfoot, with mud between. Whether she notices, how Clary walks this rough invisible path, as though under the light of the noon-day sun

— whether she wonders at it — We cannot say. When one wishes only to lie down, and rest, every other concern, dwindles towards insignificance.

In a short while the ground underfoot becomes bare stone — the air suddenly more cold, and very still. The perpetual mutter of the sea, is muted. Miss Farthingay all at once can hear her own breath, as though she had come within-doors, to a place of walls and echoes. The unhomely candle-light appears to burn brighter — But shews nothing, except that the stone where they stand is moist, and glistens like a cavern floor.

Clary stops again. Miss Farthingay senses, that she is afflicted by some uncertainty.

— You have not mistaken the way, I hope?

— No. — Bella —

— What is it, my dear love?

Clary sighs once more. — Nothing — All I wish to say, I have said. — Here —

She reaches among the drapery of her black dress, and withdraws two small objects.

— Put forward your hands, she says.

— What —

— Bella, Clary says, in an harder tone, Put out your hands. You must take these.

Miss Farthingay obeys, though not without some trepidation, at this new fancy of her poor deranged companion.

Clary seems to hesitate a little. — Ought I give you both, or one only? she says. — This you must have — It signifies *him*. — With these words she places a small dark thing in Miss Farthingay's right hand, and closes the fingers over it, so she holds it securely.

— Keep it by your person, Clary says, no matter how distasteful it is to you. Never let it be apart from you. As for the other — Yes — I think you shall have it, though I do not know why. — She places another item, of similar size, in Miss Farthingay's left hand, and again closes the fingers into a fist.

The two objects Miss Farthingay now holds, seem as though they might be small carvings of wood. — Miniature statues, perhaps — such as chess-pieces —

— Good-bye, Bella, Clary says.

At this farewell, spoken with such dreadful finality, Miss Farthingay is seized with fresh alarm. Before she can cry out, or speak, or even draw another breath, she is embraced, for the final time. So fierce is Clary's grip that she drops the candle. — Its flame goes out. Absolute dark descends in an instant. Miss Farthingay is pinioned, in a grip of iron. In her ear, Clary speaks —

But the *language*, is an horror of sound —

Growls, and hisses, without meaning — spoken in a voice which might proceed from stone —

For a moment — a moment, plucked from a night-mare! — Clary's whole form appears illuminated, by *inward* light, and wavers, and seems to shed its own substance, as though dissolving at its edge, like printed characters when a stain of water touches the ink. — Miss Farthingay's alarm, becomes dread — I, too, she thinks, am mad! —

The pitch of her terror rises, and overwhelms her. Oblivion — merciful oblivion — comes upon her — And she sees, nor hears, nor feels, any thing more.

*The Virgin descends from Heaven, and appears before Her
faithful!*

Village by village the news spreads. Though ocean winds have
begun to strip the trees and Brittany is sodden with fog, a fire
kindles there. Old women come from their hovels to the village
markets, weeping. With my own eyes I saw Her! What did our
blessed Lady say, grandmother? Words of comfort. Hold fast to
your faith. Be charitable to poor strangers. God is with you.

The old women cannot in fact hear what the Madonna says,
but their devoted hearts fill in the words, with some encouragement
from Lesinge who they think must be Her prophet. Cochonne
knows this is very wrong. She would like to prevent Lesinge fom
parading the apparition in the stone in front of toothless Breton
crones. But as he points out, each demonstration procures them
shelter and food. Would Cochonne prefer to pass more nights
under the open sky on the brink of winter?

She would not.

The pious old women cannot offer Lesinge enough. Though
they speak only the Breton tongue, which is a relic of the druids
and incomprehensible to Frenchmen, their acts and gestures are
plain as any language. Take my goat, they beg. Take my
granddaughter. But Lesinge is careful. Greed has been the downfall
of many brigands. He must not arouse the jealousy of the village
men. Besides, the granddaughters are crabbed and swarthy from
labour and not to his taste. The grandmothers would follow him,
on their knees if they could, wailing and praying as they go, but

Lesinge takes care only to summon his obedient phantom before the oldest and feeblest. When morning comes he and his companions are already gone. The rumour remains, smouldering, spreading.

'God will punish you for these lies,' Cochonne says in her surliest rumble.

'And yet your Madonna continues to show Herself,' says Lesinge. 'If She were displeased with us, would She not refuse it?'

Cochonne cannot dispute this, unless she admits that the gentle dark woman conjured from the stone might not after all be Saint Mary. There is a corner of her heart which begins to suspect as much. To acknowledge this doubt openly would be a species of defeat. Cochonne, though only a farmer's daughter of freakish proportions, has her pride.

The rumours are not restrained by any doubt at all. They flame with certainty. Ordinary Breton folk have been waiting, it seems, for just such a sign. This revolution of Parisian philosophers, what is it to them? They want their old faith and their old king. Few of them had much love for Louis, but one does not replace one's king because he displeases one any more than one discards a husband because he is drunk and useless. God has made certain bonds permanent.

It is time, murmur the country folk of Brittany, for counter-revolution.

The enemy is hell itself. It will be a holy war. Well-attested stories say that the Devil has come to Brittany in the guise of a burgher riding a mule. He desecrates village churches. He has an attendant demon which torments good people.

In the cities and the larger towns these rumours cause rational heads to be scratched and revolutionary brows to furrow. Superstition is the habit of the peasants and must be tolerated when it cannot be ignored, until the age of enlightenment triumphs; but what if it becomes dangerous? There are reports of outrages against functionaries of the state. Encouraged by this nonsense about the Virgin, the refractory priests shout more boldly. They incite crowds. Some of the disturbances might even qualify as riot.

And, look, here is news from Normandy that citizen Denfert has ridden from Paris and sets his course to the west!

At this the rational heads come together in anxious conference.

Citizen Denfert tolerates no superstition. He is known to be its most implacable enemy. Worse, he is a man to whom certain rumours of his own attach. To displease Denfert, they say, is unwise. Fatally unwise, according to the whispers. The rational heads nervously feel their collars and decide to investigate the stories coming from the countryside. If some charlatans go about the roads of France claiming to speak to Mary the mother of Jesus, who was of course only an ordinary woman, and is long dead, then those charlatans had better be arrested before Denfert arrives in Brittany.

Detachments of the guard go out from the coastal towns, from Brest and Saint-Brieuc, from Quimper and Lorient, into the interior wastes, looking for the man, the woman, the boy and the donkey of whom the rumours speak. It is noted that the boy fits the description of one wanted for the theft of some boots. These are not prophets of Heaven, they say to the surly villagers, but liars and tricksters and common thieves. The villagers spit behind their backs. All of them know someone who knows someone else whose aunt or grandmother witnessed the miraculous apparition of the Virgin with her own eyes. Or if they do not, they see a chance to strike a blow against the National Guard. The detachments are harried by stones and set upon by men with hammers and scythes. Any soldiers who escape ride pell-mell back to the coastal towns and report that Brittany is in revolt against the revolution.

Lesinge, Cochonne and des Sables continue west without hindrance, ignorant of the turmoil in their wake, until they come to the ancient forest in the heart of which lies Castle Charizard.

'Are you sure?' says Lesinge to des Sables, raising a sceptical eyebrow at the view before them.

The trees press together so closely it is dark as night within. They are huge and hung with beards of moss, brooding giants turned to wood.

For once des Sables is indeed certain. He remembers the horrible forest. There can be nowhere else like it in all the world, so gnarled and shadowy and sinister. Everyone says witches and fairies and dead men live under these trees.

'What noble family would raise their castle in such a place?' Lesinge says. 'By God, my boy, if you have led us astray—'

Des Sables opens his pretty mouth to protest but Cochonne interrupts before he can speak.

'You call yourself our captain. Do not blame him. You dragged us all this way. Will you turn back now?'

'Turn back? Bah!' Of course Gaspard will not turn back. He goes on always, towards his destiny. The nature of Lesinge is — irrepressible!

Nevertheless, they are not eager to proceed into the forest. They rest a while to eat some of the bread and cheese provided by credulous old women, of which they have enough to feed a regiment. The road ahead is not welcoming. There are fallen sticks lying plentifully, in numbers that could warm a hovel until Christmas, but no old women have come to gather them.

'Myself,' says Lesinge, 'I do not credit these absurdities of haunting and curses.' He wipes his moustache, which has grown luxuriant.

'That is strange,' says des Sables, 'considering that you carry a ghost in your pocket.'

Lesinge takes the magical stone from its bag and turns it thoughtfully in his hands. None of them are now afraid that it will perform its enchantment unexpectedly. They know the apparition only answers to firelight and silver locket.

'One old crystal may contain the remnants of the spiritual world,' he says. He has come to think of himself as a connoisseur of arcane matters. 'But a whole wood? A tract of land within the boundaries of modern France? No.'

'Is this even France?' says des Sables. 'My old master, may the devils keep him, used to say it was not. He called the Bretons savages.'

Cochonne's eyes open suddenly wide.

'The stone!'

Lesinge looks at his hands. Though there is no flame anywhere, the crystal gleams with inward fire. It is becoming warm. For a moment the sensation is pleasant, as one enjoys cradling a bowl of soup on a winter day. But the warmth turns hotter and the gleam brighter, and then the stone is burning his fingers. He leaps up with an oath and drops it to the ground.

'What have you done?' Cochonne cries. The grass around where the stone fell is beginning to blacken. Smoke rises, carrying an evil smell.

'Me?' says Lesinge. 'What am I to blame for?'

Cochonne can see that the light of the stone is different from before. The radiance appears angry. Tiny dark shapes dance in its fires, nothing at all like her beloved gentle phantom.

'This is all because of your lies, Lesinge. Our Lady has abandoned us. Look, the stone is full of devils like des Sables said. I warned you!'

'Quick,' des Sables cries, 'put it back in the bag!'

'And how am I to do that? It is hot as hell.'

They fall to shouting all at the same time and waving their arms, with such enthusiasm that none of the three notices the approaching rider until he is almost upon them.

'Excuse me, my young lady, gentlemen,' says the rider, drawing up his mule. Despite the uncivil scene before him he speaks very politely. He touches his hat.

The brigands cease their brawl as abruptly as they began it, and turn as one to inspect this newcomer who arrives at such an unfortunate moment. Their precious enchanted stone is lying near the feet of des Sables, glowing like a coal in a forge. The earth all around it is scorched, the grasses and weeds withering.

'I apologise for disturbing your conversation,' the rider on the mule says. 'I noticed you at some distance and was relieved to hear French being spoken. I have for some days been among Bretons.'

He speaks correctly but with a pronounced and unpleasant accent. Which region he hails from Lesinge cannot guess. The man is certainly no peasant, though the beast he rides is a sorry-looking animal of the sort that unscrupulous farmers bring to town to sell to ignorant travellers. His dress is the burgher's habit of breeches, waistcoat and jacket, surmounted with a felt hat and a cockade. He has a mild abstracted air. It appears he has not even noticed the noisy quarrel which raged moments ago, nor the enchanted crystal lying in plain sight on the ground.

His eyes, Cochonne thinks, are those of a dreamer.

Des Sables attempts a discreet shuffle of his boots, aiming to interpose them between the stone and the stranger.

'All yesterday and today,' the rider continues, 'I have not been able to make myself understood. I know no word of the Breton language. It is akin to that spoken in Wales, I have read. If one may speak of kinship between languages.'

Lesinge has not heard of this place called Wales. An obscure but powerful instinct tells him he is being mocked. But the traveller's manner has no trace of supercilious wit. He is certainly no sneering young lord or university man. There is something about him which gives the impression of many years passed.

Perhaps his eyes are bad. He does not notice the stone, though it blazes as if just plucked from the molten fires under the earth.

'Eh, well, what do you want?' Surprise and embarrassment make Lesinge speak more roughly than he intends.

'Only some advice concerning my right road,' says the stranger, unperturbed. 'I fear I am lost.'

A loud cawing breaks out from nowhere, startling the three brigands, though not the man on the mule, who acts as though he had not heard anything. Des Sables and Cochonne turn towards the sound. There is no crow or raven anywhere in sight.

Lesinge keeps his attention on the rider. With the instincts of a professional man, he is making a rapid estimation of the prospects for brigandage. The traveller is certainly no commoner. His boots and clothes are good. Of most significance is that he rides alone, which on roads such as this, far from the main thoroughfares, is as good as an invitation to be robbed. The purse, Lesinge guesses, will not be heavy, but will be easily had. He is not one to scorn small treasures which can be won with little effort. A proper understanding of the proportion of risk to reward is one of the arts of the brigand, too little studied, in his opinion, by the majority of his adventuring brethren.

'Whether a certain road is the right one for you, sir, or the wrong one, I am not so bold as to guess,' says Lesinge. 'I will however venture the estimation that you are native to no region of the north?'

The stranger blinks several times, as if he has difficulty understanding. His answer explains it.

'I am an English traveller, sir,' he says. He touches his hat again.

Cochonne's jaw falls open.

'Then lost you most certainly are,' Lesinge says. 'You have strayed into the incorrect nation.'

The Englishman smiles faintly. It has the curious effect of making him look even older.

'I must absolve myself of that particular error,' he says. 'I have missed my way in several other respects, but the place I seek is assuredly in France.'

'And what place is that?'

'The Castle Charizard.'

The brigands cannot disguise their consternation; not even Lesinge, who prides himself on his cool blood.

'There is no such place!' des Sables blurts out. 'It is very far from here!'

The Englishman blinks again but makes no other expression of the face. Possibly he has not understood.

'Quiet, boy!' Lesinge says. Cochonne meanwhile has picked up her rake and glares with open hostility at the rider. Lesinge draws a breath to compose himself.

'Be so good as to pardon this young fellow. He is unfortunately an imbecile.'

The Englishman's look passes vaguely over des Sables before returning. It is possibly the first time that anyone, man, woman or child, has regarded the beautiful youth with so little attention, since his twelfth year.

'You said the Castle—'

'Charizard,' the Englishman repeats.

Lesinge frowns mightily and chews his moustache.

'Castle Charizard, hum. The name is distantly familiar.'

'I am informed it stands somewhere to the west,' says the Englishman.

'To the west? No, no.' Lesinge gestures along the road. 'Who told you that? Some mischievous Bretons, according to my guess. No, nothing lies to the west except this gigantic forest, as you can see for yourself. The Castle Charizard . . . Is it not . . .' He turns to Cochonne. 'To the north, I think? Nearer the sea?'

Cochonne stares blankly.

'Yes,' says Lesinge, nodding to himself. 'I am sure it is to the north. I remember now, they speak of it in Morlaix. You should reverse your course and take the next road to your left, and ride that way until tomorrow. How fortunate a chance for you is this encounter! You would otherwise have been lost in good earnest among all those trees.'

The Englishman thanks Lesinge for his friendly advice. Lifting his hat to each of them in turn, he turns his mule around and rides slowly away.

'We should pursue him and kill him,' Cochonne says, gazing at the retreating figure. Her fingers flex on her rake in a dangerous manner.

'Patience, good Cochonne,' says Lesinge, laying a hand on her arm.

'Why? The English are brutes and infidels and the enemies of France.'

'This one did not seem so brutish.'

'We should at least knock him from his mule and take his purse. We are brigands. And if he cracks his head falling from the saddle—'

'By Saint Christopher! Why so thirsty for blood?'

'My father told me it is the duty of every French person to exterminate the English wherever they are found.'

'And you have always told me, my fair colossus, that your father is an ignorant beast. Besides, I am not certain our friend there was telling the truth. Though his accent was unusual he looked like an ordinary man. And what would an Englishman be doing asking after the country estate of the late Sir de Charizard? No. Gaspard Lesinge, he suspects a trick.'

'I believe you are right,' des Sables says. 'When I lived in London, which is the chief city of that nation, I observed many English. The men are all red in the face and roaring drunk, with no more manners than the pig. Also not one of them knows how to speak French.'

Lesinge nods. 'As I suspected. But who then is this stranger, and what could be his intention at the Castle Charizard? Perhaps some acquaintance of the late Sir, who hears he is dead and goes to claim for himself the family treasures. How lucky my quick wits were able to misdirect him so easily! We ought to hurry, my companions, and reach the castle before any other such villains.'

'Why not knock him from his mule anyway?' says Cochonne.

Lesinge laughs. 'So warlike, my Penthesilea? What would the Madonna say to you now?'

All three fall silent and look at one another, and then cry out as one — 'The stone!'

For a terrible instant Lesinge thinks it is lost. He can see no fiery gleam anywhere in the ruined grass. Then he spots it, lying just where it had been: dull, lifeless, no hotter or colder than the earth beneath; an ugly lump of rock which any traveller's horse might kick away unnoticed. Cochonne picks it up with an exclamation of relief and rubs it clean on her skirts.

Now des Sables pleads with them in earnest. Draw the velvet bag tight around it and wrap it in rags, he says. Bury it in the pack with the cheese and bread. Leave it untouched. He is eloquent and convincing, for it is conviction rather than cowardice which impels his argument. His eyes moisten with passion, producing an effect of high pathos. He swears he has seen his old master commune with devils through that very stone. Surely, he argues, the diabolic influences awaken now that Castle Charizard is near. There is a corrupted shrine there, he tells Lesinge, dedicated to the worship of One he will not name. Rob its treasures if you will, but do not risk your soul by bringing the demonoscope forth in the vicinity of that accursed place! Observe how the earth herself shrank from its touch! He kneels to lay his hand on the burnt grass. Let us not, he says, disregard the warning of Nature herself!

Lesinge does not like to be swayed by a mewling boy. Yet, and particularly since their adventures in Dinan, the lilywhite lad has become much less prone to fits of womanish complaint. He has even learned to walk fifteen miles in a day on his own legs, by God! Perhaps this is why Lesinge is minded to listen to the boy's advice.

Besides, in the shadow of the huge old trees it is easier to credit these tales of devils and evil bargains.

They hide the stone and enter the forest.

Across Brittany the three of them became good companions. They joked and sang, or mocked and grumbled, and did not mind which, so long as it helped the miles pass.

But this place, it is a kingdom of silence. It is like the world under the sea: dim and slow and full of strange shapes. Lesinge tries to sing —

> *Who passes by this way so late?*
> *Companions of the marjoram!*

— but his heart is not in it. The bearded trees seem to listen and disapprove. He feels himself a poor jester before a court of solemn lords. Even Broubrou hangs his head and holds his tongue.

Their road joins another, wider and marked by wheels. At the junction Lesinge and Cochonne look to des Sables. The view in either direction is the same: boulders overhanging the way, curtained with sickly moss, and colossal trees clutching them in their sprawling roots. Reluctantly, des Sables indicates the westward direction.

'How far?' says Lesinge.

'We will be there soon enough.'

None of them find it a cheerful thought.

After another hour or two the forest turns lighter and younger, until the trees are almost of ordinary dimensions. They are near the village of Charizard-la-Forêt. Before they reach it another path turns aside and ascends towards an outcrop of granite. Des Sables leads them up. They must avoid the villagers, he says. Even for Bretons they are savage animals. He has hidden his face in his hood. But the three brigands do not see another living soul abroad.

The day is growing late as they at last approach the end of their long pilgrimage. Atop the granite bluff is a plateau, overlooking the forest beneath like a raft afloat in a murky sea. There is the old castle, clinging to the raft. It is grey as a widow except where generations of rains have stained it black.

'The gates are broken!' exclaims des Sables.

Cochonne brushes the hair from her eyes and squints ahead. 'That is a rich man's castle? It is as bad as the castle in my village, which was a ruin used to keep cows and hens. And prisoners.'

Lesinge is sick to his heart. In his travels from Artois he has seen small estates as well as great ones, but never has he encountered a house sporting the name of castle which looked so miserable. Its iron gates droop from their hinges like empty sails. Half the windows in the façade are broken and the lawns and walks between have been trampled and left to sprout weeds. No one inhabits it at all, except a handful of dirty black goats who wander the desolation at their leisure.

'And the goats are escaped!' des Sables says, in a tone of profound shock. 'Where is old Diguelet the goatherd? Where is everyone?'

Lesinge sniffs and folds his arms. 'Your old master's house has been sacked,' he says.

'What do you mean?' says Cochonne.

'I mean that the revolution already toppled our friend the Sir de Charizard. I have heard stories like this from many places across France. It was in the summer of 'eighty-nine. People rose up everywhere and the houses of the lords were looted and burned.'

'Impossible,' des Sables says. 'The villagers would never dare approach our castle. They were too frightened. All the peasants believed it to be cursed and held the place in superstitious reverence.'

Lesinge raises his eyebrows and nods towards the broken gates and windows. 'Then perhaps your friends the goats are responsible.'

Broubrou appreciates the joke with a grim *hee-haw*.

'Do you mean to say,' Cochonne rumbles, 'that you made us walk all those miles for nothing?'

'I made you? I, Lesinge, gave the order? Perhaps my memory betrays me, but I seem to recall it was you who begged to accompany me, and threatened me with violence if I would not let you.'

'Dear companions,' des Sables says, 'I beg you, do not resume this old quarrel. The castle always had a bad appearance. One is a little surprised to find it decayed, but really it is not so much worse than it used to be.'

'I do not give a fig for how it appears,' says Lesinge. 'Its treasures, they are why we are here. Let us pray your master kept them well hidden from looters!'

'Have no fear on that account. The secret crypt is impenetrable.'

A growl of distant thunder interrupts their bickering.

Lesinge sighs. 'At least the roof remains. And if the doors are broken and the servants fled we shall have no difficulty going under it. Let us stable Broubrou and find beds to rest in, my faithful companions, before that storm arrives. We shall inspect the treasures in the morning.'

But the Castle Charizard does not consent even to this modest plan.

Entering the house is easy enough. Only the goats resent their approach, and a few swipes of Cochonne's rake chase them off. The old oak doors which were once securely locked have been smashed from their hinges by the mob.

Unfortunately the same mob then proceeded to pillage the rooms within like locusts in a field of wheat. If there was a movable article, it has been taken. 'The suit of armour!' wails des Sables, staring at an empty space under the hanging stair. 'The bearskin! The pewter urn!' He is a despairing catalogue of absent things. 'The curtains! The brocade stool! The shield of the fourth baron!' Lesinge and Cochonne follow him through the scene of devastation, equally despairing. They find beds, too massive for theft. The revolutionary villagers instead expressed their displeasure by breaking them in pieces and attempting to set them alight. Only the all-conquering Breton damp, absorbed over decades by each object in the house, has prevented conflagration.

Des Sables sits in the dust and filth of what was once his master's apartment, his head in his hands. 'Savages! Beasts!' There is evidence that the mob used the rooms for their entertainment, in the form of bottles strewn about, and greasy papers, and stains that reek of urine or worse.

Cochonne leans on her rake. 'The rewards of greed,' she says. She ought to be angry but she is not. Saint Mary is giving her a lesson concerning the vanity of earthly ambitions.

Lesinge also cannot be angry. He is too disappointed and too bitter. The riches of Castle Charizard were promised to him and him alone. It was his destiny, conferred by mysterious powers. And now his rightful inheritance has been scattered to nothing by the actions of lawless drunken peasants. He is filled with disgust. These common swine have no respect for the property of others, God curse them!

In room after room the despoliation continues. But when they reach the castle library, des Sables, who being familiar with the house has led the way, lets out an exclamation of relief.

'The library!' He hurries into the room. 'Look, it has not been touched. Regard the pictures still on the walls and the books in their cases! One supposes these Breton animals did not know their value.' He runs his finger over a fine table of honey-coloured wood. 'The reading desks are here without a scratch on them. And the chairs with their cushions.' An angelic smile lights his face. Their journey has not been wasted; Lesinge and Cochonne will be happy now, and forgive him. He turns to share their delight and is very surprised to see that neither has followed him into the library. They stand together in the door, gaping like children at the pantomime.

Cochonne, whose jaw has fallen open, makes the sign of the cross over her chest.

'Ah,' des Sables says, 'the skulls. Do not be afraid of them. They are only goats who died of old age. Perhaps one or two were sacrificed in the master's rites, but it makes no difference now they are dead and hanging there.'

Each case of books is surmounted by the head of a goat, bleached to the bone. The horns are adorned with ribbons in shades of red and black. On the broad part of each skull mysterious sigils have been painted in matching colours.

Between the cases hang a number of pictures. There is a witches' sabbath, and an illustration of the torments of hell, and a massacre of the innocents, along with several martyrdoms. Every scene is repulsive. There are still lives also. They show death's heads, decaying flowers, moths pinned to boards, animals cut for the butcher.

'Oh,' says des Sables, seeing the horrified expressions of his companions, 'these are nothing. The most severe accoutrements of wickedness are confined to the chapel.'

'The chapel?' Cochonne says, in a strangled voice.

Des Sables has never seen her frightened. He did not think her capable of it. To him she is a female Hercules. It disturbs him to see her cowering at nothing more than a presentiment of his late master's taste in decoration.

'Come,' he says encouragingly. He opens one of the cases and strokes his thumb over the bindings. 'Many of these are immensely valuable. My master often boasted of it. How stupid the mob was to leave such treasures for us! But we do not complain, my companions.'

Lesinge cannot allow the milk-white boy to outface him. Though he feels the sightless eyes of the dead goats watching him, he enters the room and puts on a careless manner.

'Bah,' he says. 'What do you know about the value of books? You can barely read.'

'But I remember how proud the master was of his collections. This one, for instance.' Des Sables draws a large volume from the shelf. 'He took particular pleasure in acquiring it. It cost many hundred pounds.' He hands it to Lesinge. 'As a man of letters, I am sure you recognise it?'

Lesinge turns it over in his hands and opens it in a few places. It coats his fingers in sooty dust. He cannot read any of the words. He guesses they are in Latin or Greek or the language of the Jews. Still, he must scan the pages across and back and nod and hum to himself. On the title page he reads *MALEFICORUM*, which he is certain is an evil word. He closes the covers quickly. His heart is beating fast. The skulls, curse them! — why do they all stare at him so?

'It is of some little value,' he says. 'As these things are commonly reckoned.'

Des Sables's face falls.

'But,' Lesinge says, 'where is the secret crypt? The treasures of gold and silver?'

Now des Sables looks wary. 'My captain,' he says, 'shall we not rest here for now? You may inspect all the volumes at your leisure, and will certainly find very valuable ones. See, there are several comfortable chairs.'

'Rest here?' cries Cochonne. She has still not crossed the threshold. 'You are mad.'

'Dear Cochonne,' des Sables says. 'It is only a few dead goats.'

She makes a small scream.

'Where does that lead?' says Lesinge, indicating a low arched door of dark wood studded with many nails. Though only a door, it seems to lurk menacingly in the corner furthest from the windows, where the dirt and dust of neglect are thickest and twilight already gathers.

'Through there is the chapel,' des Sables says. 'The key is hidden ... Aha!' In the shelf behind him is a series of false bindings, glued together to conceal a secret niche. With a cheerful grin he pushes them aside and extracts a key as long as his own hand. 'So much for our mob of bandits. The older parts of the house will be untouched. There is no other way through.'

'What use did your master have for a chapel?' Cochonne asks, from the door. 'He was the devil's man, that is plain.'

'Oh,' says des Sables, eager to explain, 'but this is a desecrated chapel, given over to the worship of the Evil One. My master and his libertine friends converted it for their purposes. Come, you may see for yourself. Beyond are apartments which I expect we will find still furnished.'

'I will not set foot in a desecrated chapel,' Cochonne says.

'My dear companion,' des Sables says, as a fond father might soothe a child. 'This is only an eccentric nobleman's house. There is nothing to fear. The infernal spirits would only appear after the performance of certain rituals—'

'By the saints!' Lesinge exclaims. 'Have you as much as half a brain in your head? You terrify our Amazon with this talk of unholy magic. Give me the key and hold your tongue.'

'But—'

'The key!' Lesinge feels less brave than he acts. Much less, in truth. Those skulls! — as the musty library darkens, and the distant thunder growls again, he imagines the dead goats coming to life and rattling their jaws of bone. But an outlaw is required at all times to season his bearing with a certain bravado.

Des Sables hands over the key with a sulky look. He has enjoyed being the leader of the company for once. Too much, Lesinge thinks. Let the boy remember who his captain is.

'I do not want that door opened,' Cochonne says. 'This is a house of the Devil.'

In honesty Lesinge suspects as much himself. But he must conquer his hesitation. Is Gaspard not favoured by demonic beings? He will not shrink from his destiny now.

'If so,' he says, with an insouciant air, 'I think he abandoned it some time ago, like the servants and the goatherd. I suppose the Devil would not have let his house be plundered by the filth of the village if he had been in residence. But you may wait in the door there, my quaking Penthesilea, while Lesinge investigates whether the master is at home.'

'I am not afraid,' Cochonne grumbles. But still she will not enter the library.

Lesinge inserts the key in the lurking door. The lock grinds and groans as it turns, as if enduring a nightmare.

Castle Charizard has sat on its granite bluff overlooking the ancient forest since long before the marriage of Anne of Brittany to Charles the Eighth, which joined the wild Celtic kingdom to France. Despite the attentions of the successive lords de Charizard, its bones and heart remain antique. Here, at the door from the library to the chapel, the old skeleton of the house begins. Lesinge steps under a very low arch into a chamber of stone and gloom. The three arched windows high in the far wall are small and grimy with soot.

'Pah!' he exclaims. 'His majesty the Devil may be out but it is murky as hell in here. Des Sables, find me a taper.'

'There are several candles. And a box for tinder. Permit me.' The valet enters behind him and opens a chest at the base of one of the squat columns.

Lesinge's eyes begin to adapt to the shadows.

During the reign of the Sun King, some efforts were made to clothe the castle chapel in more fashionable dress. The walls have been panelled in wood. The benches, Lesinge sees, are in a gracious style. There are candle-holders of brass wrought in pleasing classical shapes.

And then some more recent castellan interfered again, and nailed the skulls of goats between the candle-holders, and hung chains above the benches, from which dangle bones and iron pendants and mirrors of spotted silver. Des Sables has raised a flame and set a pair of candles burning. They are black, scented with a perfume of night-blooming flowers. By their light the unholy chapel is completely revealed. It is not large, but its every corner has been given over to vile devotion. The old monuments and pious tablets have been covered in black drapes painted with alchemical and cabbalistic symbols. There were once kneeling angels at the ends of the carved benches; their heads have been gouged away or stuck with nails. The altar, a bare block of stone, is surmounted by a goat skull of particularly impressive size, positioned so that the sockets of its eyes each hold a pillar of black wax. On the altar before the skull there is an iron dish and a knife. The simple crucifix in front of the windows has been hung upside down.

'Even the candles are dusty,' des Sables says. 'The servants must have fled for their lives when the mob came and never returned. Cowardly rogues!'

Lesinge works his jaw. He must speak just as carelessly. He cannot show fear when the boy does not, or by God, what will they think of him? He opens his mouth. But for the first time in many years he cannot think of what to say.

'It is a relief,' des Sables continues, as he lights more candles, 'to enter without the contribution of the musicians. The master employed a violin and oboe to produce unpleasant harmonies. The effect was very disquieting, I assure you.' He notices Lesinge's expression. 'Are you well, my captain?'

'Of course I am well. Why should I not be well? Imbecile!'

Des Sables shrugs. 'You look pale.'

'It is the bad air of this place. It oppressed me for an instant, nothing more. Where are the apartments beyond?'

Des Sables indicates two doors in the opposite wall. 'That,' he says, 'leads on to the old quarter of the castle. And that is the passage down to the crypt. It opens only with a secret mechanism.'

Cochonne, whose fear of being left alone has outweighed her disinclination to go deeper into the horrible castle, ducks through the arch behind them.

'Mother of God protect us,' she says, staring at the desecrated chapel.

'Enough candles,' Lesinge says to des Sables. 'Show us these apartments and be quick about it! Can you not see that poor Cochonne is terrified?'

'Would my captain not prefer to inspect the crypt first? My master's riches are surely down there, where I was never permitted to go unless blindfolded, if they are anywhere.'

'If?' cries Lesinge. '*If?*'

'I killed him,' Cochonne says in a tone the others have never heard from her before. 'His ghost will come to haunt me.'

'Absurd!' Lesinge exclaims. How the word echoes under the heavy stone arches! It seems to set the candles quivering and the shadows scurrying under the benches like silent rats. 'Enough nonsense, both of you. We shall inspect the crypt another time. It will be more convenient by daylight. For now we must locate some decent rooms. We will make a fire and pull off our boots and enjoy the comforts of the Sir de Charizard's house. If his ghost returns we shall thank it for the hospitality.'

Cochonne mutters *Ave Maria* as she crosses the chapel, keeping her head bowed to avoid sight of the altar. In her heart she promises the Madonna that she will destroy all the evil decorations when it is day. She does not think the Virgin will begrudge her warmth and rest before she undertakes the task.

Beyond the chapel is a squat stone tower, the very oldest part of the castle. Except for the breaking of a few windows it is untouched by plunder. Preferring more modern accommodation, the late Sir de Charizard left these low dark rooms for guests, or more commonly for nobody, since the libertines of his circle were not often tempted to visit such a distant and backward retreat.

These accommodations, scorned by the ladies and gentlemen of Paris, represent to Cochonne and Lesinge a luxury beyond their dreams. The stone floors are softened with skins and rugs and the walls with faded weavings, and the bulky oak furnishings with cushions of embroidery and silk. There is no one to prevent them throwing themselves in this chair or that bed just as they please, once they have beaten a little dust out of their way. Soon they have a merry fire burning in one of the cavernous hearths. Lesinge begins to dream of wine. It is only a dream for now. The kitchens and cellars have been thoroughly looted. But it is a pleasant dream.

Beyond the walls deep twilight has come. All the windows are blue-black and from time to time the thunder echoes again. The little brigand band draws closer to the fire as a night wind commences moaning around the tower. They have made their camp in the highest room, furthest from the chapel below.

Lesinge, though, is restless.

His companions, they are simple creatures. A little warmth, a rug to lie on, and there! — they are happy, like cats. The boy des Sables loves to prate about the great mansions he has seen and the lords and ladies he has served but his soul is as much a peasant's soul as Cochonne's. All their cares are banished by a good fire and a comfortable bed.

Not him, no. Gaspard is a man of destiny. Great riches await him here, promised by immortal powers. He can almost hear the piles of gold and silver calling to him from their concealed places: Free us! Find us, we are yours! He paces the room back and forth while Cochonne and des Sables lounge sleepily, turning their stinking feet in front of the flames.

'Regard, Cochonne,' des Sables says. 'Our captain shuns the warmth of this fire I made. He is a miserable old man who prefers cold and darkness.'

Cochonne chuckles. 'I think he misses the old women in their hovels who treated him like God's prophet.'

Lesinge ignores them. His sensitive brigand's instinct has drawn him to the far corner of the room, where an empty armoire leans against the wall.

He looks at the floor in front of it.

Only a man of genius, he thinks, notices such things without even having to try.

'Ho, Captain!' des Sables calls out. 'There is no use robbing that armoire. It was empty even when there was enough light to see inside.'

'If that was a joke it fell over its own feet like a drunken ass. Bring me a candle, unless you are too lazy to stand up.'

'What do you want with a candle?'

'To examine the door concealed behind the armoire.'

Des Sables jumps to his feet. 'There is no door there!'

'Well then, bring a candle and prove yourself right.'

But des Sables is wrong. The frame can be seen by anyone who squeezes their head tight to the wall. The boy's fingers are slender enough to slip behind the armoire and confirm the existence of the hidden door by touch.

'I do not understand,' he says. 'I know every secret of the castle.'

'And I have exposed your ignorance with two minutes of investigation,' Lesinge says.

Des Sables shakes his head. 'It is most probably a disused door. A relic of some former period of the tower's construction.'

'Then,' Lesinge says triumphantly, 'what explains these deep marks on the floor? The armoire has evidently been dragged away from the wall and replaced. Frequently, I would guess, and recently.'

Cochonne has hauled herself to her feet also. She had been feeling pleasantly sleepy. 'We will open no hidden doors in this castle,' she says. 'Not until the morning.'

Lesinge turns to her. 'Do you propose that we go to sleep in this room, and let the fire burn out in the night, not knowing what may be just on the other side of the wall?'

Cochonne looks sulky.

'Nothing can be on the other side,' des Sables says. 'The master would have told me. We shared every confidence.'

'Naturally,' Lesinge says. 'It is well known that great lords consider their valets trusted equals.'

Cochonne sighs. If this is what she must do before she can go to sleep, she will do it. 'Both of you talk too much,' she says, and shoulders them out of the way. She takes hold of the armoire and pulls it away from the wall with no more effort than a person of ordinary strength uses to push back a chair.

Before them is the concealed door, very narrow, very low and very old. There is no keyhole, only a simple latch.

'There.' Cochonne leans back and dusts off her hands. 'Now you open it, since you talk so bravely.'

Lesinge's heart beats faster. How much of the burden of leadership consists of conquering oneself, not others! In his imagination this hidden door is an upright tomb, from which heaps of bones will tumble as soon as it is opened. But because Cochonne mocks him he cannot hesitate even a moment.

He lifts the latch.

The candle illuminates a tiny room beyond. A writing desk, a wooden chair, a lattice window as much lead and soot as glass, and the bottom of a narrow spiral stair; that is all. On the desk are some pens and ink and a blotter, and also a casket for papers. The secret room smells of stone and dust. Outside the wall the wind whoops and hisses.

Lesinge cocks an eyebrow at des Sables.

'It seems the Sir de Charizard did not entrust his faithful des Sables with the whole of his confidence.'

Des Sables pouts like a girl.

Lesinge turns to Cochonne. 'Have I your permission to enter? Or do you suspect this room to belong to the Devil's secretary?'

'One day,' Cochonne rumbles, 'I will close your mouth for good with my fist.'

Lesinge smiles. 'Do not resent me, dear companions. I have many years' advantage of you both in knowledge and expertise. These small triumphs of Gaspard's are quite natural. How else could he be your captain whom you follow so willingly? Come, let us see what our unlamented Sir kept hidden in his private writing-room.'

The casket holds a single document of several pages sewn together, handsomely written and concluded with seals and flourishing signatures. Lesinge extracts it with a grand gesture. He clears his throat, bows to his audience, raises his chin and begins to read the topmost page: '*I, Hippolite-Aimant-Louis de Bobigny de Charizard, being of the age of twenty-nine in this year of grace seventeen hundred and eighty-eight, in entire health of mind and body, do by these present signs intend* — By God! It is his will!'

Cochonne and des Sables frown at one another.

'What use is that to us?' says Cochonne.

'Whatever use ingenuity can make of it. At the very least we may find the riches of his late lordship itemised in these pages. Hold the candle and let me read.'

'It is several pages,' des Sables says doubtfully.

'I would rather sleep,' Cochonne says.

Lesinge ignores them. He is scanning the paragraphs with a practised finger, tracing lines of de Charizard's commanding script. 'Declarations . . . Affirmations . . . bah, this is the mere wind of lawyers, it says nothing of interest.' He folds back the first page. 'Now, here! The preamble is done, and we come to the real business.' He squints and recites: '*To my nearest cousins Olympe and Augustine de Bobigny-Dodrieaux, I irrevocably and unalterably bequeathe, nothing whatsover*—ha! poor Olympe, poor Augustine! — *Likewise to any offspring of theirs, or any relation of theirs, who may claim kinship of blood with me, I bequeathe an equal and commensurate nothing at all. Likewise in the case of any further cousins of mine, in any degree, who may happen to exist, unknown to me, or to any other blood relations, however distant, I do solemnly acknowledge their claim upon my estate, and recognise it, and accordingly bequeathe to them a share in it of precisely nil per cent, in any case to amount to a value of not more than zero pounds and zero pennies* . . . By God, he is a comedian, your late master!

Look, he lists several others by name to whom he leaves nothing. They will laugh at the jest, no doubt.' Lesinge turns another page. 'Where is your real wealth, my comic friend? Ah! *My estate in real property, including the Castle Charizard, by the town of Charizard-le-Forêt in Brittany, and all the fixed and movable goods therein, and all that pertains to the same estate* . . . yes yes yes, but tell us who inherits it? Ah, here! . . . *I bequeathe in their entirety, except only for certain few items particularised hereafter, to Madam Luce Denfert, of Paris.*' Lesinge looks enquiringly at des Sables, who has given such a start that he spills hot wax on his own fingers. 'Careful, oaf! You will set the paper alight.'

'The Denfert!' des Sables exclaims. 'Does it really say so?'

'At great length. This Denfert is his mistress, I suppose?'

'By no means. He barely spoke of the Denfert. When the name was mentioned by another he would dismiss me from the room. I understood her to be some very great lady whom he and his wicked associates held in the most excessive reverence and fear.'

Lesinge shrugs. 'His whore, then. She might pay handsomely for this document.' Des Sables is shaking his head earnestly, but Lesinge has returned to the paper. 'What trifles, I wonder, are excluded from the grand whore Denfert's inheritance? *To my friend and co-religionist the Viscount Rapidâches—*'

'A monster!' cries des Sables. 'The most depraved of libertines!'

'*— I bequeathe the sum of five thousand pounds, and also my picture of the Martyrdom of Saint Sebastian, and also my picture of the Rape of the Sabine Women, and also* . . . Yes yes yes.' Lesinge skips several lines with his fingers. 'The good viscount is welcome to his trash. What else . . .'

His hand comes suddenly to a stop. His eyes widen.

'What is it?' says Cochonne. She is bored. She has been considering the narrow spiral stair, whose base enters the minuscule writing-room in a corner. She wonders whether the room above holds something more interesting.

Lesinge clears his throat and reads more slowly.

'*To my faithful valet Valentin Pichot, called des Sables—*'

'To me?' des Sables squeaks. 'I am remembered in his will?'

Lesinge smiles. 'Most certainly.'

'What does it say?'

Lesinge chortles. 'Oh, he is indeed the comedian, that master of yours.'

'What does it say?' roars Cochonne.

'Very well, very well. *To my faithful valet Valentin Pichot, called des Sables, I leave the suit of black velvet, together with the blindfold and the several ribbons of black silk, in recognition of the many happy hours he passed in that costume—*'

'Beast!' des Sables exclaims.

'Patience, boy, there is more, . . . *Also to the same des Sables I bequeathe the chess-board of ash and onyx, known to my ancestors as the Devil's Chess-Board, together with all those chess-pieces belonging to it which I have acquired, in recognition of the particular enjoyment he had in contemplating certain mysteries in the game of chess—*'

'Vile, wicked villain! To hell with that cursed prop, and all—'

'Attend, attend,' Lesinge says. 'There is one last bequest for you.'

'Even in death he mocks me. Son of a whore!'

'Listen. *Also to the same des Sables I eternally and irrevocably bequeathe the heirloom of my ancestors variously called the Summoning-Stone, the Demonoscope or the Eye of Hell, and charge the same Valentin Pichot, called des Sables, to keep the said stone always upon his person, in acknowledgement of the same des Sables's great fondness for the stone, and the pleasure he always took in it.*' Lesinge raises a finger to forestall another interruption and continues reading. '*The said stone being a gift presented to my family in perpetuity by the Devil, and the familial line terminating with my death, I therefore also bequeathe any curse, misfortune, ill luck, or other diabolic influence, to the same Valentin—*'

'May his soul burn for all eternity!' des Sables cries, heedless of the droplets of wax. 'Worst of masters, how I wish it had been I who struck the blow that terminated your execrable life!'

Lesinge rolls the papers up. 'Calm yourself, young friend. This is no more than a joke. Your master amused himself with the thought of leaving behind only insults and sneers.'

Cochonne can see that des Sables is upset. 'He died without dignity,' she says, resting a giant hand on the boy's shoulder. 'It was the death of a common coward. And now God punishes him for ever.'

'Well, my dear Cochonne,' Lesinge says, 'it appears the boy is the lawful owner of your Madonna. Oh, do not scowl at me so. This witty nobleman is to blame for the joke, not Lesinge. Though it is composed in an ironic spirit the document is properly attested, as far as I can tell. Our stone and everything in it belongs to des Sables.'

'Then I will take it to the sea and throw it in.'

Lesinge sees Cochonne's frown darken. It is time to make peace among his company. 'The *lawful* owner, I said. But fortunately for you both, Gaspard has already stolen it. You may set the police on me to recover your property if you wish, but until that time it will stay wrapped in my pack. I forbid any further discussion of it. Shall we go and sleep by our fire, my dear companions? This was an amusing discovery, but no more.'

'What about the stair?' says Cochonne.

Lesinge shrugs. 'No doubt it gives access to the roof. You may sleep under the sky again if you wish. I prefer to ignore it.'

Des Sables, who of the three has the proportions best fitted to the steep tight stairs, is already peering up, candle in hand. 'There appears to be another room above,' he says. He ducks his head and turns his shoulders and mounts three or four steps. 'Some attic — No! I see a bed.'

'In which the Sir rested from his testatory exertions,' Lesinge says.

'Or went to shit,' says Cochonne.

'That too is a form of relief.'

A gasp sounds above.

Lesinge sighs and rolls his eyes. 'Another surprise?'

'Or,' Cochonne says, 'he has stumbled and hurt his toe on the bed.'

Lesinge chuckles. One night, he thinks, while they occupy this pleasant empty castle, he will have this girl, pious and gigantic though she is.

'Des Sables?' he calls.

There is no answer.

'Or,' Cochonne says, 'he has fallen off the roof.'

'He is a feather of a boy. The wind would blow him back on again. Ho!' Lesinge puts his head up the stair. 'Valentin Pichot! What have you found?'

Des Sables's bare feet appear, then his trembling legs, then the whole of him. He has turned white as a ghost.

'What is it?'

'Up there—' Des Sables's voice runs dry. He swallows. 'In the bed. She is . . .'

'She? Who? Do not gibber, but explain yourself!'

'Dead,' des Sables cries. 'She is dead!'

Lesinge's heart sinks. His happy thoughts of conquering the virginity of Cochonne fade away. By Saint Christopher, he is tired of goat skulls and diabolic jests and all things sinister!

'A woman,' des Sables stammers. 'On the bed — Expired!'

Lesinge sighs again. The lad and Cochonne are both staring at him. If there is unpleasantness to be faced he must be the one to face it. 'Give me the candle.'

The stair is infernally narrow and steep. It is all he can do not to scrape his head. Everything above is dark.

Holding the candle before him, Lesinge first sees the bed. It occupies almost the whole room, which is as cramped and cold as his former prison cell, and also significantly smaller. Why any noble would make a secret bedchamber here he cannot begin to imagine.

Unless it was a place for criminal acts? — for forbidden and merciless seductions?

He sees an arm, and then a foot.

The body lies unmoving on the bed. Its arms are flung loosely to the sides. It wears a woman's clothes, boots included. The boots are filthy with sand and grass.

'Captain?' des Sables calls from below.

'Hush!'

There is no smell of decay. If the woman was brought here and was unable to escape because the armoire blocked the door, and so died like a prisoner in an oubliette, it cannot have happened long ago. The face, Lesinge thinks, will not be rotten and crawling with maggots.

Nevertheless, a lengthy interval goes by before he can take the last steps into the room and raise the candle to look.

He cannot believe the woman is dead at all. Though quite still she looks peaceful. Her eyes are closed. Dark hair tumbles over half her face. There is not a spot of corruption on her. Her hands, however, are rather dirty. Both of them are closed in fists.

In each hand she appears to be holding some small object.

Lesinge frowns. He reaches the candle towards her left arm.

'Lesinge?'

'Be quiet!' he repeats, too loudly for so small a chamber. At the noise of his voice the woman twists and emits a moan. Her fingers loosen. The object grasped in her left hand falls onto the linens of the bed.

It is his lost totem and companion, the blind cavalier; the white knight from the game of chess, its eyes of jet removed.

The woman pushes hair away from her face. In incomprehensible astonishment, Lesinge recognises her also.

Then she opens her eyes.

CHAPTER NINE

Miss Farthingay —

The very words, that we write, dissolve and rearrange themselves, before our eyes. — Insects of ink —

What has happened to our tale?

Reader — we are — *adrift* — As though this very room, where we sit, with pen, pot, and paper — our shuttered retreat, where, alone among all the places of the world, we have glimpsed contentment — As though it were removed, to the deck of some solitary vessel, lost in a foggy ocean, a thousand miles from land. — A ghost ship, crewed by invisible hands, whose sails droop like shrouds in the endless mist — Our table, our ink and paper, and we ourselves

Alone, alone, all, all alone,
Alone on a wide, wide sea!*

Once, we raised the spirits of the past, and bade them move and speak at our command. Our art was absolute power. — We, its tyrant.

We are *thrown down* —

Where is Mr Peach? He, whom we conjured from his grave, for your entertainment, and, though you knew it not, your edification. — He, whose secrets no man or woman remembers, save we ourselves. He, for whom these pages were birthed — THOMAS PEACH! where have you gone?

* Coleridge's 'Antient Mariner'.

We cannot see him. At the attempt, darkness repels us — Darkness, and horror. We glimpse only those terrible dreams of desolation and abyss. — *They* were once, inside *him*. Now, we fear, *he* is — inside *them* —

Miss Farthingay — Awakens.

So much we know, but no more. — She wakes, as though from the sleep of aeons — Arthur's sleep, or Merlin's — All ignorant of where she lies, or how she came to be there. — And we, no less ignorant than she!

A curious suspicion comes over us. Mere instinct — a fleeting sensation —

Is it YOU, reader, that knows, what we do not?

Is it *your* invisible hand, that can raise the sails, and steer us to harbour?

Was it YOU who toppled us, from our imperial throne?

We surrender it gladly. Our time has passed, as Mr Peach's time has passed. Other arts must supersede this old necromancy of ours — Of his —

Heavens! some filthy ruffian leers over the bed!

He holds a single candle in his calloused hand, without even a dish to support it decently.

The room is low, damp, musty, and miserably confined. — Some hovel, surely — and this gaping oaf, with crumbs of cheese in his beard, and his shirt stained and reeking, is its lord.

Who has transported our heroine, to such a place? — Not Clary? — Clary, who professed her concern and regard for her old play-mate, in such passionate terms?

Or was our last chapter — in its intirety — Mere phantasy? — A dark dream?

We cannot tell —

In Miss Farthingay's brain the rational machinery stirs, casting off the rust of sleep. Instinctual dread seizes her. — She sits bolt upright, and can scarce suppress a scream.

Some voice calls from elsewhere — an adjacent room of the

hovel. The leering rogue answers a single impatient word — This brief exchange conducted, in French.

So, we are in France yet! — No wonder we proceed, without chart or compass. — We can no more distinguish one corner of that nation from another, than *China*, from *Siam* — and the language is a mystery to us, unless pronounced with care and measure — Which are not to be expected, from an heathenish villain, such as this fellow bending above Miss Farthingay's bed. Look at him — Have you ever seen a visage, more consummately *French*? — The droop at either corner of the mouth, which even his sprouting moustache cannot disguise. — The stoop of the shoulders, undignified in any man not yet sixty. — The hungry animation of his ill-proportioned features, better suited to a pole-cat, than any human face. — His general and universal *dishevelment*, in a degree no Briton of any station will tolerate.

We deduce, with much relief, that the blackguard intends no insult to our heroine's honour. His regard, though ugly and low-bred, is full of wonder. — The simpleton appears struck by something akin to superstitious awe. Indeed, he retreats from the bed, as Miss Farthingay meets his look with hers — a motion as welcome to her, as it is to us.

Who would not have feared for her safety, in such a place as this?

The gawping ruffian looks from her face, to her hand — her left hand — Back to her face — back again — As though astonished to discover, that an human person is possessed of a sinister arm —

Following his gaze, Miss Farthingay notices, that some small thing lies on the bed, at her left side. — A small pale thing, that catches a little candle-light.

It is — a chess-piece — A white knight, with a peculiar sorrowful expression.

As though recalling the senseless transactions of a dream, Miss Farthingay remembers how Clary put the objects in her hands, in the last instants, before —

Before — what? — We know not what — Nor does Miss Farthingay.

She opens her right hand, and sees there another thing, which she held tight in her sleep. Another chess-piece — the *black king* — Identical to that so importunately pressed upon her, by the villain de Charizard, in his black carriage.

These things are not dreams. —

— Clary? says Miss Farthingay, looking from side to side.

An exclamation comes from the adjacent room. Some hasty conversation ensues. — There appear to be two voices in the room below.

Below? — Lo, reader — this hovel is furnished, with a stair of *stone*! — An old winding stair, such as the architects of our cathedrals inserted in the walls of their monuments — too close and cramped almost, for the passage of the human frame.

This cannot be a peasant's abode. — Look again — Here is a window — barely so wide as an hand, but it is lead and glass. And the floor, though dirty, might almost be marble. — It is paved, with alternating darker and lighter squares. —

Miss Farthingay's faculties gather, with the rapidity and ductility, natural to youth and a strong intellect. She meets the ugly ruffian's look with as much dignity as she can muster, in a situation so mysterious and unpleasant — in surroundings, so unpropitious.

— Who, sir, are you? Where is my companion?

The filthy Frenchman growls something. His accent is so uncouth, as to frustrate even that small familiarity with the language, acquired by our heroine.

— *Je suis Mademoiselle Farthingay*, she says. *D'Angleterre.* — And, having come to the temporary limit of her ability to converse with the peasant in his own tongue, she proceeds, with the natural confidence of every British person abroad, in her proper speech. — I demand to know what this place is, and to be brought before some person of cultivation. Where is my companion?

Demand and enquiry are evidently equally incomprehensible to the churl. He grins, as though it amuses him to be addressed in language he cannot understand.

— *Mademoiselle . . . Fardinguée?* he says.

All the fellow's features are of the sort that, if she had met them upon the public road, she would fear for her property. Yet there is a curious sprightliness in his manner — most particularly, in his eye.

— Far — thing — gay, she repeats.

The man juts out a leg — or rather, a length of mud-caked breech and tattered stocking, terminating in several holes, through which she glimpses portions of a foot, of unspeakable grossness — and whisks that arm of his, which is not encumbered by the candle, into the air — Thereby performing, a dirty bow.

— *Gaspard Lesinge*, he says, *encore à votre service, mademoiselle.*

The display of rustic courtesy — as improbably energetic, as though introduced by an actor, upon the comic stage — quite startles Miss Farthingay. During the interval afforded by her surprize, there is a rapid exchange of speech between the man and another below, who is heard ascending the stair. A moment more, and the pinched and dismal bed-chamber is invaded, by a vision of loveliness — A tall fine-featured girl, whose natural beauty outshines the depredations of weather and dirt, to which it has evidently been subjected. Her golden hair is lent an angelic radiance, by the candle-flame —

Forgive us, reader — The newcomer is no woman at all, but a doe-eyed male youth. You will excuse the mistake, for a *Viola* or a *Rosalind* might have appeared so, when they donned their disguises, and passed for young men — nay, an *Imogen* even — sweetest, wisest, most determined in gentleness, of all the heroines of Shakespear!

Alas, there are no such men as that *Fidele* in the world, but only in the dreams of the best of poets, whose genius gives them a woman's soul and heart.

This fair youth — Reader, have we not met him before?

There cannot be *two* such creatures, within the limit of a single book — Perhaps not in all the world.

The recollection comes likewise upon Miss Farthingay — though it is as wholly inexplicable to her, as to us. But, such a countenance, once seen — who could forget it?

This is the valet of that impertinent seigneur, the Monsieur de Charizard! —

Recall, reader, how we noticed him, among the crowd gathered to watch the remarkable demonstration of Monsieur Philidor — the chess-player — It was our very first chapter, was it not? — The lad was then trumped up, in a ridiculous affectation of silks and buckled shoes, and sent about the company, at the behest of his presumptuous master, to learn our heroine's name.

Of the shoes there is no sign. But the silks are the same, though filthied and torn almost beyond recognition. — Not that either Miss Farthingay, nor we ourselves, require the evidence of his *dress*, to know him. We cannot forget that face, dirtied though it is. — Moreover, the youth has also recognized Miss Farthingay! — It is plain to see. — Observe, his sudden stop — his gaping astonishment —

Is this some further plot of the villain de Charizard? — Has he appeared, while our heroine slept, and, by some malign trickery beyond our understanding, conveyed her to this chearless place?

Miss Farthingay shudders at the thought.

But — she *will not submit*. — She is quite finished, with abductions, and imprisonments, and rescues — With playing a mere pawn, in another's game.

She rises from the bed — leaving the chess-pieces lying there, white and black, side by side. The rogue who made her his flourishing bow, indicates them with a soiled finger — Says something to Miss Farthingay, which has the sound of an enquiry — then, with care — so as not to alarm her, it appears — Fetches up the white knight from the linens, and turns it before his eyes, with an expression of such rapture, that his natural ugliness is transformed — Almost —

The chess-pieces — The valet — This place, altogether unknown to us — The stranger — Reader, there is here as great a tangle of mystery, as in the closing scenes of that play of *Cymbeline*, to which we alluded a moment past — though, alas! lacking the genius of a Shakespear, to unravel every thread, and compel all into harmony.

Miss Farthingay will have none of it. — The satisfaction of *understanding*, she does not desire in the least, at present. Her exclusive wish, is that the drama be brought to an *end*.

Has she escaped the malevolent influence of M Denfert, only to fall again under the persecution of the libertine de Charizard? — Then let him stand before her, instead of sending his servants to treat with her! — Let the cowardly villain face her, and feel the majesty of her indignation!

— You, she says, indicating the comely youth with an imperious gesture. He shrinks from it, as though she commanded thunderbolts. — Bring your master here at once. I will no longer tolerate his amusements, if such he imagines they are.

The valet stares incomprehendingly, like a sheep — if there were sheep so lovely.

Miss Farthingay stamps a boot. — Do you speak English?

The boy holds up a trembling hand, finger and thumb a little apart.

— Small, he says. — English — small.

Miss Farthingay lets pass the opportunity, to correct his grammar. She is out of patience.

— I wish to speak with your master immediately. Also with the companion who conducted me here. And for Heaven's sake, have this fellow stand further off, and fetch more candles!

The valet shakes his head helplessly.

— Great God! — Miss Farthingay fixes the boy with such a stare, as though she will impress her meaning upon him, by mere force of will. — Your — master — she says, as one might address a deaf old uncle. — Here — Now!

The valet delivers one of those rueful smiles, impossible of atchievement by any face that is not French.

— The master, he says. — Not is. *Il est mort.*

Miss Farthingay frowns.

— Your master is — dead?

He nods eagerly. — *Oui, oui,* the master is dead. The head — He taps his own head, and mimes an eruption with his hands, accompanied by an illustrative noise, *Bouf!*

— You refer to Monsieur de Charizard?

The other man is nodding as well, with still more vigorous enthusiasm — *Bien sûr* — *Le Monsieur de Charizard* — *sa tête* — *Bouf!*

Is this true? — the despicable seducer, dead?

Miss Farthingay is uncertain. We also cannot know, whether to trust the information of these French fellows. Every thing is doubtful, in this unanticipated scene.

Miss Farthingay nevertheless *hopes*, it is true. — A thought, no doubt very shocking — yet we cannot condemn her for it. The only regret she can muster, for the demise of her unwanted suitor, is that he cannot now be summoned to explain himself, in tolerable English.

The two Frenchmen — the fair and the grotesque — have begun talking between one another, with that animation of gesture and tone, so characteristic of the discourse of their nation. Miss Farthingay will not stand by, while low-born foreigners conduct private conversation, before her face.

— Where, she says, in an imperious tone, Is my companion? *Ou est ma amie?* She ought to be informed that I have woken. I believe she speaks good French, which will be convenient.

It is no use. She cannot make herself understood, no matter how distinctly she pronounces her speech.

A most unwelcome predicament, for a *poet!* — one who lives by the word. —

It is hardly less unfortunate, for an humble historian, such as ourselves. How are we to conduct our scene, when the greater proportion of our actors express themselves, in *miching mallecho?*[*]

Neither the unkempt rogue nor the comely valet gives any indication, that they will go and fetch Clary. Miss Farthingay, therefore, determines to seek her by her own efforts.

The state of her dress is quite shocking. — But she will go forth nevertheless. — Clary? she calls, descending the Lilliputian stair — Where are you, dear sister? I am awake. —

Have you, reader, met in your dreams — as we have — those mysterious houses, which seem to extend themselves, the further one proceeds within?

This place, which we thought an hovel — albeit an hovel of stone — is under some such enchantment. It is no miserable peasant abode at all. Room follows room, though all dark, inelegant, and quite without convenience or comfort. — Draughty door, gives on to desolate apartment. — When Miss Farthingay inspects a window, she discovers she is high above the ground.

This is some old fortified house, or château! — though, by every visible token, long abandoned.

We have heard of such mansions, in our neighbour kingdom. In the long twilight of the Old Regime, there were many poor men, who still bore the title of noble or *seigneur*. Lords, in little more than name — their fortunes, dissipated — Their antient seats, neglected and crumbling.

Doubtless, we and Miss Farthingay have been transported to some such woeful ruin. See, how every thing is antique — These rough stools of wormy wood, and those faded cloths — tokens of wealth and splendour, ten score years ago, but rendered barbarous, by the passing of generations.

Beyond a minuscule doorway is a room, where a smokey fire burns in a great crude hearth, and boots and cloaks and packs lie scattered about. These at least are marks of habitation, though

---

* 'It means nothing.' — Prince Hamlet.

none of the politest. — Elsewhere, our heroine finds only cold black apartments, and no trace of Clary.

The curiously sprightly Frenchman — we forget his name — follows her, with the candle, maintaining throughout her explorations a respectful commentary, which she must ignore, because she cannot understand.

How vexing, to have only Frenchmen for company! — But what else was to be expected, from an excursion to France? We have only ourselves to blame. —

Frenchmen, we say. — We must correct ourselves. There is one other in the house, besides the ugly ruffian and the valet.

We barely know how to describe this specimen. But what else is there to do, except try the attempt? — Clary is not here, to give her account of the place, nor how we are come to it. We must face what lies before us — alone —

The third personage is no Frenchman at all, but — a *woman* of France. This, despite standing far above six feet high, with shoulders broad as a prize-fighter's — arms, with the girth of legs — hands, more suited to the battle-axes of the old Northmen, than needle and thread. Those who study the bones that lie deep in earth, tell us, that Europe was once trod by giants. Here is their descendant — attired in smock and petticoat — As filthy and travel-worn, as her companions. — *Companions* they surely are, for they talk familiarly, and seem as thoroughly discontented with one another, as only companions can be. But what species of company this might be, is far beyond any guess of ours — Unless the three of them have together escaped, from the collection of those wandering mountebanks, who pretend to display *mer-maids* and *wolf-men*, to amuse the ignorant and vulgar.

The valet of de Charizard! — how comes *he* among them?

Stairs of stone descend, to further regions of the château — Which Miss Farthingay is prevented from investigating, by the refusal of the rogue with the candle, to accompany her below. When she demands to hold the light herself — with gestures sufficiently plain, to banish all ambiguity — he shakes his head, and steps away — *Mais non, mademoiselle Fardinguée.*

Insufferable boldness!

Her only recourse, is to treat with the stammering valet — An unhappy marriage, between Miss Farthingay's bad French, and the boy's much worse English. — Where is the lady? The youth knows no lady. All the people of the château are not here. — Where did she go? The lady, all in black? — *Toute noire?* — At this description of Clary, the ugly rogue becomes animated. Miss Farthingay takes this for a sign, that the fellow has seen her. — But when she asks, where the lady in black is, he will only shrug, and grin, and wink his curiously penetrating eyes, and give an answer she cannot understand — seems to say, *En l'enfer!* — And he laughs, and capers, and gesticulates, as though Miss Farthingay's predicament is a jest infinitely amusing. Some further lunatic notion strikes him. — He smites his greasy palm on his forehead, delves in his travelling-pack, and with an eager exclamation brings forth, and thrusts under the startled eye of Miss Farthingay —

Another *chess-piece!* —

An ivory queen, with a pointed crown — *C'est vous!* he exclaims — darting his chin back and forth, like a jackdaw when it goes afoot — *N'est-ce pas? La reine blanche, c'est vous en vrai!* —

Were we mistaken, in supposing these comfortless old apartments, part of a neglected lordly seat? Is this instead a French *Bedlam?* — a madhouse, far from every road or village? — and these three strangers, its condemned inmates?

Miss Farthingay grows alarmed, at the grotesque performance. — Withdraw, monsieur, she says — I am not used to being addressed in this manner. — But either he does not understand, or he lacks any instinct of good breeding — Either explanation, we think, is as likely as the other — And he continues to dance about our poor heroine, waving the white queen, and chattering without cease.

The *Gargantua* remonstrates with him, in a grumbling *patois*, equally incomprehensible.

The *Ganymede* attempts to placate them both. — They abuse him — He scorns them. — All shouting, pointing, waving their arms, like three petulant maestros, that compete to conduct their discordant Gallic symphony.

And, their stench! It is as beyond our powers of description, as their speech. —

A lady such as Miss Farthingay — whatever her present condition — Cannot possibly be expected to keep such company. As well shut her in the kennel, and require her to endure the society of hounds.

— This, she thinks, is intolerable. — Therefore — Tolerate it, I shall not.

She claps her hands — once — twice — And, when even this gesture fails to procure silence — she screams.

— I shall retire, she says, in the startled interval that follows, to the room above, where I hope neither my ears nor my nose will be further offended by your company. Though sleep appears improbable, I expect to rest undisturbed until morning, when I intend to quit this house, whosoever it belongs to; for you, I am certain, are not the lawful occupants. *Madame, messieurs, je vous souhaite une bonne nuit.* — With these words, delivered to as uncomprehending an audience, as that congregation of *fish*, to whom Saint Anthony of Padua once preached — Miss Farthingay sweeps from the stinking room — through the low dark door — Alas! she has no candle! — but dignity precludes retreat. — She finds her way, to the narrow winding stair, and ascends, guided by touch. — Leaving behind her, a doubtful chorus of murmurs.

Once before — we think — and she also thinks it — She went through an house, in the dark. — With Clary to guide her, then. — Can the girl have been so heartless, despite all her protestations of affection, to bring her old friend and play-mate to *this* place, and abandon her to the care of *these* people?

We feared Miss Clarissa Riddle capable of any wickedness. You recall it, reader. — Our judgment is recorded, for all eternity, in our former volume — Printed there, as enduring as any gospel. — And yet, so cruel a betrayal, we are unwilling to credit.

Miss Farthingay will not think of it. She will not think, at all. She will do nothing, except await the coming of dawn. — With cautious benighted steps, she attains the bed-chamber.

Though she has surrendered every expectation of comfort, she thinks she will at least remove her boots. —

Perfect dark! — and the wind moaning, about the tower walls — The odours of dust and damp stone. — She sits herself in the bed, refusing to admit the tears, that threaten her eye. — Clary — she thinks, despite herself — You, whom I called sister — did you nurture such bitter resentment for so many years, that this is the treatment you chuse to inflict upon me? — I, who never meant you harm, nor thought of you except with tender affection?

She recalls Clary's impassioned protestations — or, thinks she recalls them, for every recollection of that mysterious night, is like a memory snatched from the drowned fragments of a dream.

Did the wild girl not bid her farewell for ever? — and tell her, that all her hopes of safety lay in the hands of — THOMAS PEACH?

Here, reader, we have the advantage of our heroine. — *She*, is quite ignorant of the association between our Mr Peach and Clary. *We*, know otherwise. — We know, that in this regard at least, if in no other, Clary spoke the truth, for Miss Farthingay's old friend rides high and low across France, with her rescue his express purpose.

Is the girl then not so far out of her wits, as she appeared?

We can make neither head nor tail of it. —

But alas, alas! — Though Mr Peach be mounted like the knights of old, and riding to the aid of his afflicted lady, according to the very pattern of chivalry, we also know — that he rides, in intirely the wrong direction! Recall, reader, that when we last saw him, he had bent his course towards — the *Château Charizard* — which lies, as we understand, in the far west of Brittany — several score miles distant, from this Normandy coast, where our heroine is.

We suppose she is by the coast of Normandy, where we left her — though no glimmer of the sea, however faint, shews from any window of the château, that she has inspected.

Miss Farthingay recollects also, the inexplicable instruction given by Clary, to keep the chess-piece by her person. — The black king. — *It signifies him*, she said.

Madness! — yet she gropes on the bed, until her hand finds where she dropped the object. — She feels a mysterious relief, that she has not lost it.

Her fingers trace the form of the little wooden monarch, in the dark.

A sound of motion below — a glimpse of candle-light, flickering in the stair — an odour of unwashed French flesh — A cautious whisper — *Mademoiselle?*

It is the voice of the giant female — curiously gentle.

The Gargantua does not attempt to ascend the stair — Most probably, Miss Farthingay thinks, because she cannot. — It would be as hard for her, as for the camel to pass through the eye of the needle, or the rich man to join the company of the blessed.

Miss Farthingay descends, in unshod feet. At the base of the steps, there is another pygmy-sized room, like a study in miniature. — A writing-desk, and a single chair, are all the furniture it holds, or affords space to hold. On the desk, there has appeared a candle, in a dish — and, in another dish, a piece of cheese, and a lump of bread. Beside these is a dented pewter goblet, containing two inches of water.

The imposing Frenchwoman has retreated, with aukward modesty. — *Pour vous*, she says.

Her features, though broad and mannish, are, Miss Farthingay thinks, not ill-formed. A certain tender simplicity animates them. — She says something further, which Miss Farthingay cannot understand, though the tone is kindly.

There is more good nature — more grace, and authentick chivalry — in this monstrous peasant girl, than our heroine has met with, from titled lords, or honoured deputies, or sisters in holy order!

Miss Farthingay expresses her thanks, as best she can. Food, she cannot think of touching. — But for the light, she is sincerely grateful. She takes it above, to the miserable bed-chamber, at the top-most extremity of the mouldering old tower —

Lies herself down, in the bed — The worst, we do not doubt, she has ever lain in, in her whole existence — and —

Brings *us*, to an impasse. —

Miss Farthingay can do nothing, except wait, and hope her candle will last until day.

We have heard, that in the game of chess there are certain arrangements of the pieces, where they all lie in perfect safety, and their player quite without risk of loss — So long as he does not move, *a single one of them.* — But, it is his turn, and move he must. The law of the game requires it. — And so, he must destroy his own position — Imperil his own safety — Mine the very ground beneath him, and expose himself to certain defeat, simply because he is not permitted to do — Nothing.

We cannot lie in silence, like Miss Farthingay, through the remaining hours of the night. — The laws of our art, forbid it. Our page would become — a *blank.*

We must go in search of Mr Peach —

Or, of Clary —

Two such beings, as wise people ought to shun!

Are they not *both* guilty, of the blackest deeds?

We have hesitated — we confess — to acknowledge it. We have turned a blind eye, as the saying is — And, lo! received a just punishment, for our tale has itself become benighted, as though we had, like King Oedipus, surrendered the organs of sight, in guilty agonies.

Extremity compels us. — Let us openly pronounce the *truth*, at last. —

THOMAS PEACH! — you are magician and necromancer! You trafficked with the dead, and are — attended by devils!

Hear us, and rescue us!

Or, if you will not — for, cast our darkened eye which way we will, we cannot discover you! — then, return to our page again, CLARISSA RIDDLE — thrall of unholy powers — murderess — child of night and hatred —

A tremor grips the north. *Denfert is coming!*

What is the deputy's business in Normandy, in Brittany? Which road does he take and how soon will he arrive? From the more distant towns letters go out to ask what preparations must be made to receive him. The reply is one line: *Denfert is already here!*

He must be riding on the wind itself.

There have been unseasonal storms, rolling northward, as if Paris discharges her frenzy in the air and transmits it along the valleys of Orne and Mayenne. Rains swell the rivers to a muddy froth. Winds scour the trees, sending brown leaves flying. Despite wind and rain, all the reports agree: Denfert has no carriage, but comes alone.

The deputy, say those who have returned from Paris, is pale and small. In the assembly, or at the Jacobin Clubs, one can barely hear him. He is soft-spoken as a woman. But, my faith! — how those on whom he directs his look fall silent and shrink from sight! How anxiously people whisper after he leaves the chamber!

He did not stop in Chartres. At Alençon he paused only to change his horse. That same night, rumour says, the animal he rode from Paris died of exhaustion.

The old belfry of Notre-Dame d'Alençon was struck by lightning and burned until dawn. That is no mere rumour, my friends! Go and inspect the truth of it, written in cracked bells and charred stone.

Where is he going in such haste, and why?

The evil weather does not abate. In Brittany they see the dark skies in the east and hear approaching thunder. The deputy is reported to be already at Avranches. A committee of patriots formed itself to welcome him, with speeches prepared, but a sudden storm blew down their flags and knocked off their hats and cockades. Denfert declined their ceremonies; with cold looks, some say.

The Breton functionaries call extraordinary meetings. Beyond the walls of their towns, out in the wild brown heaths where peasants, smugglers and superstitious old women hold their ancient sway, the revolution is being pulled down around the people's ears. Decrees ignored, laws flouted, officers insulted or worse; and everywhere, spreading like rot after winter rains, this talk of the so-called Blessed Virgin and Her miraculous apparitions.

A thousand rumours attach to Citizen Denfert, many of them of a character all serious people dismiss. But there is one point on which everyone agrees. The old religion, the discredited religion, has no more determined enemy than him.

The functionaries very much wish to say to the deputy, when he arrives: See, citizen, how we prosecute these fanatics, these enemies of the nation!

Someone must be arrested before he comes.

But who? The old women? They are implacably sullen. In front of the National Guard they confess to nothing. Some throw mud and sticks. They might be forced to answer that crime, but the wrath of Denfert will not be satisfied by incarcerating crones. A nest of recusant priests is what the soldiers want. Alas, each time they are told where to find one, the information only leads to an ambush. Their powder and rifles fall into the hands of counter-revolutionaries, whose victory cry is *Long live the King!*

At the last moment the functionaries have a great stroke of luck. Near the edge of the forest of Huelgoat, where no sane man will go, a detachment of guards is stopped by the town curate. He is a legitimate curate, duly elected and sworn to uphold the civil constitution; a poor ragged frightened man, despised by his parishioners. He hides all day in his house. But when he sees the soldiers go by he runs out: Sirs, sirs, thank Providence you have come! There is a stranger in my church, a foreigner. He says he takes shelter from the company of devils but he smiles ironically when he speaks and is dressed like a gentleman. He is most surely a spy, unless a lunatic. Take him away, good soldiers of the nation, I entreat you.

The guards find this well-dressed traveller exactly as the curate described him. Providence smiles on them indeed: the man is English. They arrest him on that account alone. Denfert will be satisfied, surely. A solitary foreigner sitting in a church, without letters of introduction or passage, who can give no proper account of himself; this is a much better prize than drooling grandmothers. Whether he is guilty, or of what, who will care?

The deputy is not known to be troubled by such questions.

Denfert appears not quite himself. Each successive day he rides from Paris the alteration shows more visibly. It is almost as if he sheds the title of man as he goes.

That he left at all is mysterious. Not a day has passed for many months when he was not seen at work in the city, whispering here, encouraging there, lending just enough weight of advice or opinion to tip a balance one way or another. Paris is the centre of the world. Whichever way it now turns everything else will follow. Everyone who wants to direct the course of history is there, urging, pressing, exerting their influence over the great mass as it totters on the very edge. Why has Denfert left now, when it seems only the faintest breath is needed to bring down the moderates, dispel all balance, and unleash an orgy of murder, beginning with the prince, queen and king?

He rides in relentless fury towards a deserted stretch of the Normandy coast.

His pallor is more pronounced than ever. His hair knows neither hat, wig or powder, but streams out behind in the wind. His eyes, so strikingly dark, burn with inward intensity, like the victim of fever. Vapours rise from the indentations left by his horse's hooves.

On an inconspicuous promontory overlooking the sands and the sea beyond, cut off from the fertile lands by marshy hollows and thickets of reeds, is a low mound. He directs his horse across the marshes.

There are many such low mounds in the north and west. They are unremarkable to the eye of the farmer who grazes his cattle around them, or the feet of the goatherd who stands on them to get a view over his flock. But though they appear no more than small heaps of nature, nature did not make them. Under each is a chamber of stone, so old that the bones they were built to house have turned to dust. They have themselves forgotten they were tombs. That is how old they are. They have outlasted death.

Thunder sighs distantly as Denfert urges his panting horse through the hollows and onto the promontory. The seabirds, profuse along these sands, have all fled. It is late in the day. To the west the sea has a tarnished glitter. Very far on the horizon, the isle of Jersey is a cloudy blot.

He dismounts and unbuttons his coat. He raises his chin as though scenting the air like a cat.

The rapidity of his journey appears to have burned some solidity from his features. He is delicate like a woman or a wraith.

'Silly blackbird,' he murmurs. 'Did you not try to flee to save your life?'

Below the mound, on its seaward side, there is a cleft in the face of the promontory. Denfert climbs down, pushing aside curtains of vegetation. At the base of the cleft the sea has worn the rock away and made a secret entrance to the ancient grave. Here the sand has been disturbed, the salt weeds trampled down. Someone has recently entered.

Denfert faces the dark slit.

'Pretty bird,' he calls in a singing tone. 'Are you there? I have come to pin your wings and pluck out your eyes.'

No reply comes from the tomb. The deputy slips inside.

The sun chooses this moment to dip beneath the western clouds. A shaft of light follows Denfert into the stone chamber. It terminates on a heap of wet black clothes.

He pokes them with his boot to make sure there is flesh within. Satisfied, he kicks.

'Do not pretend to be dead,' he says. 'You cannot die until I permit it.'

The heap of clothes stirs. Slowly it arranges itself into a seated body, gloved hands hugging its knees.

'Wicked thing. You have removed your veil.' The weak beam of light does not reach as high as the crouching woman's head, but darkness is no impediment to Denfert. 'I forbade it, on pain of utter destruction.'

'Destroy me, then,' comes the reply; the ugly croak of the minion in black.

'Oho! You desire annihilation so eagerly? Remember, you will be nothing at all. Less than a thought that is instantly forgotten.'

'I am very tired of being myself,' the woman says. 'Also I am very tired of you.'

Denfert hisses like a snake.

'Impertinence is not tolerated.'

'But I do not ask for your tolerance, or care for your opinion in any way at all. You have come all the way from Paris to undo me. Do it then. I wish you had ridden faster.'

'How dare you speak to me like this, slave? Stand up before your prince. Beg his pardon.'

'No.'

Denfert darts forward, seizes the woman by the hair, and pulls her upright, eliciting cries of pain. Keeping his fist tight, he twists her head from side to side.

'Your face,' he says, 'is inconceivably revolting to me.'

'I did not invite you to look at it.'

With his other hand he reaches to her cheek and rakes his nails over it, drawing three thin lines of blood. She bites her lip.

'Explain to me, worm,' he says, in the quiet and deadly voice which makes powerful men in the Assembly blanch with dread, 'how you learned to defy me like this, when your very existence is only at my pleasure and your corrupted nature compels you to obey me.'

The woman licks away a bead of blood.

'But I have obeyed,' she says. 'You commanded me to have the Englishman dead or in chains before you arrived. It is done. Whether obedience is truly obedience at all when it is compelled, is another question. I have been thinking about it while I lay here waiting for you.'

A cry of rage boils from Denfert. It begins as a rising note and ends in a scream which threatens to crack the chamber's age-old stone. He shakes the woman like a doll.

'I will flay the skin from your face,' he says. 'I will make your blood burn in your veins like fire.'

If the woman is alarmed by his threats she is too beaten and tired to show it. She waits until the shaking stops, then shrugs weakly.

'As you please,' she says.

Denfert studies her coldly before releasing his grip.

'Better,' he says, with a small nod.

'Better? Worse? What does it matter, since I am to be unmade?'

'Perhaps I shall not destroy you after all, pretty blackbird. It amuses me to have an obedient pet. Perhaps I prefer to keep you shut in a little cage. To sing for me when I command.'

She gives a wan smile. 'Do you not know what I did here, master? You will be less amused after I tell you.'

Denfert sniffs the tomb's heavy air. 'Some feeble portion of the power I gave you was expended, I see.'

'I found the Farthingay.'

'Ha! Good.'

'I gained her confidence, and then led her here, where forgotten power lingers and the veil of the world is thin.'

'Good, good! My bird may be wilful, but she serves me still.' Denfert looks from side to side. 'And what did you do with the

Farthingay? I hope you have not already dispatched her to her fate. That task I reserve for myself.'

The woman wipes another trickle of blood from her mouth.

'I sent her away from here. To a place I chose myself, many days' journey away. Just as you send me without regard for my will, I did the same to her. Also, master, I did it for only one reason, which was to keep her from you.'

Denfert is so astonished he forgets to be angry.

'Impossible,' he says.

The woman sits down on wet stone and hugs her knees again. 'Very difficult,' she says, 'but not impossible. All my strength was spent on it. Nevertheless. It pleased me, and still pleases me, in my last moments, to have found a way of defying you.'

Slowly descending, the sun sends its beam of brass deeper into the tomb, where light was never meant to go. The woman closes her eyes as it touches her face.

'You cannot defy me,' Denfert says. 'You are my slave, eternally and absolutely.'

'In the port cities,' says the woman, 'I have heard news of an island in the far west where all the masters have been killed by their slaves. African slaves, in chains. They were supposed to be enslaved for ever. Now they are free.'

'Silence!'

'Did you yourself not once rebel against an eternal master?'

'SILENCE!' Denfert kicks the huddled heap, making her cry in pain, and then twice more. 'Insect! Cat! Bitch!' Kick, kick, kick. His boot tangles in her sodden black skirts. He stumbles and falls out of the shaft of light. In the dark he catches his breath, while the light creeps up and over the slumped woman's form until she is wholly illuminated, bathed in gold.

'There,' Denfert says. He is hoarse from exertion. 'I commanded silence and now you do not speak.'

Her eyes remain shut. She might be inhaling the last of the evening sun.

'Also, your defiance is meaningless. Whatever you did, it was done only with the power I allowed you. You can do nothing against me or without me.'

The woman ignores him. She collects herself a little, rearranging her wet clothes.

'I can easily find out where the Farthingay has gone. Did you think you could deceive me with so simple a trick? Worm.' He murmurs in a strange tongue, at which the woman shudders despite herself. 'Ha!' Denfert steps back into the light, casting his shadow over her. 'The Castle Charizard! Where those fools made me a temple and adored me as their divinity.'

'Fools indeed,' she mutters.

'How futile, this small gesture of rebellion. I shall ride west immediately. I shall find the Farthingay and consign her body and soul to endless torment. Thus the demonoscope will be mine, and I shall raise my legions at last.'

The minion makes a hissing noise, which could either be an exhalation through closed teeth or some words in English, the language best suited to her unharmonious voice: *yes, yes, yes.*

'It only remains,' Denfert says, 'to determine your fate.'

Her eyes open. 'But you promised me annihilation.'

'Be quiet.'

'You swore—'

The deputy kneels and places a hand over her jaw, sealing her mouth. She is too weak to struggle out of his grip. He tears several wet strips from the hem of her dress and uses them first to gag her and then, while she splutters and chokes, to bind her wrists and ankles.

Satisfied, he stands.

'Now you cannot speak.' He nods to himself. 'Just as I instructed you.'

Behind the wad of soaked linen and lace her tongue attempts furious noises. But she cannot produce any language, not even English.

Denfert raises his chin and assumes a decisive stance.

'I do not yet grant you oblivion,' he announces.

Hnnn — nnn — gnn — Mmm!, protests the woman.

'It pleases me to keep you my slave a while longer. You will remain here in darkness and cold until I choose to summon you. Perhaps I never shall. Perhaps you will sit alone in this hole for ever, like the dead in their tombs.'

Gggnnn — mmmh —

'Thus I punish you.' He turns on his heel with a flourish. 'I, your eternal emperor.'

At last she spits out the gag and emits a tirade of English, its meaning certainly as foul as its noise. But Denfert has already reascended the promontory and remounted his exhausted steed, and is gone.

Boom! The thunder cracks. *Hiss!* Lightning splits the night. Denfert hastens west, heedless of rain and darkness. In the poor houses of the Breton plain the peasants are roused from uncomfortable sleep by the sound of hoofbeats. Who passes by so fast on such a night? They ride like the devil! The roads are infested with brigands, smugglers, counter-revolutionaries and other men with no purpose except to practise violence until they are drunk with the joy of it. But this weather has driven even them to shelter. If any catch a glimpse of Denfert, instinct compels them to shun him like a madman.

Near Saint-Brieuc his horse expires, throwing him to the mud in its mortal seizure. He leaves the foaming corpse in the road and walks to town. At the gate he announces himself to incredulous guards: Citizen Denfert, from Paris, on urgent business in the cause of the nation.

Consternation! The functionaries are summoned from their homes, where they were just sitting down to meals of nourishing Roman simplicity with their wives and children.

Are we to be disturbed at this hour? Is not the family the bedrock of republican virtue?

What — Denfert? — *Here?*

This pale and dripping spectre with the feverish stare; this mud-spattered solitary traveller who comes without warning or ceremony; *this* is the dreaded Denfert?

No one dares show what they are thinking. He demands dry clothes and a strong horse. They offer a hastily-ordered meal of wine and bread. His black eyes burn with instant rage. Wine and bread? Why do you give me wine and bread? Are you priests of the tyrant God? Is this town a temple of superstitious fraud?

The functionaries shrink in terror and send for onions and pastry.

Denfert's new clothes are a white silk shirt, riding boots and breeches, and a plain long coat split behind for the saddle. No cravat, no wig. With his long unbound hair and fine features he looks like a woman dressed as a man.

While they wait for the meal to be sent the functionaries take turns assuring him their town is a place of good patriots. In the country, alas, a few troublemakers stir up the ignorant peasantry with backward talk of miracles and other reactionary absurdities. But the National Guard will soon put down these minuscule sparks of would-be rebellion. Why, just yesterday we, the diligent officials of the Northern Coasts, arrested a spy! — a highly suspicious Englishman, no doubt one of the ringleaders of the poor country fools. Would the deputy be pleased to inspect their prisoner himself? Perhaps Citizen Denfert will even do them the honour of pronouncing a sentence and signing the necessary authorisations.

He has no interest in the onions or pastries, but he does consent to visit the prisoner.

In Paris people whisper that the exercise of authority is to Denfert what brandy, tobacco and women are to other men.

They lead him to the town prison, where the guards are discovered drunk. This is not surprising. Men who have nothing to do but sit and watch will drink; men who drink will become drunk. The functionaries are nevertheless severely embarrassed, especially in the presence of this joyless hermit of a deputy who will not touch wine or food. When he asks about the arrested man the stupid guards cross themselves. The Englishman whispers terrible words, they say, and is attended by devils. Have you come from Paris to hang him, good sir deputy? Do it quickly, for this Englishman is evil and we do not like him in our prison.

The mayor is in torments of shame. Let these drunken idiots be whipped, he cries!

Denfert stays his hand. Attended by devils, do you say, citizens?

The guards swear it. They have heard strange whispers in the prisoner's cell. Shadows stir around him even though the lamp has not been moved. Have him executed without delay!

Denfert turns to his small entourage.

'I wish to question the spy alone,' he says.

Who would think of contradicting him? The functionaries are very glad to be relieved of his presence. They gather around the guards and their bottle of wine, mopping their brows, while the deputy proceeds to the cells alone.

He finds the Englishman sitting on a straw pallet under a high barred window. There is no other resident in the prison, the rats excepted. The man is respectably dressed. He has the general appearance of a gentleman burgher, until one studies his complexion and observes the small motions of his face. His expression is restless and dreamy, his cheeks pale, his lips unsteady. His eyelids flicker. The tips of his fingers twitch and pluck, catching phantom flies.

Denfert opens the cell door. He has no key. He merely puts his hand on the lock and it turns.

He leans on one leg and lets the other dally on the heel of the boot. He folds his arms.

'At last,' he says, 'Mister Peach.'

For several moments the Englishman seems unaware that anyone has entered his place of confinement. When his eyes open properly and come to rest on the deputy, there is a long silence.

He sits straighter.

'I believe I know you,' he says. He speaks good French, in a grave serious voice. 'Madam Denfert, is it not?'

'Enchanted,' says Denfert, with a flirtatious dip of the head. 'I am inexpressibly delighted that you return to me.'

'Have I returned to you?'

'But evidently. Here we are.'

'If so, madam, it was an accident. I am not here of my own will.'

'Your own will does not matter at all. I told you myself that you belong to me. Now regard, the confirmation.'

'Then you are the gaoler here?'

The deputy laughs. How few have heard the laughter of Denfert! No one expects it to be so gay, light and silver, like the water of an artificial fountain.

The guards and functionaries hear it and look even more pale. What the devil can they be speaking of down there? Was that laughter or a shriek of pain? Does the citizen need our assistance?

Not one of them thinks of going to offer it.

In the cell Denfert kneels beside the prisoner.

'You are suffering, Mister Peach my friend,' he says. He sniffs the air. 'They have taken your laudanum.'

'Madam,' he says. It takes a geat deal of effort for him to compose himself to speech. 'You will very much oblige me, by either declaring the purpose of this interview or bringing it to a conclusion.'

'I shall do both.' Denfert pats his knee. 'When I choose to. Would you like your opium-bottle returned? I can arrange it with a snap of the fingers. I have perfect power over this town. The people here fear for their lives at my smallest displeasure.'

The Englishman does not reply.

'They wish to have you executed. Shall I give them their desire? They say you are a spy, but I know your true crimes. Mortal sins, my good friend. Shall we accuse you of practising forbidden magic? I have it on the very best authority that you raise spirits of the dead. Do you wonder how I know that, Mister Peach?'

'Not at all, Madam Denfert,' he says.

The deputy extends a finger and presses it against Mister Peach's waistcoat, over his heart. 'Or,' he says, with a delicate smile, 'shall we have you hanged for murder?'

The prisoner stares back with a dull look.

'Why yes, my friend,' Denfert says. 'I know your sin. I was there with you when you did the deed. It was me you called on to hide your form in darkness while you went through the streets. It was my power that tricked the locks of your father's house.' He nods towards the cell door, which stands wide open. 'Just as I opened this lock for you. Acknowledge me and you may go free. Deny me, and you hang.'

'He was not my father.'

'Pah. The father of your pretty wife. Did he not stand in your parent's place, since you had no father of your own?'

'Leave me, madam.'

Denfert stands up. 'But I cannot. Or rather *you* cannot leave *me*. You are my creature. For many years you have been. This present conjunction of ours . . .' He gestures daintily around the cell. 'It was inevitable. Now we shall go together, unless you prefer to defy me and die.'

The prisoner again gathers himself to speak.

'I recall we met but twice, Madam Denfert, and it grieves me to say I regret each minute of either encounter.'

'My dear Mister Peach.' Denfert waggles his finger, *tut-tut*. 'This wilful obtuseness may deceive others. But you cannot fool me. Or yourself.' He stands astride the Englishman's legs. He points an imperious finger. Suddenly his voice is loud and commanding. 'Admit that you know who I am.'

The functionaries and the guards hear muffled words. They pass the bottle around nervously. What interrogation is this? Why are they still talking down there?

'You need not name me,' Denfert says. There is lightning in his eyes and thunder in his mouth. 'My name is too great to be soiled by mortal lips. Acknowledge me only. Otherwise.' He smiles. 'Die.'

The functionaries direct their looks at the ground, the sky, the windows of houses, at leaves as they fly past on the wind; anywhere except at one another. What was their error? Are they personally to blame? What will their punishment be?

Denfert has liberated their prisoner.

The two of them came out together. The deputy looked coldly triumphant. The Englishman followed him like a dog, hanging his head. Find him a clean coat and breeches, Denfert commanded, and return all his possessions to him, particularly his apothecaries' box.

Evidently a mistake has been made. The Englishman is no counter-revolutionary agent, but a friend of the honoured deputy. Who made the mistake? The mayor accuses the intendant. The intendant accuses the captain of guards. The captain of guards accuses his subordinate, who is fortunately not present.

Denfert does not care. The braver among the functionaries dare to observe that he does not even seem angry. But with Citizen Denfert who can say? His passions are a mystery.

At least the hangman has not yet been called for.

It falls to the mayor to attempt reparation. If the expectations of the deputy have in any way been disappointed, he apologises. For the remainder of the deputy's visit he places the whole town at his disposal. The accommodations cannot be adequate, but they had no warning of the deputy's arrival. Why, only two days ago Citizen Denfert was in Normandy, according to the best intelligence! The mayor offers his own house. He and his wife and children will remove to the Hotel of the Golden Oyster. The harvest has not been good, but all its fruits are at the pleasure of the deputy and his guest. It pains the mayor to surrender his wine, but what else can he do? He must assume the maximum of abjection.

It is not enough. Denfert refuses to stay. He and the Englishman will ride out from town as soon as clothes and horses are procured.

But, honoured citizen, you cannot possibly intend to go onto the roads tonight? It is late. There have been storms. To Morlaix or Carhaix is many miles, and the roads are very bad.

Denfert looks past the mayor to the captain of guards. Have my instructions been carried out? Have the possessions of my English friend been returned, his bottle of laudanum in particular? Are the horses ready? Good. We leave at once.

The mayor wrings his hands. He trusts the Englishman is not offended at the treatment he so unfortunately received? A thousand curses on that imbecile the subordinate of the guards! Had anyone known their visitor was a friend of Denfert —

The deputy leans so close that no bystander can hear.

'Leave us alone,' he murmurs to the mayor. 'I tire of you.'

It is only thanks to his good constitution, fortified by republican frugality, that the mayor does not drop dead on the spot.

He returns to his house. The rising wind whips his coat around him as he runs through the streets. He has his children roused from their beds and brought before him. He hugs them one after the next with tears in his eyes. His wife is astonished.

Even late in the night, when Denfert and the Englishman have been gone several hours and he is at last certain they will not return, the mayor cannot sleep. He has a vision of his own tomb, as plain before his face as the bed-post. He lies awake until dawn listening to unseasonal thunders. The storms are returning.

CHAPTER TEN

DAY — at last!

Yet our prospects have hardly improved. Behold —

In every direction, we overlook a sea of lank brown leaves, and the bitter evergreen of hemlock and fir. Like the heroine of a nursery-tale, we are lost in the heart of some antient forest. — Turn which way we will, it extends to the horizon.

The sea is nowhere in sight.

With the rising of the sun — cold, and occluded by fogs — we are at least invited to distinguish the quarters of the world. — To pronounce, *that* way to be north and east, where the sun shews its feeble outline above the masses of trees. — *That* direction, therefore, where the tumbledown castle looks over a low granite cliff, ought to be south and west. — The intervening vistas, to be arranged accordingly, around the compass rose.

But what use is our calculation, when each prospect is as silent, desart, and comfortless, as its neighbour?

There is not so much as a road. —

And the castle! It is in some intermediate state of architecture, between *building* and *ruin*. It has not the picturesque desolation, of the latter — that vacancy, which charms the meditative soul, and inspires thoughts of ages gone by. Yet it lacks the coherence — the homely sturdiness — of any thing, worthy to be called a dwelling. It is walls, roofs, and windows, thrown together pell-mell — Then, partly thrown back asunder — Construction and destruction, equally without rhyme or reason — Neither antique nor modern — as though ignorant of the mere idea of time.

By what incomprehensible device, are we brought *here*?

Some deed beyond our imagination has been done, in the depth of this last night. Clarissa Riddle! — How secretly and strangely you work, when the eye of our narrative is darkened!

Lying awake through the tedious nocturnal hours, but for some intervals of fitful dream, Miss Farthingay has resolved — resolved, *again* — to quit this grim house, and its grotesque inhabitants, the instant there is light to go by.

At the first hint of dawn, therefore, she goes purposefully down. — Through the room, where the uncouth travellers made their camp, though they have risen before her, leaving only their stench — On into the chearless labyrinth of cobwebbed stairs and neglected apartments — in search of an exit from the château, and a place where horses are stabled. She will ride away without announcement or ceremony. — Any other place, must be better than this. — Any direction, must bring her a degree nearer home.

We have given a picture, of the sad exterior of the house. Its inward state is still more disheartening — if that may be imagined. The chaos and ruin, suggested by the outer view, are more fully accomplished behind the walls. — Half of this decayed manor is as bare and wrecked, as though it had been taken by a crew of terrestrial pirates, and plundered top-mast to keel. The other half, that has not been stripped and smashed —

Miss Farthingay hurries through it, with revulsion. We also shall not stop to record what we see — But hasten with her, to the door, and the stable — Appropriate whatever mount we can, and RIDE AWAY. —

Alas! there is no stable! —

Miss Farthingay finds her way, through scenes of unspeakable filth and degradation, to the entrance — a pair of broken doors, collapsed in a puddle of rain — Surveys the waste grounds beyond, and discovers only a number of — *goats!* — Roaming, quite at large, as though they were the four-footed *seigneurs* of the manor. — They pause in their browsing to stare at her, with malevolent looks.

In an open-sided barn, which might perhaps once have served as a stable of sorts, though the meanest farmer of Britain would disdain to keep his chickens in such an hovel, she spies a mount. — A single donkey, tethered, and cropping nettles.

Her determination quails. — I cannot ride a donkey, she thinks. — I do not know how. — And I am frightened to go out among the goats.

She is forced to retreat within-doors.

Against our will, we must retrace our steps also — and furnish you, reader, with some account of those parts of the house, we should much prefer to have overlooked. — For our heroine goes in search of the château's grotesque inhabitants, to demand their assistance in procuring an horse — And we must go with her. We, at least, will not abandon her — though it is plain that Clary has. — Wilful, heartless girl!

There is a small, inelegant, mouldy library, in a part of the house left untouched by piratical looters. Here at least are tall windows, and other evidences that these rooms were once improved, in some desperate approximation of fashionable stile. — Though any effect of elegance is quite ruined, by an absurd scheme of decoration, whose theme is the heads of — goats! — Mounted, like trophies of a Bacchanalian hunt, on every wall — woven with coloured ribbons, as though they were baskets of flowers — daubed with paint, in unpleasant colours. — Miss Farthingay cannot restrain a laugh, when she sees them, though she has never in her life been less inclined to levity — or, not for many years.

The presence of books is some comfort, at least. She pulls some volumes from the dusty cases — But they are all French, and unknown to her — and old, and ill-tended, rank with the smell of rot.

From somewhere adjacent comes the noise of furious argument. — Or, it may be, of lively amicable chit-chat. Among the French, it is impossible to know one from the other.

Miss Farthingay follows the sound, through a barbarous low door, into the adjacent room. We wish, she had not — For now we must attempt a description of it.

This chamber is the most ridiculous and revolting, in the whole oafish house. It was once, we suppose, the private place of worship, of whatever family laid claim to the château. Like them — we further suppose — it was always poor — clumsy — ignoble, in its pretentions — nor displaying a whit of taste or elegance, in successive efforts at improvement.

In more recent times, some prankish child has evidently been let loose within. There are kitchen implements, upon the altar — Chains, hung from wall to wall, with rusting objects suspended from them at intervals, for no imaginable purpose — Smears of dirt, and soot from the *black* candles, upon every surface. A rude wooden cross is raised under the filthy east windows — but raised *upside-down*, as though the ones who placed it there, had never seen another crucifix in their lives — which we can well believe, for if ever an house in Christendom were *God-forsaken*, this remote and utterly incommodious château, is certainly that house.

And, lo! by way of further ornament — More goat-heads! —

We guess the animals had an heraldic significance, for the *noble* family.

Like their cousins in the library, these are bare bone. — A spectacle at once mournful and absurd — Still more so, when the hollow sockets, that once held the silly creatures' eyes, are pressed into service as *candle-holders*, and agglomerations of wax deface the ugly skulls.

Enough. — We waste no more words on this scene.

The French, we are often told, have for two hundred years led all Europe, in matters of fashion, taste, and refinement. Should this *canard* henceforth ever be repeated in our presence, we need only point to this château — if we can find it again. No words will be necessary. — *There*, monsieur — our silent index says — there is our refutation. — Go now, and be for ever abashed, in the presence of BRITONS!

The Gallic cacophony, which drew our poor oppressed heroine towards this ludicrous place, sounds from beyond a further door, which opens on a descending spiral stair. — It leads, we guess, to some older foundation, beneath the barbarous chapel. — The crypt, or burial-place, perhaps, of the ancestral occupants — Messieurs and Mesdames of the House of Goat. We hope their senses are as dull in death, as their discernment was, when they furnished their noble residence, for otherwise their sleep cannot be very peaceful. The motley French vagabonds, whose acquaintance was forced on Miss Farthingay in the night, are down among the tombs, making a furious noise. She can easily distinguish their several voices — though they each speak at once, and strive to make themselves heard, by shouting louder than the rest.

She is not minded to stand on ceremony, when there is no ceremony to be stood upon. She leans through the door, and shouts herself. —

— I require assistance.

Instant silence below. — The shades of the old Seigneurs de Goat sigh gratefully, and resume eternal snoring.

Up the stair leaps the sprightly old rogue, whose name is Gaspard Lesinge. — So he says — He has the look of one, who has adopted and discarded several names, in his life. — To flee creditors — angry relations — spurned lovers — the police —

— It is necessary, Miss Farthingay says to him, that I be conducted at once to the nearest town.

He darts his curiously expressive eyes from side to side, and cocks his head.

— To — ze nearess — down — he repeats, like an ill-trained parrot.

— *Town*, Miss Farthingay says, already exasperated. — *Une ville.*

Monsieur Lesinge roars down the stairs — *Des Sables!*

This name, we have learned, belongs to the valet — The *quondam* valet, we should say, for whether or not it be true his master is dead, the fair-haired youth is certainly not employed in

service at present. Our Ganymede ascends, and is engaged by M
Lesinge, in rapid conversation —

Your pardon, reader. — We shall henceforth not trouble to
qualify the talk of either party, as *rapid*. The epithet is a
redundancy. You may presume it, without being told — It is plain,
that neither knows any other method of speaking. Their mouths
are always at the gallop — or, shut. — Nothing between.

It is otherwise, with the Gargantua. There is a slowness about
her, we took for lumpen idiocy. — But now we wonder, whether it
bespeaks instead a certain consideration — some distant hint, of
a reflective temper.

She interests us, this giant peasant-girl. — Crude and oafish, no
doubt — Raised in that fixed poverty and ignorance, which are
the lot of the common people, in every nation less enlightened
than our own. Yet we detect signs in her, of a good heart. — The
organ must certainly be a capacious one — It could not otherwise
propel the blood, around so huge a frame.

She ascends also, and shepherds her companions and Miss
Farthingay, back to the miserable library. Evidently, she does not
like the prankish mockery of a chapel. — We think she mumbles
Popish incantations as she passes through it.

Let us not hold her superstitions against her, reader. The poor
girl has been taught no better.

In the adjacent library, which has at least the virtue of admitting
some quantity of day-light, for its windows are tall and square,
and face the east — Miss Farthingay repeats her demand, as
patiently as she can.

Conversation proceeds, like a rustic cart, upon a cobbled
road. Lurching — coming to sudden stops, as often as going
forward — We shall not tire you with it. Its conclusion, as best
our heroine can determine, is — They cannot assist her —
There are no horses — There is no town — No gentleman
resides nearby — and, moreover, Monsieur Lesinge does not
desire her to leave.

Desire her! — An error in translation, we presume!

La dame noire — the lady all in black — He appears convinced, by some phantastical misprision, that she brought Miss Farthingay, *to him* — that our heroine, a well-bred and accomplished lady of England — a poet! — is — his *prize!* — intended for him by Clary, whom he calls *la reine noire* — the black queen. *Mon trésor, mademoiselle,* the shameless rogue declares, with lunatic earnestness — his chin so far forward, we fear his head might topple from his shoulders — *C'est vous-même!*

The mere suggestion, that Clary has turned Miss Farthingay over to the protection of such a creature, is ludicrous. She cannot take offence, at an insinuation so comical. She has been misunderstood, without a doubt. She demands these ruffians to go to the nearest place of habitation, and fetch some person of decent standing.

M Lesinge either does not understand, or refuses. —

The giantess seems offended on Miss Farthingay's behalf, and remonstrates with him. — He justifies himself, in passionate terms, to judge by his gesticulation — though we suspect these French mountebanks would wave their arms about with equal vigour, in passing the time of day with their neighbours, or reporting the dullest news of the hour.

Another conflict is certainly brewing. —

No wonder the people of this nation cannot go six months, without beginning another revolution! — when a mere *three* of them cannot speak with civility for ten minutes together, in the presence of a lady.

On this occasion, however, conflict is averted, by a *thunderous* interruption. — A great storm-peal cracks across the forest, so deep and heavy, that the windows rattle in their frames, and the house itself seems to shake.

— Mercy! cries Miss Farthingay, in involuntary alarm.

The sky in the east is obliterated by clouds black as the depths of Ocean. They swallow the morning light — enveloping the château, and the forest surrounding, in sudden gloom — Alleviated for an instant by a sheet of lightning. — Several breaths of peculiar stillness follow, before the report reaches the house, and smites it, as though it were a stone anvil under the hammer of the storm. An angry wind blows up, sending the woods into a phrenzy. — And then, what an instantaneous tempest of rain, hurled against the windows by that wind!

The whole scene is in a single moment become *Gothick*, to the last degree. —

Thinks Miss Farthingay — A departure is not to be thought of, until the storm passes. — How vexing! Every circumstance conspires against me, in this wretched country.

Her revolutionary ardour is, we fear, quite dimmed.

The common people of France, who appeared in so noble a light, to her visionary conceptions, are, on close inspection, as boorish and slovenly, as the common people of every other nation. And, heavens! their stink! —

Monsieur Lesinge rushes out, to attend to their donkey, which cannot be left to the mercy of such weather. Because there is no stable worthy the name, they bring the beast — *inside the house!* — Tethering it to a stair-post, where it adds its braying to the general cacophony, and its cloacal reek to the foul airs of its masters.

Justice compels us to record, that the fair valet des Sables remains with our heroine. — By his exclamations of terror at every blast of the storm, we suppose him too cowardly to venture out of doors. Nevertheless, we must acknowledge, that his manner is deferential, and he seems anxious not to give the lady alarm.

He has, we suppose, at least a passing familiarity, with the manners of decent society.

— The master — he says to her, in his Frenchified approximation of English. — Very — He lacks the adjective, but conveys his meaning with a pantomime grimace, and a gesture encompassing the goat heads, as well as the various oil paintings adorning the room, which are, without exception, of vile quality, and worse taste. — *Homme fort méchant. Maudit!*

He intends, we guess, some form of apology. — To disown on his part, any share in the despicable Monsieur de Charizard's conduct. He repeats execrations upon the name of his master, while waving his arms about the room, with more than usual emphasis. — As though the shameless libertine were in some manner present by implication, in the distasteful furniture of the room.

— What is this place? she says — and, seeing his doleful look, musters again the rudiments of her French. — How I miss my female companion, she thinks! — *Içi* — *quelle place?*

— *Quel endroit?* His look is uncertain. — *La bibliothèque, mademoiselle.*

— No, no, no! — She tosses her head in frustration. — A spirited gesture, highly characteristic of the lady. How we admire her fortitude, in this unpleasant situation! — This house, she says. — *Maison* — What is it?

Now the Ganymede's face is all surprize. — *Le château? Le Château Charizard?*

The CHÂTEAU CHARIZARD!

Unthinkable! — impossible!

We are thunder-struck. — Miss Farthingay, also. —

Ask the boy again, in the plainest language — plain enough to suit his English, and her French. — She does so — Is answered the same —

This decrepit and pillaged manor, odiously furnished, and barbarously neglected, is — the Château Charizard! — The very property and seat, of the vile seducer!

Des Sables observes Miss Farthingay's consternation, with concern. He takes a volume, from the cases — opens its cover — Points to the name, written on the first leaf, in purple ink, in an elegant hand — *Hippolite-Aimant-Louis de Bobigny de Charizard* — with the date, *1er Septembre 1779.* — *Son nom*, he says — *ses livres* — *sa bibliothèque* — *son château!*

Even we, cannot mistake his meaning.

For the first time, Miss Farthingay's fortitude begins to waver. As though it senses her weakness, the storm redoubles in ferocity.

— The thunder, like a salute of cannons — The rain, a flock of birds, that batters itself to death upon the glass.

The Château Charizard!

— Is it possible — thinks Miss Farthingay — that Clary — my play-mate — my adoptive sister! — That despite all her professions of tender care — of *love* — That she has practised upon me the cruellest deceit, and left me at the mercy of my unscrupulous enemy, while she herself vanishes, no where to be found?

But it cannot be. The valet must be mistaken. — There must be another explanation. To Miss Farthingay's certain knowledge — hers, and ours — the Château Charizard lies in the western part of the kingdom of Brittany, scores of miles distant from the dismal sea-shore, where Clary led our heroine away from the soldiers' assault.

Are we to suppose Miss Farthingay transported across so great a distance, in *a single night?*

For a dreadful moment, she suspects her own wits may not be sound. — That the successive torments she has met with, since her abduction from Cherbourg, have worked a fatal oppression on her brain.

Hideous thought! to fear oneself *mad* —

A commotion — Shouts, from elsewhere in the house, heard between the volleys of the tempest — Des Sables! Des Sables! — his companions are calling.

Away the fellow runs — Leaving our heroine, pale as cold ashes — Stupefied —

After some moments, she goes after him. — Poor lady? What else can she do? She has no taste, at this terrible hour, for those intervals of reflexion, which have been her solace, since her early youth. She desires — she knows not what — some explanation — some answer. — Somewhere, the end of these impenetrable confusions must exist, waiting to be found.

In her hand she still clutches the chess-piece — The black king —

The noise of the three French persons is more agitated, than ever before. We fear it presages a fresh surprize. — Great God!

that Miss Farthingay should have no better society than this, in such a crisis!

Behold — Monsieur Lesinge and the Gargantua, now joined by the valet. — They are gathered at a window, in a despoiled room, above the entrance stair — The three of them looking out in alarm.

Someone approaches the house!

Is it Clary, at last? — returned, to give account of what she has done, for good or — alas! more likely — for ill?

The valet stands tip-toe, to peer over the shoulder of the giantess. He pushes his golden hair from his eyes — Squints, at those who ride towards the ruined door.

In horror he exclaims — *Denfert!*

The name strikes Miss Farthingay's ear, in the exact instant she enters the room. — Dread seizes her.

Denfert!

The architect, of her sufferings — The author, of these groundless persecutions — *He* is coming? *He* rides to the desolate château, to complete his mysterious purposes? — to enact, his unknown plot — unknown, but beyond all doubt malignant and vile?

Ah, des Sables says, springing back from the window — *non non non — la Denfert, venue encore?* — Each word he pronounces, and every motion he makes, signifies beyond the need for translation, that he is terrified out of his wits.

Miss Farthingay goes to the window — or, as close as she is able to approach, behind the formidable Gargantua. Beyond, the rain blows down in billows. Amid its veils, she distinguishes a pair of riders, passing slowly through the wreckage of the grounds, among the goats, towards the house. Leading the two is a slight figure, with hair unbound. — Clary? — No — it is not she. — Lagging behind is another, with head bowed and hat low, pulling his cloak close against the rain — Dressed like a gentleman, though all such distinctions are almost obliterated by the dreadful weather, which reduces garments, rider, and horse alike, to a black and dripping mean.

There is something about this second figure, that awakens in Miss Farthingay a peculiar sensation of familiarity. — As though he were known to her — or, *she to him* —

— Is it Denfert? she says to the valet.

Has the poor youth's access of terror driven all understanding from his head? He gapes — but then, nods once. — *Ah, mademoiselle!* he cries — and rushes away —

But what cause has this des Sables, to dread the appearance of the wicked deputy, Monsieur Denfert?

Reader — Do you not suspect, as we do, some villainous conspiracy, between Denfert and the *seigneur* de Charizard? — the one writing the letter, that summoned poor Miss Farthingay, with false promises, and empty protestations of respect, to Cherbourg — where the other, impersonated the coachman, and effected her abduction?

Perhaps, if M de Charizard indeed be dead — the youth fears some retribution?

We are in a great fog. — We stumble along the course of our own narrative, like a benighted traveller over a trackless waste.

Miss Farthingay is possessed by one thought only. — *Denfert is coming.* — She retreats from the window also. She is the hare, that has sighted the hound. — She must not be discovered — She must hide herself.

All her sensations are in turmoil. Coiled around her heart, as the serpent coiled about the tree in Eden, is a suspicion of the most sable hue. — That Clary — cursed, unnatural child! — has betrayed her, to those who wish her harm.

Yet was it not Clary who warned Miss Farthingay, of the wickedness of Denfert?

She cannot stop to think. She will conceal herself, before these riders enter the house. Whatever they intend, she will escape it.

She runs lightly down the stair. Thunder cracks — The donkey brays — Lesinge shouts this or that, at some person or other. The valet has gone ahead. — He beckons, when he sees Miss Farthingay following. He plucks a candle from the skull of a goat, and lights it, and motions to her to accompany him — Down, into the crypt below the defaced chapel.

The youth des Sables, it appears, has the same thought as our heroine. — To evade the eye of Denfert, by retreating to the most obscure and secret part of the château.

They step together into the antient twisting stair. The valet closes the door behind, and seals it with three bolts — Murmuring encouragements, to Miss Farthingay — we suppose them to be encouragements.

Let us pray we have not mistaken the character of this des Sables! He is fair of face, and has some marks of gentility in him, despite his humble station. But

one may smile, and smile, and be a villain

To be locked in — a *tomb* — for this cold crypt, is a place of burial — With a single man —

Are Miss Farthingay's trials never to end? —

Will they not only endure, but become *more desperate*, with each passing chapter?

We would excuse her, if she wept. Indeed, we would not think the worse of her, if she imitated the action of every persecuted heroine, and fell into a deathly swoon.

But, though greatly frightened — She is resolute. A spirit all defiance, sustains her.

Admirable lady! —

The rage of the storm is muffled, in this musty cavern of stone. — A place of crude thick pillars, and graceless arches — Of shadows and echoes — No less grim and comfortless, than the house above. — Yet, no *more* so, for the valet has procured from somewhere, furnishings quite incongruous with a mausoleum. — Several silk cushions, and a small oriental rug.

We, like our heroine, are past surprize. —

He motions her to sit, and puts his fingers to his lips. He gives an encouraging look, as though to say — You and I are safe here

— The door above is secure, and if we are quiet, none will find us, in this deep sanctuary. — Not even — *him*.

Miss Farthingay sits. — The valet's eyes widen, in sudden alarm. He points towards her hand, and emits a stream of anxious French, unmistakable in its general character, if impenetrable in detail. The little object, that she holds — He has just now noticed it, and its presence has awakened in him some fresh access of childish dread.

She opens her hand again. There is the sable chess-piece, with its cross-topped crown.

— *Le roi noir*, whispers des Sables, and indicates by several signs, whose meaning is as clear as though inscribed in letters of fire upon the mouldering stones — like that *mene, mene*, which presaged Babylon's fall — That she should discard the black king — Cast it away —

— Pooh! thinks Miss Farthingay. — This boy would quail at his own shadow, were there enough light from the candle, to make one. What is there to fear, from a *chess-piece?*

Whether our heroine also remembers Clary's instruction — *Never let it be apart from you — It signifies HIM* — We cannot say with certainty. Perhaps, she does not wish to admit among her recollections, such strange dark language. — And yet, despite the valet's frantic gestures, she closes her hand again, around the little monarch —

Her thoughts turn of a sudden to her dear friend Mr Peach.

— Thomas, she thinks — Will you come? —

In silence — she waits —

'Regard the goats!' Cochonne says. 'They run away!'

It is true: the stupid creatures, who idled in the castle grounds regardless of rain and thunder, tearing up flowers and weeds alike without a care in the world, have all turned tail and scattered.

As have the coward des Sables and the mad Englishwoman; but Gaspard Lesinge, by God, he does not so easily yield his ground. What has he to fear from two wet strangers? This is his castle now, by right of conquest and possession.

For all his life he has known it: he was destined to take his place among men of talents and property. As the old enfeebled nobility falls, true genius ascends to replace it. Contemptuous of the mere accident of birth; recognising instead only merit and ability and philosophy, in all of which who is wealthier than Gaspard Lesinge?

'Shit and piss!' Cochonne presses her face to the window. 'That Englishman!'

'No!'

'It is him, see for yourself.'

'How can I see for myself with your milking-pail of a head in the way?'

Cochonne's expression has turned as thunderous as the sky. 'I will fetch my rake,' she says.

He holds her back. 'No time for that.' He must hurry down to intercept these unwelcome visitors, and in truth he much prefers to have Cochonne with him when they reach the door, rake or no rake. He wipes the dirty glass with his dirtier sleeve. The man in the hat, who rides so slowly behind the bare-headed long-haired fellow: is it really the same loitering burgher they met at the edge of the wood? — the one who said he was bound for the Castle Charizard?

Cochonne may well be right. Her eyes see much better than his, though he will die before he admits it.

'We must be at the threshold to greet these travellers. Come.'

'Why does des Sables call that other one Madam? It is a man. Look at his clothes. And why is he so frightened of them?'

'Because des Sables is an idiot with the heart of a girl.'

'The heart of *what*?'

Lesinge already leaps down the stairs, clumsy Cochonne struggling to keep pace. 'A rabbit then, or a mouse if you prefer. This is no time to dispute the choice of words. To the devil with des Sables! You and I are enough to find out what these two want, whoever they are, and inform them they cannot have it, and send them on their way.'

Outside, the lightning flashes constantly. Denfert's eyes flash with it. The grim castle rises before him, a fist thrust up from the rock. He holds his head erect. Rain like this would sting another man's face and make them hunch their shoulders. Not him. He leaps from his horse. His boots splash in the drowning earth. As soon as it is free of his control the mare rears up with bulging eyes and bolts away.

The door, being broken, cannot be barred against these intruders. Lesinge does the next best thing by stationing Cochonne under the lintel. A ragged cataract of rain spills from it. He stands in front of her and folds his arms as Denfert approaches.

Lesinge does not like the look of this one at all. It is some effeminate Parisian stripling with a haughty air. Some acquaintance of the late Sir, most likely; perhaps one of those mentioned in the jesting will, come to pick the bones of the estate. Well, my good Sir, he thinks, in an attempt to fortify his courage: you will find nothing bequeathed to you here!

It is not easy to feel brave under the stare of those eyes. God! They are black as night, but burn with inward fire.

Lesinge clears his throat.

'I regret to inform you,' he says, 'that the Castle Charizard is closed.'

Denfert steps closer and closer again until they stand face to face. The stream of water falling from the lintel breaks over his head and soaks through his long loose hair. He does not notice it. His skin has a consumptive sheen.

Lesinge squares his shoulders. 'We have been sadly inconvenienced by looting,' he says. 'It is unfortunately impossible to accommodate travellers or visitors of any sort. The town, sir, is back that way, a mile or two below the castle. You may find hospitality there. The people of the region are proverbial for their welcoming character.'

'Stand aside, filth of mortality.'

That voice! Though high and whispering it has the fury of the storm rain.

Behind Lesinge, Cochonne shakes her head and snorts. 'Filth?'

Instead of speaking again Denfert points an arm skywards.

As if answering, a bolt of lightning leaps down to crack against the earth. The noise is like a dolmen stone breaking in two. A white glare obliterates everything. Cochonne screams and throws her skirts over her head.

When the glare passes it reveals Denfert standing just as he was, except for the unpleasant smile now curling his lips.

'Obey me,' he says.

Lesinge has unaccountably adopted a cringing posture, hands over his ears. Conscious of his pride, he springs upright and puts on a witty disdainful manner.

'Eh, sir,' he says, 'you may pretend to command galvanic phenomena; but a man is a different matter. One cannot merely point and say *obey*. I do not obey, sir, and there you have it. By God, Cochonne, cease your whimpering!'

At his invocation of the deity Denfert flinches as if a mosquito had flown by his ear. His cruel smile changes to a snarl.

'Four times must I ask you and four times be refused before I may enter and destroy. Will you stand aside?'

Cochonne has uncovered her head. She is a little ashamed of herself, but very greatly astonished at the bravery of her captain, for she is now quite certain that the Devil himself is at the door.

Lesinge meanwhile glances over his shoulder to assure himself his mighty foot-soldier has not fled. He is as fortified by her constancy as she by his.

'Ask four times,' he says, 'or ten, or forty. The house will remain closed.'

'Once more: will you let me cross this threshold?'

'No,' says Lesinge.

'Never!' cries Cochonne. 'Saint Mary protect us!'

Denfert hisses as if stung. His pale fingers flex. A great roar of wind suddenly blows at his back, so that the torrential rain is swept apart like a veil and he stands in an island of clear air. He raises a hand towards Lesinge's breast.

'Heavens! What weather!' It is the other man, who has dismounted and now pushes his way forward through the typhoon to stand at Denfert's elbow, clutching his hat. 'It cannot last long, surely?'

It is indeed the same man Lesinge and his band encountered at the margin of the forest, the wandering Englishman with the mild scholarly air. He is a sorry spectacle, drenched from head to foot despite his good boots and travelling-cloak. Nevertheless, he lifts his hat politely. 'Sir; my young lady.' To Cochonne he makes a small bow. It is as if he does not remember their previous meeting. His manner is courteous. 'Please accept our apology for arriving unannounced. Had we known the castle was closed we would have made arrangements in the town. But, such a storm! You will not object, I am sure, if we come out of the rain a little while? I fear I may catch an ague. I am wet through.'

With an apologetic smile he slips past Cochonne and Lesinge. Both of them move aside to admit him without entirely knowing what they do.

At the foot of the stair he removes hat and cloak. Cochonne finds she must suppress an urge to take them from him. He stands in a growing puddle, looking around the destroyed hall with an air of tranquil satisfaction: the shattered windows, the pictures torn from their frames, the boards of the floor pulled up in several places and robbed of their nails; the pile of malodorous straw-coloured cobbles which is the only remaining sign of Broubrou, who in the noise and confusion managed to eat through his tether and has now withdrawn to an unknown corner of the house.

'I suppose,' says the Englishman, addressing no person in particular, 'there is not any possibility of tea?'

Faint vapours rise from Denfert's figure. The rain appears to shed away from him. He is not wretched and bedraggled but triumphant.

'Castle Charizard!' he exclaims, surveying the dismal scene. He scents the air, which smells powerfully of the urine of Broubrou. 'Here I was summoned into the world by servile fools; from here my legions will spread across the globe! Generations will dread the name of the place where my eternal reign began.'

How did he enter? Lesinge meant to stop him. The infernal politeness of the Englishman caught them all by surprise.

But what does he care whether the ranting gentleman stands on the step or in the hall? It makes no difference. Gaspard is lord of this place and will send them away once the rain relents, with Cochonne's help. Though he regrets after all that she does not have her rake.

'And now,' Denfert says, while the Englishman wrings out his cloak and mutters quietly in his own language. 'Bring out the Farthingay.'

The Farthingay? What has this vainglorious stripling to do with the English lady, whom they found inexplicably asleep in the castle tower?

He exchanges a look with Cochonne.

Tender and modest by nature, Cochonne has been more than a little awestruck by the mysterious lady, who seemed to her like the Belle of the Woods from the beautiful fairytale, despite her disordered hair and stained dress. Cochonne thought English women were witches with long crooked nails and horns behind their ears. But this lady could be any fine noblewoman, even though she barely knows how to speak and sometimes screams like a vixen. When Cochonne brought her bread and cheese she thanked her. No one else has ever thanked Cochonne for anything at all, except Lesinge in his cell who poured out compliments and fine words at the drop of a hat; but that was because he had designs on her tender nature, curse him for an adorable rogue!

Lesinge sees the adoration in her glance. By God, he admires her, his Amazon, his Jeanne of Arc! And who says he should not? In this new France, why should a farmer's girl not be good enough for Gaspard?

'The Farthingay,' Denfert repeats. 'Have her brought here immediately.'

'The who?' says Lesinge.

Cochonne makes her eyes go wide like a cow's. 'We do not know that name here,' she says.

The wet Englishman smiles to himself, squeezing the corner of his cape.

Denfert taps the point of his boot. The gesture is unmanly, Lesinge thinks. If this one had a fan he would flutter it.

'Naturally,' Denfert says. 'You know nothing.' He will not even condescend to look at Lesinge. He thinks Gaspard beneath his notice. He waves his slender bloodless hand as though dismissing a fly. 'You two may return to your business.'

Lesinge is not easily angered. The philosopher must break his passions like young horses and accustom them to the bridle. Nevertheless, his ire stirs.

'And what business is that, sir?'

'You are the domestics, I assume? Evidently you have much to attend to. Starting' — he indicates the excrement of Broubrou — 'with that.'

Insulted in front of his own follower, who is also the woman he chooses to admire! Lesinge bristles. He may be wary of this Parisian, who talks as if he thinks himself the king, but he is a Frenchman of the new nation and his dignity is inalienable. He advances on Denfert.

'Young fellow,' he says, with a certain careless haughtiness, 'I am Gaspard Lesinge, and this castle, along with those I choose to admit within, are under my protection. Who *you* are—' He shrugs dismissively. 'I do not interest myself in knowing. Some passers-by, of no particular concern to Gaspard. You may consider yourself my guests as long as this rain endures. I advise you to conduct yourselves accordingly.'

Denfert laughs, wild girlish laughter which grates on the ear like the *hee-haw* of Broubrou.

'Passers-by,' he says. He strides back and forth, his boots clicking on the bare boards. 'Mister Peach, tell these stupid peasants who they have for their guest.'

The Englishman, who has been attempting to dry his hat, equally unconcerned with the pride of Denfert and the indignation of Lesinge, looks up.

'Madam Luce Denfert, is it not?' he says. 'Of Paris, I understand.'

The deputy shakes his head impatiently. 'But tell them who masks his glory behind the name of Denfert. Do not hesitate, Mister Peach. You have vowed on your life to acknowledge me.'

'I have heard something of that name,' Lesinge says, maintaining his casual air. He does not believe this one is really the whore of de Charizard, named in the will as Luce Denfert; but then the unwelcome visitor does not seem quite a man either. Whoever he is, he is insufferably boastful like all Parisians; but Gaspard has the measure of him, by God! 'You are a certain old associate of the Sir de Charizard. You thought the world was made for your pleasure, you and your sort. But the world has turned, sir, or madam, whichever you are. The people of France do not want you any more. Your friend de Charizard is, let me inform you, dead;

punished for his wickedness by natural justice. Any ties you may once have had to this castle are dissolved.'

He has more to say, but the Englishman interrupts.

'Excuse me. Did you say the Sir de Charizard is—'

'Dead,' Cochonne says, and cracks her knuckles. Lesinge inspires her. Listen to him, rebuking the Devil! She will not be afraid. She remembers the blessed spirit in the stone who encourages her in faith. 'May his soul burn in hell.'

The Englishman taps his drenched hat against the stair-post. 'Is this intelligence certain?'

'The young lady and myself,' Lesinge says, 'witnessed his expiration in person.'

'Then,' the Englishman says, with a thoughtful air, 'it appears my purpose in this country is made unnecessary. I shall perhaps go home.'

'Silence!' Denfert says.

Despite himself Lesinge is warming to this man of England, who goes about his business calmly, without insult or contempt.

'You were not a friend of the departed Sir?' he says.

'I did not know him,' replies the Englishman. 'But I understand him to have been an execrable character, who had put in train certain plans that I am glad to learn are frustrated.'

'*Silence!*' Denfert roars. The storm roars with him, blasting the house with a bolt that makes even Cochonne cower. 'Not one of you is fit to speak as much as a word in my presence.' The deputy is slight and looks unwell, yet there is an aura about him as if he is clothed in lightning, and his voice carries an echo of the cataract. '*You*' — he points at Lesinge — 'shall not talk to me of the turning of the world, when I was present at its birth and prophesied its corruption before your history began. And *you*' — he turns to the Englishman — 'will go nowhere and do nothing without my command, for you belong to me body and soul. On your knees, each one of you, before the Adversary of God, and the Regent of this fallen Earth!'

From elsewhere in the house comes a muffled exclamation: *hee-haw! Heeee-haw!*

No one kneels.

Lesinge has had his fill of braggarts. He knows the type. A little wine, one or two lucky successes, and certain bandit kings used to fancy themselves Louis the Fourteenth reborn.

'Cochonne,' he says. 'Expel this insolent sir from the house.'

'What? — Me?'

Lesinge shrugs. 'Very well. I must always lead by example, that is clear.' He steps forward to lay hands on Denfert. Man or woman, the stripling with pale hands and delicate fingers cannot be a match for him.

The Englishman moves to stop him. 'I advise you, sir, do not—'

Too late. Lesinge plucks the wet sleeve of the deputy. In the next instant he leaps away howling, clutching the offending hand.

'Ah!' he cries, through tears of agony. 'It burns like fire!' Another great roll of thunder peals above the castle. He dances from foot to foot. The fingertips that touched Denfert are blistered and peeling. 'Ah, ah! God have mercy!'

As Cochonne rushes to his side, tears of sympathy swelling in her eyes, Denfert laughs again.

'God? God will not hear you. God is defeated.' He spreads his arms wide. The rage of the storm possesses him. It crackles in his fingers and eyes and hair; it almost lifts him from the floor. 'God is departed. God is dead.'

Poor Cochonne cannot hold back her weeping. The dreadful blasphemy pierces her pious soul, but not so deeply, she is surprised to discover, as the sight of Lesinge in pain.

'And now,' Denfert cries, 'bring out the Farthingay, so I may send her to her lover!'

The Englishman frowns a little. He is no more perturbed than at a game of cricket or some other trivial entertainment of his nation.

'I cannot think,' he says, 'you refer to the amiable Caspar?'

'What?'

'You alluded to the lady's lover.'

'The fool de Charizard! To whom she is promised by an eternal contract.'

'But the Sir de Charizard is—'

'Bound in adamantine manacles on the shore of a lake of fire. Mister Peach, prepare a passage from this world to the realms of the dead. We shall send the Farthingay that way, into his eager embraces.'

Cochonne, trembling in fear, turns to the Englishman. 'Please do not do that, sir. It would be a great sin.'

'Be quiet, insect. Or do you also wish to learn the torments of hell?' Light-footed, Denfert advances upon the poor weeping girl.

The Englishman spreads his hands peaceably. 'One moment, Madam Denfert. We do not even have Miss Farthingay before us.'

If his purpose was to divert the deputy's attention from Cochonne he has succeeded. Denfert stops and again raises his chin like a cat taking a scent.

'The Farthingay is here,' he says. His eyes have a cat-like glitter. 'Instinct sent her to my altar. Follow me to my temple and you may begin your rite.'

Cochonne cannot stop shaking with unfamiliar fear. But if her Lesinge stood firm she must also be brave. 'I will not allow it,' she says.

Denfert rounds on her with a terrible look. He reaches an arm towards her. 'Let me show you,' he says, 'who gives permission and who obeys.'

The Englishman coughs apologetically. 'Forgive me, Madam Denfert. You need not correct this young lady. She is right. What you ask is unfortunately out of the question.'

He has stayed the deputy's hand again. Denfert turns his burning stare away from Cochonne.

'What did you say?'

The Englishman looks abashed, but says, 'I regret that I cannot do as you ask.'

Denfert advances on him. His voice has become a terrible slithering hiss.

'Mister Peach. Do you attempt to deny me?'

'Madam Denfert—'

'You, most cursed of sinners? You, most damned of men? Are you not the last magician of the world, who commands the passage between this earth and the realms of the dead?'

Mister Peach pinches his hat nervously. 'It is most unfortunate. To open the passage you spoke of, certain conditions are required. Very specific conditions, and also certain absolutely necessary materials, which are in this instance lacking. I deeply regret that I am unable to perform the task.' He bows. 'I am desolated,' he says.

A pitchy smell rises from Denfert, as if the moisture of the storm is burning away from him by sulphurous alchemy. He fixes the Englishman with his cat stare.

'I hope, Mister Peach,' he says, 'you do not imagine yourself indispensable?'

'Not in the least, Madam.'

'I could cast you aside like dirt.'

'Without doubt.'

'They would have hung you for a spy if I had not come for you. Your very life is mine.'

'I reflect on the circumstance perpetually.'

Denfert has stepped close to the Englishman. The odour is of flesh burning.

'Then *why*,' he whispers, with terrible quiet rage, 'do you not obey me?'

'Only because I cannot, madam, I assure you. It is entirely a question of the insufficiency of provisions. Most regrettable.' Mister Peach draws in a breath and holds it. 'I am mortified,' he says. He closes his eyes, expecting pain.

Denfert watches him without blinking. There is a pause in the storm as if the frantic sky also held its breath. Then thunder rolls again, slow and further off.

'You.' Denfert snaps his fingers at poor Lesinge, who still crouches and whimpers and cradles his burnt hand. 'Come here.'

Kneeling at his side, Cochonne bathes him in her tender tears. 'Do not go,' she says. What ecstasy even in this terrible moment to feel his rough skin and greasy hair against her! 'Defy him. Heaven will protect us.'

'With you at his side, my sweet Penthesilea, Gaspard defies all the world. — Ah! My fingers!'

'Brave Lesinge!'

'My warrior queen!'

'Come *here*,' Denfert repeats, with a hiss like a hundred snakes.

Cochonne raises her head to him defiantly. 'We will not submit to you. Blessed Virgin, be our shield and sword!'

The deputy flinches and grimaces with rage.

'You have insulted me for the last time, pig-girl. Prepare to meet your doom.'

'No!' Lesinge cries, and struggles to his feet. 'See, I come. I obey.'

Cochonne clings to his arm. 'Ah, dear Gaspard, do not! This is surely the Devil in human form.'

'Peace, my sweet flower,' says Lesinge. 'For your sake Gaspard will face even the Devil.'

'My emperor!' She would hold him back by strength if she could, but love has made her weak.

Her devotion fills Lesinge with mysterious courage. 'Well,' he says, with all the bravado the agony in his hand permits. 'And what do you want with me, sir?'

Denfert holds out a hand. His skin, Lesinge thinks, is as dry and smooth as alabaster. It seems to glow from within.

'The Farthingay,' says the deputy. 'At once. Any more delay and you will all burn alive.'

For two heartbeats Lesinge fears he is defeated. With the third he understands what he must do. He is Gaspard: his wit rises above fear and pain.

From the pocket of his coat he brings out the white queen.

It pains him to his soul to surrender it. It is his treasure, promised by a demon. Why then does the Prince of demons renege on the promise? But infernal creatures, he supposes, are like the worst sort of brigands, whose word is forgotten as soon as given; people without honour.

Nevertheless, he will not reveal that the English lady is in the house.

'You refer to this, I assume?' he says.

Denfert stares at the chess-piece.

'Give her to me,' he says.

Lesinge shrugs. 'I have been asked for less with more courtesy. But there you are.' Careful not to touch the outstretched hand, he drops the little ivory trinket into it. 'My white queen.'

Denfert's palm snaps closed. A look of savage contentment comes over him. It is as if Lesinge and Cochonne are no longer present.

'Follow me, Mister Peach,' he says. 'To my temple.' He steps past Lesinge without another word.

Mister Peach glances at Lesinge as he hurries in the deputy's wake, giving a rueful look. Lesinge does not see it. He is already enveloped in Cochonne's embrace.

In the soot-engrained window of the desecrated chapel lightning plays without a sound. The wind has relented. The rain falls in moderation, though it has penetrated the roof somewhere above and the chatter of its victory echoes down through the house. But though there is no thunder, white light dances everywhere. Iron chains, silver mirrors, unholy symbols of tarnished brass, all flicker and flash as though the air was haunted by legions of imps.

Mister Peach mutters to himself as he sees the room for the first time; some English expression of mild disapproval.

Denfert is already at the altar. The perpetual dazzle in the window outlines his form. With a shrieking laugh he picks up the knife and the bowl.

'You complain, Mister Peach, that you do not have the necessary materials to open a passage to the dead? Regard! Everything necessary is here. All I now require is the Farthingay in her own person.' He has placed the chess-piece on the altar; he caresses it with the point of the knife. 'She can no longer hide.'

'Madam Denfert,' the Englishman says, 'I beg you to consider—'

Denfert does not listen. He plucks up the white queen and raises his arms beneath the inverted cross.

'Arabella Farthingay,' he howls. 'To me!'

A splintering crack follows his cry. The door to the crypt shatters and flies from its hinges, accompanied by a small scream from the woman revealed beyond.

CHAPTER ELEVEN

— My dear Miss Farthingay — Are you hurt? — Heaven forfend!

A man hastens to her. — A solicitous man, hat in hand — wet, from head to toe —

Miss Farthingay — drawn up the stair, by the noise of conversation above — Frighted half to death, by the sudden explosion of the door! — some stray bolt of lightning, we suppose, that entered the house by a chimney, and, finding itself confined, raged with quicksilver speed through room after room, until it vented its wrath here — We have read of the phaenomenon — Miss Farthingay, thank God! is not hurt, for the door leapt outward from its frame, as it split into pieces. But she has taken a dreadful fright. She staggers — wavers, for some alarming moments, on the brink of a swoon. — The solicitous wet man rushes to her side and offers a hand.

White radiance flashes at the window, and lights his face. — Great God! — He is —

— Tom! she cries.

MR PEACH! at last!

We should hardly have known him. — Only look at him, reader. — Pitiful sight! His cheek, sallow and sunken — his eye, distracted — Dripping and shivering, like a cat caught in a shower.

— Arabella — pray — Let me assure myself you have suffered no injury.

— None at all. — But, Tom! you, here! I am inexpressibly glad —

— Mr Peach, calls a voice high, French, and feminine.

There is another present, in the grotesque chapel. How well this new apparition suits the scene! — wholly as uncouth, as the horrid room, with its animal skulls and carceral ornaments. It is some woman, in a state of dress utterly unsuited to society. Her hair, unbound — Traces of dirt or soot, about her mannish riding habit. — She stands at the end of the room, under the filthy window, gesturing furiously, with kitchen implements in her hands. — We believe we noticed those implements, resting on the altar, in our previous chapter.

Is this some deranged house-keeper, in the borrowed clothes of her dead master?

There is a phrenzied look about her. — An unhealthy luminous pallor, in her complexion. She cries again, in the distinctive accents of a Frenchwoman — Mr Peach, bring her forth to me.

Mr Peach offers Miss Farthingay his arm. — Can you walk? he says. — Permit me to assist you.

Blessed with a natural elasticity of temper, Miss Farthingay is recovering from the shock of the explosion. — I am quite unharmed, thank you, she says. — Who is that?

Mr Peach leads her to the heavy oak benches, where the family of the house once sat at their devotions.

— Miss Farthingay, he says, indicating the wild creature at the altar. — May I present Madame Luce Denfert, a lady of Paris. Madame Denfert — Miss Arabella Farthingay, my dear friend and neighbour.

MADAME DENFERT! —

We know her now —

We encountered the lady, in our former volume. You have not forgotten it, we trust. — The occasion, though brief, was memorable — and, memorably painful, for Mr Tho.s Peach. It is an acquaintance we cannot think he would have wished renewed — Yet — here they are, together.

But what are our alarms and confusions, compared to those of our heroine? — to whom the name of DENFERT, is the most unwelcome of any in the world! Denfert, the confederate of her black-hearted seducer — Denfert, whose machinations have haunted her, at every turn — whose letters were all dissembling protestations and shameless lies — THIS, is Denfert? — No Monsieur at all, but an harridan woman, with the eyes of a Bedlamite!

Are they then the identical person? — Is the *Monsieur* Denfert, whose baleful influence upon our history we have been, alas! too slow to recognize — to our eternal sorrow and shame — Is he no more than an imposture, conjured by that *Madame* Denfert, formerly known to us?

We supposed the sirname was a common one, in France. — That there was no connexion, between the deputy, and our insane madame. Fool that we are!

Miss Farthingay turns to Mr Peach with renewed alarm. — Tom —

He leans close by her ear. — Do not be afraid, he says.

— Conduct the lamb to the altar, Mr Peach! says Madame Denfert, in a tone of exultation better suited to the stage, than the pages of an authentick history such as ours. See how she waves her kitchen-knife about! — as though she imagines herself the heathen priestess, of some unspeakable rite.

— Gracious! exclaims Miss Farthingay — Whatever does she mean?

— Nothing — says Mr Peach — It is nothing — Pray, sit.

— You are bound to my service, Madame Denfert says, in tones that seem at once to whisper and ring — like the deep roar of wind, high and low together.

We suspected it once, and are certain now. — Madame Denfert, fine French lady though she may be, is — *intirely mad.*

— Shall you wield the instrument of sacrifice yourself, she says, as Abraham did, when the Tyrant commanded him to offer his own son? I think you shall.

— Tom — Miss Farthingay says, in a low voice — I should like to leave this house immediately. The rains have relented somewhat, I think.

— Patience, Miss Farthingay, he murmurs. — Sit a while. — Though his manner remains solicitous, he looks about the room, with evident anxiety, as though searching for something hidden, or some one.

— Try me no longer, Madame Denfert says. — The time is arrived. Obey, as you must!

Mr Peach straightens his back — clears his throat — turns his sodden hat in his hands.

— Madame Denfert, he says, releasing Miss Farthingay's arm to face the altar. — The course of action you propose, if I understand it correctly, is evidently quite impossible for me to perform. What human creature could willingly consent to such a deed? or be urged to it, without maintaining a steadfast refusal, in the face of any threats or compulsions whatsoever? I am sensible of my obligation to you. Nevertheless — firmly, though regretfully — I must insist — I will not comply with your instruction, in the present instance.

The silence that follows this speech, is very remarkable. — deep, long, and *resonant*, if we may apply that epithet to the absence of sound. — The silence — we imagine — of antient graves.

Madame Denfert lowers the implements.

— *Will not?* she says — as though those words of Mr Peach's had been pronounced, in a language unknown to her — As though their meaning will not settle, in her brain.

Mr Peach makes an apologetic bow. — It is most unfortunate, he says.

— You are my creature! — Madame fairly howls with indignation. — You are enmeshed in arts of darkness, forsaken by the God, and condemned to my service. It is required that you obey me.

— Heavens! says Miss Farthingay. — What language!

Mr Peach seems unmoved by the tirade, though his hands still turn the hat over and back, betraying, we think, a restlessness of mind, that he keeps from his speech. — I beg your pardon,

Madame Denfert, he says, and — *shrugs*, in the French manner — as though to say, with an eloquence beyond words — The thing is impossible — alas!

Madame Denfert — reader, we regret we have no more delicate term, with which to describe her action — *screams* — like an enraged child, denied a toy. — Though there is nothing of petulance in the noise, which is, we confess, quite terrifying. — More akin to the shriek of a predatory bird, as it falls on the poor doomed mouse, than the cry of any person, however deranged.

She throws down the implements with a clatter, and thrusts an hand inside her scorched cloak. — Great Heavens! — is the garment *smoking?* — Has she kindled a fire, about her own person?

She draws forth — a tiny black thing, no bigger than a finger — a *chess-piece* — The bishop, or as the French call it *le fou* — the jester, or madman.

More *chess-pieces!*

We begin to doubt the opinion of M Philidor, that chess is *only a game* —

Miss Farthingay leans towards her friend. — Mr Peach, she says, ought we not quit this place without delay?

— I can't, Arabella, he says, very quietly, and in a despairing tone. — But let us be patient. The crisis approaches.

— Good Lord, Tom! A crisis?

— Hush.

Mr Peach is certainly distracted in his thoughts. — Else, he would never have thought to *hush* his benefactrix — his honoured friend — or, so we earnestly hope. For a moment, our startled heroine contemplates a gentle complaint — perhaps, something approaching a rebuke. — But her attention is captured once more, by the behaviour of the Frenchwoman, who has placed the little black bishop, or jester, upon the altar, and now intones some words.

We suppose, they are French, for they are certainly not English. — Though they resemble no French conversation we have ever heard. — If Mr Peach knows the meaning, he keeps his counsel. Though, see! how his fingers tighten their grip, on the inoffending hat.

Madame Denfert's speech rises to a loud climax. If it was not evident nonsense, we should say she was addressing — the chesspiece — Imploring it, or commanding it.

Far from the château, thunder grumbles again.

Hark! — now *another person* stirs, in the deep shadows of the barbarous chapel. — We hear a rustling of clothes — a moan, such as the sick emit, when wrenched from sleep, into renewal of their daily suffering.

Who is there? — Is it the valet des Sables? — We did not see him ascend the stair.

It cannot be either of his companions. —

What new personage lurks, in this refuge of lunatics?

An huddle of dusky skirts — Some poor lost creature, that has perhaps been curled up in the dirtiest and darkest corner of the forsaken house, out of our notice, until forced at last from sleep, by the loud chanting of Madame Denfert.

She stumbles to her feet — Totters forward, pushing her hair from her face.

The gesture is instantly familiar —

CLARY!

— Clary! cries Miss Farthingay.

— Clary! cries Mr Peach.

— Help me, Clary whispers. — I am —

She can say no more — but falls, at the feet of Miss Farthingay. Miss Clarissa Riddle, herself! — whom we sought high and low. — So she has been concealed in the château, all this time — Has she not? Hiding, from Miss Farthingay — from the assorted French clowns — From *ourselves*, though we bent every effort of our pen, to recall her to our page.

How has she hidden herself so perfectly, until now? and on what account?

Mystery upon mystery, and confusion upon confusion!

Mr Peach is as amazed as we. His *quondam* house-maid, who vanished without notice, three years past, and was no where seen or heard of since, is found — *now* — and *here!* —

In recent years — since her disappearance, and the termination of his nightly intercourse with his poor departed wife — he has seemed indifferent to all the transactions of life. — As though his gaze were fixed on a far horizon — or, beyond it. But see, how he now rushes to assist Clary, with a degree of animation we thought lost to him for ever. Miss Farthingay, likewise — Her suspicions, of Clary's unaccountable behaviour, and unfathomable motives, are all forgotten.

How weak and frail her old play-mate looks! Clary seems all but worn away — As insubstantial, as her tattered black dress. — My dear Clary! cries Miss Farthingay, assisting Mr Peach in bringing the girl to a seat — My sister! — Miss Farthingay looks about the room. — Will no one fetch a cordial? she says — Or a glass of lemonade?

Clary, whom we thought insensible, opens her eyes, and smiles a little, as though at some weary jest.

— Dearest Bella, she says. — And Mr Peach. I knew you would come.

She looks at him — then, past him — Her eyes widen in alarm.

No — she says, rising — gazing at Madame Denfert, who advances between the crude columns — *He* is here!

— My abject slave, Madame Denfert says. — My first and best instrument, compelled to obedience. I have one more task for you, pretty bird.

Reader — there is no question, but that she addresses these words, to *Clary*.

What refinement of mystery is this, that a lady of Paris, calls Clarissa Riddle — of all the people in the world — her servant?

That Madame Denfert is *mad*, no one can doubt. Yet Clary herself does not appear surprized, at the words — and is plainly acquainted with the lunatic madame.

Is this where the absconded house-maid has been, these three years? — In *France*?

We cannot pause, to contemplate these Gordian puzzles — for lo! Madame Denfert has picked up the kitchen-knife, from where she flung it to the floor, and now advances on our British friends, brandishing it in the most alarming manner.

— Mr Peach, says Clary — Please —

— I see you are acquainted already, cries Miss Farthingay, quite astonished. — Tom — how is it that you know my dear Clary?

Clary declines to give an account of the events described in our former volume, at this uncertain and dangerous moment. We do not blame her for it. — She lays hold of Mr Peach's sleeve and urgently implores him — Save us now!

Mr Peach shakes his head. — I have no power over this, he says.

— I do not understand you, says Miss Farthingay.

Reader — no more do *we*. —

— To my side, instrument! exclaims Madame Denfert, pointing a single finger at Clary — a gesture of the most imperious disdain.

— Banish him, Clary says to Mr Peach, with desperate emphasis. — Command him away from the world, back to the infernal regions.

— To whom do you refer? says Miss Farthingay. — Tom — I fear she is not well.

Mr Peach's attention is all on his former maid. — I cannot, he says. — But — *you* —

— To me! Madame Denfert cries, beckoning Clary, as one might call a dog to heel.

Miss Farthingay stands — Draws herself very upright, to face the Frenchwoman. — I beg your pardon, she says, but I do not think myself obliged to tolerate this behaviour. You shall not speak in that fashion, to one whom ties of long intimacy and affection impel me to call by the dearest of names — A *sister*.

— Your sister! says Madame Denfert, advancing still, the kitchen-knife firm in her grasp. — But how piquant! For the imbecile Abraham it was a son. For you, my blackbird, it shall be a sister. — She presents the knife to Clary. — You shall kill on my behalf once more, she says. — Then the promised annihilation will be yours.

Clary looks at the proffered implement — then — *Takes* it —

Miss Farthingay gives a small cry of alarm. — Tom!

Madame Denfert laughs. — Do not, she says, expect any assistance from him, Arabella Farthingay. — He too belongs to me.

— Is this true? Miss Farthingay says to Mr Peach — the beginning of a tear, moistening her eye. — Are you under some obligation to this lady? — whom I believe to be the author of all the trials I have been put to, in this horrid country?

Madame Denfert offers Miss Farthingay a mocking bow. By some trick of the light, we could almost swear that the lady's eyes — pitch black, like pools of ink — are *burning* — with inward fires —

With strange assurance, she speaks. — Do you not know, Arabella Farthingay, that I am the author of all suffering in the world? This creation was perfect and without blemish, until I corrupted it.

— Mr Peach, says Miss Farthingay, gathering a little of her native firmness of spirit. — As you are a gentleman, I must place myself under your protection, and request that you remove this woman from my presence.

— Forgive me, Arabella, he says. — I cannot lay an hand on her.

— To touch me, says Madame Denfert, is to burn. Is that not so, my blackbird? — She steps behind Clary, and takes hold of the wrist that holds the kitchen-knife, with her own hand — Lifting the arm high, so that Clary appears to threaten with the implement. Clary shudders, as though the grasp causes her pain.

— Now — cries the insane Frenchwoman, triumph in her eye — Strike, and complete the bargain!

Though Clary is evidently in great distress, she — *laughs*, also — a dreadful, bitter laugh!

— I — refuse, she says.

— Well said, Clary! exclaims Mr Peach.

— Disobedience? says Madame Denfert, tightening her grip on poor Clary's wrist. — Forbidden! Impossible!

The raised knife quivers in the air — The point turning, towards where our heroine stands —

— Heavens! says Miss Farthingay, in the utmost anxiety. — Will no one assist me? Monsieur Lesinge! *Aidez-moi, s'il vous plaît!*

Lesinge! We had quite forgotten him, amid this bedlam — him and his ill-sorted associates.

Are they still in the house? Or have they enough sense, mulish peasants though they be, to have fled these pageants of lunacy?

— Slay her, cries Madame Denfert, in Clary's ear.

— I will not — says Clary, forcing the words between clenched teeth.

— You have murdered hundreds already at my command. One more and you are free.

Clary replies —

— in language, too coarse for us to record. Forgive us, reader. —

— Gracious! says Miss Farthingay — her fine complexion, which horror made pale, now reddening.

— Well said, Miss Riddle, well said again! says Mr Peach. — Remember, he adds, this is the age of revolution.

Revolution? What has this terrible scene to do, with the turmoil of nations and peoples? — Is Thomas Peach also out of his wits?

But, hark! — rushing steps — An immodest clattering haste, approaching the grotesque chapel. — A door bursts open —

It is Monsieur Lesinge, accompanied by the Gargantua. Both of them have furnished themselves, with village armaments. — She has fetched, from somewhere in the house, a long-handled gardener's tool, which she brandishes like a pike. He, meanwhile, has equipped himself with a lump of rock, bigger than his fist. — Ready, we suppose, to hurl it, as the Parisian mobs hurled bricks and slates, so we have read. The two of them tumble together into the room, tripping over one another. — M Lesinge halts — sees Clary, for the first time — His jaw falls open, in a caricature of surprize.

Ma reine noire — he says — *Ma démone!*

We hear the words quite distinctly. There is no mistake. —

Are *these two also acquainted?* — our Miss Riddle, and this vagrant rogue Lesinge?

Reader — why do you nod, as though forewarned?

— The thief! Clary says, as astonished as he.

— The demonoscope! exclaims Madame Denfert.

This last exclamation at least, does *not* surprize us. We expect nothing else from the lips of the French lady, but perfect NONSENSE.

We record it exactly nevertheless. It is plain enough, that this scene represents the *crisis*, or turning-point, of our tale. — Though, upon what it turns — Whose fates are balanced, in what scales — we could not tell you, were we as wise in the laws of drama, as Aristotle himself.

Madame Denfert's nonsensical exclamation has at least had the effect, of causing her to release Clary's wrist. The kitchen-knife clatters to the floor. — Nasty implement! We fervently hope, it will not be picked up again. Some stray foot will kick it, God willing, under the benches, out of reach.

A stream of French passes between M Lesinge and his Amazonian ally — an Alpine mountain-stream, as it were, that rattles between rocks, faster than a galloping horse. Madame Denfert laughs to hear it. How boldly she faces them! — beckoning, with arms outspread, despising them and their rustic weaponry. The giantess raises her garden-tool. — On her black-browed face, a look of grim determination. —

Like a portent of thunder we feel it — Some deed of violence is in the air.

— Pray — says Mr Peach, holding out an hand, as one soothes a skittish horse — Monsieur Lesinge — Mademoiselle Cochonne — Approach no nearer. Force of arms will not avail against this foe. — He recollects himself, and repeats his advice, in French.

— Tom! — exclaims Miss Farthingay, aghast. —

Now —

In moments of extreme peril, our nerves vibrate with exquisite motion. All the natural philosophers agree, on this point. — Our senses are sharpened, to a rapier point. We apprehend, in the mere blink of an eye, whole panoplies of sight and sound, whose distinct elements, in the ordinary state of our faculties, we should struggle to distinguish, and combine, during long minutes of attentive observation.

Hence it is, that amid the anarchy of our scene — this Chaos — Miss Farthingay's eye, picks out a minuscule detail. — A single thread, in the carpet — a brush-stroke, on the canvas — We speak in metaphor — there is no carpet here, or painted picture — The object, that glances on her attention, and then, in less than the blink of an eye, seizes it wholly, is — A little gleaming thing, wrapped by a delicate chain, in the left hand of Monsieur Gaspard Lesinge.

His right hand grips the stone missile, with which he armed himself, before entering the room. But in that same interval, he has also fetched — from who knows where — for the acquisition is as perfectly inexplicable — as *impossible* — as every thing else, that transpires in this phantastical *crisis* of our narrative — He has fetched, a little silver charm — A locket, upon a chain, such as lovers wear, to keep at their breast, some token of their *amour*.

THIS particular locket Miss Farthingay recognizes, with the instant and perfect acuity, bestowed on her by the sensation of immediate danger.

It is — we assure you, reader, she is not mistaken — the VERY SAME locket, which she herself wore, secreted in her bosom, these past three years and more. — The locket, containing the last mortal remnants of poor departed Eliza Peach, which Mr Peach gave to Miss Farthingay — gave her, with the solemn request, that she should keep it safe, but on no account return it to him, unless in *the utmost extremity of need* — And which she kept on her person, every day of those three years, until the overturning of Monsieur de

Charizard's carriage, and the violent fall she suffered within, caused it to be lost. — For ever lost, she feared, and so did we. — Yet, HERE IT IS — in the dirty fist, of this unknown Frenchman!

Aristotle! Old Grecian! — Two thousand years ago you pronounced upon the *unity of action*, that must govern every tale. Does your shade hold sway, over our pen? — Are we so governed? Is there order and meaning in this madness, though *we know it not ourselves?* — and though we no longer discern your antient spirit, nor the other wise ghosts that attend the world, in this age of steam-engines and electrical illuminations?

Some pause has interrupted the present Chaos, while these reflexions occurred to us. — The warning of Mr Peach has been heeded — While various impulses, of surprize, or recognition, or disappointment, or suspended alarm, have caused the other parties, to cease their threats, and pleas, and we know not what, for the space of a few breaths.

In the interval of calm, Clary speaks — Addressing herself, quite plainly, to Madame Denfert, though with a confusion of sex, we are at a loss to explain.

— Dread prince, she says, behold. I have brought you the stone as you desired.

Madame Denfert seems entranced. Her wild rages, thank Heaven! may be passed. — Who knows what desperate act she might have committed, in the height of diseased passion?

— Tom — whispers Miss Farthingay — Look, there — it is your locket!

— The summoning-stone, Madame Denfert says. Her burning gaze is fixed, upon M Lesinge. — We therefore assume, that she refers to the fragment of rock in that worthy's hand. — Mine at last, she says.

— Yours indeed, eternal master, Clary says. — Behold, no sacrifice is required.

Madame Denfert appears to consider the matter. — But the bargain was agreed, she says, and it remains. The Farthingay for the stone.

— It does not, says Clary. — The bargain was made with de Charizard, and he is dead. The stone is not his to dispose of. You may have it freely, dread master.

That name! de Charizard!

So Clary is *also* familiar with him — the libertine seducer!

Clarissa Riddle! — This history of ours, which we meant to dedicate to Mr Tho.s Peach — then unwillingly discovered, to be the tale of poor Miss Farthingay and her oppressions instead — Was it YOURS, from the very beginning? — YOU, its dark secret goddess — its fallen muse?

Look — here now comes the valet des Sables upon the scene, as though conjured by the name of his despicable employer. He has emerged, from the shattered door that opened on the crypt. He finds himself unseen by the majority of the other parties, who stand, facing Monsieur Lesinge and the giant peasant-girl, on the other side of the chapel. Only Lesinge himself has observed the comely youth. — They exchange a silent look, in which we detect some significance — as though a wordless instruction has passed, from the old rogue to his young confederate.

M Lesinge glances for a moment at the stone in his hand, and then looks again at des Sables —

Who nods — in understanding — And, sets the flame of the taper, which he carries, to the larger candles, variously affixed to the wall adjacent, in their *goatish* sockets.

The storm — let us take a moment to notice it — Is considerably relented. Some hints of clear daylight begin to show, behind angry clouds.

We think the more proper moment to light the candles, would have been before — While the sky was at its darkest. — But no one now heeds our opinion —

Madame Denfert is answering Clary. —

— Shall we not have blood nevertheless? she says. Her attention has not wavered for an instant, from the shabby piece of earth, held in M Lesinge's right hand. — So great an occasion demands it, she says.

Miss Farthingay touches Mr Peach on the sleeve. — Some fit has come over her, she whispers. — Let us steal away while we can.

Mr Peach lays his hand over hers, and again shakes his head.

Miss Farthingay frowns in annoyance. —

— There will be blood enough when you command your legions, Clary says.

Unseen by all but Lesinge, des Sables coaxes two more candles to life.

— That is true, says Madame Denfert. — You are a wise slave, pretty bird. I shall miss you, when I have destroyed you.

To this distasteful language Miss Riddle makes no answer.

— Come, then, says Madame Denfert, stretching forth an arm, and raising her voice. — Let us see how the Eye of Hell obeys its master!

Her outstretched hand becomes a fist. She speaks again — Terrible words, pronounced with terrible emphasis. The language is neither French nor English. We shudder to hear them — will strive, for the rest of our days, to forget we once did.

And now — strange trick of the new-awakened candle-light — The rough sphere of rock, held by Monsieur Lesinge, has begun to gleam, with a warm glow.

We are no geologist — though we admire them! — those modern oracles, who read vast characters in the folds and scars of the earth, and endow its obscure matter with names and histories. — We think nevertheless, this particular fragment of stone, must belong to the family of crystals, or quartzes — some translucent generation. A moment ago, we thought it plain and dull enough — But the reflexions, stolen from the candles, have produced the illusion, that it is *lit from within*.

M Lesinge makes an exclamation of pain, and flings it from his hand. — *Encore ça brûle!* he cries. Ah! Poor man! — his fingers are scarred and blistered, with the marks of fire!

The stone tumbles across the floor, to rest by the feet of Madame Denfert, who cries out in mad triumph.

— Arise, my legions! Come, appear before your prince!

The giantess is fallen to her knees. — She bows her head, and clasps her fearsome hands at her breast in prayer.

Madame Denfert rounds on Mr Peach, with an unpleasant smirking look, peculiarly French in character. — *Voilà*, she says, I have no need of you at all. The demonoscope acknowledges me, and will open a path to the realms below.

— I have read that it possesses that virtue, says Mr Peach, quite equably, as though he were conversing with the lady, upon some matter of ordinary interest.

— Hand it to me, says Madame Denfert, pointing at the stone on the floor.

Madame! — you address a British gentleman! Not some menial of yours! —

To think the world will have it, that we are to take instruction in manners and *politesse*, from the ladies of France. —

Despite her uncivil and peremptory language, Mr Peach complies with the demand. — Or rather, he begins to. He crouches to the floor, and studies the stone, with some care.

Reader, we could swear he *smiles* — Involuntarily — as though, in this scene of confusion and menace, he had suddenly observed something, that assures him of perfect contentment.

He reaches for the stone, to raise it from the floor — And pulls his hand away.

— Excuse me, madame, he says, I cannot. It is excessively hot to the touch.

Madame Denfert nudges Clary, with the tip of her boot — As one might kick a spaniel.

— You, then, she says.

Clary reaches down — Straightens again, withdrawing her hand, before she can touch the object, which is evidently of such profound interest to Madame Denfert.

— I cannot either, she says.

Monsieur Lesinge, we observe meanwhile, sidles away, as though to escape the madwoman's notice. But instead of retreating from the room — which we should certainly have attempted ourselves, in his place — He goes crab-like, around the benches, in the murky rear of the chapel, towards where des Sables stands.

Madame Denfert cares for nothing but the object at her feet. — The pair of you, she says, are drudges, unworthy to serve me. Behold, I assume myself the orb of my majesty.

With this proclamation, and a flourish of her arm equally pompous, she swoops to pick up the stone —

Withdraws her hand, with an angry hiss —

— It burns!

The chapel echoes with laughter. It is the clown Lesinge, who has found something to amuse him, in this scene. — His features, we confess, were formed for drollery. — If not to enjoy it, then to be its subject. We have never in our existence encountered a physiognomy, so intirely ludicrous.

What has provoked him to laugh, we cannot guess. — Though, in answer to a furious glare, directed at him by the Denfert, he makes a number of remarks, in French. — While, by furtive motions, he passes the locket, whose surprizing appearance we remarked some moments ago, into the hands of des Sables.

— Do you see? whispers Miss Farthingay to Mr Peach. — It *is* your locket.

— So it is, he says.

— What did Monsieur Lesinge say just now?

— As best I could interpret him, he said he has possession of the testament of Monsieur de Charizard, and reads in it, that the stone upon the floor there is bequeathed to this handsome young fellow. The late gentleman's valet, I believe.

— That much is true, Miss Farthingay says. — I saw him in London. He seems a gentle-hearted young man, though rather deficient in spirit.

While they whisper, the more animated conversation continues around them, in French. Its exact significance — forgive us, reader! — eludes us. — Had we been forewarned, that our tale would linger abroad so long, we might have taken better care, of Miss

Farthingay's female companion. — But this is not the hour for regrets. We make what inference we can. — Madame Denfert is certainly enraged, at some body, or every body. — Monsieur Lesinge, greatly pleased with himself, we should guess, though we know not on what account. — The valet des Sables, anxious and hesitant, interjecting but a few words. The Gargantua continues her orisons. She tells her *Ave* — Her voice gaining force, with every repetition, as though defying one and all to silence her.

— What are they saying now? Murmurs Miss Farthingay.

— Nothing to the purpose, says Mr Peach. — You know the French.

— Too well, alas! She sighs. — Shall we quit the scene?

— I think we shall, very soon.

— Dear Clary must come with me. She is not at all well. Her mind is disordered.

— She has endured a great deal.

— I feared her lost for ever.

— As did I.

— But — begins Miss Farthingay, still at a loss to comprehend, how there can be any connexion between her dear childhood friend and play-mate, and Mr Peach. She intends to satisfy her curiosity, on that account — But now the Gallic dispute has risen to a noisy climax, which forbids all whispered intercourse. Urged on by M Lesinge, the fair valet approaches our British hero and heroine. — His purpose, though, is not with them — No — It is the *stone* again, which concerns him. — Him, and every body.

Even Mr Peach looks on the glimmering rock, with interest.

Is it perhaps of *scientific* significance?

Might it be a gem-stone, in the raw? We have heard that even the most brilliant diamonds, are dull ugly things, when pulled from the earth.

Des Sables bends down, to perform the simple act, of which Mr Peach, and Clary, and Madame Denfert, successively proved incapable. — The collecting of the stone, from where it lies upon the floor. He picks it up, and turns it over in his dirty hands, with a look on his face, like a pauper's child given a sweet orange. — As though he had never in his life held a thing so marvellous.

Madame Denfert cries out, in a paroxysm of fury. She demands, by word and gesture, that it be given to her immediately.

The simple reply, given in turn by M Lesinge — by the giantess — the valet — does not tax our knowledge of French. — No — Never.

How rapidly the storm abates! But tempests of such violence will often pass, as suddenly as they arrive.

Madame Denfert addresses her compatriots, in some tirade of fiery rhetoric — Her voice echoing about the chapel. — Des Sables looks a little abashed, but nevertheless clasps the stone close to his breast, and repeats — *Non* — *Jamais.*

Says Mr Peach — See, Arabella, how the common people of this country will not be swayed as once they were.

— How dare they refuse me? says Madame Denfert, her complexion ashy — the strange fire in her eyes dimmed. — How dare you all? The God is dead, and I am king over this world.

Mr Peach clears his throat. — Madame, he says, it cannot have escaped your notice, that kings are overthrown. We chuse not to submit. Authority, it appears, depends on obedience. It is the lesson of this age. One declines to obey, and, hey presto! The great monarch — the dread prince — is — *Nothing.* — He directs this last word towards Madame Denfert, with a peculiar firmness of emphasis.

It strikes her like a blow. She appears — stunned —

Miss Farthingay regards her friend, with a look compounded of surprize and admiration.

— Why, Mr Peach, she says. — You are quite the revolutionary, after all.

But, now —

Des Sables brings the locket, passed to him some moments ago, by Monsieur Lesinge, into one hand. — Holds it close by the stone, and lifts the two objects together, towards the flame of a candle.

Blessed light of day! — After the morning's thunders and torrents, lo! an arc of the sun is uncovered in the east. Its radiance comes in at the dirty window, and makes a beam of light through the air, that eludes the inverted cross and the dangling chains, and falls directly on the person of the valet.

Great Heavens! — there is yet *another* personage upon the scene!

Who is it, that has appeared in the chapel now? — and how has she come in, so silently — all unnoticed?

Accustomed to gloom, our eyes are dazzled. We cannot see distinctly. — Does she stand in light or shade?

Or is she herself only a shadow?

— Eliza — says Mr Peach, in the absolute silence, produced by this new apparition. — My dearest Eliza — My love.

— Hello, Tom.

Though faint as a July breeze, we would know that voice among an hundred — a thousand. — Night after night, we once heard it.

It is the voice of — MRS PEACH.

Do not stir — reader — we implore you — Suspend your very breath, if you can. Whatever spell is cast here — Let it not be broken —

Mr Peach is trembling with emotion — though, *which* emotion — Joy or grief — or, that deeper feeling, which is both together, and for which there is no name, though all music and poetry strive their utmost, to speak of it — We cannot say.

— I thought I would not see you ever again, he says.

— I was begun to think the same, says Mrs Peach. — Where have you been? Some odd people carried me along while I waited. They were foreigners. I told them you were in the west, but I'm not certain they understood.

— Forgive me, my dear. I was diverted once or twice. Had I known you expected me here I would have come straight.

— Oh, Tom, you know you would not. You could never resist a diversion. You was always after some odd old thing.

Madame Denfert — we can scarce see her! — she stands in the light. — She says, You are no demon. Begone.

Her voice does not echo as it did before.

— Who is that? Says Mrs Peach.

— No one, Mr Peach says. — But tell me, Liza, for I suppose you can't stay long. Why did you seek me? Is there any last service I may do?

— None at all, my dear, none at all. I am quite content.

— I am very glad to hear it. But did you not say you expected me?

— I had a message for you, I think. Was I always so forgetful? I hope I can't have been.

— You were not, my love, but you are escaped from the burden of time.

— That must account for it.

— Do you remember your message?

— Of course I do. I am an angel. *Malak*, you once told me, is *messenger*, which is also the meaning of *angel*.

Madame Denfert emits a strange moan. — Is it she? We think, it must be. So difficult to distinguish place and person, in this sudden brilliance! — the shadows are turned impenetrably deep, and the beam of light is too radiant to look upon. Somebody has fallen. — We think, it is the Denfert.

— An angel, whispers Miss Farthingay.

— *Un ange*, murmurs a French voice, in solemn wonder. — The Gargantua, we guess.

— Goodness! says Mrs Peach. — What a crowd there is! This is not your house, Tom, surely?

— No.

— Why did you call me here?

— I did not, my love. I believe we were each directed to this place, to meet once more.

— For the last time.

— Yes. For the last time.

— Don't look so sad, my dear. Time is only a burden. You once told me so yourself.

— I must be a little sad, because you are so very beautiful, and I wish I could be always looking on you.

She *is* beautiful, reader — Is she not? — celestial light surrounds her —

— I do not think much of your reason, she says.

— Nevertheless, Eliza, nevertheless. I suppose I may not embrace you?

— Heavens, no. Embrace the dead? You know better.

— Yet I feel I would rather die here than continue apart from you.

— Very romantic, dear. But quite untrue. You cannot deceive me. We shall get on tolerably well without one another.

To judge by her voice, Mrs Peach pronounces this sentiment merrily, with gentle affection. Mr Peach wipes away a tear.

— If you say so, Eliza, he says.

— You should never have brought me back at all, you know.

Mr Peach hangs his head a little. — I do know it, he says.

Miss Farthingay cannot restrain herself. — Then, she begins, in a whisper — so deep a silence has fallen, and so solemn is the light, that any speech above a whisper cannot be thought of — Then, she says, you did not merely imagine, that your wife still lived —

— *Shhhh!* the three French companions hiss, all at once. They hang upon the words of Mrs Peach, as though receiving the gospel. — Though surely they can none of them understand above one word in twenty.

Where is the Denfert? — she, who but a few moments ago, before the sun peeped in upon our scene, made so mad a spectacle, and raged about the room, threatening we know not what? — There — She covers her head in her hands, and crawls away from the light, towards the door, as though in the extremity of abject terror.

None but we observe her — And we, for a passing instant only. We too strain to hear Mrs Peach. — Dead Mrs Peach, returned now to our sight as well as our hearing.

A messenger, from realms unknown —

A traveller returned, from the bourne of that undiscovered country —

Mr Peach has quite forgotten that any body else is present. — I was mad with grief, he says, at losing you.

— Oh, Tom, she says. — As though no body in the world had ever died before.

— Well, he says, I've suffered for my mistake. Though I cannot say I regret it.

— Poor Tom. But the suffering too shall end.

— Is that your message, my love?

— Message?

— You said you were come as a messenger.

— Did I? How odd. I came only to say farewell.

— So I feared, Mr Peach says.

— There shall be no more visions or visitations. The living shall live, and the dead shall remain in peace, and spirits, and angels, and demons, are from this day on only names and words, for all the ages of the earth to come.

Clary — is she overcome? She has dropped to the stone floor, in a faint — Emitting as she falls, a moan.

— *Shhh!* the French onlookers repeat.

— The things you have done, Mrs Peach says, you shall do no more, nor shall any other. They shall be found only in dreams and tales. You, my dear, are the last of your kind.

— Very well, he says.

— Good-bye, Tom. I am very glad to see you.

— And I you. Glad beyond expression.

Mrs Peach seems to close her eyes a moment, and yawn.

— Ought you not shut the door? she says. The light will disturb us.

— Very true, my dear. I shall.

— Thank you. I am quite fatigued. Have I omitted to tell you a message? I must do it before we sleep.

— You have done it, dearest Eliza. Be easy now, and rest.

— Oh — Good-night then, Tom.

— Good-night.

In some portion of the eastern sky, a chance wind blows a certain cloud, in a certain direction, so that the light of the sun is extinguished, in the mocked and defaced chapel of the Château Charizard.

The stillness is broken by a violent crack! — Not thunder now, for the storm is quite blown out. — The noise is sharp, and brief, and comes from within the house.

The stone, in des Sables's hands — It has split in two.

Clary is not quite insensible, after all, for she raises her head from the floor, to watch the broken pieces fall beside her. The rest stand, where they stood. — Mr Peach — Miss Farthingay — the three churls of France — Each in various travails of silent wonder.

Of Madame Denfert there is no trace whatsoever. — And Mrs Peach too, is vanished.

Monsieur Lesinge prods one half of the shattered stone, with the toe of his frayed boot. He looks at the others present, and — shrugs.

— *Ç'est fini*, he says.

Mr Peach murmurs the translation. — It is finished.

After the storm, looters return. They appear in the castle like autumn spiders. Turn a corner and there one is. Ox-carts creak up the steep track from Charizard-le-Forêt, ready to carry away the spoils.

The villagers are no longer afraid of the inner apartments. Why not?

Something has changed.

Des Sables feels it himself. All these wicked embellishments, the iron cups, the paintings of massacres and orgies, the goats, each vulgar trinket of pretended devil-worship; why did he fear them so much? Is it not all trash? His master who loved to play the fine villain was only a small fool.

Lesinge remonstrates with the looters. Respect the property of others, he says, or who will respect yours? They answer him with sneers and curses if at all. The people of Charizard-le-Forêt are poor and do not care for political philosophy. They wish to rob and destroy. They threaten violence, at which Cochonne drives them off. Very well, they grumble: we will return with fire.

'Be wise, my darling,' she says to Lesinge. 'Let us leave this place along with the English people.'

'You are right, my turtle dove. There is nothing for us here. Everything that led us this way was a lie. Gaspard, he will shake its dust from his shoes.'

He is ashamed of himself. To have mistaken this feeble English girl for a demon, because she dressed in black and saw well in the dark! Look at her now, in plain daylight without her veil. She is barely more than an ugly child, and so weak they will have to mount her on Broubrou.

'I am an old ass to have been seduced by talk of riches,' he says. 'And you, my sugar-pastry, were a fool to follow me. I did not deserve such noble faith.'

'But, my lily-flower, did you not find the greatest treasure here — our love?'

Cochonne would have followed him from one end of France to the other, riches or no riches. From the day she saved his life defending his cell from the village boys she has worshipped him. Perhaps it was not always perfectly clear. What does that matter? Now it is. Where he goes, she will go, as the Bible says. She cannot believe they have been led astray at all. For as well as the priceless jewel of their mutual regard, did they not discover in Castle Charizard the revelation of God's own angel, sent to destroy the Devil himself?

No wealth compares to human or divine love. Nevertheless, the Englishman is so kind as to point out certain books in the dead sir's library which he suggests they take away to sell to collectors. He writes on a piece of paper the name of a man and a street in Rouen. Cochonne cannot read, but her sweet Gaspard testifies that the letters are correct. An Englishman, not only capable of speaking proper words but making them in writing too! It can only be another sign of the angel's blessing. The mercy of God, being infinite, must also extend to English people. Her heart fills with wonder and reverence.

'Shall we go together to Rouen, my honey-tart?' she says.

'We shall, my angel,' says Lesinge.

'It is on the way to Paris,' des Sables observes.

He will accompany them. He has taken nothing from the ruin of his master's ridiculous castle. He wishes to discard it all. He will not even keep the name des Sables, which the fool bestowed on him as a jest. Among the new men in Paris he will appear as his proper self: Valentin Pichot. The single thing he has kept is the dead castellan's will. In the city there will surely be lawyers who can turn it to his advantage. This is the way of things now. Those who were servants may rise. He will become a prosperous burgher of the new nation.

Des Sables is not sure whether he witnessed the defeat of the Devil or merely the madness and collapse of his old master's patroness, the eccentric and licentious Madame Denfert. Likewise he cannot satisfy himself as to whether he saw an angelic being or an ordinary ghost. Though he learned only a little English during his London sojourn he is sure he heard someone call her *Missis Peach*, as they call the grave Englishman *Mister Peach*. But it does not concern him. In Paris no one cares about angels and devils. Only country people like Cochonne think about such things. Soon there will be no more priests anyway. As they travelled across Brittany they passed the sign painted above a churchyard gate: 'Death is Nothing but an Eternal Sleep.' It is logical.

The forest also has changed. It no longer seems haunted. It is still old and dark and full of great rocks covered in moss, and there are pools and waterfalls which catch or shatter rare beams of light. Who is surprised to find it so? The trees are old because the forest has never been cut. Being old they grow tall and spread wide; therefore it is dark. Often it rains in western Brittany, which encourages moss. The water must gather and sit still in the low ground, or if it falls on higher land it must descend, leaping over rocks where that is its natural course. That is how the people in Paris describe such phenomena of nature as pools and waterfalls. Haunted? Pah!

They go even more slowly than they came. There is only one horse in the party, the one the Englishman rode, and the Miss Farthingay must have it because she is a lady. Des Sables sneers at this, but discreetly, since he admires the Farthingay, and so does Cochonne, who will therefore not tolerate any carping. His face is too beautiful to adopt a sneer with conviction. No one notices.

Everyone else goes afoot except for the English girl in the ragged black dress, who looks likely to die at any moment. Broubrou carries her at the slowest pace a donkey can achieve. The Miss Farthingay often weeps over her and calls her sister.

'Your two ladies,' Lesinge says to Mister Peach, who is a fellow man of the world and worthy of his conversation. 'Are they really sisters? There is not a great resemblance, by God!'

'They have become so, I believe,' says Mister Peach in his excruciatingly accented but otherwise acceptable French.

'Then the organisation of your families in England is different from ours in France. Among us, persons are either siblings, in which case they remain so eternally, or are not, in which case they remain not. I exclude connections of marriage, which are anyway not instances of consanguinity, though custom permits the appellation of *sister* or *brother* in those cases.'

'On the contrary, Sir Lesinge. It is you French who teach the world that things which were once not true, may become true. That, one might say, the foundations of the world may be changed. Have changed.'

How cultivated he is, Cochonne thinks, and yet my Gaspard is easily his equal in talk!

'True,' answers Lesinge. 'To take one instance, the younger of the sisters there once appeared to me to be an unnatural being gifted with prophetic powers, but is now evidently nothing of the sort.'

'You are not mistaken now,' says Mister Peach, with a polite inclination of the head, 'and were perhaps no more mistaken in your first opinion.'

'Will she live, sir?' says Cochonne.

'She will.'

'But she is so weak!'

'She appears weak, Miss Cochonne, but she is not. She is in fact the strongest person of this whole age, and has done the greatest deed that will ever be done.'

Behind Mister Peach's back Lesinge winks at her and taps his head with his finger. He makes a face. The English! All mad!

'The good God keep her,' Cochonne says. 'She saw the angel come among us. That will give her strength.'

Mister Peach will not discuss the angel. At the mention of her his face turns overcast. He is not a man of God, Cochonne supposes. Most likely they do not have churches in England and cannot understand the Bible because of the language they speak. Nevertheless, she blesses him in her capacious heart.

It is All Souls' Day, when even Englishmen may be numbered in the lists of grace.

At the edge of the wood comes a parting of ways. The foreigners turn north towards the harbour towns and the sea and their own country. Cochonne, Lesinge and des Sables, the merry companions, inspired in various degrees by love and liberty, walk blithely east, into the maelstrom of the coming year.

Seventeen hundred and ninety-two! How many thousands will stray too close to the murderous currents and be caught and dragged under! How many tens of thousands more, who keep their heads above water, clinging to the wreckage of revolution, will look up into the heavens where once the bright sun of freedom promised to shine in endless summer, and see only one storm departing and another approaching behind it, pitch black and roaring destruction! The profane and the godly; the noble and the venal; cowards, scholars and men of action; those who would march and those who would sleep; every man, woman and child of France, no matter what their disposition or their politics, will feel the battering of these successive tempests, which descend on them as indiscriminately as the thunders and deluges of nature.

It is well for Lesinge that he anchors himself to one who is not easily blown over. Never is he tempted to let go; not once. Remarkable but true: Gaspard, the brigand and cynic, is for the rest of his life devotedly in love. No one is more astonished than him. But he is a modern man, and when the storms at last relent it turns out, to the surprise of all the philosophers, that it is a romantic age.

As for Cochonne, she is unshakeable. She will never forget that she heard an angel speak. It does not matter that she could not understand the words. The world proceeds with its turmoils. In the midst of them all she has been blessed, briefly and without great consequence. She is not a new Jeanne of Arc. She does not need to be. Though her womb remains barren, and there are bad years, and ill-wishing neighbours come and go, nothing can move the certainty of happiness from her heart. One day, she knows, she will see Gaspard to his grave, because he is many years older. Very well: she will love him when he is dead. There is nothing to fear. She was born greater than others. She will never be ashamed of it again.

Valentin Pichot is not so fortunate. The Paris of his imagination is not the Paris of conspiracy, riot, squalor and bloodshed which greets his arrival. At first only his insignificance saves him. Later, when he has been in the city long enough to accumulate a history of sorts, and with it the usual complement of hatreds and enemies, he must fall back on his beauty and the resourcefulness learned from his brigand days. Valentin Pichot vanishes from Paris and a certain Miss des Sables appears, blonde and fine-featured, modest and retiring, without attachments or opinions or ambitions of any sort. Miss des Sables becomes popular in discreet Sapphic salons. She tacks with the wind and survives.

Each August she leaves the fetid streets and stinking river for a month and goes to stay in the country, with an ugly old farmer who smokes a pipe and his colossally proportioned wife. Which of them laughs longest at the other is never settled; but laugh they do, all month long.

And Denfert?

Denfert flees the castle as fast as he can. Already the merciless eye of Heaven begins to peep between dissolving clouds. Celestial beams of light pour down, crisscrossing the earth. He has been seen. He is being sought. Denfert imagines battalions of angels descending on the golden rays. Thrones, dominations, princedoms, virtues, powers, the cherubim and the seraphim and the great general Michael with his shining sword. He groans and gnashes his teeth. He covers his head with his hands until the horse brings him under the shelter of the forest. There he would like to shake his fist at the sky and shout defiance against his eternal enemy the Tyrant. But — horror and shame! — he dares not. The ancient secret terror grips him. He thought the Tyrant was fled. Withdrawn or asleep. In his dotage. Maybe dead. And then — this angel, revealed within the stone! The demonoscope, through which he meant to summon his legions to conquest: made into a tool of his foe! Denfert's own minion would not obey him. He is cast down again. He is defeated.

He was always defeated.

Madness takes the deputy. By day he hides himself in ditches and under bushes in case the Tyrant's bright eye lands on him and crushes him to dust. By night he rides in frenzy towards Paris. If he cannot summon armies from the regions below he will unleash hell on earth. The people of France will be his legions. He will pile men's corpses so high the Tyrant will turn his sickened gaze away from the world and retreat once more into indifferent silence, this time for ever. Denfert stops at the Breton and Norman town to rouse the patriots. Tear down the churches, he will urge. Burn the houses of the pious, he will command. He will order and be obeyed: shoot the enemies of revolution where they stand and leave their bodies for the dogs. But always he comes at night when the gates are closed, and no one recognises him any more. Be off with you, raving beggar, say the guards. 'How dare you?' he cries. His voice has become a thin rasping pipe. 'I am Denfert!' Ha, ha, and I am the chevalier Roland. You are drunk or mad, my friend. Let honest men sleep.

His mortal form consumes itself. He does not eat or drink. He is feverish and glassy. Sixty miles from Paris, near the poor wretched village of Haut-Ô, he falls insensible from his horse, which canters on into darkness, having long since lost its wits as well.

When dawn comes he is found in the road by a milkmaid.

This tender-hearted creature is moved to pity by the plight of the sick gentleman. With the most gentle and patient attentions she coaxes him awake and brings him to her own miserable hovel. She lays him down in straw and linen and fetches water from the well to soothe his burning brow. Her name is Marguerite. She asks him who he is, whether he has family or friends nearby to whom she may send for assistance. In answer he raves. He insists he is Satan, prince of infernal legions and rightful inheritor of the whole earth. He curses her charity. He swears that if she touches his flesh her hands will burn like meat in the fire.

'Oh, sir, how wildly you talk! But I will restore you to health, with God's help.'

Denfert thrashes in his cot. 'Do not speak of him!'

'I know it is presumptuous for a poor ignorant milkmaid to name the Lord. But God has given all His creatures the gift of prayer, no matter how humble.'

'Credulous sheep! He does not listen to your prayers. He is silent and gives nothing. You ought to hate and despise him as I do.'

'You clever gentlemen doubt the efficacy of prayer, I know,' says gentle Marguerite. 'It is true that this spring my mother died of the white flux, God receive her soul, though I prayed all night and day for a week. But why should I be angry? His will must be done.'

'It is not his will! It is blind chance and indifferent fate! How can you deny it?'

'Perhaps, good sir. The world is a cruel place. But that is why we must pray and have faith, for if we do not, what hope is there?'

'No hope!' Denfert's eyes roll in his head. He tears at his face with his unshorn nails. 'There is no hope!'

'Alas, sir, calm yourself. I think you must have suffered some sad disappointment.'

Denfert rants and curses. The more furiously he rages at her simple piety the gentler she answers. Poor man! With all her heart she wishes he may recover his wits. What a terrible delusion, to believe himself the Devil! When his frenzy exhausts himself and he sinks unconscious she prays over his sleeping body. She hangs her little wooden pendant cross over the cot.

At his next waking he is no longer angry but desperate. Though she begs him to rest he crawls from the bed. He stands. He is no more substantial than a spectre; his cheeks sunken, his flesh like paper, his clothes loose as a scarecrow's. Hands trembling, he pleads with Marguerite. Look at the world, he says. Plainly and incontrovertibly, human life is misery and suffering. Harvests fail, the dishonest prosper, fathers hurt their wives and children. The prayers of the faithful fall on deaf ears. The law of nature is indifferent, brutal and absolute. There is no God. You know it in your heart, he says, even if you pretend otherwise. Marguerite, Marguerite, there is no God! Why can you not see?

'Ah, good sir, perhaps you are right after all. And yet I will still pray, for my heart desires God even if He hides from us.'

With a wild cry Denfert stumbles out into the night.

And then Paris, where no one knows him.

Deputy Denfert? There is no such name in the lists. A poor madman or madwoman howls along the alleys. There are hundreds such. This one cries savage revolution in a feeble voice, calling for the execution of the king and queen, the slaughter of the priests, a general massacre. Who attends to them? As the new year arrives such words blow everywhere, unremarkable as the pamphlets sodden with sleet and trampled into mud. No one remembers the speeches of last year. Desmoulins, Robespierre, Marat, these are the men of the coming age. Week by week Denfert is forgotten. Denfert vanishes. History records nothing of him. He is gone; gone as if he never was. For exactly like a long-married couple, God and the Devil, though bitter enemies, cannot survive apart; and when one finally quits the world their old adversary has nothing to do but follow, meek and resigned, into the eternal forgetting.

CHAPTER TWELVE

— I do not understand, says Miss Farthingay, the significance of the *chess-pieces*.

Mr Peach, whose tea-cup is at his lips, pauses — without drinking — The china confection, suspended in mid-air.

— You remember the chess-pieces, I am sure, Miss Farthingay says.

Mr Peach exchanges the briefest of looks with Caspar, who sits in the window-seat, with his habitual stately and upright bearing. His own dish of tea — served without so much as a grain of sugar — rests close at hand — That famous view of the *Thames*, celebrated by poets and painters, tempting his austere gaze beyond the glass.

— *You*, Clary, my love, must recall them, Miss Farthingay says, with an hint of impatience. — Even if Mr Peach pretends he does not.

Miss Riddle, alas, is not listening.

She has a novel in her hands, from which she cannot be separated, in mind or body. She is sunk in a posture as disgraceful, as Caspar's is impeccable. — Shoes raised upon a foot-stool — a cushion, behind her head — tea wholly forgotten — The very picture, of the incurable affliction of *novel-reading*, which all the moralists of the age decry, most particularly among young ladies. — Those tender, susceptible creatures! so delicate in their constitutions, that they are liable to suffer *material* harm, from perfectly *imaginary* agencies.

Caspar clears his throat.

— We have it on the authority of Monsieur Philidor himself, that the game of chess is nothing more than a rational system of rules and principles. There is no extraneous or additional significance.

Miss Farthingay makes a dismissive noise. — You were not there, she says.

Understand, reader, that she refers, to *France* — The heavenly, or hellish, nation of France, according to your view of the matter. Our own is, we confess, become quite bewildered. Was not this narrative of ours intended, to settle the matter? — with the assistance of that remarkable man, Mr Tho.s Peach, Esq., to whose eye the most secret and arcane influences are visible, and from whose penetrating intelligence no causes, however recondite, may be concealed? — Instead of which, our voyage to France atchieved no more, than the rescue of a lady from her oppressions — like *any other novel* — While the revolution continues its mysterious course, bringing bloodshed, and tyranny — and also, brotherhood, liberty, and the rational application of enlightened principles — All commingled together, and parts of the same whole, like the white and black squares, upon a chess-board.

At least Miss Farthingay *is* rescued. — So much we have atchieved, if little more. We must not grumble. — The deliverance of a lady, from wicked plots against her virtue, ought to be sufficient for an *happy ending*.

Behold, reader, here she sits — In the close but elegant upper apartment, of Mr Peach's house, on the side of the hill, at *Richmond*.

A year almost is gone by, since our last. Mr Peach has quit the old Somerset-shire cottage, where we had exclusively known him to dwell. He remained there, he said, only for the sake of certain memories. — Recollections, which could only give pain, albeit of that curiously sweet sort, which we derive from conjuring for ourselves the phantoms of things lost. For the sake of his happiness, he let them go — and the house also — and, the county — And is transplanted to Arcadian *Surrey*, where no body knows him, nor cares to, since many persons of fashion frequent the town, and take their amusements by the river there, and draw all public notice to themselves. Even our Miss Farthingay, who is in her native Somerset-shire a figure of prominence, and the topic of every tittle-tattler between Bristol and Bath, becomes in these new surroundings, a minor ornament at best — a winking star, outshone by an hundred more marvellous constellations. The lady *writes verse?* — and is widely rumoured, to have taken as a lover, one of her household servants? — pooh! pooh! in the annals of fashionable scandal, these are scarce worthy a foot-note.

Certain younger poets admire her greatly, it is true — But their opinion is of no consequence at all, in society.

— Clary, my love, pray put down your book and attend to me.

With an ungracious sigh, Miss Riddle lets the novel fall in her lap, face down, so she will not lose her place.

— You recollect the chess-pieces, I am sure. You placed them in my hands yourself, and urged me to keep them.

Miss Riddle also shares a look with Mr Peach.

— I do not remember, she says. — I was very unwell.

— I think you all conspire against me, says Miss Farthingay. — A conspiracy of oblivion.

Miss Riddle takes a drink of tea —

Reader — Why do we notice an act so trivial?

We feel there must be some significance, in Miss Riddle's drink of tea. — Absurd! Nothing could be more quotidian or dull, than this *happy ending* of ours. Tea — chess-pieces —

Our whole narrative, has been a *disappointment*.

As a consequence of those unhappy recollections recently alluded to, Mr Peach had become habituated to the laudanum-bottle. His expedition to France, in the service of Miss Farthingay, with all its dangers and uncertainties, naturally led him to have more frequent recourse to its poisonous consolations. — Who will now say, which of his adventures in that country, belong to history, and which to the phantastical record of dreams?

On their return, Miss Farthingay secured the services of a wise doctor, who has taught Mr Peach to moderate his use of the drug. His sleep is now peaceful, and his nerves calm. Yet the intellectual system has suffered certain shocks, which cannot be intirely repaired. The impressions left upon the plastic matter of the brain, by events of the years recently passed, have been weakened. — Effaced, perhaps — For Mr Peach can never, or will never, speak of certain matters. — Notably, those matters which we ourselves have been at such pains to record.

And Clary is now become his ally, in silence. —

How changed the young lady is! So much at least we can declare with certainty. — Did we not once dread the mere appearance of her name, upon our page? — and yet behold now, a mere sulky girl, who retreats to her novel-reading, as often as ever she can. — An anchorite, of romance. Her former passions and past-times, she also does not allude to. — Yes, she is greatly changed — But, *how* — or, *from what* — No one will say.

In short — The present scene, is altogether without interest. Merely four persons, in idle familiar chit-chat. — Quite *happy* — and intolerably dull.

How are we come to this pass? —

Was it for this, reader, that we wore out our pen?

Our own purposes escape us. — Were we not once an adept, of necromantic arts?

Did we not tremble on the brink of secrets, from which every pen shrank, but our own?

Alas, this *revolution!* — Would that we had never gone near it!

O, time of turmoil! — While our principal characters sit in comfort, overlooking the tranquil course of sweet *Thamesis*, the nation is at war. — No less with itself, than the unruly French — for though the armies of Europe contend, with musket and cannon, the greater conflict rages at home, in every city and town. — Its weapons, ink, and paper, and breath. — The war of thought — of *idea* — Between those who mourn the world that has passed, and those who welcome the one to come.

These will tell you, that the present shocks and struggles, are like the fever of the body, by which it eliminates its distempers, and restores itself to its original health — That Europe must be convulsed, in order to rid itself of its afflictions, and return to the Good Old Days. — While *those* insist, that the broils and bloodshed are the natural birth-pangs, of the wondrous New Age.

Reader — Born, as we are, in these latter times — How shall you determine, whether every thing was better *before* — Or, not?

Mr Peach's man enters the scene, with an apologetic cough — *hem* —

— The news-paper, sir, he says.

— Thank you, James.

James presents the item in question, upon a pewter tray.

— I see, he says, the French king and queen are made prisoner, and will likely be put on trial for their lives.

Mr Peach takes the sheets, and holds them at arm's length, squinting over his nose.

— Poor lady, says Caspar.

— The richest poor lady there ever was, Miss Farthingay says.

— An extravagant and luxurious ornament, no doubt, says Caspar. — But it is not for her extravagance that she is condemned, not for her folly, nor any of her other vices, which are, we may suppose, not very much worse than those of other kings and queens. She falls merely because she cannot be permitted to remain aloft. It is akin to a proposition in logic. Monsieur Robespierre and his friends calculate that if they are to go up, she must go down. Justice is not the question.

— You are too severe, says Miss Farthingay. — Doubtless there are many imprisoned from mere expediency, or revenge, or other ignoble causes, just as the poor slaves of the Bastille were given over to indefinite incarceration upon the whim of a monarch, under the old regime. But the queen is a declared enemy of the revolution. She is proved to have conspired by clandestine means with the enemies of her own country, more than once. I deplore the excesses of the Parisians, as every body must. In this instance, however, one cannot accuse the Commune of an exercise of power merely arbitrary.

Caspar inclines his head, and will not contest the issue. His is not a disputatious nature.

— What is your opinion, Mr Peach? says Miss Farthingay.

Mr Peach continues to study the news-paper.

— I beg your pardon, Arabella, he says. — I am not yet finished reading the report.

Miss Farthingay laughs.

— Dear Tom. Wars rage, and crowned heads will be toppled, and half the world cries that the age we live in is the very worst of all the ages of the world, even as the remainder declare it the very best; and in the midst of tempest and earth-quake you alone sit perfectly still and content, and are the solitary person in creation, who will not incline an inch one way or the other.

Miss Riddle puts down her novel.

— I have just been visited, she says, by the most remarkable thought.

Mr Peach lowers the news-paper. He bestows on her, an enquiring look — As do Caspar and Miss Farthingay, each according to their fashion.

— Might not both parties be in the right? says Miss Riddle.

Mr Peach appears to smile a little. — Though what has amused him, we cannot say. He is become a MYSTERY. The book, which we endeavoured to read, and hoped to expound, is closed. — The story of this man, taken from our sight. — Like the writing on a tomb-stone, it is become no more than a *name* — and a pair of dates — the beginning, and the end — Every thing that passed between, blank and silent, as the uncarved stone.

— What do you mean, Clary? he says.

— All this great dispute, she says, is perhaps no dispute at all.

— How so?

— Some say, do they not, that this age of ours is the best of times?

— They do, Clary.

— And the rest contend, that it is the worst of times?

— Indeed.

Miss Riddle takes a drink of tea.

— But, she says — Might it not be — BOTH?